REALM OF
SHADOWS

Books by Shannon Drake

THE LION IN GLORY

KNIGHT TRIUMPHANT

SEIZE THE DAWN

CONQUER THE NIGHT

COME THE MORNING

REALM OF SHADOWS

DEEP MIDNIGHT

WHEN DARKNESS FALLS

BENEATH A BLOOD RED MOON

Published by Zebra Books

REALM OF SHADOWS

SHANNON DRAKE

ZEBRA BOOKS
KENSINGTON PUBLISHING CORP.

For Moraima, with deepest appreciation for the support.
For Vanessa Molina, the songbird, with love and best wishes
and total faith that she'll fly high, and for Sean Abreu, with
thanks for the laughter, and the tango!

ZEBRA BOOKS are published by

Kensington Publishing Corp.
850 Third Avenue
New York, NY 10022

Zebra and the Z logo Reg. U.S. Pat. & TM Off.

First Printing: October 2002

Printed in the United States of America

PROLOGUE

The Trenches
Germany
September 1944

A shell exploded not ten feet in front of the line. Despite the days and nights the men had spent in their hellish hole in the earth, some jumped at the sound.

Others barely twitched.

They'd been holding the line nearly a week, waiting for reinforcements. Though word kept coming through that the men from Airborne would be shoring them up, none had arrived. Some of the men were bitter, but Brandon Ericson shrugged at their comments without replying. He was certain the men from Airborne had been sent out.

They just hadn't made it yet. Gut instinct warned him that the paratroopers had been dropped from their planes with all good intentions. Some of them had tangled in the trees. Others had been shot down while their chutes were still billowing in the absurdly blue skies. Some of them had met death on the ground. And some were wasting away in the enemy's prison camps. No lack of intent or valor left them as they were now. Just the brutal determination of a foe determined to conquer all Europe.

"Jesu! That was close!" Corporal Ted Myers muttered, crossing himself. His pale blue eyes were bright against their red rims and the dark grime on his face. Beside him, Jimmy Decker started to shake. What began as a trembling turned suddenly into a full-force spasm. Then Jimmy slammed forward, crashing against the wall of earth that shielded them, and back again.

"Better get him out of the line," the lieutenant said quietly. "Back to the infirmary."

"Ain't no infirmary anymore, Lieutenant," Sergeant Walowski said. He leaned back against the earth and sank to a sitting position, drawing a cigarette from his pocket. "Caved in last night."

"The medics have something else rigged up. Myers, get Decker out of here," the lieutenant said. He stared across the earth. Pretty soon, dusk would fall. Until then, there would be another barrage of mortar fire. After that, the enemy would make a run at their position again. He didn't need anyone in the line who was cracking. They'd held here now for nearly two weeks under impossible odds. They'd done so because, for the most part, the men were crack shots. They weren't budging, and from where they were, they could have a field day with troops approaching them—even the trained professional German soldiers who had been ordered to root them out.

Still, they could only hold so long. The enemy powers had ordered those soldiers—family men, many of them, like their French and American counterparts—to give their lives, as many as need be, for the Fatherland. They'd just send more and more troops, night after night. Even if fifty of the enemy were killed for every one of his men, eventually, they would fall. Unless reinforcements could reach them. And quickly.

A whistling tore through the air.

"Take cover!" the lieutenant ordered. Myers, running with the shell-shocked Decker, ducked and kept running. The men remaining in the trench flattened themselves. This one didn't explode quite so close.

"Keep down!" the lieutenant warned, and sure enough, the first explosion was followed by a second, and then by a third. On the last, great piles of earth fell like rain upon the already filthy men, but there were no cries of pain, no shrieks indicating an imminent death among their shrinking number.

"They'll be coming through the dusk and fallout," the lieutenant warned. "Remember that ammo is low. Hold your fire until I give the command."

"Don't shoot till we see the whites of their eyes," Myers muttered.

"Hell, we'll never see the whites of their eyes in this powder and dirt," Lansky said. Lansky was something of an old timer. Forty-five when the war had broken out. He'd joined up anyway, two days after his son was killed in Italy. By then, the recruiters hadn't cared much about his age. He was a damned good man to have on the line. He'd learned to shoot hunting in Montana and he rarely missed his mark, no matter what the conditions.

"Every shot counts," the lieutenant reminded them

all. He was less than half Lansky's age, but Lansky never batted an eye at an order. Lansky had proven to be his best friend out here. He'd seen action at the end of the First World War. He'd learned a lot about digging into the trenches, and he had a way of giving damned good suggestions. Quietly. Without irritating even the officers with higher ranks than the lieutenant's.

He saw Lansky's eyes now. "They're coming," Lansky said. "I can feel it."

The lieutenant gave him a nod. And a moment later, Lansky was proven right. From out of the dusk, powder, and drifting dirt, the soldiers suddenly appeared. Knowing that they were within sight, they let out strange cries, like warriors of old. Maybe battle never changed, the lieutenant thought. Just the time, the place, the argument. Maybe men needed to scream, to run into a maelstrom of bullets, even if they were armed and prepared to deal out death themselves. Perhaps a battle cry was a man's last roar to heaven or hell that he was, indeed, alive.

"Fire!" the lieutenant shouted.

The earth seemed to split apart with the roar of the guns. The line coming toward them stumbled and broke. The eerie battle cries turned to screams of pain as men fell and died.

And yet, where the line had been broken, new men came rushing in, and the battle cry they had taken up seemed to soar and echo into the darkening sky. "Fire!" he roared again, and another barrage filled the night, and more men fell. But like ghost soldiers, the enemy kept coming, more soldiers filling in where the others had been. The line was coming closer and closer, and the enemy soldiers were firing as well, aiming blindly for the trenches.

"Fire!"

Again, the roar of bullets. Powder filled the night so thickly that it was almost impossible to see anything. They heard screams, and knew more men had fallen.

And knew that they were close.

A soldier burst into view, throwing himself into the trench, gun aimed at Lansky. The lieutenant used his own weapon instantly and instinctively as a mace, cracking the enemy with a vengeance on the back and neck. The man fell before he could get off a shot, but others were coming, almost upon them.

"Fire at will!" he roared in the night. In a minute, it would be a melee, the enemy would be in the trenches, a man wouldn't know who the hell he was shooting anymore. Rifle fire rattled explosively in the night as the defenders shot almost blindly at the enemy encroaching upon them. A soldier caught a bullet in his gullet and fell into the trench, on top of Lansky. Lansky pushed the dead man aside and took aim again.

Then, out of the night, came a howling. It wasn't the battle cry of the enemy. Eerie, uncanny, like the scream of a thousand banshees, or a cry from the damned in the deepest pits of hell. It was so startling, so deep, so soul-wrenching that, for moments, neither side fired a single shot.

The silence was as eerie as the hell-hound cry that had stilled them all.

MacCoy, the boy from Boston, spoke softly. "May all the saints bless us and preserve us!" he whispered.

All hell broke loose; the baying began again, along with the sound of wild shots, shots fired from the trenches into the dust and darkness, shots fired at the approaching enemy, shots that whistled into the darkness.

Then . . .

The thunder against the earth. As if cavalry were upon them . . .

The screams began, screams coming from the German soldiers, while they could still see nothing in the whirl of powder, earth, and dust before them.

"Hail Mary, full of Grace . . ." MacCoy intoned.

"Blessed Lord!" Lansky cried, and it was a prayer and a curse, for a German soldier burst out of the haze, covered in blood, falling in upon them and to their feet. Their eyes fell instinctively to the man in the muck.

And that was when the creatures came.

Creatures . . .

Wolves, but not wolves. Some were silver, some were black, some were tawny. They had the form and structure of the canine beasts, but they were larger, and their eyes . . . their eyes were different. Their eyes saw, and knew, and the machinations of thought and cunning could be seen in them as they sprang, seeming to sail and fly above the soldiers in the trenches and then they came pouncing down.

"Fire! Fire!" the lieutenant roared.

Guns blazed, animals fell, men fell, the trenches themselves became a mire of men and blood, German uniforms, American, cloth so bloodied, ripped, and torn, it couldn't be discerned. "Fire, fire, fire!" the lieutenant thundered again and again, and he heard the deafening rat-a-tats as his men obeyed his command. At his side, Lansky's body was suddenly wrenched up and away. He saw Lansky fall before the trench just as another bloodied, terrified member of the German elite came hurtling in upon them, eyes open in death.

"Lansky!" He went flat, crawling, down, down against the dirt, determined to drag Lansky back to the relative safety of the trench. Bullets, wild and stray, whistled above his head as he inched along.

He was struck. He didn't know by what. He felt the weight, a terrible crushing weight, upon his back. Then the stinging at his nape. A bullet, a bayonet, a knife . . . he didn't know what. He just felt the stinging sensation. Not even real pain . . . just the thrusting . . . and the sting.

He'd been hit.

By fire? By one of the rabid wolves? But he was breathing. Alive and breathing. And still crawling.

Lansky lay just ahead, at his side. Lansky, the crack shot. He had to get him back. Sweat dripped into his eyes. Not sweat. Blood. His vision was blurring. He refused to die in the mud; he refused to lose the battle this way. He inched forward, aware that more and more of the dust and haze seemed to be filling his vision from the inside. He looked where Lansky lay and saw his countryman's hand. He reached out, catching his friend, dragging him toward him.

As the body came near, he screamed aloud himself, recoiling. Lansky had no head.

Despite the horror, his scream faded. His lungs burned. His entire body seemed to be afire, and yet, in seconds, that fire seemed to be fading to a strange cold. Cold.

Death was cold.

He was dying. It was his life's blood dripping into his eyes. Oozing from his veins through the stinging gash at the back of his neck. What dim light there had been was fading away completely. Just as sound. He could no longer hear the screams of his men. He could no longer hear the sound of rifle fire. Time stood still, and cold, and it seemed that sound kept ebbing, and ebbing . . .

There was stillness. He didn't think that he had blacked out yet. And he didn't think that he had died. Yet.

But still, time had passed. Sped like light, drifted like a slow current . . .

The stillness remained.

Then there was a dim sense of sound and movement again.

Footsteps. Walking. Hard on the ground. He tried to turn. He felt something on the earth at his side. Heard language that didn't register in his mind.

He blinked hard. His sight seemed to be dimming to a tiny peephole surrounded by a haze of red and black.

Yes, something by his side. He blinked again, fighting to remain conscious, yet knowing that he would lose the battle any minute.

Yet, there, yes . . . a boot. A man's black boot, planted against the muck and mud and blood of the earth. Black, and something shining despite the caking mud that spattered it.

Just as his eyes closed completely, he recognized the shining insignia on the boot.

A swastika.

The thought registered . . .

Then there was no more thought. The world faded into a haze of crimson, and then . . .

There was nothing but blackness.

CHAPTER 1

"He has changed since you last saw him. He has simply changed." Ann waved her hand in the air as she spoke, the plume from her cigarette creating a swirl of smoke.

Tara stared at her cousin blankly. She was exhausted—she had managed to cross the Atlantic without even a catnap, despite the overnight duration of the flight when traveling eastward. She wanted nothing more than to reach her grandfather's little chateau on the outskirts of Paris, but after picking her up at the airport, Ann had insisted they stop for petit dejeuner before heading out of the city.

And now, though she wasn't putting it in so many words, Ann was trying to tell her that their grandfather was senile, or suffering from Alzheimer's disease.

Tara narrowed her eyes, perplexed, as she watched Ann. She shook her head, taking a long swallow of her café au lait. "Ann, if Grandpapa is ill, then perhaps he should come back to the States—"

"Phui!" Ann wrinkled her nose, inching it higher in the air. "Why must you always think that there will be something better in the United States?"

"I didn't really mean that," Tara said, then lowered her eyes, biting her lip. The medical care in France was excellent. She did have that tendency to think that the best of everything had to be in America.

Except for croissants, perhaps. And café au lait.

She looked at Ann and grimaced ruefully. "Sorry."

Ann shrugged.

"But if you're trying to tell me that he has lost his mind completely—"

Ann sighed deeply. "No, no, it's not that! Really, it's not that at all."

"You think, though, that he is becoming senile? He's certainly old enough to be allowed some eccentricities."

Ann shrugged again at that. "Mais oui. He claims he does not know how old he is himself. He said that he was older than most of the boys in the Resistance, and lord, World War II ended in nineteen forty-five! So, yes, he is up there in years. He has had the respiratory trouble, as I told you on the phone, but I've had him out of the hospital now for several days, and though I chide him and tell him he must be careful, he is up and about a bit each day. But he sits in his library when he is up! He shuts himself in, and he talks about something that he calls the Alliance all the time."

"Perhaps he is reliving his war years."

Ann appeared troubled, drawn, and weary, which was not like her. Tara had always thought her cousin was one of the most beautiful women she had ever seen. Her eyes were deep, penetrating blue. He hair was dark, her complexion very fair, and the contrast was startling and appealing. She was tall and elegantly slim, with curves just where they should be.

There had been times in Tara's life when she had hated the visits of her French cousin. She'd had too many friends in high school and college who all but drooled openly when Ann came around. She could admit to a certain amount of jealousy over the years, but she also loved her cousin, more so once she had gotten older, when high school and college were long in the past. Ann had spent enough time in her house when they were growing up to make it a rivalry that sisters might have shared—except that in Tara's case, her "sister" had come with a fascinating accent and the allure of being an exotic foreigner. Ann came to the United States frequently; Tara and her family went to Paris just three times in the years when she was growing up. Ann spoke both French and English perfectly, while Tara's French was poor and her accent far too obviously American. Jacques DeVant had fallen in love with their grandmother, Emily, an American nurse, at the end of the war. The two had married, and moved to the United States. Their son, David, had, in turn, fallen in love with a French artist, Sophie, during a summer term of college in Paris. He had remained, while their daughter, Tara and her brother Mike's mother, had married Patrick Adair, a first generation Irish American.

Their cultural differences therefore, despite their grandparents, were great.

But those old times seemed long ago now. When Tara graduated from college, she had spent a summer at the old chateau. Her grandmother had died and her grandfather had moved back to Paris by then, taking up residence in his family home, where Ann had grown up. Ann's parents had retired, and spent most of their time in a little house on the beach at Costa del Sol.

To call her grandfather's house a chateau was, perhaps, a bit presumptive, but it had been called Le Petit Château DeVant since it was enlarged in the seventeen hundreds, and thus it remained. The war had basically destroyed what hadn't exactly been a family fortune, but a decent portfolio, and now, though somewhat decayed, the little estate did have tremendous charm. The house itself was two stories with an old-fashioned hall rather than a parlor or living room, a magnificent library, and beautiful upstairs bedrooms with balconies that overlooked a courtyard. The carriage house still housed a small buggy and Daniel, an incredibly old, gentle, gray draft horse who did little more these days than amble around the adjoining pasture.

Ann suddenly shook her head and crushed out her cigarette, leaning forward. "It's not the war. Perhaps his writings have gotten to his mind. Maybe he read too many American comic books. He is distressed, thinking that he deserted . . . something. He does talk about the war, saying that the realities of it made him forget what he was, who he was. And then, going to America, and he should have known, because it was there, even in America."

"What was there—even in America?" Tara asked.

Ann threw up her hands. "I don't know. He suddenly becomes disturbed, as if he has spoken too much. Maybe you will do better with him than I have. I took time off from work when he was so sick . . . but I can't now, or I won't have a job anymore. I don't make a fortune, but I love my work."

Tara felt a twinge of guilt that it had taken her so

long to make it to France. But she had a few deadlines of her own.

She and Ann had taken different paths, but oddly enough, wound up working on similar projects. Ann was an editor with a company that purchased and translated English and American titles. Tara was a commercial artist who was frequently hired for book covers.

"You can do a lot of work at home, though, right?" Tara asked her.

Ann laughed. "I have to come home to work half the time, what with the phones and the meetings all day long. But that's just it—I have to be at those meetings."

Tara nodded. "Well, I am here now." She yawned. "And really tired."

"Does that mean I'm not taking you celebrating to any local bars tonight? There are some exciting fellows around now. You said on the phone that you had split with the stockbroker."

Tara nodded. "Yes, we split. But should you really go bar hopping? What happened to the new love in your life?"

Ann wrinkled her nose. "We, too, have split."

"A nasty split?"

"Nasty?" Ann raised a brow with perfect contempt. She sighed. "There was an art meeting in my office that ran very late. You know, of course, that I met Willem when he came in to take over as head of the sales force. About a week ago, he was to lock up for me—he was finishing some business with the art director and the models hired for the ad campaign—and meet me at—well, meet me at a hotel room. I left to pick up some food for a romantic dinner, but I had forgotten a manuscript I wanted to work on, and went back to the office. He had not been expecting me, nor had the model for the advertising campaign. I found him in a compromising position with the girl. I left."

"It was your office?"

"I assumed he'd be out of it by the time I went back the following Monday," Ann said dryly.

"And he was, I take it."

"Yes."

"How bad was it? Did he call? Did he try to apologize? Did he have an excuse or an explanation?"

"He called. I assured him he had nothing to say that I would like to hear."

The man had hurt her Tara decided. But Ann also had a tendency to see the world in white and black. She could be totally unforgiving when she chose. Pride and direction were important to her.

"It must be difficult. I mean, he's still with the company. You two still work together."

"He does not work in my office."

Tara was silent for a moment. Ann had talked about Willem with such great enthusiasm. She had expected to hear that her cousin was engaged at any time.

"All right, let me get a little more personal here. Just what was he doing?"

Ann flashed her a glance and rolled her eyes. "The girl was on my desk. He was bent over her. What more do you want?"

"Everything," Tara said. "Were they—dressed?"

"They had clothing about them."

"Then maybe—"

"Don't make excuses for him!" Ann said irritably. "They were kissing and pawing one another, at the very least. And that is too much for me."

"I'm not making excuses for him. But . . . perhaps the model forced him into a compromising situation.

Or maybe he was showing her a pose that he particularly wanted." Tara grimaced, wondering why she was trying to defend a man she didn't know, who had been caught in a situation she knew nothing about.

Ann laughed curtly. "There were no photographers in the room. Nor was the male model there. So . . ."

"You ended it then and there?"

"I said that if he stepped in my office again, I would quit. I meant it, and he believed me. Of course, I also said that I would skewer him with my letter opener. I meant that as well. Now, what about your stockbroker?"

Tara hesitated. Ann already thought that she was dealing with madness where their grandfather was concerned. She wasn't sure how to explain the feelings that had caused her to break off her relationship with a really nice, attractive guy.

"Well?" Ann persisted. "I've certainly laid my heart and the truth on the table!"

"It just wasn't right."

"Just wasn't right? You said that he was good looking, polite, charming, and sexy! Did he become unsexy?"

"No."

Ann shook her head. "He made a decent income, he wasn't a starving artist, he didn't play ridiculous music in a coffee shop?"

Tara laughed. "No, there was nothing in the least wrong with Jacob. He's a great person. I can't really explain this. He wanted to move in together, buy a ring . . . and I backed away. It just wasn't . . . right. I don't know how else to explain this . . ." she finished lamely. She really didn't know how to explain why she had broken up with Jacob. He had understood about her coming to Paris. And yet . . .

She'd had the oddest feeling about coming here. As

if she'd been waiting for this trip—this time—all her life.

And . . . there had been the dream.

She had plans to come to Paris, a little bit later, but while she was working on a deadline, trying to decide on the right date, she'd gone to sleep and . . .

Been in Paris. She had seen the city beneath her as her plane landed. She had seen the city she loved, the spires of Notre Dame, the rise of the Eiffel Tower. She had seen herself with Ann, sitting at the café, driving out to the village. And then . . . a mist had rolled in, and she was walking. Walking through the woods in the surrounding countryside, intent on her destination. And as she walked, she had been afraid.

Afraid of the shadows that surrounded the place, shadows that twisted and moved and formed strange shapes, and seemed to whisper. She didn't know if the whispers were words that beckoned her onward, or if they were warnings. But she had to get to the house, and it had something to do with her grandfather. Every step brought greater fear, and greater determination. Through a field of tangled trees and shrubbery, she could see a structure ahead. It seemed to glow with a strange yellow light, like that of the moon sifting through clouds and mist. And in her mind, she was repeating the words *help me* over and over again, though she wasn't sure who it was she was calling to, only that she believed, had to believe that he would be there.

She had awakened with perfect logic, explaining to herself that the dream was all about her grandfather. She adored him. And he was in trouble. She needed to reach him because of his illness. She was being selfish and foolish by not getting on the first plane she could in order to be with him. The dream was a warning that her grandfather needed her, and her fear of shadows was her fear of illness.

And at the same time, despite all her logic, she felt that some cycle in life was ending, and that another was about to begin. Oddly enough, whatever it was, she had been waiting for it all her life, and now was the time.

Which brought up Jacob. She did care for him. He was wonderful, full of fun, sensual, a down-to-earth bastion to balance her flights of fantasy. But there was simply something else out there, and she had to go to Paris, and discover what it was.

Somewhat insane. And yet . . .

The right thing to do.

Crazy, but right. How, she couldn't begin to fathom. She didn't intend to stay in Paris forever. It wasn't her home. New York was.

Yet the call to Paris, and whatever she was seeking, was ridiculously strong.

"Maybe I should go to New York with you and meet Jacob," Ann said, wrenching Tara out of her reverie.

"Maybe," Tara said, "I guess I just wasn't . . . in love with him." Ann could be so totally down to earth and practical. There was no way that Tara could explain her feelings to Ann.

Ann shook her head in confusion. "Great. You give up Mr. Perfect, and then you give me a hard time? The man I love cheats, and you think I should listen to him. You have someone open, honest, and loyal, but you're just not in love."

"I do care about him, a great deal. But not enough."

Ann was silent a few minutes, watching her, and then shrugged. "Well, look at the two of us! We definitely should go bar hopping. It's not the way to meet the right man, but work is definitely not the right place either. And I do nothing else except work, so it seems."

"We really should go out—only semi on the prowl—and we will," Tara said. "But not tonight. I'm so tired. I don't think that I could deal with the excitement of a good-looking man. Or a nice one. Or even an ugly fellow who wanted to buy me a drink."

"Tomorrow night, then."

"Sure."

"Well, then. Let's get on to the chateau. You can hear for yourself what Grandpapa is saying. You can talk to him this afternoon, and I will go back to work."

"Maybe you and Willem will work it out."

"I carry my letter opener with me always," Ann said, lifting her hand to the waiter to signal for the check.

Ann insisted on paying. As they were rising, she suddenly froze for a moment, then caught Tara's arm, turning her about on the sidewalk.

"What? What is it?"

"Let's just go. Hurry."

"What is it?"

"Willem," Ann muttered.

"Willem? Where?"

Tara tried to turn, anxious to see the man her cousin had been so deeply involved with. Ann kept dragging her along, but she was able to catch a quick glimpse of the man. He was tall and blond, wearing a designer business suit, very suave. A lock of hair fell over the darkness of his sunglasses as he paused to light a cigarette before choosing the café table they had just vacated.

"Don't stare! Let's just get out of here."

"Well, you still work with him. You could introduce me. Then I could be a better judge of his character."

"He has no character. Let's go."

Ann dragged her along. Tara couldn't help but look back. As she did so, she was certain that the man was watching them leave, though she could see nothing of his eyes through the glasses. He was appealing in a very smooth way that would have fit very well with Ann's cool veneer of sophistication.

His attention was taken from her as he was joined by another man at the table. Willem apparently knew the fellow he was meeting. He rose, and, American style, shook the man's hand. The other fellow was light as well. Tall, with sandy blond hair, and, beneath his business suit, he appeared to be in excellent condition. They were moving too quickly for Tara to make out his features; he, too, wore sunglasses.

Nearly tripping, Tara looked forward for a moment. She was startled by an uneasy feeling, a sense of being watched—or stalked, even. Goose bumps rose on her arms, and a bolt of icy adrenaline shot through her, causing her to shiver.

She looked back.

Neither of the men was at the table. Tara stopped where she stood on the busy street, staring back, puzzled. The two had simply vanished.

"He met someone," Tara said.

"He's the head of sales! He's always meeting someone," Ann said impatiently. "And I have to get you home, and come back in and do some work. Please, let's get moving!"

Tara gave herself a shake. She was tired. She hated the long flight over the Atlantic. She loved Europe, but hated getting here. She smiled ruefully at herself. It was really a beautiful Paris morning.

"Tara!"

"I'm coming."

Moments later, they were in the car, heading out of the city.

"He has an interesting look," Tara commented, watching her cousin.

"I don't care to talk about him anymore." Ann still seemed distracted. "There is more to worry about than a lying, cheating, man. There is Grandpapa."

"Is there more you should be telling me?" Tara asked.

"I have told you that he is a lying cheat. Is there *more?*"

"I meant about Grandpapa."

"Ah." Ann glanced at her. "We'll be home soon enough. When you see him, you'll understand."

"But his health is good?"

"Not good, but better. He has made a sound comeback from his bout with pneumonia. It's as if he's willing himself to get better and be strong. One thing that has bothered me is that he's incredibly concerned with an archeological dig going on in our village . . . seems they've dug to the crypts of the ruins of the old church. Grandpapa wakes first thing in the morning, looking for the newspaper. He's asked me to go see what they're doing. He pores over those ancient books of his, and gets all excited. He wants to go himself, but the doctors have told him that he mustn't, that the air in such a place would be extremely bad for him. When he heard it might actually kill him, he realized that he couldn't go. He is determined to stay alive. He is trying to stay healthy, and guard himself, but he has been driving me crazy to go down there."

"And have you gone?"

Ann shook her head. "I am not feeding into his fantasies! I told him that the crypts are off limits to tourists and that I have no way to get into the dig."

"Is that true?"

"It was true," Ann said, flashing Tara a little smile of guilt. "They were worried about the integrity of the underground structure. I don't really know what the situation is right now. There were a few write-ups in the paper when they began, but now, there may be a column or two every few days." She glanced at Tara and shrugged as she drove. "Okay, I think they have opened the dig to tourists. I'm not sure why. We're really nothing more than a little village on the outskirts of a big city—Paris offers the visitor so many major attractions that a small dig doesn't usually get much attention. Some professor involved is certain that he's on to a major historical find, but he doesn't seem to generate much enthusiasm from his colleagues. And most people come to Paris to see the art and beauty. Those with a morbid twist to their minds can crawl down into the catacombs and see thousands of bones."

"Perhaps Grandpapa is all excited mainly because the ruins are in our little village. He grew up here, lived a lot of his life here. Maybe he feels that there is a family connection to this dig."

"I asked him that," Ann said. "He was appalled, assuring me that we had nothing to do with ground that was deconsecrated. But then, hey, you're not exactly a seasoned Parisian, but you have been to what's world famous and historical here. If you want to tramp around in a crypt, be my guest."

"But you said you were afraid that it would feed into his fantasies."

Ann shrugged. "Well, I'm still afraid. But I'm also trying to catch up with work. And trying to keep the old place going with little help. I don't mean you, your folks, your brother, or my folks. I mean on a day-to-day basis, simply keeping bathrooms clean, straightening out, keeping the roof on, and the ivy down. We've only got Katia running the house and Roland keeping up the grounds. Debbie, his old assistant in the States, has written to say that she wants to come to look after Jacques, but it will take her a while to put her affairs in order. So, you see, I really haven't had any extra time to go running around to ruins. And I'm really glad that you're here. You said that you were actually all caught up and would do some painting that you wanted to do—rather than what was commercial and paying the bills—while you were here. Maybe you'll find inspiration in the crypt. Maybe they'll even let you set up an easel. I don't know. I love old Jacques with my whole heart. Remember when we were kids? He wrote popular fiction, but people were always interviewing him as if he were a great scholar or literary writer. He's always had such a grip on the world, on human nature . . . I don't want to lose the grandfather we've known and loved all our lives."

"I love him, too. He was always magnificent, larger than life. He gave me my love of art, and you've certainly learned a lot about writing and publishing from him. He means the world to us, and he loves us very much as well."

"Yes, but you are the one with the love of stories and tales and fantasies. I am far too logical and straightforward for him. So you talk to him. See if you can make sense of it all."

"I'm here to do whatever is needed."

Ann nodded, falling silent as they drove.

They had left the city behind and were driving

through beautiful countryside with little clusters of charming old houses. Minutes later, Tara saw the drive to the chateau before them, and then the home that had been her fantasyland as a child. The drive wound haphazardly through trails of flowers—Ann's babies, as she called them. Then they came around the gravel drive directly in front of the old stone steps.

The front door opened and Roland, who was close to her grandfather's age, came hurrying down the steps, throwing open the car door before she could do so herself. He burst into a warm and enthusiastic greeting so quickly spoken that she could pick out only one word in every few; it didn't matter, she knew she was being welcomed. She hugged Roland, then insisted she was perfectly able to handle her own bag. By then, Katia, a few years younger than Roland, had arrived at the door. She wiped her hands on her apron, ran down the steps, and folded Tara into a massive hug as well. Tara struggled for the right words in French to return her greeting, gave up, and hugged her back. It seemed that the cheek kissing went on forever.

"I've got to get back to work," Ann called to her. "I'm not going inside. You're in your old room."

Tara had her own firm grip on her bag again; she wasn't about to let either Roland or Katia try to take it from her.

"Your grandpapa is in the library!" Katia said with stern disapproval, shaking her head with such vehemence that little gray tendrils of hair escaped from her neat chignon and whispered around her face. "You mustn't excite him too much; he can be such an old fool!"

"I'll tie him down if he gets too frisky," Tara assured her.

Ann continued around the gravel drive and headed for the street, returning to the city, and Roland and Katia followed Tara back into the house. In the once grand foyer, Tara paused. She looked around at the beautiful woodwork, and the fraying tapestries on the wall. The long, claw-footed table in the hall held Ann's computer surrounded by mounds of paper.

Tara smiled. It was good to be here.

Far across the Atlantic, Jade DeVeau woke with a start, and then wondered what had caused her to do so.

It was still night . . . or the wee hours of the morning. For a moment, she lay tensely, eyes narrowed, as she tried to ascertain what danger might have stirred her survival instincts while she slept. And yet . . .

She heard nothing.

She opened her eyes farther, twisted silently around.

Moonlight streamed through the window above the charming courtyard of her Charleston home. Lucian sat in the rocker by the window, looking out at the night.

It wasn't strange that he should be there. Jade had changed her own natural sleeping schedule to coincide with his, and he had learned to lie down and rest in the darkness of the night. But still, many a night she woke, and saw him there. Sometimes, he read, with a book light, so as not to disturb her. Sometimes, he sat, rocking, watching the moon. Most of the time, he was at ease, simply a quiet night owl, who, when really restless, went downstairs to work or watch one of the twenty-four-hour news stations or an old classic movie.

Tonight . . . there was something different.

Jade sat up, reaching for her robe at the foot of the bed, still afraid, though she knew not why, and feeling strangely vulnerable in the naked state in which she slept. She knew that he was instantly aware that she had wakened; he could sense her slightest movement.

He turned toward her, and even in the dimness of the moonlight, she saw that he smiled apologetically.

"I woke you. I'm sorry. I thought I was quiet."

She shook her head. "You didn't wake me. I just woke."

He pulled her down to sit on his lap. She drew her fingers through his hair, wondering if it was a sin to love anyone so much.

"What is it?" she asked him, her voice a whisper.

He shook his head. "I don't know."

A shiver shot through her. His arms tightened around her. "Don't be frightened. It's . . . whatever it is, it's away. Far away. Of course, that's what bothers me. I can feel something. But I don't know what."

As if he were afraid that he might be sending his tenseness straight into her soul, he stood suddenly, setting her upon her feet. "I'm in the mood for a hamburger."

She looked up at him dryly. "At five in the morning?"

They were interrupted by a sudden wail. "The baby," Jade said. She turned, hurrying to the next room down the hall. She knew that Lucian dogged her footsteps, though she didn't hear his movement.

She flicked on the light and hurried over to the crib where six-month-old Aidan slept. At the moment, he was wide awake, tufts of blond hair standing straight up from his tiny skull, cheeks red, little fists flying, tears streaking down his little face. Jade scooped him up into her arms.

The hardest thing for her to face when she married Lucian was the fact that she couldn't have children. She

had decided not to adopt; she wouldn't put an infant
into danger. But then, she heard about Aidan, just days
old at the time he was orphaned.

And now . . .

It didn't matter that she couldn't bear children. Aidan
was her child. She loved him as fiercely as she ever could
any child who had been born of her own flesh and
blood.

She cradled him gently in her arms, crooning to him.
He began to calm down, making little gulping sounds.
"Little boy, little boy, little boy . . . you're all right. It's
all right. Mommy is here."

His sobs subsided, then began again.

"Here," Lucian said, and took him from her arms.
Lucian looked down at their son. He spoke softly in
French. Aidan looked up at his father, fell silent, and
slowly closed his eyes, sound asleep.

Jade took him from her husband and slipped him
back into his crib, then came back to Lucian. "I should
resent your ability to calm him so easily, you know,"
she said.

"I cheat. My French is excellent. And it's a soothing
language."

She smiled. "Don't worry, raising him, trying to keep
working . . . to keep up . . . I'm far too exhausted most
of the time to be resentful."

He kissed her on the forehead. "Go back to bed, my
love. Get some sleep."

"I'm not tired anymore. Let's have hamburgers."

"You don't want an omelette?" he asked. "It is veer-
ing toward breakfast time."

"I'm in the mood for beef, very rare. How about steak
and eggs?"

"That will do."

They went down the stairs, hand in hand. Jade was proficient in a kitchen, and good scrambled eggs were one of her specialties. But she noted, though Lucian spoke to her, his words casual, that he kept staring out the rear windows. The pool—not much of a pool, but enough of a little lap pool—was in the back, surrounded by latticework and vines, a beautiful area. And a high stone wall that dated back more than a hundred and fifty years surrounded the backyard. She couldn't understand what he was watching so intently.

Or perhaps she did.

He watched the moon.

Moments later, she came out to the dining room. "Steak and eggs, and a wonderful Burgundy to accompany the meal."

"Burgundy—at this hour of the morning?" he inquired.

"You bet," she told him.

They sat down to eat. She tried to be casual. She talked about Aidan's smiles. The book she was reading. He responded with all the right words but he wasn't really listening.

The deep darkness of night began to lift.

He stood, stretching. "Well, that was delicious. We should try to get a little sleep."

Jade nodded. She started to pick up the dishes. He caught her arm, and his deep brown eyes touched hers.

"We'll get them later," he said.

She nodded, feeling a jump in her heart, in all her senses.

Her husband was an expert lover.

A vastly experienced one, but . . .

He loved her, and she knew how deeply, and the past didn't matter at all.

She followed him up the stairs, her hand in his. And at the foot of the bed she shed the robe she had wrapped around herself. In seconds she felt his hands upon her bare flesh, and as always, it was as if she was set afire, as if she melted . . .

As if nothing else mattered in the world at all . . .

No matter the darkness, no matter the light, always, she felt his eyes, liquid fire, traveling over her, into her . . .

And in the end, always, she would be amazed that she could still feel such passion, time after time, as if the world burst into gold, and sometimes, after the volatile climax seized, seared, and sated her, the brilliance would fade to black.

Finally, exhausted, she slept in peace.

He lay awake, and when he was sure she was completely into a world of dreams, he rose.

He closed the curtains, and went down the stairs, then down again, into the basement.

He kept a computer there. He started toward the desk, determined to send an e-mail.

Then he decided against it. He found his place in the dark coolness of the lowest section of the house. There he closed his eyes.

And receded into the depths of his mind.

"Tara!"

Jacques DeVant might be aging, and his health might not be the best, but he could still offer his granddaughter a bone-crunching hug. He didn't go on and on welcoming her, he just said her name the way only he could say it, and hugged her. And she hugged him back.

Then, of course, there were the inevitable kisses, one on each cheek, and he held her out at arm's length, studying her.

He was a handsome man, even at his age. He'd never lost his hair. It was thick and snow white glinting silver in the light. His eyes were incredibly blue, and though his features were weathered and worn, there was a nobility in his facial structure that gave him a tremendous dignity and appeal.

"Terrific hug," she told him, ushering him back to his library chair. "And you look wonderful. But you have to be careful, you know. You have to rest. And not go about throwing away too much energy."

He arched a furry white brow to her, looking at her skeptically. "I'm doing very well. And trust me, I'm extremely careful of my health. I intend to live until . . . well, you know, until I reach a ripe old age. A riper old age."

He had been going to say something else, Tara thought. *I intend to live until* . . . it was as if he meant to say that he was going to live until he was done. Until some task was completed.

"Honestly, you could be a young dude of only sixty," she assured him.

He shrugged and smiled, accepting the compliment. Tara perched on the edge of his library desk, looking at the old volume he had been reading.

She decided to cut right to the chase. "What are you up to? Ann is upset because you want her to go down and find out what's going on at a dig in the village."

His smile faded just slightly, becoming rueful. "She thinks I am a demented old man."

"No, she would never think that. But she is worried."

"I have to know what is happening there, and Ann has resisted me, and . . . well, thank God you're here!"

He spoke the words so fervently that Tara immediately understood her cousin's concern. "What is it about this dig?" she asked

"I have to know what they're after. And what they've found."

"A bunch of old bones, I would imagine, if they're digging up the crypt of a deconsecrated church."

"I have to know exactly what they're digging up. I need the plans to the crypt. I need to know if the professor has other scholars working on the project, who, just exactly who, is involved. I believe that the work must be stopped. And if I don't have all the information, I won't be able to do anything. Tara, you must go for me. You must be my eyes and ears. I have to be so careful, you see. My own grandchild thinks I am losing my mind. If I am not careful, others will see that I am locked away. That can't happen."

"Grandpapa, you are a scholar. A well-known author."

"An author of fiction. Of far-fetched tales."

"With tremendous messages," she reminded him.

That compliment only irritated him. "Fiction. They will think that all the fiction of my many years has slipped into my mind, and that I am crazy. Of all the times to be old and ill and weak!"

"I don't understand," Tara said.

He didn't appear to hear her. He was staring into the old stone fireplace where logs burned and flames danced, rising in blue, orange, yellow, red, and soft gray plumes of smoke.

"Grandpapa—"

"I need you to go to the church," he told her.

"I'll go tomorrow," she said. "I promise—"

"Tomorrow may be too late. Perhaps today is too late, and yet I haven't heard of anything terrible happening."

"What terrible thing can happen in an old church crypt?" Tara asked. "Are you afraid that there is something of immense value down there and someone may be after it? Are the men in charge of the dig in danger? Is there something that you really know?"

He stared from the flames into her eyes. He shook his head. "You wouldn't understand. But you must find out for me what is happening."

"I told you that I would. But you know me, I can't sleep on planes. I'm exhausted. I'll go tomorrow."

"Today." He looked her up and down. "Katia will get us some strong coffee. If you keep moving, you'll be fine. It's once you lie down and rest that jet lag gets to you."

"You don't understand. I'm wiped out. I had to turn in a project before I got on the plane. I haven't had a lot of sleep in days."

"Then one more day won't matter."

"Hey! You're my grandparent, you're supposed to be concerned about my health and welfare."

"I'm extremely concerned. But you will go this afternoon and bring me back every possible piece of information they have on the dig. The name of everyone involved. You must somehow get in right where they are working."

"They may not allow—"

"Good heavens! Flirt your way in."

"Sure you don't want me to just sell my body on the street?"

He let out a sound of impatience, giving her a stern frown. "This is not a matter for joking."

"Jacques!" she said, using his first name, as she had always done when pretending to be among the literary community he had known so well in New York. "I don't know what I'm doing. If I could understand, it would help. What exactly do you think is going on that you feel you must stop? Ann says you've spoken about something called the Alliance—"

"Yes, the Alliance. I am one of the Alliance, and there are not many of us left, not many who have understood the calling. Surely, there are others. But perhaps they don't know as yet. There are those I may be able to find . . . but first! I must stop the dig."

"Jacques, what is this Alliance? A group from the war? A group of writers?"

"The Alliance . . . there isn't time. Yes, perhaps you could say we're a group from the war. Now please, we can talk for days on end. You must do this for me. If you do not, I will have to risk another bout of pneumonia or respiratory failure and go myself. If I'm right about what they may find . . . who they may find . . . you've got to get down there."

"If you know something, you should call the police."

"The police would not understand. They would have me locked up. Please, if you love me at all, Tara, you will help me now. I need you." There was a desperation in his tone that made her seriously wonder about his mental state.

"The police cannot help," he went on. "Not now. We are not in danger from any thief or ordinary murderer."

"Grandpapa, what is the danger, then?"

"Evil, pure evil. Tara, I'm begging you. You must do as I ask."

She was startled by his words. She wanted to open her mouth, to protest the things that he was saying.

Yet, she suddenly could not.

A chill had settled over her. A chill that seemed to sweep straight through her, blood, flesh, and bones.

"You will go?" he asked. "You will go for me. Today. Please?"

"Of course I will go."

CHAPTER 2

The gloom in the crypt seemed overwhelming. Despite the many portable lamps hung around the vault deep in the earth, the corners were cast in shadow, deep and gloomy, shadows that moved in a macabre dance, making angels, saints, gargoyles, and grotesques come to life in an eerie profusion of darkness and light.

"Dig carefully!" Professor Dubois admonished.

Carefully! They could barely see.

"Carefully, carefully!" Dubois repeated.

The man was distraught. But then, to Jean-Luc, Dubois always appeared on the edge of a frenzy, as if his explorations in the crypt were world-shattering and his findings would change the shape of the globe.

Down in the ground, in the area of deconsecrated ruins of the old St. Michel recently rediscovered foundations, the workmen were tired. Jean-Luc Beauvoir stared at the professor with his thick glasses and wild gray hair and bit his lip to keep silent. He and the American, Brent Malone, had been working tirelessly for hours, slowly, slowly digging away the age-old rot around the coffins. Professor Dubois was expecting an incredible archeological find. He was certain he was going to unearth not only the dead, but worldwide recognition, honors and awards, and naturally, the fortune to be made from the book he would write, and the lectures and speeches he would give. The professor gave little thought to the fact that most learned men thought he was a raving lunatic, or that he had bought his way into the excavation either by bribery or by making a large donation to the current St. Michel. Little money had been left to pay for the highly trained archeological staff Dubois had wanted, and so the professor constantly shouted orders and ridicule at the two-man team of laborers he had managed to obtain, and forced them to keep working once the afternoon began to wane toward evening. The American seemed able to silence the professor with a single stare from his strange, gold-tinted hazel eyes, but the professor would merely start all over again.

The St. Michel now standing in the little village just outside Paris dated back to the sixteenth century; the crypt in the old ruins they now worked so laboriously to probe and restore predated the new church by three or four hundred years. The work was treacherous, but they had shored up the area enough to allow tourists to pay extra francs to come and view the dig in process. Now, to add to the aggravation of the professor leaning over their shoulders, directing the tedious and back-breaking labor, there were the curious stopping to ask questions every other minute. The Americans were easy to ignore; he pretended he spoke no English. The

French were more annoying because the professor would pause to speak with them, then shout at his laborers again that they were working far too roughly; they might damage coffins that had survived for centuries.

Jean-Luc stared over at Brent and rolled his eyes as a young woman began a conversation with the professor. Not just a young woman. A beautiful one, with a smooth cultured voice and a knowledge of the area, and the church. American. Her accent was definitely American. And though her words were curious and knowledgeable, there was also a friendly charm to the very sound of her voice. It was not lost on the professor. The old man was not without a lascivious nature; he would hold the young woman to balance her over the opening so that she could see better, and so that he could get his bony hands on her young flesh.

Brent didn't seem to catch Jean-Luc's look. He was distracted, not noting the young woman talking to the professor, either. He was studying the area in which they worked, which connected to the underbelly of the new church through a maze of vaults and corridors, many of which had housed the bones of the noble dead. This area, some distance from the new foundations, was different in its style and decor. Typical Gothic arches created both support and architectural features, but the walls and crypts were decorated with a strange combination of the customary and bizarre. Large crosses, in various metals, surrounded the grave sites, but were joined by myriad demons and gargoyles.

In the pit where they now dug, they had just come to an obstruction. He knew it, and the American knew it. As the professor chatted with the young woman in French, Brent at last gave Jean-Luc his undivided attention. He gave a little shake of his head, indicating that they should not tell the professor just what point they had reached.

Jean-Luc grinned. The American was smart. The corpse they were about to exhume might be laden with precious jewels and adorned in gold. Let the professor have his accolades. They would take the riches.

But the American frowned, and Jean-Luc frowned as well. What was Brent planning?

The young woman was lingering, speaking with the professor, but watching the American as he worked in the crypt. Why not? Jean-Luc thought with a shrug. The woman was young. Tall, sleek, elegantly, sensually built with full curves and a slim waist. She had long, sandy hair, and wickedly long legs. Large, luminous eyes, and a perfectly fashioned face. Smooth flesh. Professor Dubois was as wrinkled as a prune and as wild looking as an electrocuted Pekinese. The American worker was a tall man, wiry and powerful with an easy grace of movement and finely honed muscles that seemed to swell and tighten each time he used a tool. His features marked him as somewhere between twenty-five and thirty-five, while his eyes were that strange green-gold color and his hair, neatly long, almost to his shoulders, frequently tied, was a dark sable. Rich, probably tempting to a young woman. The world didn't change. Women might marry a man with intelligence and riches, but when it came to a man with whom to find pleasure, they tended to hunt out a man with physical power. Animal instinct. The American, however, still wasn't giving the electric beauty of his countrywoman much notice. He was pretending to dig deeper now, but making no real moves to disclose whatever treasure they might have come upon.

Jean-Luc had simply paused; now he wondered if it was the American, or the grave, to which the young lady was giving her sharp attention while casually making conversation with the professor.

"Professor," Brent said suddenly and impatiently, interrupting the conversation and leaning on his shovel.

"What is it?" Dubois demanded.

The American looked at his watch. "It's late. We have to begin again in the morning."

"Not so late. We shouldn't stop. I have studied the old records. We must be nearly upon the grave."

"And if you are upon the grave you seek, you'll want experts in here to move the final layers of dirt and sand, and you will not get the professionals you will need at this time. As of now, we have nothing here, nothing to bring in grave robbers by night. If we start again by morning, you will have ample time to do your discovery justice. It is nearly seven. We have already worked hours overtime. The church is closed. We must get this young lady out, and shut down for the evening."

"Oh, I have overstayed!" the young woman exclaimed. "I simply find it all so fascinating. Forgive me."

"Forgive you? Not at all, my dear," Dubois said, drawing Jean-Luc's greater attention to the woman. She wore jeans and a sweater and handsome black loafers, now covered with the dust from this realm of the dead. Simple clothing, but worn very well, hugging the form that had so drawn the professor's interest. Her hair was a sandy blond, long, but drawn back in a smooth, sleek ponytail that heightened the fine sculpture of her features. Her eyes, deepened by the murky light and shadow, appeared to be almost turquoise, the color of the sea off the French coast. They were never going to get the professor to let this morsel go . . . Jean-Luc could almost understand the old man's desire to hold on to something so simple as conversation, just as long as he could.

"Shall I see our guest out?" Brent asked bluntly. He stared coolly at the woman. "She needs to be *out.*"

"Yes, of course, she must be seen safely out, but you must finish up. I will see the young lady out," Dubois said. "My dear, if you will?"

"Oh, please, don't worry, I can make my way," she said pleasantly. "I am simply so intrigued. I'll be back, if I may?"

"Please, you are so very welcome, Miss . . ." Dubois said.

"Marceau. Genevieve Marceau, Professor. And thank you, you've been so kind."

"A French name. But you're an American."

"Of French descent. And I'm familiar with such vaults—"

"But still! Alors! You must not go alone. The flooring is tricky. And despite the lights . . . well, it gets late, and though we are underground, it seems even darker once the night has come."

"I am absolutely fine. I will see you then, Professor. Thank you so very much."

She shook the professor's hand. The professor was loath to let go of her hand. She managed to retrieve her fingers, and repeated, "I'm fine. Please!" She started out then, quickly, determined to exit on her own. The professor looked after her for a long while. When she was gone at last he stared with narrowed eyes at the American. "Make sure that the tomb is secured when you leave. Totally secured."

"Of course."

The professor glanced at this watch. "You're right. I must make calls . . . find the right people. And you!

Jean-Luc! Keep your heavy hand off the work from now on. You hack away as if you were plowing weed-strewn fields. This is great work going on here."

Without another word, the professor turned and started from the tomb.

Brent looked at Jean-Luc. "I have to open this tomb tonight," he said quietly.

"Yes, yes, of course. We have done the work. The professor will take everything; we are nothing to him but muscle. He is like a slave driver. But what will we do? If we rob the tomb, he will know. The government will be called in."

"No, no, pay attention to me," Brent said impatiently. "We will open it carefully, and reseal it."

"And rob it first, of course."

"No."

"But—"

"There will be a trinket, something you can take. But we are not robbing the tomb."

"Then . . ."

"There will be a reward for you, and Dubois will never know. All right? Help me with the last of the dirt. Quickly."

The dirt was easy to shift, but the sarcophagus was covered by a huge stone slab.

"We will never shift this," Jean-Luc muttered.

"Take the side."

Jean-Luc hefted his huge frame against the slab, grunting and groaning, sweat immediately popping out on his brow. The American set to the task with him. The stone shifted and Brent shouted that they must be careful; they didn't want it crashing to the floor and breaking. The stone settled. They could see the coffin itself.

It was black. Crosses abounded over and around it. Brent immediately set to work removing them. Jean-Luc joined in. "There is strange writing on the coffin. Look, how odd, I cannot make it out completely, but the words speak of the devil while the coffin is covered in signs of the Lord! Sacrebleu! How very strange!"

Brent had picked up a crowbar.

"I don't think it will work. It appears as if the coffin has somehow been sealed with some kind of adherent . . . like a soldering."

"I will open it."

Brent shoved the crowbar against the coffin. The creaking sound it gave out caused even such a man as Jean-Luc to feel a prickle of fear at his nape. The silence that followed the creaking was deep and complete.

So deep, in fact, that they were both startled to hear a sound . . . a furtive, rustling sound, coming from the exit to the vault. One of the portable lamps suddenly burned to an end; in the wall sconce at their side, there was a popping sound, and the area went dark. And still, they could hear something . . . footsteps, stealthy, careful, coming from the exit to the vault.

"It's the woman, surely," Brent said, and swore impatiently. "I'll get rid of her. Touch nothing, nothing, do you hear me, nothing, while I am gone, Jean-Luc, on pain of death. I mean it."

"Of course! Never. I swear that I will not," Jean-Luc said, and crossed himself. But as he watched the American silently disappear into shadows that seemed to close around him, he felt the birth of resentment in his soul. The American wanted to rob the tomb without getting caught. Good, sane concept. But the American wanted the finest riches in the coffin to be for himself.

The lid had been pried open; it was surprising that

the American had managed it so easily. A sumo wrestler might have struggled with such a task.

Jean-Luc looked toward the stygian darkness of the exit vaults. Brent was not returning, yet.

He edged his away around the coffin to the side where his work partner had stood. He could not resist. He lifted the lid of the coffin, hearing again the blood-chilling creaking as the hinges, hundreds of years old, gave way. He steeled himself against the ghastly look of the ancient dead; he had become quite accustomed to skulls; to open jaws that appeared to have been captured in a victim's last scream against death. Decayed flesh, withered flesh, gray and moldy, fragments of clothes, boots, with bits of bone poking through . . . this would be nothing new.

Yet he gasped as he stared into the tomb. There was no scent of decay, not even the musty smell that came when centuries had passed since death. There was no bone to be seen. What he stared upon was . . .

Eyes.

Eyes wide open, black as pitch, but open. Staring, staring straight into Jean-Luc's own. As if the corpse had never died but slept, and waited . . .

And then . . .

The corpse moved.

Jean-Luc let out a shrill, bloodcurdling scream that might have wakened the dead not only in Paris, but in all of France . . .

Darkness, wavering light, filled the tomb as the lamps suddenly swung. The black of the grave, the white of the flickering light . . .

The brilliant crimson of blood . . .

All filled' the tomb.

* * *

Standing in the vault, about to accost their unwelcome visitor, Brent heard the scream.

And he swore, damning himself. And damning *her*.

"My God!" she cried.

The woman had been returning to the vault. Sliding along the vaults with their smell of rot and decay, she had been returning to the site of the dig. *Why? Who the hell was she? What was she doing . . . at this site, here, and now?*

She forgot to hide as they heard Jean-Luc's scream tear through the corridors of the vault like the haunted shrieking of the damned.

And so she cried out herself. Cried out, and . . .

She saw Brent, saw his eyes . . .

Her scream echoed Jean-Luc's.

She turned to run.

Too late . . .

Oh, yes, by God.

Far too late . . .

Tara had never heard anything quite like the sound that still seemed to echo within the walls of the crypt.

She had felt a strange sense of the ages while going down into the underground ruins, and she had felt a sadness for all the lives gone by, and even a bit of awe for lives lived so very long ago, and the intense history of mankind. She hadn't felt entirely comfortable with the mausoleums and graves of the dead, but she hadn't been afraid. Not even in the darkness and the gloom.

Then she heard the scream.

The shadowy light in the bowels of the earth gave life

to the savage grins and leers of gargoyles, grotesques, and angels alike.

Sound seemed to rise from the dead.

The walls to grow closer, darker.

And there, ahead of her, as frozen by the sound as she, stood the American.

And the look on his face as he stared at her, in that split second when they were both paralyzed by the echoes that seemed to rise from hell, from the shrieks that still seemed to fill the hellish world of the dead in which they stood, transfixed her.

He stood some distance away, and she knew that he had come after her, somehow aware that she hadn't left the tomb, that she had an agenda of her own.

He was some distance down the corridor, where the tombs had been laid out as shelves. The shadows had grown darker as the work lighting had dimmed, as lamps had shattered. She couldn't possibly see his face, not really, he was just a silhouette there, and yet one filled with menace. And she was certain that he was staring at her with fury, and with a vengeance that seemed to make the hair at her nape rise. Seconds, flew by, seconds, and yet in that time, she could feel his tension, as if it were an ancient wind, roiling down the length of the tunnel toward her. *He would come after her, he wanted to kill her, do to her what she had heard in that bloodcurdling scream, still seeming to echo against stone and concrete.*

But he didn't come toward her.

He turned, racing back toward the sound of the scream, as if hell had come bursting through the earth below the crypt, and if he could stop exploding fires that had risen from hell.

And yet she knew. He had seen her face. And every

single line and nuance of her countenance had been embedded in his memory.

He would still come after her.

She turned and ran. As fast as he had run back toward hell, she ran away from it. Down the corridors that had been home to centuries of the dead.

Down through the darkness. Desperate, almost blinded by fear. The stairs to the new church at last loomed before her. She flew up them, barely aware of her feet touching the steps. She arose near the doors at the rear, raced across a length of marble and threw herself against the doors that would lead back into the sanity of the French night.

The doors were locked.

Brent felt as if he had been physically torn in two. And in the minuscule span of time during which he had heard the scream and stared at the woman down the corridor, eons of thought had passed through his mind.

He'd been the biggest fool in the world to leave Jean-Luc alone with the coffin.

But he had known that the woman remained in the crypts, and he knew he must get her out. He hadn't even been certain that he had been right about the tomb. He had taken on the job of digging just as a precaution. Because of a vague legend that had circulated hundreds of years ago, a nightmare story told by schoolgirls and boys around the fire on a cold winter night.

And yet . . .

He should have known.

Despite her loafers, the woman could run. She had

been far ahead of him. And she had run like a cougar, and he knew, even as he raced back to the tomb, his heart sinking, that she had taken off again, and she was sure to be trouble.

She had heard the scream as he had. And no one with any sanity or instinct or sense of self-preservation could ever be fooled into thinking that it was the sound of an owl in the night or a wolf howling in the far off woods.

He swore, even as he ran.

The scream . . .

As much as he had heard, had seen in life, the scream still seemed alive. Within the walls, within his soul.

He swore to himself. He should have come to know Jean-Luc better. The scream that had echoed throughout the ancient stone had indicated that he had been a greedy fool, that he had opened the coffin.

That legend was true.

And Jean-Luc had already paid the price of greed.

Brent raced with lightning speed back to the site of the excavation. But as quickly as it had all occurred, he was too late. Which, of course, he knew. Too late for Jean-Luc. And yet had hoped that he would not be too late for . . . others.

Yet he knew that he would be.

Time might have been a trick of the light.

The lanterns that had illuminated the room had been cast down, broken, shattered. Only a few, down but not broken, remained to provide even a trickle of sickly, ash-colored light. Shadows ruled.

Brent damned himself over and over for leaving.

In the near darkness, he moved cautiously, all his senses attuned to the slightest movement. Yet even as he took reasonable care, he was certain that it would not matter. The tomb was empty of the living.

Of any creature . . . with even a semblance of life. Even the rats had fled.

His eyesight was excellent in darkness and shadows. He found his way back through piles of earth and stone and around other craters of the dig.

He found the hole in the floor. So carefully dug. The centuries-old tomb.

In the pit, the open lid displayed an empty coffin. Jean-Luc lay on the floor beside it. Brent bent down, touching the shoulder of the man, seeking to roll him and try to find any facsimile of a pulse.

The head rolled to the side at his attempt, completely detached from the body. Jean-Luc was like a doll seized by a child in a frenzy, ripped into pieces.

Brent noticed the stains on the floor. Blood vessels had been completely severed, but there were no great pools of blood.

He stood, closing his eyes. He held dead silent, taking a moment to listen, but the crypt was empty. He couldn't hear so much as the scratch of a rat's claw or the scamper of a spider across the floor.

But then . . .

There was something, a sound, far above him.

A banging. He closed his eyes and listened intently. Far, far above. From here, in the bowels of the earth, the next sound was faint, almost like the crying of the wind. It was the woman, screaming.

The crypt was empty.

The coffin's occupant was gone, and despite her years of incarceration, she would be carefully testing the new world now. Hidden in the night, in the shadows. Carefully exploring.

A long night lay ahead. Yet . . .

He stared down at the remains of Jean-Luc.

She had feasted. He might have the night, and the following hours of daylight, to find her before she felt the thirst again.

There was nothing else to do here . . . except see that he was not arrested himself. He turned, and moved with fluent speed back along the corridors he had followed earlier. He moved in silence, still.

He noted the bag against the wall and stopped. A small leather shoulder bag. It belonged to the woman in the crypt. He knelt down beside it, feeling no qualms as he dug into its contents. She had said that her name was Genevieve Marceau. She had lied. Her name was Tara Adair. He studied her passport, her other IDs, and the contents of her purse. He stuffed the contents back into the small leather bag, and fit the bag into the leg pocket of the painter-style denim jeans he wore.

She hadn't realized that she had lost her purse.

Hadn't known? Or hadn't cared.

She had been desperate to escape. Naturally. Anyone would have wanted out after hearing the pure, unadulterated terror in Jean-Luc's scream.

But just what the hell had she been doing here? What did she know? And more importantly, just who the hell was she, and why had she come here the way she had, questioning Professor Dubois, hiding after she had said she was leaving?

Her name meant nothing to him. Adair . . . he wondered if had ever known anyone named Adair.

She had said that she was of French descent. Not through anyone named Adair.

And yet . . .

He stopped, turning back, aware that she was still banging against the doors and screaming above him.

There was a cell phone in her purse.

She was probably realizing just about now that she didn't have it.

He turned back quickly, dug into the purse once again. He quickly hit the buttons on the cell phone, memorizing the last number she had dialed. He scanned the contents of the purse again, but there was nothing that gave an address in or around Paris.

She had come from New York City. That morning.

Still, she spoke French decently enough, with a few hesitations and an atrocious accent. But she had a good comprehension of the language.

Then, digging in her wallet, he found a half-ripped luggage tag. It gave an address on the Upper East Side of New York City. It also listed an address in the village here, in this little place on the outskirts of Paris.

He narrowed his eyes. Wondering.

He thought he knew the place.

From long ago, but . . .

He rose, and started down the corridor again. He had to reach the woman. One way or another—even if someone reached the door to the main church before he did.

There was no way out of it. She had to be hunted down. Stopped.

But not until he knew what she had been after in the crypt.

The man arrived at the café just after dusk.

Fashionably, casually dressed, self-assured and aware of his assets, he sat sometimes aloof, and sometimes offering a smile for the one female server at the café. He was not the type of man who invited casual conversation, and yet he was not averse to talking to strangers when the occasion warranted, nor was he particularly severe. When he chose, he gave that smile, and when he chose, he engaged in discourse about the weather, travel, and the beauty of the country when autumn approached.

As evening came, he sensed a strange disturbance in the air around him, and he felt a knot of tension building within him.

That evening, he waited.

He had waited before, and he would wait again.

The girl came by his table, asking if he would like more coffee. He drank it black, a large cup, like many Americans. But his French carried no accent. If he were not a Frenchman since birth, he had long ago mastered the language with all the smooth fluidity of a native Parisian.

"Monsieur, another coffee?" the girl asked.

His eyes lingered upon her for a moment. She was young, slim, wide-eyed and pretty. He smiled in return, and saw the way that his smile touched her face—she was flattered, she felt instantly close, and warmed.

"Another coffee, certainly . . . Yvette, is that what your tag says?"

"Yes, I am Yvette," she answered. Her words had taken on a slightly breathy quality. Ah, the young ones! So easily drawn to the attractive and powerful. Admittedly bored from his constant vigil, he felt the urge to play.

"Yvette . . . always, one of my favorite names," he said softly. "Can you sit a minute?"

She glanced over her shoulder nervously, looking for her boss. Indecision touched her large, deep brown eyes. Ah, but the lure was greater.

She sat.

"How late do you work?" he asked.

"Midnight, monsieur."

"Ah, but tell me, how old are you?" he queried.

"Old enough," she assured him. "Nearly twenty-one."

"Wonderful," he told her. She had placed her hands upon the table—perhaps ready to push against it and jump up should her employer appear. He brushed her fingers with his own and leaned closer, just a little tête-à-tête, something the few other customers lingering about the café would not notice. She shivered at his touch. Her eyes came to his. She seemed to be fighting to speak. "Your name, Monsieur?" she managed at last.

He crooked a finger toward her, beckoning her to lean in, toward him. She did so, a pretty fall of brown hair covering her face, and his.

Yet even as he played, he felt a sudden jolt rip through his body. He pulled back, leaving the girl as she had been, mesmerized. He stood, and looked around.

Then cursed himself. Something had gone wrong. Terribly wrong.

He threw francs upon the table, lifted the girl's chin, and muttered a quick thanks to her, and a promise that he would see her later. He knew, even in anger, that he wanted the friendship of this place, across from the church . . .

And near the police station.

He hurried across the street, still cursing himself, and wondering what the hell had gone wrong.

The rugged American digger was behind her before she ever even realized it.

She hadn't heard him come up the steps, hadn't had the least idea that he was there until he came directly behind her and spoke.

"If you stand aside, I can try to break it."

She screamed, jumping away from him, clearing a space.

The glance he gave her seemed disdainful. "We've got to get out of here through this door. Someone at the café down the street should have heard you by now. Of course, they're always playing loud music."

Tara kept her distance from him, feeling her tension running the entire length of her body. Every cell of her flesh seemed attuned to danger.

The night lights left on in the church were dim, but offered far more illumination than the trickles of light down below that had done little more than turn blackness into murk. He was moderately tall, probably about six-one, and though he appeared wiry and well-muscled, he was no sumo wrestler. Yet there was something about him. She could almost feel the heat of his energy, the tension in his muscles. She had a feeling the man could snap a neck with the flick of his wrist. There was an underlying sense of sleek and steadfast power to his least movement. It created a complete contrast of emotion within her. The first, to get away, to keep her distance. The second, to come closer, to stand behind the bastion he somehow seemed to offer. To trust in the strange, compelling urge to come closer.

She remembered the scream she had heard. Her mistrust of everything and everyone within the crypt.

She was staring at him, she realized. Almost hypnotized by the yellow-gold color of his eyes. *They were hazel, simply hazel.* She had watched him work in the crypt, heedless of her appearance there, or annoyed by it, one

or the other, and still, she was fighting the strange urge
to trust in him implicitly.

Fight it? Hell, yes, she possessed the logic to do so,
and she was furious that she had stood so long, staring,
and yet, she thought, in truth, probably only seconds
had gone by.

Then he moved.

And so suddenly that she was startled into jumping
again as he slammed a shoulder against the door.

Once again, his strange, near-yellow eyes fell upon
her. To her surprise, the door shuddered as he did so,
the wood sounding as if it was about to give.

Then she remembered that she had been ruing the
loss of her phone just as he arrived. He slammed against
the doors again.

They might be hundreds of years old, even in the
"new" church, but they were heavy, solid, and strong.

"My—my phone is back there."

"Your phone?"

"In my purse. A cell phone. I—dropped it back there
somewhere."

"Do you want to go back there for it?" he queried.

She felt whatever blood had been left in her face
drain from it at his words.

She moistened her lips. "What happened back there?
What was going on?"

"Why don't you tell me?" he asked, pausing a
moment and rubbing his shoulder. He leaned against
the door as he did so, studying her with a direct gaze.

Strange sensations swept through her. Fear, for one.
Because he was part of this. Because he had raced after her.
Because she had seen his eyes in the crypt.

Fear.

Again, she wanted to run. She didn't want to tell him

the truth. The ridiculous truth. That she had promised she would find out everything. That her grandfather thought he was part of the "Alliance." That she had been told to find out exactly what and *whom* they had been looking for, to bring back names, dates, anything she could discover. To try to listen when the professor and the workers talked, to make sure they were not yet close to an important discovery.

Fear . . .

And yet, he was leaning against the door, keeping his distance, trying to help her escape, the same as he was doing himself.

And there was something about his appearance . . .

Classic looks that were somehow rugged as well. An all-American appeal with a touch of European sophistication. Something very basic about him seemed to demand trust . . . and to compel her to move forward. Her mind warned her to keep a good distance. She stepped closer anyway.

He was wearing a denim work shirt, the sleeves rolled up, hinting of solid muscle in the biceps above. He was covered in dust, and still, somehow, his appearance was essentially neat and businesslike. And he appeared calm and stalwart in the face of . . .

"What happened back there?" she demanded. She had stepped forward again. She was just inches away from him. His jaw was square, his eyes direct. Cheekbones high and somewhat broad. There was a hint of five o'clock shadow on his jaw.

He didn't reply, but slammed a shoulder against the doors once again. To her amazement, there was a loud cracking sound that time, followed by a snap.

The door opened.

"I've got to get the police," he said flatly. "Perhaps

you should go." Those yellow eyes were on her, as if he knew . . .

That she didn't want to explain her grandfather's strange demands, especially in light of . . .

She shook her head determinedly. "I need to know what happened."

"What the hell do you think happened?" he asked impatiently. "Jean-Luc is dead."

She stepped back again, and he let out an oath of impatience. "Obviously, I didn't do it. I was chasing after you when we both heard the scream."

"Then . . ." She couldn't swallow. She couldn't make another word follow the single syllable she had uttered.

"Someone broke in. Of course. This is a dig. Someone out there knew that there must have been—something—in the tomb. The coffin in empty. I don't know what was in it because Jean-Luc opened it when I ran after you. Now Jean-Luc is dead, and I'm going to the police. Now, are you coming with me, or are you going home? Are you going to tell the police why you were running around at a closed architectural site? Wait! Never mind—don't answer yet. I'm not staying in this place any longer. I don't know about you, but I'm getting the hell out." He shoved at the door, creating a gaping hole. Broken wood creaked and groaned again.

She crawled through, trying to force her numbed mind to function.

Dead, a man was dead. Well, she had known that, had known it since she had heard the scream. *And, of course, one thing was true. This man hadn't killed his French coworker. He had been in the corridor, chasing after her, just as he had said, when they both heard the scream. She was an American, snooping around an excavation site she had been asked to leave.*

She would have to explain . . .
What she didn't understand herself.

"A man is dead," she said, the words coming from her painfully. "I can't run away."

"A man is dead, and there is nothing you can do," he reminded her. "You were where you shouldn't have been at the time. Trust me, I intend to report the matter." He swore again. "Listen, I'm trying to let you out of this mess."

It was night. Her grandfather's old Citroën sat in the lot by the café. People were milling outside it. She heard music, laughter.

She needed to see Jacques. She could always go to the police.

He must have read her mind. He was about to speak when he stiffened suddenly, almost as if he had seen something.

But he hadn't.

It was more as if he had sensed something, like smoke on the air, a promise of a devastating fire.

"Drive home," he said, his words suddenly tense. "Go home. If you don't like what you see in the newspaper, you can run to the police tomorrow. Tell them what you saw."

He turned away from her, starting down the walk from the church to the street. She ran after him. "They had best find out who did this," she said firmly, her words a warning.

He nodded, letting her go as she passed him.

"Tara."

She stopped and turned back.

"Be careful. Get in your car immediately. Now. Lock the doors, drive straight home, don't pause for anyone.

Don't invite anyone into your house who is a stranger. Don't go out alone at night. Do you understand?"

"Why?"

"Obviously, there is a murderer loose in Paris. One who might have seen you."

He walked past her. She saw that his determined footsteps were bringing him up the slight hill to the village center, and she knew that there was, indeed, a police station there.

She started across the street. Suddenly, she panicked, wondering how she was going to drive home when she had lost her purse in the crypt, then realized that the keys to the car were in her pocket.

But as she got into the Citroën and gunned the engine, she realized with a sinking heart that the police would know that she had been in the crypt. They would find her purse.

But as she was about to go back, a chill shot through her.

Tara.

He had called her by her real name when she had introduced herself to the professor with an alias she had pulled out of thin air.

Her mouth went dry.

She needed to stop, get out of the car, go to the police.

She turned. He had stopped, he was down the street staring at her. *Staring at her, or watching over her, like a strange sentinel?*

She couldn't go back. Not now. By tomorrow, she would know if he had indeed gone to the police, and if he hadn't, she would do so. And she would be able to describe him. And insist that although he had not committed the murder, he might know something about it.

This was illogical. She should go to the police immediately.

But an instinctive voice was rising inside her. *No. Do as he says!*

Shaking as she was, she pulled the car out onto the street, and headed for the chateau.

She needed to talk to her grandfather.

CHAPTER 3

There would be little that the police could do.

As Brent Malone sat in a chair before the desk of Inspector Henri Javet, he answered every question with complete honesty.

He didn't attempt to offer his own insight into the bizarre murder.

He admired the detective, and the speed with which the man worked. Within minutes, police officers had scoured the tomb. They had done so with competence and efficiency, being careful not to compromise any evidence that might be discovered by crime scene detectives and the forensic team. Then, when the site had been roped off and officials set in place to do all that they could, the questioning had begun.

And it hadn't been difficult to tell the truth. He and Jean-Luc had been closing down. He was afraid that a tourist might still have been on the premises. When he went in pursuit of the offending visitor, he heard the screams. The visitor had departed. Professor Dubois had left by the excavation route, but after finding the remains of Jean-Luc, he had panicked himself and departed by crashing through the church door.

Javet, a man with dark eyes, slick dark hair, and a build that spoke of many nights in a gym, was amazed that Brent had been able to break down the door.

"Adrenaline," Brent told him, lifting his hands in a rueful explanation. "I'm embarrassed to admit this, but . . . I had no thought other than to get out, and get to the police."

"You're certain that Professor Dubois had departed?" Javet asked him.

Dubois had been a total asshole through much of Brent's association with the man. That the professor was going to face intense questioning from the police himself seemed to be a beacon in the darkness.

"I believe he was gone. I can't be certain. Jean-Luc and I were working to finish for the night. And then I heard noise and knew someone was not out of the church. I thought perhaps a kid, a tourist. Maybe even someone who had been dared to spend the night in the crypt. You know how crazy people can get. I hadn't started along the corridors long before I heard the screaming. But I have no actual time frame. When I emerged from the church and came to you, it was dark already. I might have been walking along the corridors for several minutes . . . or more."

"And then you raced back?" Javet said, though they had been over this before.

"He screamed. My first thought was to help. Then I went to him, and I knew I couldn't help. My next thought was to get the hell out and get to the police."

"You were working legitimately in France?" Javet asked sharply.

Brent produced all his papers. Javet nodded. "This is your correct address in the area?"

"Yes."

"You don't intend to leave the country?"

Brent smiled. "No, sir. I have no intention of leaving at all."

"You might be out of work for some time."

"Yes, of course. I'll be all right."

"And that is how?"

"Family money . . . I dabble in the stock market and real estate back home."

"And yet, you were doing manual labor on a dig."

"I'm an eternal student of history, Inspector. I was fascinated by the dig, and glad to take any work to be a part of it."

Javet nodded. "While it seems that the man who was killed was working to keep food on his table."

"I realize that I remain a suspect," Brent said flatly.

"You were there. In fact, you were the only one there. Except for this tourist or student or whomever it was you were chasing when you say the murder occurred. What else can you tell us about him—or her?"

"There is practically nothing I can tell you. I didn't have a chance to find the person. Perhaps they had managed to get out. When I heard the screams, I went back to the site. And found Jean-Luc. I touched him to see if he was still breathing, but I touched nothing else at the site. I got out of there as quickly as I could."

"Dead is dead. And still, the way the man looked . . ." Javet wasn't an old man, but he had a drawn look to his features, as if he had seen many evils in his years as a detective. "Such a heinous murder. And all for an empty coffin," Javet said, shaking his head sadly.

Brent shrugged, lifting his hands again in a hopeless expression.

"I touched nothing after I tried to see if Jean-Luc had a pulse. When the head . . . well, I was quickly certain that he was dead, and, as perhaps you can imagine, I felt a surge of pure self-preservation. And I also wanted to get to professionals like you as quickly as possible."

Javet nodded. Brent forced himself not to look at his watch. Hours had gone by.

Hours he needed.

"I will be holding on to your passport," Javet said.

"Naturally."

"Now," Javet said, leaning back, "we will go over it all one more time."

"Again?"

"Indeed, the entire event from the beginning to the end."

He had waited and waited, and all to no avail. Watched when the two had run from the broken door.

Watched, cursing and angry, as the police had arrived, swarming over the place.

And he had stood there and tried and tried to fathom . . .

All for nothing.

So he had listened. Listened to the officers talking. And then he had known what was about to occur, and hurried to position himself properly.

Shadows were easy to find in the dark streets of the village. By the train station, they were numerous. And so he waited, watched, tensed and ready, using every sense within him.

They weren't needed. The man arrived on the train from Paris in full uniform. He immediately began to follow him. When they were on the streets alone, and the shadows were dense and tight, he approached him.

"Monsieur!"

The man, assured of his office and his own abilities, stopped impatiently. "Yes, where are you? What is it?"

He stepped out of the shadows.

And approached the impatient officer.

"I have information for you," he said quietly, coming close.

A cloud covered the bit of moon in the sky, and all the stars, and the two were swallowed up by the shadows.

Brent again looked at his watch, damning this man who went over and over every small detail.

Javet spoke. "I must tell you as well that, as you were the only person known to be present, I could hold you now for suspicion of murder."

"If I had murdered the man myself, I would hardly be running to you now, telling you all that I know."

Javet shrugged. "I usually have a sense for certain things, Malone. And I sense that you are telling me the truth, and that you are not a murderer. But the village, and perhaps all of Paris, will be in great alarm. They will be demanding an arrest, so that they can sleep tight in their own beds at night, unafraid. There may be many as well who think that you should be arrested on the spot."

"Are you going to arrest me?"

"Not at this moment. Every word you spoke rang true

when we came to the crypt. The coroner says that you must have come straight here upon finding the body as the man had been dead so short a time. You couldn't have hidden any riches or done away with a decaying body so quickly. For now . . . no, you are not under arrest."

"Ah."

"And what does that mean?"

"I'm assuming you'll be watching me."

"You assume correctly." Javet hesitated for a moment, as if he considered his next words carefully. "There is a sense of unease rising in the city center as it is."

"Oh?" Brent frowned. He'd been so totally concentrated on the work in the crypt that he'd paid attention to little else. "Have there been other murders lately?"

Javet had been carefully watching him for his reaction. He shrugged. "It is probably all unrelated. We've had reports of missing persons. But you know . . . people sometimes disappear because they choose to do so."

Brent leaned forward. "And sometimes they disappear because something has been done to them. How many missing persons?"

Again, Javet hunched his shoulders. "Five—in my files. One was a British tourist . . . a young woman of about twenty-five." He pulled open a drawer in his desk and produced a file, flipping pages. One young man, four young women in total. Two were prostitutes . . . the man and the other two were tourists. All three tourists possessed rail passes, so they could be almost anywhere, backpacking through Europe. As to the prostitutes . . . they worked the seediest streets of the city, had drug habits, and . . . well, they were young, but defying death on a daily basis."

"A prostitute murdered by a john or a pimp would

most probably be discovered in an alley somewhere, don't you think?"

"We've not found a single body in an alley, and as I said, the other young people might be anywhere—you know, children will forget to call home, and nervous mamas will call, and become more nervous. So, we have taken the reports, and the files and pictures are all across the entire metropolitan area."

"I haven't seen anything on the news, or in the paper."

"You must not read past the first page. There has been mention."

"Perhaps there should be more mention made."

"Paris is the City of Light. We need visitors from around the world. We try not to panic the public irresponsibly."

"Warning them might be nice as well."

"Perhaps you should walk out before I do decide to arrest you."

Brent leaned back. "You're not going to arrest me, because you actually believe that the disappearances might have something to do with this murder. And you do know that I didn't kill Jean-Luc, so there is an unknown murderer out there. He—or she—might be afraid that I did see something, and therefore, on the streets, I might be bait to lure the real killer."

Javet shrugged. "Perhaps." He kept staring at Brent as if he could read something from watching him.

Brent stared back.

At last Javet lifted his hands. "You are free to go. As long as you do not go far, of course."

"Well, I can hardly ask you to trust a stranger, but I am as anxious to see his murderer brought to justice as you are, sir," Brent said, rising.

Javet rose as well and shook his hand. Brent was aware that he spoke very softly to one of the men who came by his desk as Brent started out. The inspector was aware that his French was fluent, and he didn't want Brent knowing that he was to be followed.

Even if he hadn't heard the whisper, Brent knew that men would be sent out to watch his movements.

He left the station, lit a cigarette on the street, and then paused.

There was something . . .

A strange sensation touched him again.

He had felt it before, coming from the crypt, onto the street. When he had insisted that Tara Adair get in her car and leave quickly.

Now . . .

For a moment, the feeling was strong.

And close, very close.

Looking back, he frowned. The station suddenly seemed to rest in a large shadow. Down the block and across the street, there was still much police activity around the outer entrance to the dig.

He looked back at the station, and went over his conversation with Javet again. He considered everything he had seen and sensed regarding the man.

It didn't make sense.

And yet it was there, the feeling of unease. That something wasn't quite right.

Here.

He walked back in. The sergeant at the desk stopped him. "Sir?"

"I need to see Javet again."

"He has just left with another inspector. You'll have to come back."

The sense of unease remained. And yet . . .

It was as if something had been . . .

And even as he stood there, it faded . . .

And was then gone.

He could do no good, standing there, arguing with the desk sergeant on duty.

He walked down the block to the café, took a table outside, and ordered coffee with a whiskey, neat. He paid when his drinks arrived, then pretended to linger, staring at the crime tape around the crude stairway that led down to the excavation site from what had been a garden square area before the church. The front of the new St. Michel was also cordoned off now, around the door he had broken down.

He waited, then spoke to his waiter about the toilet facilities, and rose. Once inside, he followed an EMPLOYEES ONLY door out a hallway to the delivery entrance in the rear.

He was not followed.

His car was on the street. He chose to leave it while he walked on to another bar. Once inside, he used the pay phone, though he had a cell phone in his pocket.

He wasn't certain that the phone even rang. He heard the deep voice answering almost instantly. "Hello?"

"I need you," he said.

"I know. I've felt it coming. It was today . . . tonight for you."

"I should have known. I suspected. I--failed," Brent said flatly.

"There is no blame. Unless I were to take it myself."

"One is dead. That I know of—for certain—so far. I'll be on the prowl."

"We have tickets already. You'll get us at Orly?"

"No, I've been to the police. I'll explain when you arrive."

"We already have tickets on the overnighter."

"Tomorrow then. I'll do what I can tonight. But . . . it's a big city."

"I'll do what I can as well."

He hung up, walked outside, and made certain that he wasn't being followed.

He stood very still, feeling the breeze, listening.

There was nothing. Nothing on the air. Nothing in the wind.

Not even a sense of direction.

Still, he had to move.

Five disappearances. Five that were official. Paris was a transient city. People coming and going all the time.

There could be more. Many more.

And now, this girl in the tomb, if she had been seen, if they knew that she might even begin to suspect . . .

He considered taking his car, then decided against it.

For a moment, he closed his eyes, and saw her as she had stood in the tomb. Slim, blond, erect, beautiful features, intelligent, suspicious, and determined eyes. Unnerved, but not a coward, dignified even in fear. He had barely seen her, barely spoken with her.

And yet . . .

A sudden urge to protect and defend her gave him new direction. It was, of course, because he was pretty certain of just who she was.

And because he was fairly certain that the disappearances had plenty to do with the murder that had occurred tonight, he had good reason to worry about her.

The night was long. He need only see that those in the greatest danger were secure. And then the hours of darkness would stretch on.

And there were, of course, those things which must wait until dawn.

Determined on his course, he started out of the center of the village, seeking the darkness of the roads in the more rural region beyond. He walked and looked up at the sky. Not a full moon . . .

A waning moon. But it was riding high in the heavens.

He moved more quickly, ever searching the village, and those now stopping to gawk at the police activity at the dig site.

More and more, he became certain of the reason that the girl had been there. There was so much she didn't know, and still . . .

She would.

He knew the address of where she was staying.

He knew where she lived.

They did not; not yet. And still, that sense of danger remained.

He began to run.

In seconds, he was swallowed up in the darkness.

Tara jerked the car to a halt in front of the chateau and went flying in, noting that Ann had not come from work. She rushed through the hall to the library, but her grandfather wasn't there.

She raced up the stairs to his room.

With pillows piled behind his back, he had been sleeping. The sound of her arrival woke him, and he opened his deep blue eyes, staring at her intently.

She had never been disrespectful to her grandfather, and she didn't really mean to be so at that moment, but words spilled from her lips before she could stop them. "What the hell did you send me into?"

He stiffened, all attention, rheumy eyes as sharp as tacks.

"What happened?"

"A murder."

"A murder? You've got to be explicit. Exactly what happened, who was murdered, and where did it happen?"

His determined calm forced her to breathe a little more slowly, but she could be as stolid as he was, and she meant to understand what was going on.

"I went to the church, and they were allowing tourists into the ruins. I flirted with that ridiculous Professor Dubois, and learned that he was certain he was near to discovering the coffin of a noblewoman who had lived during the reign of the Sun King. She had been his mistress, but she had been ordered buried in unhallowed ground because of her evil practices. I kept at it as long as I could, and yet I was being urged out. They were closing down for the day. Still, I lingered, wondering if I could sneak back and eavesdrop on the workers. One of them came after me. When he did, there was suddenly the most god-awful scream I have ever heard. The fellow who had followed me went back. I went blindly racing for a way out. While I was banging away at the church door, the worker who had come after me suddenly reappeared and broke the door down."

"You heard a scream—but how do you know that someone had been murdered?" Jacques asked.

"Because his coworker said he had been murdered and that he was going to the police."

"But . . . he didn't urge *you* to go to the police?"

"No, he urged me to go home."

"Could the one fellow have killed the other?"

"No, I just told you, he had come after me. We were staring at one another when we both heard the scream."

"And he insisted that you not go to the police?"

Tara let out a long sigh. "He swore to me that he was going to the police, and seemed to think that he was doing me a favor by insisting that I not go with him. Now, I think that I was an idiot. I should have gone with him, and told them what I know."

Jacques was shaking his head. "What could you have said? What do you know? You know that you heard a scream, and that was it. There's brandy on the dresser there, get yourself some. Take a few deep breaths. Settle down."

"Where is Ann?"

"Delayed at her office. Thank God."

"Why do you say that?"

"She thinks I am losing my mind. She would be furious that you took my words to heart and put yourself in danger."

"Did you put me in danger?"

"I didn't intend to," he said softly. He was frowning. "But . . . at least you were out of the crypt, and you did not go to the police."

"Wait, a minute. As a decent citizen—"

"You're American, not French."

"As a human citizen of the world—"

"There's nothing you could have done."

"I still think I should turn around right now and go back and talk to them."

"No!" he said with an alarm so great it worried her. His face had gone ashen; he looked weak and frail.

"But—"

"The fellow who urged you to leave was doing you a great service. You must keep your name out of any investigation. Someone went into the dig and murdered a worker. Perhaps that someone is very dangerous. If your name were associated with the case, you could be in great danger."

"Grandpapa," Tara said, "you must explain to me what is going on here. The professor thought a noblewoman was buried there. Was she buried with a tremendous fortune? What would cause someone to commit murder over a corpse?"

"Get your brandy," he commanded her.

Because she was still shaking, she did as he said. She swallowed the contents of a small snifter without pausing for breath. Warmth flooded her. She hadn't realized that she had felt so cold. She poured more, then took a seat by his bed.

"Tell me—"

"What about this fellow who insisted you leave?"

"What about him? He was one of the diggers."

"Old, young? French, English, Italian—"

"American. Somewhere between . . . I don't know . . . twenty-eight and thirty-five, I believe."

Jacques was frowning again. "And what did he look like?"

"Dusty."

Jacques frowned.

"Tall, wiry build. Strong—he broke down a very heavy door for us to escape from the main church. Brown hair, I think. Hazel eyes."

"Short hair?"

She shook her head. "Probably below collar length. It was tied back."

Jacques shook his head, frowning, not looking at her, but seeming to search somewhere in his mind. "Ah, well, hair, it changes."

"What are you talking about? Jacques, I mean it. You have to tell me what is going on!"

He stared straight at her. "There is evil in the ruins of the old church."

She sighed and clenched her teeth. "Jacques—that won't cut it!"

"You're safe," he said, as if he were speaking to himself. "Thank God. I had not imagined they had come so far. I'd not have sent you if I hadn't believed that I still had time to . . . to stop it. To know. Now, I know. I was an old fool. Yet it's so difficult to become involved. And there are so few of us left. Because the world has changed, you know. That's immaterial. Go to the top drawer of my dresser."

She sat stubbornly. "Not until you tell me what is going on."

He closed his eyes and grasped his chest suddenly.

"Grandpapa!"

He opened one old rheumy eye.

"Go to the dresser."

"I am not! I'm calling the emergency line."

"No! Dammit, I'm just exhausted, I'm not having any kind of an attack! But I beg of you, do as I say."

"I'm not letting you get away with this!" she told him firmly.

"Open the drawer."

She opened the top drawer. Her grandfather's things were neat and organized.

"Open the little brown box."

She did so. There was a cross in it. A beautiful cross. Eighteen-carat gold, she thought, large, and elegantly fashioned.

"Put it on."

"I'm wearing a birthstone pendant."

He shook his head, appearing deeply upset. "Please, I beg of you, wear it. Wear it for me."

She unhooked the necklace she had been wearing and replaced it with the cross. When she walked back to the bed, she was startled by the strength of his grip as he took her hand.

"Sit."

She sat.

"This must be between you and me for now, please. You must swear not to talk to others about me behind my back, no matter how senile you think I am."

"I never thought you were senile—"

"Well, then, you're the only one who hasn't. But swear to me, swear on the cross that you'll say nothing about this, whether you believe me or not. I cannot afford to be locked up in a mental institution at the moment."

He sounded perfectly rational. His gaze, fixed upon her, seemed as sane as any she had ever seen.

"I swear, I won't repeat any of this."

"I believe that they have dug up a vampire."

"What?" she cried, incredulity heavy in her voice.

He sighed deeply. "There are such creatures in the world, you know."

"No, I don't know. There are sick people in the world, I do know that. There are people who think they are vampires, and there are people who think that dogs and even gods speak to them, and command them to go out and do terrible things. But Grandpapa, there aren't real vampires."

"I knew you would not believe me. And I'm very afraid that in time, you will."

"I'm lost, here, Grandpapa. Help me. I want to believe you, or to at least find a logical explanation for what you're thinking, believing. Because I know you're not crazy, and you've always been the brightest man I have ever known, sane, intelligent, ready to think and reason."

Once again, he was shaking his head. "Would that age were not such a brutal hindrance!" he said. "Listen to me, there is evil in the world."

"I'm afraid there are few so innocent and naive any more that they don't recognize that fact. Man himself can be more evil than—"

"Indeed, sadly that is true. But this goes beyond your concept of what evil may be."

She looked at him steadily. "Grandpapa, I don't believe in ghosts, spirits, or vampires."

"All right; I know that I am asking a lot of you. But you must promise that you will pay attention to what I ask you to do."

She sighed. "You know, we've just agreed that you're not a senile old man. Therefore, I shouldn't have to humor you."

"You must do what I ask."

"And what is that?"

"Wear the cross. Never take it off. And let no one into the house that you don't know. Be wary. Be rude. Don't make new friends while you are here. Think of the things you have heard in legends, in books, in movies, but don't count on them all. Oh, no. They can walk by day. They may be weak, and there are those among them who love garlic, though many do not. Holy water is strong against those who are evil, not against all of them mind you, but those who are evil. And a cross . . . a cross is a symbol. It is the same, it means nothing against those who aren't evil, and everything against those who are. Are you listening, paying attention? It's important. You must keep the windows closed. And ask no one in. That's very important. Ask no one in."

"Jacques, please, I'm going to try to do as you say, but you must admit yourself that you're sounding like a madman."

"But you must listen to me. I think, I still think, there are things that must be done, she must be stopped. There are others in the Alliance, it has just been so many years, I thought myself crazy sometimes in the States, as if I had imagined it all from the Old World as well. And then there was the war . . . and more wars. Always, wars. And that's when you see the evil of man, and sometimes learn the goodness of the Alliance. In the modern world . . . but they are out there, and now she is out there, and you must listen to me."

Tara was listening, and she loved him, but the more he spoke, the crazier he sounded. Except that maybe he was right about one thing. If a brutal murderer had killed a poor worker to get into a coffin, there had to have been something in it of incredible value. And to keep from being caught, the murderer might well make her a target, if he knew that she had been all but a witness in the crypt.

"Lord!" she exclaimed suddenly.

"What is it?"

"My purse. It is still in the corridors of the dig somewhere."

"Perhaps not."

"It must be—"

"Perhaps the young man found it."

"He didn't have it when we left the church."

"Perhaps you didn't see that he had it. Don't be

afraid. If it were there, most probably, our phone would have rung by now, the police would have found you here. Let us hope it is gone, as I have said. If it is found, you must say that you lost it when you visited the church and the excavation site. You must not let on that you know anything about the murder."

"This is still wrong, my not reporting what I know. If I could help—"

"You can't help. Not by going to the police."

Tara heard Ann's car in the driveway below. She walked to the windows that looked down on the courtyard.

"Tara!"

She turned back. "You mustn't tell Ann about anything that I have said. She will not believe. She is beautiful and smart and loving—and entirely pig-headed! And I fear . . ."

"You fear what?"

"I fear that I can't keep her from danger. You must watch out for her as well. Never risk yourself, but watch out for your cousin. She is all sense and fact and what the eyes can see, and this will not help us now."

"Grandpapa, what exactly will help us?"

He closed his eyes. "I have to think . . . I have to think . . . if only the old Alliance were still about. We have grown so weak with time, with the horrors of today's world. Men fight other battles, and they forget . . . easy to forget because so few believe, and then again, if they did believe, what would happen would be frightening."

"Ann is on her way up."

"You must say nothing."

"What do you mean, say nothing? She told me this morning that you wanted her to go to the church."

"Tell her that you went, that is all."

Ann came up the stairs, hurried into the room, and spoke so quickly herself that Tara wasn't called upon to say much.

"Did you hear? Dear Lord, I had the radio on while I drove home. I never do, I usually listen to CDs, music, you know, after endless meetings. There's been a murder. At the church. Something really horrible, someone broke in, apparently stole the contents of a coffin including the corpse, and murdered one of the workers. Horribly. The man was decapitated!"

"We heard," Jacques said, shaking his head.

"Tara, did you go there today?"

"Yes."

"It makes me shiver, just to think of it! My God, you must have seen the poor man who was killed! Were they working when you went?"

"Yes, I suppose I did see him. But the workers ignored me, mainly. I struck up a conversation with the professor running the dig."

"Dubois," Ann said, rolling her eyes.

"Do you know him?"

"I've met him. He is a wild-eyed fanatic with wild hands as well. Hm. At least now, he will be stopped. And they will hold up the excavations, so that will please you, won't it, Grandpapa?"

"This is all on the news already," Jacques murmured.

"Well, yes, of course. A terribe murder was discovered. The one coworker discovered the other and went to the police. Of course, he is under suspicion. They don't say so on the news, but he must be. It was just him, and the dead man, who remained at the excavation."

"I wonder," Jacques murmured.

"You wonder what?" Ann said.

"I wonder if Dubois was really gone. Have they spoken to him since this happened?"

"He was called, according to the report I heard. He was shocked when he spoke to authorities, having been interrupted at his dinner after a long day. And, of course, he was deeply dismayed, but it didn't sound as if he was as dismayed about the worker as he was that his dig would be halted. But I certainly don't think he was guilty of killing his own worker. Nothing in the world meant more to him than that dig. He is disturbed because his great scientific work will be held up by crime scene detectives." She looked at Tara. "You're all right? The fact that you were even there today gives me shivers. I'm bringing Eleanora in from the stable tonight. She will sleep in the hall." Ann paused and shivered again. "This is horrible. Horrible. Such a brutal murder to have taken place so close to us!"

"There is an alarm on the chateau," Jacques reminded her.

"Of course, Grandpapa. I'm not a silly little chicken. It's just unnerving."

"Very unnerving," Jacques agreed.

Ann frowned suddenly. "You look exhausted, Grandpapa." She looked at Tara, as if her cousin's arrival and time this late with their grandfather was foolish and discourteous and Tara certainly should have known it.

"I'm fine. But I will sleep now. And Ann, you are not a foolish little chicken—you must bring the dog in, and, of course, you must see that the alarm is carefully set. And as I have been telling Tara, we must not invite any strangers into this house. You understand that? We mustn't invite any strangers in."

"Of course not," Ann said. "We'll leave you now to sleep."

She kissed him on both cheeks, and Tara did the same. His eyes caught hers, and in them, there was a look of pleading along with determination.

"Bonne nuit, Grandpapa," she said softly.

They started out of the room. He called after them.

"If there is trouble ever, of any kind, you must call me. I mean it. I fought in the Resistance, you will remember. And I may be old, but there's nothing wrong with my aim."

"Of course, Grandpapa," Ann said.

They stepped out of the room. Ann closed the door behind them. "You have to learn, Tara, how easily he tires," she said reproachfully.

"I just got home, and have been with him only a few minutes," Tara said. "But don't worry, I adore him, too, and intend to be very careful."

"It must be this shocking news that has so upset him," Ann said. She shivered again. "When I heard on the radio . . . my skin just seemed to crawl! Oh, Tara, I should have a wonderful dinner and sit down and be chatty, but I am so tired. I was thinking of a very large drink in the bathtub, and then bed. Would you mind? I know that I had suggested going out tonight, but the day was so chaotic, I ran so late, and then hearing about the murder . . ."

"Go to bed. I'm exhausted as well. I never got to sleep because Grandpapa wanted me to go to the church."

"If you had arrived tomorrow, it would have been too late."

"Yes, well, I arrived today," Tara said ruefully. "Go to bed, get your rest. I'm off to my room as well."

"I'm just going down for the dog. Eleanora is a shepherd, huge, and loyal, and so trustworthy!"

"Good night, then."

Tara kissed her cousin on both cheeks, and headed for her room. Once inside, she sat down at the foot of the bed. She felt numb. The worker had been beheaded.

Sweat broke out on her palms. She had been there when it happened.

She stood, trying to shake off the mantle of fear that seemed to tighten around her as she sat. She walked to the French doors that led out to the balcony and opened them to the night breeze.

Her room was to the right of her grandfather's, while Ann's room was to the left—all three of them overlooked the front of the house with the drive and the entrance to the stable to the right when she was looking down.

There were no stars in the sky, and the moon was but half full. The chill of the coming fall suddenly seemed great. She looked from the sky to the stable, wondering if she had the energy to go and give Eleanora a welcoming pat.

She heard a strange sound.

A baying. Fear seemed to clasp chilled wet fingers around her heart again.

A dog. It had been nothing but a dog.

And there it was. Down below, at the end of the drive. Eleanora?

The animal was huge. She heard the baying again. Deep, and otherworldly. A haunting sound that might have come from an entire pack of deep-throated animals, crying to the night and the heavens above.

She leaned over the balcony. It was not Eleanora. It was not a shepherd.

It was a wolf. And a wolf as large as a horse, so it seemed.

There were no wolves here, just outside of Paris, she told herself. And she blinked. Hard.

The wolf remained.

And once again, the night was split with the unearthly sound of the creature crying out to the moon and the sky.

She withdrew, standing in the doorway, away from the balcony. She closed her eyes, wishing that the sound didn't seem to tear into her soul, and bring such a premonition of danger and fear.

A man had died. A horrible death. And she had been there, down in the darkness of ancient corridors that belonged to the dead. Naturally, she was frightened. And it wasn't at all usual to see a wolf in the driveway . . .

She opened her eyes. The wolf was gone.

Neither did she see Ann, securing Eleanora.

Tara hesitated for a moment, then suddenly heard a whinnying and thudding from the stables. She turned, ready to hurry down. Across the room, she realized that she had left the balcony door open.

She often left it open when she stayed at the chateau.

For a moment she stood there, watching the breeze touch the draperies. The feeling was soft, cool, seductive, but the chill was giving her goose bumps. She walked purposely back, closed and locked the doors to the balcony and then hurried downstairs.

There was no one about. But the front door wasn't locked, and she assumed Ann had to be outside, looking for the dog.

Old Daniel was still whinnying. It was very strange, because he was the most placid animal in the world. Something had to be disturbing the horse.

She hesitated, afraid to step outside.
But . . .
Ann had to be out here somewhere.
This was ridiculous. This was her home.
She stepped outside.
The door closed behind her.

CHAPTER 4

Light fell over the courtyard, but it seemed to be an eerie yellow. As she walked across the drive as she had done dozens of times, Tara felt prickles of fear along her spine, and at her nape. "Ann?" She called her cousin's name. There was no answer.

The large doors to the stable were hooked in their open position, allowing the strange colored light to just ebb into the stables. There was a light switch immediately within the doors. Tara hurried forward, ignoring her premonition and fear. She hit the light switch, and heard a snap and then a buzz. The lights came on, then flickered. She stood poised and ready to run back to the house, but then, the lights came on strongly. And there was Daniel, back in his centuries-old stall, brown eyes very wide.

"Daniel!" She hurried to him, sliding her hand down his long silky nose. He jerked away once. With his rear hoof, he kicked at the wall. He seemed to be looking past Tara, and to the courtyard beyond. She spun around, trying to see what the horse was seeing.

There was nothing there. And yet . . .

That prickling sensation was still teasing her nape. And it seemed as if the huge horse was shaking as well.

"It's all right, Daniel," she said, her tone loud, as if she would assure herself as well. She kept stroking him. He laid his heavy head on her shoulder after a minute and let her continue to pat him. She crooned softly to him. She felt the great animal begin to calm down.

"You all right now, boy?" she asked.

He turned to his hay bin and began munching.

"Good night then, old boy," she said. Leaving the stables, she hesitated before turning off the light. Going across the drive, she saw no sign of Ann.

"Ann?" she called to her cousin.

No answer. She found herself walking, calmly at first, then racing for the door. But then she reached the house—and found that the door was locked. She cursed herself for not realizing her cousin might have come in first. She pounded on the door.

"Hey! I'm out here!"

She swallowed a burst of panic as the door opened.

Katia, gray hair mussed, a robe thrown over her nightgown, stood staring at her wide-eyed.

"What is it? What's wrong?" Katia stepped out, looking around.

Tara suddenly felt like a fool. There was nothing wrong, and nothing around her but the cool breeze of the night.

"I was just saying hello to Daniel," she told the housekeeper ruefully. "I thought Ann was outside."

"She was. She has come in—and gone to bed."

"I'm sorry."

"No, no, Tara, it is nothing."

"Well, thank you. I—uh—I didn't bring my key. I just came out to see Daniel."

Katia nodded, but still seemed to think it was crazy that she had suddenly decided to see the horse at that time of night. No wonder the woman seemed to think she was daft.

"I'm really going to bed," she promised.

"Bonne nuit," Katia told her, locking up, hitting the alarm buttons, and yawning as she headed to her own room behind the kitchen.

Tara walked back to her room, walked to the balcony windows, and hesitated again. She was exhausted, but she wanted a shower, wanted to wash away her fear and unease along with the dust of the crypt.

Just shower and sleep.

She let the water run over her, long and hot, then at last emerged and donned a cotton nightshirt. How long had she been up? Endless hours. Jet lag was setting in.

Maybe she would do some more unpacking.

Tara set to the task busily, hanging clothing, then taking out some of the canvases and paints she had brought with her. The easel Jacques had bought her years ago was still in the room. She set up a canvas, and found herself digging into her watercolors. She wasn't even sure what she intended to do, but she started first trying to create the colors of the night. An image of grays, blacks, and whites began to form as well. She stared at the canvas, wondering what she was doing. Then she realized that she was really something like the walking dead, she was so tired. She had to get to bed and try to get some sleep.

But once in bed, she still lay awake.

A man had been killed. Brutally, horribly, murdered. And she had been there . . .

And her purse remained in the tomb.

She had to pray God that the police were the ones to find it.

And not the murderer.

Paris had changed.

Of course, she had seen the world change before. But nothing like this.

She hated the countryside, and had always hated the countryside. She had always loved the bright lights and bustle of the city, although she would have to say that—along with the machines ripping along the streets—the country had grown up. There were people about. There were shops. There were people at tables on the streets, drinking, eating. Some of them . . .

Half naked. Ooh, la, la! The clothing these days! She loved it.

There was a freshness and freedom all about her. Intoxicating. But she yearned for the city, and it didn't take her more than a few minutes to realize that she needed only to flag down one of the yellow cars to get a ride far, far from the dowdy little church in the village. And the farther they drove, the better, the stronger she felt.

The driver was first amused with her garments, yet he seemed to realize that her jewels were real. Well aware her clothing was not at all what it should be, she quickly convinced him that she was heading for a masquerade. He was young and good looking.

Delectable. She managed to get him talking about

the city, about what was happening. She tried to be quite casual, and still . . .

It was shocking to hear about the revolution. Shocking, amazing, deplorable. They had beheaded a *king*. It was absolutely amazing. Of course, the cab driver then became somewhat suspicious, incredulous that there might be anywhere in the world that she hadn't learned something about French history of such gravity.

When he slowed to a stop, she leaned forward, and caught his eyes in the rearview mirror of the thing called a taxi. She touched his cheek, and told him that he was quite luscious. He started to smile . . .

She chose not to kill him. She did, however, relieve him of his money.

Paris had changed.

And the shops were quite incredible.

She spent hours trying on clothing, telling shop girls that she had come into town for a costume party, only to discover that the mode of dress had changed. And since she was buying things for the evening . . .

She was disturbed to find that she didn't have enough money for all the purchases she wanted to make. Anger, or the thrill of her renewed power, nearly made her forget that she was in a crowded place. But she controlled herself, and she was glad, because she then found out about something called plastic that could be made into a card that worked better than money. And, of course, at the right moment, she was able to convince the shop girl that she had paid for everything that the sweet young thing wrapped up for her. She obtained more money, and a number of the plastic pieces that made buying so easy. The shop girl was young, naive, prime.

Such a pity that they were in such a public place. The girl was adorable.

Delectable. Surely, delicious.

She would remember the name of the shop.

There were moments on the street that she did not find so intriguing. The behavior of young people had become intolerable. They didn't know when to make way. The ogled . . . ogled, as if they weren't at all aware of her position, of just who she was, and that, no matter what she had done, eyeing her so was a deadly and dangerous game. But then kings had been killed and who knew who ruled, and what the laws were and weren't these days. They knew nothing of finesse, of subtle charm, of the way to have what they wanted.

Sometimes, she would return a gaze. And do it in a way that not only sent a flush of embarrassment to a young man's face, but a flash of fear as well.

Then, she enjoyed herself once again.

Beginning to understand the value of her francs, she paused for wine at a sidewalk eatery, drank, and read from a paper that had been discarded by a previous customer. She shook her head. The changes were amazing. And yet . . .

What a world. She felt a rush of exhilaration, and yet curbed her longing to go about wildly in celebration. This time, she wouldn't make mistakes. She would jealously guard her strength, and gain greater power daily. She would send out her messages, seek within the world of dreams, and summon those who should be near her.

She finished her wine, pleased to have discovered that the French still enjoyed the best. And then, she began her explorations again.

There were old landmarks, and new landmarks. There were people and buildings everywhere. The next taxi driver insisted that he should take her elsewhere, that the destination she had in mind was certainly closed for the night. She had to insist that she did not care.

He was not particularly attractive.

They came upon the old palace, and the man asked to be paid several times before she even heard his voice. By then, she was so furious that she turned and stared at him. He, of course, fell silent, and later, he wouldn't remember that he hadn't been paid. He would twist and turn, having strange dreams that night, but he wouldn't know why.

She continued to stare, appalled.

What had they done?

Naturally, the place was closed.

Naturally, she entered anyway.

She had no interest in security guards, and kept her distance from them. If she'd been at all rational after being wakened from such a long, deep sleep, she'd not have dug into the worker in the crypt like a half-starved waif. But then, she *had* been half-starved. But now, she had consumed him, and taken from others, and she could build up her strength through the coming hours when she would rest again. This night was a time of discovery.

She spent hours and hours wandering . . . still appalled. Well, of course, there had always been art, but now . . .

What had they done to such incredible beauty? But, alas, it was a place she knew, and once loved.

Appalling . . .

Yet convenient that there were so many shops now attached. By day, she could imagine the number of people. And there were so many corridors and little rooms. It was still a fine place to seek some rest, and a good base from which to observe the new world. At least for the night.

It would be dangerous to stay too long, she realized. It was one of her old haunts.

And there might be those about who would know it. Yet . . .

There had to be someone about who knew her. Why else make such a determination to see that she was wakened? Perhaps she would have to find somewhere special near the village and the church to rest—and observe. She must be far more careful than she had been in the past. She was aware that she had overstepped the boundaries of her power before, grown careless in her belief in herself, and in her position in the world.

Indignity swept through her.

She would not be so fearful as to become *humble*. That would be far too much.

She would simply be wary, and careful. And take things slowly. Slowly, until she had gotten a firm grasp on the ways of the world. And discovered who was out there. A thrill entered into her as she wondered . . .

Yes, it could be.

She thought about the village, as she hadn't before. And her eyes narrowed as she wondered if the same dangers existed.

Surely, they did.

Ah . . .

So first things must come first. She must be careful, lie low, wait. But there were dangers she could observe, and perhaps resolve, even while she watched . . .

Waited.

But for tonight . . .

The palace.

The things that they had done! She must see it all.

And so she wandered, deep into the region where the old architecture was displayed for the common visitors who apparently inundated the place daily.

By then, she had walked for hours, looked for hours . . .

And daylight was coming.

Then . . . the night.

By morning, Tara was feeling much more rational.

Like Ann, she was deeply worried about Jacques.

No, perhaps she was even more worried. Her grandfather believed in vampires. That was extremely serious. But she had sworn to him that she would keep their conversation secret, and she intended to do so.

She wished that she dared talk to someone. Jacques had been right that there had been extreme danger in the crypt, something very wrong. But of course, now the police would know, and so it wasn't necessary for him to worry so much.

But he believed in vampires.

She couldn't share that with anyone, even if she hadn't made such a promise to him. She was very afraid that he would wind up locked away in an institution. So what should she do? Continue to regale him with logic? Or humor him.

Tease him. Tell him it was a pity they were in France and not Italy, where there was so much garlic that a vampire wouldn't dream of darkening the door.

No. Jacques did not seem to have a sense of humor about it; he was dead serious. And there had been a murder. A horrible, brutal, murder. But throughout history, there had always been enough greed and brutality among man. Perhaps inventing monsters was her grandfather's way of dealing with the evil in the world.

She could drive herself crazy with this. And with the worry that she should have done the right thing, and gone to the police.

Ann was about to leave for work when she came down to the kitchen. Katia was singing as she prepared a breakfast tray for Jacques. Roland was already out and busy about the grounds. Katia kissed Tara, who thanked her and waved her away, insisting she could get her own coffee. With cup in hand, she followed Ann to the car.

"So . . . think we should still go out tonight?" Ann asked.

"I don't know. Should we?"

"I really need a night out."

"All right," Tara said slowly. "We'll stick together."

"And it seems to me that this guy was after the riches in the crypt. I mean, he wasn't out terrorizing women or anything. Yes, I need a night out."

Tara thought for a moment and then nodded. "I'm afraid that we live in a world where murder is all too frequent. There's no reason to believe that someone who robbed a grave would be after us." As soon as the words were out of her mouth, she felt her muscles tighten. *Where the hell was her purse? If the police had found it, they would have called by now.*

Maybe the murderer had found it.

She felt the blood drain from her face.

"I don't know—"

"Yes, definitely, we'll go out. I'll bring friends from work as well. In numbers, we'll be safe." She kissed both of Tara's cheeks and headed for her car. Tara looked down the drive.

"Hey!" she called.

"What?" Ann called back.

"I saw a wolf last night."

"There are no wolves around here. There haven't been . . . forever."

"No, honestly, I saw a wolf."

"You saw a dog."

"If I did, it was one big dog."

"We have very big dogs in France, you know. It was probably a big shepherd. Maybe it was even Eleanora. I went out to get her last night, and she was off prowling somewhere. Such a guard dog!"

"I could still swear it was a wolf."

"The couple down the road have a pair of huge Mala-mutes. Maybe you saw them."

"Maybe," Tara agreed.

"You were very tired. And we were all shaken by the news of that horrible, brutal killing! Now, though, Jacques will not want us crawling around the ruins any-more!" She waved and blew a kiss. "I'll call you later and let you know about the plans."

Tara gave her a thumbs up. Then she wandered back into the house.

Katia told her that Jacques was still sleeping.

Normally, she would have spent her first morning just talking to him, perhaps taking a short walk in the small garden, or at the least, joining him for café au lait and croissants. But he was still sleeping, and, she was certain, he needed his rest. She desperately wanted him to be at his best. And having learned that he was still resting, she felt an urge, strange as it was, to get out of the house.

To spend some time alone.

To think, to observe, to be in the village again, and

look about, and see that the world around her was normal.

And she wanted to see the church. And what the police were doing.

Since no one had called yet, she needed to get up the nerve to go to the police and tell them she had lost her purse at the ruins—during tourist hours.

She was glad that she had left some francs in her luggage so that she didn't have to ask Katia or Roland to borrow enough for a cup of coffee. And since she had showered and dressed before coming down that morning, she was ready to head out just moments behind her cousin.

She parked in almost the same spot where she had been the day before.

From a table in front of the café, she could see that large expanses of the area remained roped off. The church door had been jerry-rigged back together with new wood that didn't begin to match the patina of the centuries-old wood she had seen broken the night before. But the "new" church itself had reopened. Tara was certain, however, that access to the tunnels or corridors leading to the ruins of the "old" crypt were still blocked as well.

Having chosen her table, she picked up a newspaper and ordered café au lait. She slid her sunglasses on, trying to pretend that her eyes weren't drawn to the church every other minute. Not that it mattered. Though people were speaking quickly around her and her French was very rusty, they were all talking about the bizarre murder. And few of them seemed the least hesitant to simply stare at the church.

Her eyes were fixed across the road when something suddenly fell in front of her, rattling her coffee cup.

She started, nearly cried out, and looked up to see the worker from the night before. She instantly felt a flood of heat rush through her. She wondered in amazement that she hadn't sensed him behind her, she was suddenly so aware of his presence.

She looked down to see that it was her purse that had landed on the table.

He pulled out the chair at her side before asking, "May I join you?"

He sat. She looked at the purse, and then back to him. "How did you get this? I thought you went straight to the police."

"I did. I'd picked it up and forgotten to give it you."

She stared at him suspiciously. He was wearing dark glasses. If he hadn't spoken, she might not have recognized him. He was freshly shaven and apparently just out of a shower. Whatever aftershave he wore was subtle, pleasant, and alluring. He was wearing light chinos and a dark shirt. His hair was loose, but not as long as she had thought. It reached just past his collar. He was tanned, at ease, and again gave a sense of casual physical power, not overly burdened with straining muscles, but smooth and sleek and taut as wire. Tara wondered if he was into the martial arts—or perhaps an avid member of a fencing club. She immediately found herself noting that he was more than attractive, while a million warning signals seemed to leap to her mind. He gave the appearance of a grad student or a teacher on break rather than a stockbroker, but he was neat and clean and far more than merely presentable. A long-haired executive on break.

Long-haired executives did not dig into ancient graves for hourly wages.

The waiter must have thought he gave the impression

of a man with some means or importance as well, as he hurried back to the table the minute the man was seated. "Café au lait, s'il vous plaît," he said, offering a broad and casual smile beneath the dark lenses of the shades. He was undoubtedly American, but his French was far superior to her own. She couldn't begin to detect the usual, guttural accent that those with English or a Germanic native language seldom ever lost.

"I don't remember agreeing that you should join me." The words, Tara thought, were required. She wondered what she would have done if he had walked away.

"And they wonder why we get a reputation for being rude!" he said with a mock sigh. "Last night, I saved you tremendous trouble and a great deal of time. I risked life and limb to save that—" he paused to indicate her small leather handbag, "and here I am to return it, and you're far less than gracious."

"I've been told not to speak to strangers. There's a murderer loose, if you'll recall."

"Yes, but you're privileged to know that I'm definitely not a murderer. Although to others," he continued, leaning close, "I may remain suspect. There you go. In my defense of you, I have created my own hell with which to deal."

"There was no reason."

"There's every reason."

"And that is?"

He shrugged, cordially thanking the waiter when his coffee came. Then he leaned close to her again. "There would be no sense in playing it safe for myself. Everyone in the area knew that Jean-Luc and I were the primary workers Dubois hired. But there was no reason for anyone to suspect that you were in the crypt at the time— or that you had more than a casual interest in the dig."

"I had nothing more than a casual interest in the dig," she said.

"Right. That's why you were crawling around in the underground corridors after making a point about knowing how to leave on your own."

"Quite frankly, I know nothing about the dig."

"Nothing at all?" he queried.

"I just arrived from New York."

"And you had a casual interest in what was going on. After a long flight, and probably no sleep, your casual interest brought you to the dig."

"I don't have to explain myself to you. Come to think of it, I don't even know your name. And I'm not sure that I want to know it."

"Pick up a newspaper, and you'll read it. But since you're here, you don't need to bother. My name is Brent Malone."

"And you know my name, of course, because you went through my bag."

"It's hard to return property when you don't know the name of the person to whom it belongs."

"Well, you've returned it."

He ignored that. "Tara Adair. And you gave us a far different name. Something very French, if I recall. You pretended you have French relatives."

"I do have French relatives," she said, annoyed with herself immediately for being defensive."

"I believe you. So—what is your keen interest in the tomb?"

"When I tell you that I really know almost nothing about the dig, it's the absolute truth," she said.

He ran a finger around the rim of his coffee cup, then slid his glasses to the top of his head and watched her curiously. She noted again the almost golden color of his eyes. Very unusual.

And it seemed almost impossible to draw her gaze from his.

"Why don't you tell me about the crypts and the tomb and whatever you were on to that was so important that someone was killed over it."

"It was a deconsecrated church crypt, you know."

"That much, yes."

"Another St. Michel stood directly on top of it, once. They razed the original church, and built a hundred yards to the south. The corridors had been blocked and sealed for centuries. Then, recently, there was some work done in the basement of the new church, and there had been water damage in some of the walls. While the new church was being repaired, one of the old underground corridors to the old crypt ruins was discovered. Professor Dubois had been bugging the fathers at St. Michel for years, wanting to get down to the ruins. When the chance came up, the good gentlemen of the church knew that Dubois had some money and would definitely see that a large portion of it made its way to the church if he was given sole control of the dig. He has a reputation of a learned scholar in archeology, history, and especially local lore."

Tara found herself listening to the tone of his voice; it was lulling and alluring. She had taken off her own glasses. Long ago finished her coffee.

He smiled, seeing that she was watching him raptly. "Another café au lait?"

"What?"

"Coffee. Would you like more coffee? I could use another one."

"Ah, yes. I guess." She was being less than gracious. She managed a curt sounding, "Thank you."

He smiled. Generous mouth, good teeth. She wanted to kick herself. She wasn't buying a horse. Yet she might have been looking over the qualities of an animal. Everything about him seemed to be exceptional and fine.

If she had met him at a different time . . .

A different place, a different way . . .

Yes, she would have found him attractive. Very. Even now, she found herself tempted to touch. He had an elusive quality of sexuality or sensuality or both that was almost ridiculously hypnotic. She gritted her teeth, irritated with herself. It was simple chemistry, and he was in great shape, the right age, with strong, masculine, attractive features. There was nothing in the least mysterious about his appeal.

And then again, she assured herself, the world was populated with any number of attractive men. She met many in her line of work. He was just one in the world. The same.

No . . .

Different.

But then, of course, that was because she had met him in a crypt.

He lifted a hand and their waiter nodded, returning with two more coffees. When he was gone, Brent Malone once again leaned toward her.

"The crypt was rumored to be the resting place of the damned and demons from hell."

Tara smiled slightly. "That makes no sense. I'm assuming that the original church was deconsecrated when the new church was finished. So until then, it was a working House of God. How could the evil of past centuries have been buried there?"

"Oh, not your penny-ante evil people. Only the most truly evil and abominable—and those, of course, who earned the hatred of the king. You see, it was sealed off hundreds of years ago, but there was always a way in. It was known by the kings and their most powerful lords, and by the hierarchy of the church as well. And when someone was to be entombed—someone truly wicked— the corpse was taken in secretly—at dawn rather than the dead of night, since the powers of the unholy are said to be greatest in darkness—and sealed into their graves."

"Ah." His tone had carried a wonderful, almost spooky, storytelling ability. She nodded, as if accepting it all word for word. "Well, we all have illusions, I suppose. The pharaohs of ancient Egypt thought that their wrappings and their rites would give them eternal life, that their preserved bodies would rise again, and they would live in splendor. And you can walk into the museum in Cairo and see room after room of once great rulers who lie in glass cases for the public to stare at, rather than have their bodies rise to renewed glory."

"Mummies . . . ah, well, they're a completely different story," he said with a dismissive wave of his hand and a touch of dry irony in his voice. "So, you don't believe in evil, or the powers of the dark, Miss Adair?"

"Evil? Oh, my God, yes. The world is full of it. But there are so many evil men and women out there, we don't need to go looking into old stories and legends to find more." She frowned, realizing that she had made a very similar, determined, and rational statement to her grandfather. Too bad Jacques didn't have this man to talk to—he wouldn't have to be worried about sounding as if he had become senile.

Even as the thought occurred to her, she felt a strange tension seize her. She didn't want this man near her grandfather. And yet, at the same time, she continued to feel that very odd attraction to him. Almost as if . . .

As if she'd been waiting all her life to meet him.

She instantly and angrily dismissed such a ridiculous thought. He had that rather raw, masculine appeal, and she had been alone for quite a while, determined that her comfortable relationship back home had simply not been right. Artists and stockbrokers didn't always go together well. She suddenly wished that she hadn't split with Jacob, and had insisted that he come to Paris with her. If he were just sitting here now, she wouldn't be feeling such a strange urge to undress another man.

She wasn't having that urge.

Yes, she was. She'd like to see him naked. Feel him next to her. Find out if it would be as thrilling to be touched by those hands as she was imagining.

Dear Lord, Tara! You're not that desperate! she told herself. She was thinking these thoughts about a stranger, a suspicious stranger.

He'd been in the tombs when a man was murdered. But it was true, she was the one person—other than the murderer—who knew for certain that Brent Malone was not a killer.

"I'm just telling you the history of the crypts, Miss Adair."

"And you're telling me that the man who was killed opened up a tomb while you were gone and therefore opened a Pandora's box—a coffin filled not with the earthly remains of a heretic or other, but filled with evil."

"I never told you anything like that," he said. "I repeat, I've just told you something of the history of the place. And of course, you are aware that centuries ago there were many people who did believe in the powers of witchcraft and that men and women could sign pacts with demons and devils. What happened in Salem, Massachusetts, in the United States was indeed tragic, but pales beside some of the executions in Europe, where thousands sometimes perished in a day for their practices."

She sighed. "Now you're making it sound as if it would be ridiculous for anyone to believe that there could truly be witches or other supernatural creatures—evil creatures—buried in the ruins of an old church."

"My point is, Miss Adair, that years ago, many holy people did believe in the existence of evil in many faces. Often, thousands of innocents died because of fear, greed, politics, and religion. But fear was often very real. And if someone was greatly feared and considered evil and certainly no part of any church, that person was entombed in unholy ground. Such people were usually buried with all manner of rites and perhaps physical symbols so that they wouldn't rise again, or practice their evil again. History has shown us some very visible monsters, men such as Hitler, with such a cruel disregard for human life that they could be considered evil. There have been many—not great leaders, but often nobility. Countess Bathory—no one knows how many innocent young people she had killed to satisfy her blood lust and her search for eternal youth. She is but one of many cruel, wicked—or evil, if you will—people who have passed through the centuries. And . . ." he hesitated, leaning toward her. She leaned closer, fascinated with the power of his eyes. "I am warning you, and I do with my whole heart. Stay away from the church. Never let it be known that you were there at the time of the murder. Keep that cross that you are wearing around your neck on at all times. Trust no one. Never be out in the dark alone. I'm afraid for you."

"You're afraid for me. Should I be afraid of you?"

She was startled, and yet didn't make a move, didn't jerk away, when he brushed his knuckles along her cheek. "Miss Adair, I swear it, there is no need whatsoever for you to be afraid of me."

No need? She was all but mesmerized. His touch had brought a sense of heat to her that seemed to stir senses and soul.

She needed to be very afraid.

She needed to rise, and tell him to stay away from her, and from her grandfather. But then, she hadn't even mentioned Jacques, and there was no need to be afraid that he might know anything about an old man living in a quaint chateau, even if Jacques had acquired more than a following in his day.

She didn't manage to make herself get up. Or move away. She kept staring into his eyes. She didn't know if he was still touching her or not, because it seemed as if the warmth was still with her.

She couldn't break away.

He could.

He rose suddenly. "Excuse me, some of my friends have arrived. I look forward to seeing you again."

He pushed in his chair and walked away. She saw him greeting people, a couple, a very tall dark man and a slim, elegant, blond woman. They were dressed casually, as tourists, the woman in jeans and a denim jacket, the man in jeans as well, his jacket leather. They were an attractive, arresting pair, but then, Paris was filled with attractive people. She had the feeling that their intent was to blend in with the crowd. They moved away, walking down the street.

They had gone a long way before she realized that she still hadn't moved.

And that she still felt his touch.

CHAPTER 5

There was a new freedom in sleep.

And freedom in dreams. Now, when she rested, she could fly.

Rise above the darkness, and fly in mist, in shadow. Concentration was essential, and she was glad of her chosen resting spot, for she felt completely secure, and therefore able to focus entirely on her task.

A flash of joy filled her as she felt the presence of another. Of course, they were guarded, all of them. She was careful. Yet she felt elation and a whisper in the wind that surged around her as she soared through the world of darkness.

Is it you? The air, the darkness, spoke to her. And she replied, feeling glorious and powerful.

Yes! I am back.

I know. I meant to be there for you. Now, you must come to me.

The world has changed.

The world will always change.

There is great danger. I sense it.

Yes. Come to me. We must be together. We can begin a new world once again.

I will come, of course.

There are others. You must beware.

Ah, but I am powerful. As are you!

Yes, but you must beware, there are others—and others who have changed. Who fear, who command that we deny the power we can wield.

They are cowards.

They are strong. And still, there are those of the Alliance . . .

Then they must be killed, and quickly. I am not afraid. I was always the strongest.

Ah, my love, you forget that it is I who have managed to free you. We know where to begin to create a world in which we can live, revel, love . . . and be safe. I have planned long and carefully. We will have with us those who would not cower before those weaker than we are. Come to me, and I will show you what this life can be. But come with care. You will laugh still more when you find what I have done in this world!

When Tara returned to the chateau, she found Jacques at work in the library. A large, ancient volume was open on his desk.

He looked up when she entered.

She set her purse on his desk and he arched a brow.

"The man from the dig returned it to me at the café in the village, across from the church."

Jacques looked relieved. "And everything is in it?"

"Everything."

"There are no papers missing?"

"No. My passport, ID, money, credit cards . . . everything is there."

"That is good."

"He does, of course, know my name."

"And do you now know his?"

"Yes."

"Well?"

"Brent Malone."

She watched her grandfather as she said the name. He looked down at his book. She put her hands on the desk, and made a point of staring at him so that he had to look up to her.

"Do you know him?" she asked.

"No, no, I don't think so."

"Strange. He talked about all the evil buried in the crypt as well. I found myself saying many things to him that I said to you."

Jacques nodded, then indicated the chair in front of the desk. He tapped his reading glasses on the open book before him. "Perhaps, when you see this man again, you will ask him to come here. I'd like to speak with him."

"I sincerely doubt that I will see him again."

"Oh, I believe you will. You're familiar with the Sun King? You grew up in America, so your history had to do with Washington, Lincoln, Roosevelt, Kennedy, and so on. Of course, every child in France learns all about the Sun King."

She stared at him evenly, gave him a rueful smile. "I know about the Sun King. Louis XIV. Longest reigning French monarch. He came to the throne as a child, and as a young man, much of his policy and power was held by Cardinal Richelieu. He became a very great king, carefully balancing statesmanship and religion. His father had built a small hunting lodge on the outskirts of Paris; Louis XIV determined to make it into a great palace. Versailles."

"As he aged, he determined as well that, after a life with a multitude of mistresses, he would be loyal to his wife. Alas, the poor thing died a year later. The king married again. He was supposed to have been a man of tremendous sexual prowess."

"They don't put a lot about that in the history books," Tara said.

"The point I'm making is that he was known—before his belated dedication to his queen—for having dozens of mistresses. He was a decent man in that he had many of his love children legitimized, many went on to marry princes and princesses and other royalty and nobility."

"Well, that was a decent concession, I suppose."

"Back to the mistresses . . . there were many of them. Many. Naturally, the lady of the moment often held sway over him, received honors . . . and was somewhat above the law.

"At one time, the mistress of the moment was a woman known as the Countess Louisa de Montcrasset. She was supposed to be extraordinarily beautiful, and to have the most unusual power over the king. She was the daughter of a French nobleman, but had not grown up in Paris—the records say only that she had been raised among nobility "to the east." She appeared at court one day, and as her father's daughter, she was duly welcomed. Within a matter of weeks she had usurped the place of the king's other favorites, and even at times when there were great matters of state to be decided, she could draw his attention."

Tara smiled at her grandfather. "The Sun King was ruling at the time when Charles II was welcomed back to England. The 'Merry Monarch' was loved by the good majority of his people. Cromwell's brand of dry government and total lack of frivolity was overturned by the king's love for the theater. And women. He had his decencies as well, of course, refusing to divorce his barren wife while going through a variety of mistresses. He did not legitimize his children, however. His beloved son was beheaded by his brother, James, then James was overthrown by his daughter and her husband, William of Orange."

"You're getting ahead in history," Jacques said. "Yes, of course, Louis and Charles had much in common—they were monarchs with a love for the arts, building, learning—and women. One woman in particular. Louisa de Montcrasset."

"The young beauty who suddenly appeared from the east. The daughter of the nobleman." Tara offered him a rueful smile, but felt a strange sense of unease. Her grandfather and the digger, Brent Malone, seemed to have far too strange a passion for the dead and the past.

"There were those at the time who doubted that she was who she said she was."

"Ah, and they attacked her relationship with the king, I presume."

"You see, her father had long been out of the country. He was a military man who traveled far and wide, and when he wasn't fighting on the king's behalf, he was a diplomat of sorts. He hadn't been seen in years. He had been a handsome Frenchman, so it was written, with dark hair and eyes, slender, aesthetic face."

"Then what was so unusual about him having a beautiful daughter? Come on, I don't look a thing like you. Or Ann. Genetics can be very strange."

"It's written that she had something of an exotic face. And 'cat's' eyes."

"She might have been a decadent woman, and from what you say, able to use her charms to get what she wanted. Very immoral, perhaps. But don't you think she might be hated for that fact alone, and therefore, many who wrote about her would make an attempt to demonize her?"

"Not many of those who despised her wrote about her."

"And why not?"

"They died."

"Oh?"

"The sixteen hundreds, my dear, was a time when witchcraft was greatly feared. It was suspected that she had joined a coven, that she had made a pact with the devil, that she gained her beauty through the sacrifice of others."

Tara leaned forward, arms folded on the table, posture serious. "We both know that the devil does not come with a forked tongue and tail and make pacts with people."

"We both know that whether the devil came or not, and that although surely, the many thousands of people who were persecuted were most surely innocent, there were those who did join covens, and who did believe that they could evoke the powers of darkness and do harm to others. In France at the time, as well as in many places in Europe, there were many who were executed for witchcraft. But it wasn't the suspicion of those around her that she had joined a coven that made her such a frightening entity. I just told you. People died. Soon after she came to court, dozens of people began . . . wasting away. They would be tired at first, distracted.

116 *Shannon Drake*

Then they would take to their beds. Some died in those beds, too weak to open their eyes. And then there were others who . . ."

"Who?"

"Who simply disappeared. It was a time of strange murders in Paris."

"Strange murders?"

"People were sometimes found dead in the streets."

"People have been murdering people since the beginning of time, sadly," Tara reminded him.

"These people were found in a particularly grotesque manner."

"And that was?"

"They were all beheaded."

Tara felt a strange chill sweep through her again. Her grandfather was talking about history . . .

The worker in the crypt had been decapitated. A brutal manner of murder, no matter what the year, or century, in which it had taken place.

"France is famous for decapitation, Grandpapa. The guillotine, remember."

He sat back, staring at her through narrowed eyes. Jacques had loved his years in America. Few people were so ardently in love with the country, and so determined to speak up for her, no matter what the politics of the moment.

But he had been born a Frenchman, and he could defend his native land with a passion equaled by few.

"The guillotine," he repeated, shaking his head, "was invented to be a merciful device. Unfortunately, it made execution so quick that a rebellious people found it far too easy to use. However, that is a different piece of history. You are not paying attention to the point."

"Just what is the point, Grandpapa?"

"A case was finally proven against the evil of the Countess de Montcrasset that was so strong, the king had no choice but to recognize the fact that his mistress was a murderer. She was found bathing in the blood of her victims. The chambermaid who came upon her began screaming; church officials who had long been very wary of the woman came running, armed with crosses, with holy water. She was taken into custody— with the screaming chambermaid all but dead in her arms. She was condemned by the king, and sent to prison to await execution. Certain men, sworn to uphold goodness, brought one of the churchmen with them and broke into the prison. They arrived in time to discover that she had seduced her jailor into releasing her—he was dead on the floor. They subdued her, throttled her, and then, when they believed that she was dead, they sealed her into a coffin with all the proper rites and symbols to keep her buried forever."

Tara shifted uncomfortably, remembering her conversation with Professor Dubois at the dig. He had told her that the history to be found in the crypt was invaluable, that maligned nobles were among those buried deep in the earth. He had told her that he was seeking a certain noblewoman, who had surely been buried with untold riches. Her coffin would have been sealed in a way that would have kept her dress, shoes, and jewels, and every item of her attire in a condition that would give historians incredible information. He had raved on about the historical importance of the woman.

He had not given her name.

"Grandpapa, if this woman was a mistress of the king, and buried in all her finery, it makes all the more sense that a criminal would be willing to kill to steal the body. She might have been buried wearing an entire fortune in jewels. It's horrible, yet easy to see how a greedy cutthroat might have studied the excavation and broken in when the work should have been shut down for the day. But Jean-Luc was there. And so he was killed so that Louisa de Montcrasset could be stolen. The police will, though, I am certain, find out who the murderer is."

He shook his head, sinking back in his chair. "No, they will not."

"And why not?"

"Because the murderer *is* Louisa de Montcrasset.

"I walked all night," Brent said wearily. "I searched out every alley, every café, bar, restaurant, and whorehouse in the area. I attempted the Louvre, but . . ." he paused, looking at Lucian. "I'm not quite as good as you are at sneaking past guards. Anyway, I searched the streets of Paris until this morning. Then I showered, and returned the purse to the American girl."

"The one with you at the table," Lucian said, his words more of a statement than a query.

"Yes."

"You kept her away from the police, and out of the papers?"

"Yes. Yes, well I have done so this far. She is as suspicious as a CIA agent."

"Quite a nice-looking agent," Jade said, a smile twitching at her lips.

Brent arched a brow at her. "Yes," he agreed softly. "And I think she knows . . . something. Though she is in complete denial. I'm determined to find out more about her. She is staying at Château DeVant."

"Strange coincidence," Lucian said, his brows knit in a frown.

"Yes, that's what I thought," Brent said. "She is the old man's granddaughter."

"We may have more help than we know," Lucian mused.

"Because the girl is related to Jacques DeVant?" Jade said. She looked at Lucian. "I still find a great deal of this very confusing. I don't really understand what is happening here."

"I'm afraid I've done a poor job of teaching relative history," Lucian said. "But we'll get to an explanation soon enough. He looked at Brent again. "There was the body at the church—but no other murders have been discovered?"

"No. But then . . . it's still only midmorning."

"Then she is lying low," Lucian murmured.

"Yes, it's what I think," Brent said.

"That's when she is most dangerous," Lucian said.

Again, Brent said a soft, "Yes, so I understand. But then again, you know more, much more, than I about the past."

"The problem is not so much the past, but the present. Our enemies have been stirring here much longer than I have known," Lucian said. "She is not alone out there. That much is certain."

"Five are listed as missing in recent weeks," Brent said.

"But they have found no bodies . . ." Lucian mused.

"Not yet."

They had gathered around the dining room table at the small house Brent had rented for nearly six months. Jade suddenly stood.

"We've all got to get some rest, that's imperative."

Lucian shook his head impatiently. "Every time she rests, she will gain greater power."

"But you do your best work when you're resting as well," Brent reminded him. "And you are the one who has warned that there is far more to this than what we know."

Lucian let out a long sigh. "You're right. Rest is in order. Because I have nothing right now. Nothing but the sense . . . the knowledge that there is a tremendous stirring . . . and a great deal of danger. Still, we're going to have to move quickly."

"Very quickly. There are things that I can do. Starting now," Brent said firmly.

"You've been up all night," Jade reminded him. "You need rest, too."

"Perhaps some. I don't require a lot of sleep. And there are some things I must do today. I need to see what my new friend, Inspector Javet, is doing."

"You forget, you have talents in your sleep as well," Jade reminded him.

"I'm afraid most of my talents come from more mundane sources—such as libraries," Brent said dryly.

"You can't go hours and hours without sleeping," Jade said flatly. "You'll wind up being useless. Now, though, I can do some exploring."

The two men frowned, staring at her.

She smiled back ruefully. "I slept on the plane. Listen, please, get some sleep. I'll see what I can find out. At least, perhaps, I can go to a library, read through the papers for the past several weeks, and find out more about the missing persons. But you two must get some rest."

"I don't know if I can sleep," Brent said, raking his fingers through his hair. "What happened is my fault.

I suspected . . . I just didn't know. And if I hadn't gotten as far as I had, Jean-Luc couldn't have opened the coffin. And now . . . well, I'm worried for all of Paris, and terribly uneasy about the girl. She is in serious danger, more than she can begin to imagine. Especially since she is a DeVant."

"You were there, Brent, when I hadn't the intuition to worry," Lucian said.

"Little good it did."

"Perhaps more good than you can imagine."

"DeVant knew," Brent said. "That's why he sent his granddaughter."

"He's old and ill, but his mind must still be strong," Lucian said.

"He didn't suspect what did happen, or he wouldn't have sent his granddaughter. Though . . . she has a cousin. Ann DeVant. And neither seems to understand what is really happening. They're in extreme danger."

"As far as the girls go," Jade told him, "that problem can be easily solved."

"And how is that?" Brent asked her.

"We simply get into Château DeVant. Sooner rather than later. It's something we must do anyway."

"Naturally, we must get into the chateau. Get close, and become bosom buddies with the inhabitants," Lucian concluded. He rose, then looked down at his wife. "Take care. Even by day, take care."

"I do know something about what I'm doing," she assured him.

"I'm not sure I can rest, that I dare rest," Brent said. " Tara Adair was at the crypt. She didn't want me going to the police alone. She's going to take steps with the police eventually, because she'll feel it's her duty. The police may be a danger. They may not. Who knows exactly who is out there right now. But if they get to her before we do . . ."

"They won't. Not yet. Not during the day. And though she may eventually go to the police, I believe that Jacques will stop her," Lucian said.

"If you mean to help her, Brent, you'll have to have your wits and strength about you," Jade reminded him. She was watching him curiously. "Of course, perhaps there is one way you can sleep and still protect her."

"Oh?"

"Sleep with her."

CHAPTER 6

It was an incredibly busy day.

One ridiculous meeting after another.

It was nearly two o'clock, and Ann had not had time for so much as a cup of coffee.

At two, she dropped the sheets of meeting memos on her desk, rose, grabbed her purse, and marched out to her secretary's desk. "Henriette, I'm going for coffee. I don't care who calls. I have to have a break."

"Of course—I will fend off all demons!" Henriette, pretty, young, and loyal to her boss, declared with the strength of a lion.

Ann smiled at her and hurried down to the ground level, then outside and across the street. She walked to the counter of the little café and ordered coffee and a croissant, though it was late and only one was left, and it was probably stale. The woman behind the counter was busy, and tried handing her everything at the same time while she was still struggling with her wallet for her money. She was startled when a man at her side suddenly helped out, taking the coffee and the croissant.

"Merci," she murmured.

She was startled when he answered with an accented, "de rien." She glanced at him, but then found herself staring.

He was tall, blond and handsome, with a charming smile. Her hand froze in her purse.

"You looked as if you needed a little help," he said in English. "I'm sorry—do you speak English?"

"Yes, I speak English very well," she said with a smile. "And thank you, thank you very much."

The woman behind the counter cleared her throat impatiently. Ann shoved francs into her hand, then accepted the coffee and croissant from the American.

"That's my table—there. There are no more empty. Perhaps you'll join me."

She had intended to take her coffee and croissant back to the office. No longer. Now, she was going to take her full ten minutes. Maybe fifteen.

"Thank you."

He pulled the chair out for her. She sat, extended a hand to him, "Ann DeVant. Thank you for your help, and for sharing your table."

"Rick. Rick Beaudreau. My pleasure, mademoiselle. I'm sorry, is it mademoiselle? I'm terribly rude, I guess. I'm sorry, I just saw you standing there . . . and . . ."

"I'm not married," Ann told him. "So, you're obviously a visitor in Paris. Though your name is French."

"I'm Cajun," he told her. "From New Orleans."

"Ah."

"Please, enjoy your croissant." He indicated the food

she hadn't touched. She nibbled a bite. She'd been starving. And now . . .

His smile deepened. He was a very handsome man. Striking blue eyes went with his blond hair. She hadn't met anyone so attractive since . . .

Willem.

She felt a surge of temper. For a moment, it included all men. Well, this one was just a tourist. But he was nice, and attentive. And very appealing.

"I'm not married either," he told her.

"You're on vacation—I assume."

He shrugged. "In a way. I'm in the midst of a healing process, you could say."

"Oh?"

"I've been in Europe quite a while. In fact," he said ruefully, "my French should be much better. I was in an accident a while back. A terrible fire. I'm still doing a bit of recuperating." He leaned toward her. "Paris seemed the place to be right now. I came to . . . look up some people. But now . . . well, I think I was just maybe called to be here for much more."

His appreciation of her was definitely a line. But a good one. And he was polite, his admiration in his eyes, and in his tone.

"You're very flattering," she said, forcing her tone to be dry. She was French after all, and not in the least naive.

"But truthfully," he said. "you're just—beautiful."

She laughed. "Thank you."

"Truly, my pleasure."

She stared at him, nodding with a wry smile still in place. Then she glanced at her watch. "I've got to go— I'm afraid I'm not on vacation. But it was lovely to meet you."

"Do you come here every day?" he asked, catching her hand.

She glanced down. He had great hands. Big. Slightly calloused. She could imagine . . .

"Sometimes." She didn't want to pull her hand away. She wanted to linger. She sighed inwardly. She had to get back to work. She grinned suddenly, forcing herself to extricate her hand. "I go out at night sometimes, too. Tonight. With my cousin. An American. I believe we'll be going to a place called La Guerre."

With those last words, she pulled away, hurried out.

Though she was tempted to do so, she didn't look back. Her cheeks, she realized, were flaming.

So much for her sense of sophistication!

No, she would not look back, and she would force the flush from her face.

He knew where she would be. If he was interested, he would be there.

Back at her desk, she started to work, then felt the presence of someone at her door. Willem was there. Tall, suave as ever, perfect in a designer suit. Her heart leaped. He had been there a while, she thought with amazement. There had been a time when she would have known the second he had arrived. And now . . .

She thanked God for the American. He had returned her confidence to her, and her poise. She was able to remain seated. She stared at Willem, without moving.

"I'm not in the office," he told her.

"What do you want?"

"Forgiveness."

She shook her head. "I never forgive, and I never forget." She tried to look down. But there was something about him. There always had been. She looked back up.

"I love you," he told her. His voice was husky and thick. His expression was pained, so much so that she nearly jumped out of her seat to go to him. Somehow, she remained seated. "I don't know . . . what I was doing. Maybe I was afraid at how deeply I cared about you. Or maybe I resented the fact that you'd see me, but you'd never bring me home, you didn't involve me with your family, with your life. I've tried so hard to do what you wanted. I knew I was wrong. But since we've been apart . . . Ann, I know. I want to marry you."

She stared at him, shocked. Just a little more than a week ago, such words would have had her in a swoon, shaking, delighted, on top of the world.

And now . . .

What a strange day. The American in the café, and now Willem . . .

"Ann?"

"I don't know. Let me think. Maybe we'll talk later."

She looked back down. The words on the page before her blurred. She fought hard not to look back up.

"When?"

"I don't know."

"Tonight?"

"No, I have plans with my cousin."

"Your American cousin? Whom I've not met."

The resentment was there. Maybe she had been too mistrustful. Maybe she owed him.

He'd cheated on her!

"In a few days, perhaps, we'll talk."

She felt it when he left her doorway. She heard him walk to her secretary's desk. They talked casually about a publication schedule.

Ann bit her lip hard. She wanted to stand, and race after him. No! Tonight, she was going out with Tara.

And perhaps she would see the handsome American again. And then, perhaps, know herself better. Know what she really felt, and at the least . . .

Pay Willem back for what he had done.

Dubois was infuriated.

The police could be so incredibly annoying, especially Inspector Javet. The man apparently thought he was some kind of a solid wall of testosterone with the right to meddle in things that he knew nothing about.

For the third time, he was questioning Dubois. This time, Javet had come to his house. The last time they had spoken, he had been down at the station. Then, he had been introduced to special crime scene detectives from Paris who explained to him that his dig site would be closed for some time. Well, he had simply exploded.

Javet had patiently explained that a man had been killed.

Dubois had simply blown up. "You fools! This is history. This is a find in the scientific world, a find that is far greater than the loss of one man! Do you think Howard Carter never lost a worker when looking for the tomb of Tutankhamen? You can not, must not, stop my work!"

He shouldn't have blown up. He went on to say how very sorry he was about Jean-Luc. But it was too late. The gentlemen began to question him again.

Then, of course, he had tried to make them see that they were harassing the wrong man. They should have been after the American, Brent Malone.

"Naturally, we are keeping up on his whereabouts,

but I don't believe that your worker can tell us anything more than he has already."

"Surely, if he had murdered the man, he would not walk in and tell you so!" Dubois was impatient that the police seemed like such fools.

They'd had little to say. They had been entirely cordial. They had excused him.

And now, Javet was here. Dubois didn't ask him to sit, nor did he ask if he would like wine, water, or anything. He barely let him through the doorway. Again, Javet seemed impervious to his rudeness and the blunt fact that he didn't want the inspector in his house.

"Professor Dubois, I think you can give us a great deal of help with knowledge you may not even know that you possess. We'd like to see all your notes regarding the dig. And especially, we'd like to know about anyone you approached for assistance in financing, anyone to whom you might have suggested that the dig could provide incredible treasures with a current high monetary value."

"My notes . . ." He frowned and hedged. "Inspector, I made quite a large contribution to the present St. Michel to be granted the right to the dig. And my work . . . no, no, I'm sorry. You cannot have my notes. My work is private. My work is like an artist's canvas. I allow no one to view it until it is complete."

"I must say, Professor, we were curious about that hefty donation. I'm afraid we humble policemen rather thought of teachers and scholars being much as we believe ourselves to be—woefully underpaid."

"I am capable of saving," Dubois said icily. "I live very plainly, as you can see."

"The house is quite enchanting," Javet said, smiling casually as he glanced around.

"The house is quite old, and falling down around my ears," Dubois snapped back.

"Ah, well, then, I had hoped there might be some help you could give us. If you think of anything, please call."

Javet nodded politely, turned, and left by the door which was just at his back, since Dubois had positioned himself in the entryway to keep the inspector from stepping in farther.

When Javet was gone, Dubois leaned against the door, his heart beating too quickly, his palms sweaty. He swore. Javet was an ass. But he was trouble. Pure trouble.

As was the American. Dubois smiled. The American was a problem that could be solved. He just had to say the word.

Feeling better with that thought in mind, he went into his kitchen and poured himself a large measure of good Russian vodka.

Yet as he stood at the window, his heart began to sink. His mouth and throat went dry, despite the liquor. In a gulp he finished off the double shot before turning.

He knew he was not alone.

His visitor stood at the door to the kitchen and stared at him contemptuously. "You fucked up, Dubois. You fucked up—and you're going to pay for it."

Dubois's glass fell to the floor as his visitor took a step toward him.

CHAPTER 7

At last, Jacques was sleeping.

Tara had done her best to listen, to pretend that she believed, that she understood. But he had seen her expression—one that she hadn't been able to hide when he expressed his belief regarding the murder—and he had immediately become upset. He had suddenly forgotten his English and switched to French, speaking so quickly and so wildly that she hadn't begun to understand what he had been saying.

And fear had set in.

Her grandfather was losing his sanity. He was such a wonderful man, and he had cherished his ability to think and reason all his life.

To think that his mind might be going . . .

It was horrible.

But in time she did calm him. She convinced him that she would keep an open mind. She assured him that she could find out what the police were doing without ever having to say that she had been there when the murder occurred. She could be a concerned tourist, just trying to feel safe in the city of Paris, and in the little village where she was staying. She had sworn that though she found his words impossible to believe, she would keep an open mind. And he had gone to bed.

Long after, she sat out on her balcony. She wondered whether or not to tell Ann about the incident, then knew that she couldn't betray Jacques. She had to pray that the police would find the murderer quickly. That would set his mind at rest.

She worried that perhaps shell shock was setting in, now that he had returned to Europe after having been in the States so long. It had been on the front here that he had fought, a special Resistance fighter with the Allied troops. Perhaps he needed to talk to someone, a trained professional, not a granddaughter who doted on him and was involved so deeply and emotionally.

As she worried, Katia came to tell her that Ann was on the phone. Her cousin was bright and cheerful, swept away in the workaday world. "Meetings, meetings, meetings! We have meetings about when to schedule meetings!" Ann told her. "But do you know what? Despite what has happened, we're going to go out. I have one of those special little shock weapons, you know. Long ago, Grandpapa insisted I carry it. And then I have mace, as well—which your father insisted I carry."

"Yes, I know. He insisted I have it in New York, as well," Tara said.

"The really big city."

"Paris is a pretty big city."

"Of course, but we won't exactly be in Paris tonight.

We'll stick close to home, and be smart, watchful, and wary. You're not afraid to go out?"

"No."

"Good! I need a few drinks. A few laughs. And maybe a few dances with a handsome man. Or, at least, a man. Come to think of it, just for a dance, any old geezer— or young one—will do. Listen, I'm working late, so I'll just breeze by, beep the horn, and you'll come down, if that's all right. We'll go to La Guerre—it's just in town, not too far from the church. If you're not afraid of going near the church, that is."

"I hardly think that the murderer is going to stick around the site of the murder," Tara said.

"Is everything all right there?"

She hesitated, then answered quickly, "Yes, fine. Grandpapa is sleeping."

"Bien! He won't mind that we take a night out together. He is always pleased when his family remains close."

"I'll be ready when you beep."

Tara hung up from her conversation with Ann. She needed to go out. To a smoky, chatty, loud bar.

Where there might be drunks and lechers . . .

But sane drunks. And ordinary lechers.

Sleep . . .

Sleep too often meant dreams, and dreams too often meant nightmares.

Nightmares were often made up of the past.

He could almost feet the pain again. The agony that seemed to beat continuously against him, flesh and bone, outside, inside.

He could remember the men speaking, the doctors

staring down at him. He could remember the needles, the way they injected him, tested his strength, his reaction to pain. He remembered the helplessness, the agony, the rage.

There was the doctor in charge, who saw to it that he was secured to the bed with steel clamps every time he would begin his experiments. The doctor didn't bother to make introductions, but he liked to inform the lieutenant that he could be referred to as the god of death at any time. The men called him either Doctor or General Andreson. Sometimes, when the lieutenant twisted and turned, damning him, Andreson would lean close, as if he listened to rhapsodic music rather than the screams and curses of a man in agony. Then he would touch the lieutenant's head almost tenderly and tell him, "Damn me, if you will. By any name, for I use several. Damn me . . . curse me, for your words are just a melody in my mind. Your strength is quite incredible. You should be dead by now, but you are not. Doesn't that make you the least bit curious? Ah, but it fascinates me!"

Andreson was a master of torture and pain. And as long as he lived, the lieutenant would not forget him.

But he could remember Dr. Weiss as well. The man who would stand in still silence, hands behind his back, face grim, as so much went on. And he would never forget the way that the man came to him in those times when the others were gone. The cooling cloth on his head. The pills quickly placed under his tongue, antidotes to pain.

He knew that Weiss stole the pills. And he knew that Weiss risked his own life to help in any way. When he tried to thank him, the man would redden and reply, "We are not all monsters. We are so many good people.

But we are afraid. And fear . . . well, fear is the greatest weapon on earth."

The lieutenant formed words with his lips. "Thank you. Thank you. I still believe there is a God, and he will bless you."

The slim little man with the wire-rimmed glasses reddened even more. "If you would thank me at all, please believe that there is goodness among my people. Those who love their children, who honor God, who abhor . . . pain."

The pain pill began to work. He could almost smile. "I know, Doctor Weiss. I know. I don't hate people, I hate rulers who have no regard for human life. Not that it will matter, will it? I will never get out of here alive."

"Oh, I think that you will live," Dr. Weiss said, and the sound was almost sad and bitter.

"No one else survived, did they?"

"No one, no one among the Allies, and no one of our soldiers, either."

"So strange . . ."

"You don't know, do you? You don't understand at all what happened, do you?"

"We were shooting, they were shooting, and suddenly, it seemed that every wolf in Europe was fighting its own war."

"Poor boy . . ."

Dr. Weiss smoothed back the hair from his forehead, looking to the windows. He stared back at the lieutenant uneasily.

"They want to know your strength. They want to use you. They want to know just how you have survived . . . and if and how you will continue to survive. But you see, I know."

"And how is that?"

Dr. Weiss didn't seem to hear his question. "Somehow, and soon, I must get you out of here. I must. They will realize your strength, and they will be afraid, and they will destroy you. I must think . . . must think."

He was drifting to sleep, but he could not help but think of Weiss. The man had showed incredibe kindness at severe risk.

"I am probably more than half dead already," the lieutenant said. "Don't do anything foolish. Your country will need men like you, when this is over."

Again, the doctor wasn't looking at him.

He was staring out at the night.

And he stared back at the lieutenant, his features contorted in fear. His words came haltingly. "I pray . . . I pray . . ."

"What is it?" His words were beginning to slur.

"I pray that it is not you who kills me."

He woke himself up with a jerk. Sweat was running down his back.

Sleep, rest.

Dreams, nightmares.

God, no more!

That night, La Guerre was hopping.

The bizarre murder was a topic of conversation, but not one that seemed to concern many people.

A band was already playing when Ann and Tara arrived. They were doing mostly American pop hits.

The tables were full. There were a few seats left at the bar and Ann and Tara took them. Ann instantly introduced her to Tomas, the bartender, as her American cousin. Tomas told them he had an especially good house wine that night, did they want to try it? They did.

When their wine arrived, Ann almost instantly downed her glass. Tara was tempted to do the same. She was torn between wondering if her grandfather had gone crazy, or if the whole world had done so. She was ostensibly listening to Ann talk about her day at the office, how they had gone through meeting after meeting, but she was also listening to those around her.

"I think the professor, that Dubois guy, has some explaining to do," a girl at the table behind them said.

"Dubois is all but foaming at the mouth at the police for closing down his site!" one of her companions replied.

"Well, unless he's an awfully good actor, I think that lets him out as the murderer," the young woman replied.

"Never can tell with those scientific types."

"What about the worker who found the body?" the girl said, her tone suddenly breathy. "Did you see his picture in the paper?"

"There's someone suspicious," one of her male companions replied.

"Oh, pooh! Who butchers someone and heads right to the police?"

"And we're going to publish a book on the gourmet treatment of dogs and cats as main protein staples," Ann said.

"What?" Tara demanded, realizing that her cousin was staring at her.

"You haven't been listening to a thing I've said," Ann complained.

"I'm sorry, I have been. Sort of. It's just been a long day. Grandpapa is still on his tangent. I don't know why—I was so tired—but I barely slept last night. I kept having nightmares about wolves."

"Oh, yes, you thought you saw one."

"I still think I saw one."

"I told you, there are no wolves. Well, of course, there are human wolves. Like the guy coming in the door now. Ooh la, la. There is a hot—hot—wolf for you. Except, of course, you must always be very careful with wolves. They'll consume you, unless you stop them."

"Maybe there was a circus in town. Maybe a creature escaped from the zoo."

"We would have seen it in the paper."

"Not when we have a local story like the murder at the dig!"

"Um. And is that why you have not—in the least—noted my state of excitement?"

Tara stared at her cousin guiltily. "You are excited. What happened? I'm sorry—I should have noticed right away."

"Yes, you should have done so."

"Well?"

"It was a day you would not believe! First—it was so busy! I went out for coffee, and was struggling with cups and money and food and . . . then I met an American."

Tara arched a brow. "An American in Paris. How novel."

Ann made a face. "An American like this one is novel anywhere, I'll have you know. He was gorgeous. Tall, blond, bronzed, so handsome. And he was all over me."

"Imagine that. A handsome American sees a Parisian beauty and tries to pick her up!"

Ann laughed again. "I know I'm going to see him again."

"Did you make a date?"

"More or less, but wait! Right after, I go up to my office, and out of nowhere Willem is suddenly at my office door. He is nearly in tears, wanting me to forgive him."

"Wow. A happening day." Tara sipped her wine, studying her cousin. "So, now there are two men fawning in your footsteps. What are you going to do?"

She shrugged, a small secretive smile in place. "Well, I really was shattered by what Willem did. And the American was . . . he looked like someone out of that old show . . . "Baywatch." I'm going to see him, give him a bit of a chance . . . and maybe, at some point, I'll talk to Willem. I was in love with him. But how can you stay in love with a man you don't trust? But then, again, in a week, you do not fall out of love. However, in a matter of moments, you can fall into fascination and . . . well, you know, lust."

"Lust—in a matter of moments. Wow."

Ann laughed. "Oh, come, come! You've never felt that before? I mean, just looking at someone and thinking, I'll bet he's great in bed."

"I've thought of guys as attractive without immediately wondering just what they'd do with all that attractiveness."

"You liar! You simply think you're far too discriminating for such behavior. We don't always act on these impulses, but that doesn't mean they're not there."

"Lots of people are attractive. Should we sleep with all of them?"

"Only if the urge is really there," Ann teased.

She was facing the door. Tara was facing her cousin. "Now," Ann murmured, "talk about your beautiful people! There are two of them coming in as we speak. One better looking than the next. Well, damn. There's a woman with them. Nope—don't turn! Bother. All the cute ones are always taken. And they even appear articulate. Well dressed. They must be married. One of the guys must go with the woman. Still . . . don't look now, but, I repeat, wow. And only one woman . . . can't quite tell which one she goes with. Unless she goes with both of them. No . . . she doesn't look the type. But then again, what would that 'type' look like?"

Tara laughed softly. "Are you sure you need me to listen to you? You seem quite able to carry on a conversation all by yourself."

Ann made a face at her. "You haven't seen what I've seen."

"Okay, then, I'll look—"

"Don't you dare turn around and stare! It will appear that we're out on the prowl, looking for men."

"Well, if you recall, we did agree that we both needed to meet new people. But then, that was before the American fell into your lap—or into your café au lait—and Willem made an appearance in your office. But then, what the heck, maybe there should be a third guy in the lineup."

"Don't be crass. We would never pick up strangers in a bar."

Tara started to turn around.

"No, no, no! I said that you can't look now! We most certainly don't want to be obvious."

"We're not obvious. You just said that we would never be so crass as to pick up strangers in a bar."

"Certainly not. We would become friends with them before we picked them up."

Tara sighed, "Honestly, Ann, I'm not sure I want to create any new friends to pick up. I think I'm lucky that

I'm not involved with anyone at the moment. Jacques is going to have my entire attention while I'm here."

"He went off on a tangent again, eh?" Ann murmured. "Oh, my God!" she breathed suddenly.

"What?"

"Tall . . . nicely tall. Broad shoulders. Umm . . . very sleek and agile. I could eat him up, just watching him walk across the room."

"Him—who?"

"Tall, dark, and walking sensuality. Well, both of them are dark. And the one coming this way . . . I think he's taller than anyone else in here. Lord!"

"Lord, what?"

Tara started to turn again.

"No! No!" Ann pleaded. "He's coming here. He looked over this way, and now . . . he's coming here!"

"He must be someone you know and don't remember."

"No. I would never forget that I knew him."

Tara let out an explosive little sound of impatience and tried to turn again.

"No!" Ann caught her hands, preventing her from turning on the stool. "Don't look around!"

"Well, you've got to let go of my hands! We're going to look very bizarre!"

Ann drew her hands away.

"Fine, okay. What does he look like?" Tara asked.

"Dark, rich dark hair, like sable, ooh, just shaggy enough to be very arty . . . nice frame around his face. Rugged face, but very nicely put together. And his eyes . . . My heart is fluttering right now."

With a sense of growing dread, Tara frowned at her cousin and spun around on her bar stool. She nearly slid off. Brent Malone was approaching her.

"Hello." He had a bottle of beer in his hand, and his smile was as casual as that of any friend greeting another in a public place. He offered Ann an inquisitive nod of friendly acknowledgment over Tara's head.

"Hello," she replied, the sound of her voice as stiff as her neck.

"Hi," Ann said pleasantly, awaiting an introduction. She nudged Tara. "Well?"

"Brent, my cousin, Ann—my French cousin Ann. Ann DeVant, Brent Malone."

"How do you do, a pleasure," Brent said.

"Certainly. I must admit, I didn't know that Tara had friends—other than our old family friends, of course—in the area."

"We just met," Brent said. "But the circumstances were such that . . ." his curious golden eyes studied her with rueful amusement, "well, I do feel as if we've known each other a long time."

"You never mentioned Mr. Malone," Ann said.

"Brent," he quickly supplied. "I'm with some friends. Would you care to join us?"

"Oh, I don't think that we can," Tara began.

"We'd love to," Ann said.

"But we're not staying long," Tara said.

"It's been a long day, which means that I'm not in a hurry to end a night's relaxation," Ann said.

"Then do, please, come along."

Ann was off her stool quickly. Tara caught her cousin by the back of her shirt. "I don't trust him," she whispered.

"Good, you should never really trust any man," Ann whispered back, "but I'm following that one—with you or without you!"

"Ann!"

With little choice, Tara followed her cousin to the table Brent and his companions had somehow managed to find.

"Tara Adair, Ann DeVant, I'd like you to meet Lucian and Jade DeVeau. Lucian, Jade—Tara and Ann."

The man rose, greeting them. The couple were the same people Tara had seen Brent meet at the café the other day. The woman was attractive—very—with sea-colored eyes and a length of beautiful hair that seemed a shade between brunette and blond. She had a warm, welcoming smile that seemed sincere. She didn't appear at all averse to Brent's friends coming to the table. She was apparently married to the tall man with the nearly black hair, since they shared a surname. He moved with an agile, sure, fluid power, even in the simple act of acquiring an extra chair; in manner—and in an elusive quality Tara couldn't quite pinpoint—he had a similar magnetism to that of Brent Malone. Perhaps that was what disturbed her the most. There was nothing about either man that should be alarming, yet she had the feeling that their reflexes would be faster than the speed of light, and that something that she couldn't see or comprehend remained dangerous about them . . .

"Nice to have you join us," Lucian said, taking his chair again as they were seated. "So, Ann, this is your home."

"Yes. I work in Paris, but live in the village. We have an old family . . . well, it's not a chateau in the grand sense of the word, but it's a lovely family home out here."

Tara wanted to kick her cousin. She didn't want these people knowing where they lived. But that was ridiculous. She hadn't actually told him, but she was certain that Brent Malone knew where she was staying.

"You must come and visit while you're here," Ann continued.

Tara kicked her cousin. Ann yelped involuntarily, then stared at her across the table. Tara knew that Brent Malone was watching her, knew exactly what had happened, and remained amused. She was certain as well that he had lured the two of them to the table specifically to get an invitation to the chateau.

Now, they had it.

"A chateau, how lovely," Jade said.

Lucian summoned a waiter, his French seeming as perfectly accented as any Tara had ever heard.

"Are you French?" she inquired.

Jade answered. "I'm originally from the New Orleans area," she said. "And you?"

"New York," she said, turning her attention pointedly back to Lucian. "And you?"

"Lucian likes to consider himself a citizen of the world," Brent said.

"I'm not French, but I have lived here," Lucian told her. " I've called the States home for some time now."

She turned her gaze hard on Brent to realize that he had never stopped watching her. "And me? I thought you would never ask. Originally, I come from Virginia," he said.

"There's a lot of French spoken in New Orleans, of course," Lucian said. "It's easy to keep up."

"Naturally," Tara said pleasantly, but turned her attention to Brent Malone. "But I haven't heard of it being such a commonly spoken language in Virginia."

His eyes didn't waver from hers. "I happen to be a student of linguistics," he said flatly.

"My French should be better," Jade said. "But in New Orleans . . . I haven't the purity of Lucian's accent, because I'm afraid we have a patois. I guess, over here, it's kind of a Southern-slash-French accent."

"That's fine, you speak the language, comprehend what is said," Ann told her. Tara saw that her cousin was flushed, and with the blush on her cheeks, she was even more attractive. She was chatting away at the table, but she seemed to be watching the back of the room. Tara tried to see what she was looking at, but the bar had gotten very crowded.

Now and then, Ann stared at her with amusement, and seemed to nudge her chair closer to Brent's. Tara couldn't help it; she didn't like it a bit.

She understood it; but she didn't like it, any more than she liked the fact that the man at her side was too close—and closer with every move Ann made. In truth, he was a *normal* distance away, sitting as they were in such a tightly packed establishment. But it was as if she could feel the whole of him. The stretch of his legs beneath the table, perfectly correct, yet if she shifted, she would brush against him. She hated the fact that a strange heat seemed to emanate from him, compelling her to move closer, as if she were cold.

She wasn't cold.

His scent . . . whatever the aftershave or soap he wore . . . remained compelling as well. Subtle. There was nothing overt about him at all. But it was there . . . something that beckoned at a subliminal range.

And while it lured, it also sent lightning into her system, tremendous flashes that warned her to be wary.

A man was dead.

She knew he hadn't done it.

Ah, but what if there had been a conspiracy? What if these "friends" of his who had just arrived had been in the tomb, what if they were the murderers? Surely, none of this talk of

*evil and vampires had been true, even though Jacques' mind
and the minds of these strangers were traveling along similar
courses. Maybe they even knew something about Jacques, knew
that she had been in the tomb because of his beliefs, and they
were playing upon them?*

"Tara!" Ann said.

She jumped. "What?"

"You're a thousand miles away. I'm off with that tall
fellow over there. We're all going to dance. Brent has
just asked you to join him."

"Oh, sorry. I, uh, I think I'll beg off," she said.

Lucian and his wife were already standing. Ann was
practically running—pushing and shoving her way—
heading toward the rear of the room. What tall fellow?
Tara still didn't know who her cousin had been
watching.

"Tara?" Brent was watching her. There was a definite
humorous edge in his eyes, and perhaps a challenge.
His hand was stretched toward her.

She wanted to jump up and knock his hand aside.
But suddenly, his long bronzed, work-roughened fingers
lay on her arm.

"Sure you don't want to join them?"

She tried to find her cousin on the dance floor. She
couldn't see her, and, perhaps unreasonably, she worried about her.

She stared down at Brent's hand on her flesh.

She wanted to draw her arm back, but she didn't.
She felt her heart drumming.

"I don't trust you any farther than I could throw
you," she told him flatly. "And I'm worried about my
cousin."

"I know."

"Oh, you do?"

"You're like an open book."

"Then you should know that I'm thinking this as well—I want you to leave us alone."

"Your cousin looks happy."

"But she shouldn't be. There's something . . . something slimy about all of you."

His lashes lowered over his curious eyes for a long moment. Then he stared at her again.

"Slimy?"

"It's the best word I can summon to fit the feeling."

"Slimy? Wow, I am . . . crushed."

"How can I possibly crush you? You barely know me. You're an exaggerator. And a liar."

"I don't believe that I've lied to you," he told her. "And I also don't believe that you feel that you barely know me. Are you always this cold?"

"Only when I meet a man while another is being brutally murdered."

"Look, I swear to you, we're not slimy. But let's see . . . in that moment when you were lost to us, you were thinking that one of my companions might have slipped in and killed Jean-Luc while I was chasing after you in the tomb."

She was so startled that he had divined her thoughts so accurately that she gasped aloud.

"Feel free to check their passports and airline tickets," he said, removing his hand from her arm and leaning back. "They have just arrived."

"Oh, really, and the authorities will give me that information?"

"I'm sure you can find a way to learn exactly what time—and from where—they arrived."

"Great. I am going to speak with the police."

"Don't tell them you were there," he said. The words were even. They were still a command—and a warning.

"I don't understand you at all. You're a fool. I could completely clear you."

He leaned forward, very close, and very intense. She was overwhelmed again by a strange sense of warmth. She told herself that she was not pulling back because she had no intention of giving in to such fantasies.

"Don't let your name become involved with what happened," he went on. "You don't trust me as far as you can throw me—well, I'm telling you, I don't trust Dubois. And we both know there is a murderer out there."

"You know my grandfather, or something about him, don't you?" she demanded. "You know his reputation as a writer, and you think he will be an ally of yours in insisting that there is pure evil in the ground. Well, there's not. There's a murderer out there."

"Tara, whether the murderer is human—or superhuman in some way—the danger would remain if you were to let your name become involved in the investigation."

"Your name is surely involved—and here you are, out on the town, enjoying life with your friends. Although how you managed to be in this part of town, I'm not at all sure."

"I do need to see your grandfather."

"I don't want you near him."

"I'm afraid that doesn't matter to me."

"He's very old, and ill, and I'm not going to allow you to hurt him."

Steady eyes, appearing pure yellow, stared into her own. Despite herself, she found that she believed him when he said, "I wouldn't hurt your grandfather for the world. In fact, I would defend him with my dying breath."

"You don't need to defend him. He has Ann, and he has me."

"And what if you find that you do need help?"

"Then I'll call the police."

"And what if—just what if—some of his talk—or mine—proved to be legitimate? Calling the police might not be the answer you need. You don't know what you're up against."

"And you do?"

"I found Jean-Luc's body, you'll recall."

"Tell you what. If it comes to that, I'll call you."

"You've never asked for my number."

"Oh."

He started writing on one of the cocktail napkins. "Here, my number, just in case you need it." He passed the napkin to her. "Please, it's just a phone number. Keep it."

She let out a breath that purposely displayed great impatience.

But she slipped the cocktail napkin into her purse.

"Why won't you dance with me?" he asked her.

"I think I've been fairly plain. I don't trust you. I don't particularly like you."

He extended a hand toward the tightly packed dance floor. "You're a liar. You're very suspicious, but I intrigue you, and I think that you like me just fine."

"Rather sure of yourself, aren't you?"

"Maybe. But I don't think I'm wrong."

"Let's see, I met you in a crypt at the exact time a man was being murdered."

"That's right. You know I didn't do it."

"But you do know something about it."

"Enough to know that you'll put yourself in danger if you can't learn to trust me."

"You've given me nothing to trust."

"Why don't you give yourself half a chance? Perhaps it's just in the back of your artistic mind, and maybe it's more than that, but I don't believe you really think I could cause you any harm. But all that aside, just what do you think I could do out there on the dance floor? Come on—we're appearing extremely antisocial. Be really daring, come dance with me."

He gave her no choice. He had risen, and taken her hand.

There was nothing tight or fierce about his grip at all.

And yet . . .

She wasn't at all certain that she could have broken it.

CHAPTER 8

That time between sleep . . . and the rush of power upon waking . . . could be the most wonderful.

And that was when she heard him.

My love . . .

The words, so soft at first, growing louder. Faint, a dream, imagination, longing, desire. And then . . .

I can feel you, speak to me, where are you?

She longed to reply. Longed with every fiber of her being. The fact that he was near . . . that he remained, that he was out there. Jubilation swept through her, and her reply came without thought or effort.

But then she held back.

There was something else out there. Someone. Another entity.

And when she replied, she did so carefully, already bitter, feeling a new rise of hate and determination. Once . . .

But once had been long ago.

She inhaled the sweet smell of ancient earth. She felt the power of the new life, the new blood, filling her veins. Felt the warmth of that life, real, solid, strong.

I will find you . . .

Her name again. Soft, yearning.

And then the realization on his end. Silence. They could be found.

Yes, we will find one another.

She closed off, purposely, and yet . . .

It was still out there. That hint of danger. Strong . . .

They were many around him. Many who had rallied to him. These thoughts came to her mind, and she was bitter. Because she could sense there was more behind him than even the strength and powers with which she was acquainted.

She rose. It was night now. Darkness had descended.

And it was her time to rule the earth.

Ah, well, start small. She didn't need to rule the earth. Just Paris.

Ann was having the time of her life.

Once they were on the dance floor, Tara decided wryly that Ann might have been right—perhaps she had really seen a large shepherd dog the night before—but Paris, and the surrounding villages, were full of wolves.

They all seemed to be in the bar.

Once they had begun dancing, she didn't have to worry long about being too close to Brent Malone. And she was close. They were bumped into every other second, it seemed, and with each bump, she was thrown hard against him. Then she realized that she had been sadly mistaken if she had thought him slim or wiry. He was lean, but must have been made of pure muscle.

No matter how hard she tried to prevent it, her mind kept going back to her cousin's words earlier that evening: Hadn't she ever met someone with whom she fell into instant . . . lust? Didn't she ever just wonder . . .

Yes.

Yes, yes, yes. She almost wanted to scream. Each crush against him, slide of his hand, brush of his chest or thigh, was a sensual experience. She was warm, roasting, blood rushing through her, betraying her thoughts in the rise of color in her cheeks . . .

The crowd on the floor seemed to be in a collective good mood, and having fun, and men were cutting in on one another constantly. She didn't dance with Brent long—not more than two minutes and sixty bumps—before he was forced to give way to a bearded fellow who in turn, handed her over to a young blond man.

At one point, she saw that the Lothario with the slick mustache who had just cut in on her latest partner was apparently sending his own date down the line—she had seen him with the short-haired mini-skirted redhead who was now with Brent when they had first come out on the floor.

When the song ended, she saw that he was coming across the floor for her.

But Lucian stopped him and said something to him that made him frown and pause. The two spoke for a few minutes, then he continued on his way to her.

"The others have to leave, I'm afraid."

"You're not going with them?"

"I'll catch up with them later." He hesitated. They were both slightly damp from exertion. They weren't

more than an inch apart. She realized that she had been
having fun . . .

And wanting more.

She had been hoping that he was going to come back
for her, each time their partners changed. She was as
suspicious and wary as it was possible to be, but she
knew that she was attracted to him, that, in fact, she
had never felt so compelled by anyone at any time before
in her life. She wished that she had met him differently.
She wished she was elsewhere with him. Like a deserted
island. A warm deserted island where clothing was mini-
mal, and she could reach out and touch the nakedness
of the chest she had been crushed against so frequently
tonight.

Staring up at him, a flood of warmth swept over her.
She didn't know his exact fantasy. It might not have
been a beach. Maybe somewhere in front of a roaring
fire, but wherever it was, flesh was the main thing, touching flesh, and getting closer than they had been on the
dance floor.

She took a step back. Sometimes, she thought that
she was a single sane person in a world gone crazy. She
knew friends who met guys at bars, never learned their
last names, and slept with them. Intimacy for her had
always taken time; in her life, she could count only three
relationships that could be considered affairs.

She didn't want time. Nor did she want the truth.
She wanted to know nothing about his background. She
just wanted a single hour to sate the curiosity and sudden
hunger that had plagued her from the first time she
had seen him.

But she wasn't accustomed to giving way, and she
forced herself to step back, blink, and assess the man
in her mind's eye. She forced her eyes to his, and away

from his hands, and her mind from the fantasy about what those hands would feel like if he were to touch her. Really touch.

"You don't have to stay because of us. We can get home okay. After all, we came out alone tonight, and we're both armed with mace. We didn't expect to run into an escort."

"Where's Ann?" he asked.

She turned and searched the dance floor at the rear of the bar. She could barely see her cousin through the crowd, but she saw the man. He was tall, and sandy haired. He might have been a linebacker from a football team. Her cousin was on her toes with her arms around him as she kissed him on both cheeks. Very French.

But then the man pulled her back for a moment in a long hug, his face buried against her neck, her dark hair spilling over his features.

The two pulled apart. Her cousin was flushed and smiling. As Tara stared, Ann left the man and came hurrying to the front door to say goodbye; she had apparently realized that the DeVeaus were leaving.

Ann did the kisses on the cheeks with the couple, encouraging them once again to come and see the chateau.

Tara somehow refrained from throttling her cousin. Lucian and Jade both smiled and waved to her. She forced a smile and wave in return, then turned to Brent.

"You are free to go with them!" she repeated, disturbed that words meant to be casual but firm came out in something of a desperate whisper.

"But I don't mind following you two home, I honestly don't mind," Brent said. He grimaced toward the dance floor. "Wolves."

"How do I know you're not the worst wolf of the bunch?"

"You don't," he told her softly.

She didn't have a chance to reply. Ann was suddenly between them.

She came close to speak, her voice rising above the sound of the music and the crowd as she told Brent, "Your friends are lovely."

The dark fellow with the mustache came up behind Ann, catching her hand, speaking in rapid French and drawing her back to the dance floor.

Tara stared at Brent, then pushed past him, making her way back to the table. He followed, taking a seat beside her.

"What is it now?"

"Surely, you can read my mind," she challenged.

"Actually, I believe you are suspicious, wondering what business dragged them out of a bar at night."

"Well?"

"They had things to do."

"Oh?"

"Previous commitments."

"Really."

She turned suddenly, wondering why she had come to the table. She couldn't see Ann from here.

"If you want to watch your cousin, we'll have to dance again."

"I don't need to watch her," she lied.

"You're worried about her."

She stared at him.

"Maybe. Ann isn't the suspicious type. I wouldn't want her to be too trusting—of anyone here. And she doesn't particularly believe in evil or things that go bump in the night."

"I thought you were far too logical to believe in what you couldn't see yourself."

"But I can be very suspicious."

She was startled when he didn't reply. It was suddenly as if she wasn't there. His eyes were on the dance floor. He didn't rise at first, but he was tense as he might have been if thugs armed with repeating rifles had just walked into the place.

"We've got to get your cousin out of here," he said, standing then.

"What?"

"You heard me. We've got to get out of here."

"Why?" she asked, startled by his sudden change.

He looked down at her, features taut, yellow eyes an intent blaze. "For once, trust me."

She didn't know what power of force or sincerity lay in his gaze. She found herself rising—trusting him, and just as anxious as he to leave the bar.

Trusting him . . .

For once.

They hurried out to the dance floor together, weaving their way through to Ann. While Tara talked to her cousin, she noted that Brent was studying everyone on the dance floor.

"So early? Why must we go now?" Ann shouted. "It's the best night I've had in ages. Oh, don't worry, I'm not taking any of these wolves seriously, Tara, but I am having a very good time. All right, well, maybe there is one wolf I'm taking seriously. Revenge. God, is it sweet. Tara, you could let Brent take you home, and I'll come along within an hour or so."

"No! I'm not leaving you alone."

"But, Tara, I'm out alone, meeting friends or whatever, all the time when you're not here!"

"We've got to go," Brent interrupted. He was staring at Ann.

Ann suddenly smiled and shrugged. "Sure. If you say so."

Tara was perplexed and amazed at the instantly acquiescent tone in Ann's voice. Linking arms with Tara, Ann started straight for the door.

"Oh, the bill!" she said.

"Lucian covered it before he left," Brent said curtly. "Let's go, now."

When they were out on the street, Tara noted that he was staring at the bar, still tense, and perhaps, still trying to determine exactly what it was in there that he had suddenly found so disturbing that they had to leave.

"The fellow with the very blond hair was quite nice," Ann said, walking along in the direction of the car. The girls remained together. Brent was behind them.

"Which fellow?"

"Ah, let's see . . . I think he must have been about six feet two or three. Great, sculpted features. Nice shoulders . . . different." She was smiling as she watched Tara. "It was the same man, Tara, the American I met today."

"Why didn't you introduce me?"

"I barely know him," Ann said. "I wasn't sure he would come, though I had thought that he might. And guess what? Willem was there . . . at least, I think he was there. I'm almost certain I saw him sitting at a corner table. I like the blond. I hope to see him again. He is . . . very handsome. And macho. I like broad shoulders and muscles." She glanced over her shoulder to see if Brent remained several feet behind him. "I mean, really, I'm quite old enough to judge a man for his mind and his manner, but . . . well, voilà, there it is, I cannot help but be impressed with good muscle as well. But this man, Rick, ah, he's courteous as well. With such a sense of humor! And his accent! When he speaks English, and when he speaks French!''

"The French hate American accents," Tara said absently. She paused, looking back at Brent.

"Tara! I never look down my nose at an American accent! All right, well, maybe now and then. But for this man . . .''

"Brent, where's your car?" Tara asked.

"In the lot. And so is yours.''

There wasn't a great distance between the bar and the lot where people parked for La Guerre. But once they had left the neon glow of the bar behind, the street suddenly seemed very dark.

It wasn't the center of Paris, where lights burned brightly at all hours of the day and night.

Old buildings, some ancient, and some only a century or two old, mingled with a few modern structures. By day they were businesses, some with apartments atop them, but by night . . .

They were closed. And dark. And the street lamps here were few and far between. Only a few pale lights— quite beautiful, actually, Art Moderne, from perhaps the nineteen twenties—stood guard over the parked cars.

The lamps should have created an area of light and safety.

Instead, they helped create a world of shadow and shifting dark shapes.

Brent had paused. He was listening. And watching the shadows.

Tara looked around, as he was doing. She felt a

strange dread growing in her, seeming to make her muscles heavy, constricted.

Shadows shifted.

They appeared as giant wings, dark sweeps in the night that played from building to building. The breeze suddenly seemed to stir, cold, though they were barely into autumn.

"Go," Brent said suddenly, and very softly.

"What is it?" she asked. *Nothing, there was nothing around them. It was just a shadowy street. The weather was changing, the seasons were shifting.*

And the shadows . . .

Were nothing more than shadows.

And yet . . .

She could still feel that sensation. That prickling at the nape of her neck. The heaviness of fear, the paralysis of terror.

Terror.

Of shadows!

She tried to get a grip on herself, to let her usual common sense and logic slip into place. Her certainty that the dangers in the world were known.

"Go!" he repeated.

Ann suddenly gripped her arm. She realized her cousin was feeling the same inexplicable sense of dread that had seized her.

Brent looked at her, and gave her an odd, disarming smile. "Go on, please, and quickly. I'll be by later, just to make sure you're all right."

"Allons-y!" Ann insisted, her fingers digging hard into Tara's flesh.

Then she didn't know what force galvanized her into action. She grabbed her cousin's hand and started running. They could see Ann's car, ahead.

Ann had parked under the lights that gave off a gloomy yellow glow.

Tara had never run so fast in her life, and as they streaked across the walk and the grass and onto the asphalt again, she didn't look back. She feared that, like Lot's wife, she would be turned to salt.

Or she would see something that she didn't want to see. Something that she could deny, as long as she didn't turn . . .

Into the night, into the glow by the car, she saw the sweep of the shadow. She heard something behind them, close behind them. The soft fall of padded footsteps, moving with a greater speed and force than that which drove them.

Overhead, a great wing of darkness was rising . . .

She heard . . . something.

A shriek.

A sudden cry of the wind that had been nothing but whispering . . .

Ann was rattling her keys in her hands, trying to find the key for the car door.

"The clicker!" Tara shouted.

For a split second, Ann stared at her, horrified at her own stupidity in forgetting that she could beep her locks open. She hit the clicker. The girls both jumped into the car, and slammed the doors.

They both shrieked, as something hit the roof of the car.

They stared at one another.

"Go, go, go!" Tara said.

With shaking fingers, Ann inserted the key into the ignition. The car roared to life.

Another thump came. Ann stepped on the gas. They heard the sounds of whatever had been on top of them falling from the car . . .

And yet . . .

They didn't truly hear the sound of anything falling.

Lips taut and serious, Ann stared ahead at the road. She jerked the car out onto the street, and they sped down the length of it.

Tara turned back. There was nothing behind them. Nothing at all. The neon glow advertising La Guerre continued to burn softly. Cars remained in the lot.

Shadows were just shadows.

There were no people just outside the door, nor were there any on the street. Not even Brent Malone.

"What did we hit? What was on the car?" Ann demanded.

"Nothing," Tara said.

Ann stared at her incredulously.

"There's nothing back there, nothing back there at all," Tara said.

"That's impossible."

"I'm telling you—Ann! What are you doing?"

Her cousin had nearly braked, and was turning the car around.

"I've got to see. I don't know why I was so panicked back there. But I heard . . . what if I hit someone, something? What if I've wounded a dog?"

"There's nothing there!"

But Ann was determined. They drove back down the street, hesitating near the bar and the parking lot.

Ann drew to a halt, laughing, leaning her head on the steering wheel.

"Ann, what is the matter with you? Let's get the hell out of here!"

"Why?" Ann demanded. "There's nothing here! We let the darkness and shadows make silly little geese out of us." Her laughter faded. She swallowed hard, and suddenly rubbed the back of her neck. "I don't feel really well. It's bad to drink wine, smoke cigarettes, and run like an idiot."

"Ann, drive," Tara said.

It seemed that the shadows were moving again. And the gloomy light beneath which they'd parked suddenly made a popping sound.

The shadows fell like a cloak of sweeping vengeance all around them.

"Drive!" Tara said.

Ann didn't hesitate. She hit the gas again, and didn't let up until they had reached the chateau, roaring past stop signs and red lights.

In front of the chateau, she put the car in park and sat still for a minute. "Are we crazy? Are we letting Grandpapa get to us?"

"I don't know," Tara said. "Yes, wait, I do know. At the least, there is a cold-blooded murderer out there somewhere. Naturally, we're nervous. So let's get into the house."

Ann stared at her and nodded solemnly.

Then, as one, they opened their doors and started to bolt for the house. As they neared the entry, they saw that the door was open.

"What . . . ?" Ann murmured.

Tara saw that Katia was blocking the doorway. And even at the chateau, where light was always shining on the drive at night, shadows seemed to have crept in.

Tara felt the breeze again. Cold, penetrating. Evil.

A breeze was not evil! It was autumn, and days could still be warm, but winter was coming, and a cold breeze simply hinted of the season to come . . .

"He is sleeping, I tell you!"

Katia was speaking in French, but she was determined, and enunciating each word.

"I cannot let you in . . ."

Tara blinked and saw what she hadn't seen before. A woman was standing in the entrance, next to the outer wall, and framed by ivy. Shadows fell over her from the balconies above, which was why they hadn't seen her at first.

"But then again . . ." Katia said suddenly, amazingly changing her mind, ready to pull out the red carpet and beg the woman to enter.

The breeze . . .

It seemed to grip her again, as if it could paralyze her.

Ann wasn't moving at all.

The woman was nearly in the house. Tara suddenly knew that she couldn't allow it. She raced to the door, spinning to stare at the woman.

For a moment, she was speechless herself. *And dear Lord, she didn't know why.*

The woman was a well-dressed, startling beauty. Hair almost pitch black. Eyes as green as emeralds. Her suit was impeccably tailored, the latest fashion. It was fitted, and she wore it very well. The skirt was short. Her heels were spikes.

She extended a hand toward Tara. Automatically, Tara accepted it.

"Hello, I'm from the social services department at the hospital. I'm just doing a checkup on your grandfather. It's something we try to do with all our patients, especially when they are elderly. We like to make sure that they're doing well in their home environment."

Like Katia, Tara was strangely tempted to invite the woman in. Her smile was so sincere.

And yet . . .

Tara's hand, when she shook that of the other woman, felt like ice.

And yet . . .

At the same time, it burned.

"I'm afraid it's far too late to visit my grandfather," she said firmly. "He sleeps at this hour. If you wish to see him, you must come by during the day."

In a flash . . . and only for a flash—so quickly that Tara might have imagined it—the woman's face vanished. The pleasant, hypnotic smile vanished. She betrayed a fury, a hideous expression of anger so deep and vile that Tara fell back a step.

And then . . .

She was smiling again, so pleasantly, her eyes on Ann, who had nearly reached the door.

"I am so sorry, it is late. I hadn't realized how late myself. You can't imagine the hours we work. It's just dreadful. There's not really much I need to do. Perhaps, if you were just to invite me in, I could take a peek at your grandfather and see that he was sleeping in comfortable surroundings. I'm aware of his family history, of course, and I'm well aware he has good and loving relatives. It would be such a relief to have one patient off my list."

"Perhaps—" Ann began, falling under the same spell.

But the woman suddenly straightened.

It was as if she had suddenly become aware of a touch of ice in the air.

"Never mind. It is not a big thing. I will be back."

She started down the steps.

"But—" Ann called after her.

The woman swung back to stare at the two of them. "Oh, don't worry. I will be back."

For a flash, a subliminal second—Tara saw the horrid mask of fury on the woman's face again.

But it wasn't there. She was smiling. And assuring them.

Yes, oh, yes, she would return.

Katia suddenly sprang to life and began scolding Ann and Tara.

"Come in, come in, come in! I don't know what possessed me to open the door! It's a strangely cold night, suddenly. And we'd been having a renewed burst of summer in the midst of fall! In the house, in the house, in the house! Come, come, girls. There is a maniac out there. The police have done nothing yet."

They were ushered in. Katia closed and locked the door firmly.

Inside, it was warm. A fire was burning in the hearth in the hall. "Girls, would you like hot chocolate?"

Tara gave herself a shake. Inside the house, everything seemed different. Everything. It was not just warm, it was . . .

Normal.

Ann seemed to be feeling the same. She gave Katia a rueful smile. "Chocolate, lovely. If you don't mind though, I'll take mine up to bed. I'm suddenly exhausted. And you're so right, Katia. I hope the police find the killer soon. This is quite ridiculous. We were both terrified out there tonight. Walking under lights that seemed more like dark clouds, yet armed with our mace! I hate being this nervous. The police must catch the killer. We were so frightened tonight! And so silly . . ."

"Silly?" Tara said suddenly. She looked at Katia.

"How long was that woman here before we arrived? I mean, that was absurd. Coming to visit an elderly man at this time of night."

"She said that she did not realize the hour," Katia told her.

"I don't believe—no one doesn't realize it when it's late at night!"

"Well, she's gone, and good riddance," Katia said.

Katia started for the kitchen. As Ann walked on into the hall, dropping her handbag, Tara followed Katia to the kitchen. "Katia."

Katia turned and smiled at Tara. "You know, you are here a day, and already, your French is getting so much better. You forget, and you get rusty, because you are gone so long."

Tara nodded. "Katia, the woman said that she was coming back."

"By daylight!" Katia said firmly. She sniffed, as if expressing her opinion that the woman had really had an incredible gall coming at that hour.

"Katia, listen to me. No matter what time she comes, you're not to let her in."

"Why not?" Katia asked with surprise.

"I don't know exactly. But for some reason, I don't trust her. I don't believe that she is who she claims to be."

"Really? We do have many social services—"

"I'll call the hospital tomorrow," Tara said.

Katia had the milk heating on the stove. Tara took a quick second to remember how much she loved Katia's chocolate. Made from scratch. The sweetest milk. The best cocoa.

"Why do you think she left so suddenly?" Katia asked.

"What?"

"I believe Ann was about to say that it was all right for her to come in, get it all over with," Katia went on, reaching into the cupboard for chocolate shavings. "In fact . . . she had worn me down." Katia looked perplexed. "Somehow," she said with a shrug. "But then you two came home, and you told her she could not come in, which was, of course, completely right. Perhaps she is not who she claimed to be! Ah! She could be an autograph hound! Jacques lives in relative privacy here, but he has been stalked by his fans for his autograph, you know. That's it! She must be a determined fan. Well!" Katia waved a wooden spoon at Tara. "She will not come in." Again, she frowned. "Still, so curious that she left . . . !"

Tara frowned suddenly. "How did she leave?"

"What do you mean?" Katia asked.

"I mean, how did she get here? And how did she leave?"

"Well, I assume she had a car!" Katia said.

"We came into the driveway, and I don't remember seeing a car in it."

"There must have been," Katia said.

"We would have noticed a car in the driveway."

"We are a bit out—surely, she didn't walk!" Katia said. "Perhaps her car was out on the road." She laughed. "If she did walk, I can see why she was so upset when we refused to let her see Jacques. But she could not have done so. She must have left her car up on the road. Perhaps she was not even sure she was in the right place."

"Perhaps," Tara said with no conviction.

Katia handed her a cup of chocolate, and placed Ann's on a tray. Tara followed her. Ann was staring into the fire. She did look beat. Strange. At the bar, she had seemed to possess endless energy. Now, she was almost ashen.

"Thank you, Katia. I think I'll go right up."

"Ann," Tara said, halting her as she took her chocolate and turned.

"Yes?"

"Did you see a car in the drive?"

"A car?" Ann frowned. "No . . . I don't think so. But then again . . . well, I still felt shaky when we drove back."

"Yes, so did I, but . . . that woman who was here. One would have thought that her car would have been in the drive."

"She must have left it on the road," Ann said.

"Where else?" Katia asked.

"Right. Where else?" Tara murmured.

Ann gave her a wave. "I'm off to bed."

"Good night."

Ann walked on up. Tara stared into the flames then, sipping her chocolate.

The warm drink, the fire . . . the house. Everything that surrounded her was warmth, life as usual . . .

She suddenly turned and walked to the front door. She hesitated, then threw it open, afraid that the woman would still be standing there, staring at her with the vengeful mask of hatred she had seen so briefly.

Or imagined.

There was no one there.

She chided herself, closed and carefully locked the door. When it had been double-bolted, she pulled on it, making sure it was tight.

"The rest of the house is locked up?" she asked Katia.

"Tara! Of course. Roland and I see to the lower floor

as soon as it gets dark!'' Katia assured her. "Just as always.''

"Of course," Tara said. Actually, she had never thought about making certain that the house was locked up.

"Thank you! Bonne nuit!'' she said, and started up the stairs herself.

She looked into her grandfather's room, feeling a surge of protective uneasiness.

The curtains were open; the doors to the balcony were ajar as well, allowing in a touch of fresh air.

Tara closed them, and locked them, and paused by her grandfather's bed.

His chest rose and fell in the deep breathing of relaxed sleep.

She leaned down over his forehead. She came close, but didn't quite touch him, leaving just the hint of a kiss upon his brow.

In her own room, she yawned. Like Ann, she was exhausted. She took a moment to survey her reflection in the mirror. Drawn. Haggard looking. Luckily, she wasn't as pale as Ann.

Her cousin worked long, long hours. Tara was ostensibly on vacation, but she loved what she did. And she hadn't so much as stopped anywhere to buy canvas and paints.

She left the mirror, drew back the covers, kicked off her shoes, and paused. A sense of unease had filled her again.

It suddenly seemed all-important to make sure that her room, like the main door, had been securely locked.

She walked to her balcony doors. Her drapes were closed. She didn't open them, but drew one aside.

She checked her doors, and felt a strange sense of relief to find them securely locked.

Then she stared through the panes at the night.

And there, in the strange pale glow of a half moon, she saw the wolf again.

The animal stood, as if it were a rigid sentinel, guardian of the night—or a creature at the portal of Hades.

Perhaps it had three heads, like the demon dogs of legend.

It did not. She could see the animal clearly silhouetted in the pale glow. It was massive. "That's no shepherd!" she muttered aloud.

As she did so, she suddenly heard a howl.

Deep, chilling. A howl to the sky, the heavens, the moon . . . or hell itself.

Tara started to shiver.

She closed the curtains, and turned, but had to look again.

There was no wolf on the road. There was nothing . . .

Nothing but the shadows of the night.

CHAPTER 9

The dreams were back, worse than before.

Twisting, turning, remembering. The hours of being watched. The different drugs. The shots that sent an unbelievable burning sensation streaking through his limbs, causing him to cry out with agony and strain against the steel bonds that held him to the bed.

Then sometimes, Dr. Weiss. Slipping him different drugs, drugs that ended the agony.

Nothing had impaired his hearing.

His comprehension of the language grew, and from bits of conversation, he began to glean more and more of what was going on.

For so long, the tyrant had held an advantage, but now the tide was turning.

And in the midst of agony, there was comfort to be had in that.

In another time, in another place, he had sat with

his father by a stream. A man who had fought a different war, survived, and learned in time the value of peace and freedom, he had taught his son that there were many things worse than death. And from that kind and sage old man, he had gained a certain strength. He didn't fear death. Far too often, he would have welcomed it.

Weiss gave him the will to survive. Weiss, who told him stories about his people. Those who risked their lives to save others, and those who were not so lucky as to escape detection, who had given their lives for others. He met men among those who should have been his enemies; a few guards who stood with their eyes averted when Weiss helped him, and a woman, the mistress of one of the worst of the officers, who smiled in the man's face, and did her best to help prisoners escape. Weiss would often whisper to him late at night. He would hear about the war, and about the world, and about people. People who might be judged badly.

There were those who were passionately against the regime, but were afraid. Not so much for themselves. For their wives, their children, their loved ones. But one day, the world would know that there had been heroes among those thought of as the enemy, heroes against insanity.

And he believed. It was easy, because he knew Weiss.

His will to live grew, because of Weiss's constant flow of news, and because of the bits of conversation he began to hear, and comprehend. The great tide was turning. Every day. Fighting had bogged down in Russia, and this new enemy was learning what so many had learned in agony before—the landscape itself was often more than the most powerful force could endure. Frigid temperatures, mountains of snow. The earth herself protecting her sons, a people battered by brutality and discrimination. There were other places where the great effort was crumbling, places where the people in the greatest danger began to take heart, and fight back.

In those days he learned that he would never judge any man, or woman, by their nationality. By their color, their religion, their sex. Goodness came in many guises, including this man, his friend, Weiss, and the others, whose humanity continued to override their fear.

He didn't know how long he had been there; it felt like years. Pain could make a moment an eternity.

But there was a change. And one night, and when the others were gone, Weiss sat next to him and he spoke about the collapse of the empire, and that the commanders, beginning to realize their own brand of fear, were planning to raze the camp.

The gas chamber would work around the clock; the crematorium likewise. Prisoners were to be killed, rather than left to be found. Credence could not be given to what the world suspected.

"I have to get you out . . . out . . . and yet, you know nothing yet. Nothing. Nothing of what you are, of what you have become, of what you must do, how it must be." The doctor was distracted. The lieutenant thought that the pressure had at last unhinged his mind.

"They'll come for you. They'll want you to disappear, they'll make you nothing more than ashes, and there will be nothing to know, nothing to speculate upon."

"Guard yourself, my friend," the lieutenant said softly. "Your people will need men like you."

"My people—no people—will ever believe that I did my best in my small way."

"If what you say is true, and the war is lost, there will

be trials. You will stand trial, and there will be those who have survived who will speak for you."

Tears fell down the doctor's cheeks. "I have not done enough. Like others, I have been too afraid for myself."

They were both startled when the door suddenly burst open. The head "physician," Andreson, strode in, followed by four of the guards. They were gaunt, tense, angry and—as customary—armed. There was an aura of something more about them today. It was visible in the way that their eyes flicked around nervously. In the way they wet dry lips far too often.

"Weiss!" Andreson said coldly, eyeing the good man. "Well, I knew you were a traitor! I knew all along. Not that it mattered. You did nothing that I didn't allow. But the time has come for change, and well, I didn't really intend that you should survive the war at any time."

Weiss suddenly found a great deal of courage. He stood with tremendous dignity. "No, sir! I have not been the traitor, never to my land. Never to her true heart. And never to my God. And I have never expected to survive the war."

Andreson turned to the men who followed him.

"Kill him," he said flatly, but raised a hand. "Slowly. Shoot where he will feel the pain long before he dies."

The lieutenant didn't know what it was that surged into him. But it was power unlike anything he had ever felt before in his life.

Adrenaline.

Fury.

Suddenly, his rage was such that he was able to break the bonds and shackles that had held him prisoner for so long. He didn't struggle.

He merely burst free.

Andreson shouted out orders that his men must fire quickly. He fell back.

Yet none of it was to any avail.

The lieutenant could move with a speed to match his strength. Bullets were fired, yes, he could feel them tearing into him, but they did not stop him.

He reached for Andreson. The man who had tortured him day after day. Who had threatened and attempted to humble and kill Weiss.

Reached for him . . .

He remembered that much.

Then he saw that Andreson lay before him, in a pool of blood, as if he had been wrapped in barbed wire. And the others were shouting something, words in their language that he didn't understand. They were taking aim again, and trying to kill him, trying to kill Weiss. He knew only that he had to stop them, and that, amazingly, he was still able to move as their bullets ricocheted wildly around the room.

The first two . . .

He grabbed both by the throat. Slung them together, dropped them. Then the second set of men stood before him, white as sheets, still trying to kill.

Like Weiss, they fell to the floor.

Like Weiss, they were torn to shreds.

And the sounds of bullets striking walls, floor, glass vials, bedding . . . came to an end.

All was silent.

Someone was touching him. Weiss. "We've got to get out of here. Now. You're bleeding, you're . . ."

Weiss stared at him. He was breathing hard. "Can you still hear me? Do you recognize me? Come, come, I have to get you to safety."

He realized he was hurt. Half dead, probably. He'd

been riddled with enough bullets. Weiss was pulling on him . . . strangely. He was crawling along on all fours, sliding along the blood-spattered floor. He looked back at the tangle of dead men. He blinked the blood from his own eyes, thinking he had seen movement.

"They're not . . . dead."

"God, yes, they're dead!" Weiss told him.

There was a roaring in his head. The lieutenant was afraid he was going to pass out. Weiss led him from the building, toward the rear, and the break in the back of the high, barbed wire fence.

He knew why the break was there without being told.

It was the path through which the bodies of the dead were taken for disposal.

"Guards," he managed to say.

Men started to cry out, to come rushing toward them. To the lieutenant's amazement, they started shouting hoarsely, and backing away. Shots were fired, but they were panicked and hurried, and horribly off aim.

The lieutenant didn't understand why. He was surely a bloody pulp of a mess, but he didn't know why that would make the guards stop in horror, making strange signals with their hands, and crying out that they must leave. They seemed in more fear than they would have been of the American army—or even the Russians.

"Come, come, come!" Weiss kept on urging him.

He looked back. Prisoners, gaunt as skeletons, barely able to stand, were looking on.

"We can't leave them," the lieutenant muttered. But what could they do, the fragile old doctor and himself, barely hanging on?

"We'll come back," Weiss assured him. "We'll come back. In just a few hours. When the moon is full."

The lieutenant would have smiled if he could have

done so. In a few hours! He could see the trail of blood he was leaving behind.

In a few hours, he thought, he would be dead.

And that was before they came at last to the stream, and he saw his own reflection.

She was exhausted and furious.

The evening should have been swift, and sure, but it had not been, and she had barely escaped. And the fact that she, Louisa, should have been frightened and on the run, was galling.

And yet, she thought, trying to soothe herself, she would have her revenge. She would take it slowly, and it would be delicious. She had to remember that, when dealing with a similar power, it was best to have numbers on her side. But then again, she hadn't even suspected that she might come across such a danger.

It would be met.

And obliterated.

And as to the inhabitants of Château DeVant . . . those women . . .

They, too, would be made to suffer.

Where was Claremont? She closed her eyes, and tried to concentrate. But again, she felt the presence of danger, and she closed her mind.

She walked through the streets, aware that too soon, dawn would come.

Anger churned, and with it came raw hunger. Desperate hunger.

As she traveled, senses heightened to a peak, she became aware of a presence that was near. She allowed her instinct to take flight, moved like the darkness, and like shadow.

She found the prey she had sensed.

Bearded . . .

Filthy, lying against a wall in an alley, a paper bag with a liquor bottle in it by his side. He was not awake, and not asleep. He sang softly.

She came close.

He blinked, eyes still half closed.

His song stopped.

She moved in.

The man's stench was overwhelming. Louisa thought that the drunk had not bathed in years. His clothing was caked with mud. He wore jeans that were all but stiff from dirt, spilled alcohol, and from being worn day in and day out, for however long. Bits of leaf and dirt streaked his hair and beard. It didn't matter, she told herself. In fact she would unintentionally be doing humanity a service by ridding the streets of such trash.

But as she moved in . . .

No.

No, he was simply too filthy. The smell was not bearable. He was unbelievably disgusting.

Despite her rage, she began to move on.

A second later, he was singing again. His song was interrupted by words as he laughed at himself for his folly in fearing the shadows.

Again, Louisa concentrated. The darkness still surrounded her, and she became a part of it. Then . . . ahead of her, laughing, talking, passing a bottle of wine between them as they ambled down the streets, was a threesome. Two men, one woman.

Her hunger, heightened by that rage that still burned within her, suddenly filled her anew.

And yet, she knew, rage would not serve her well. It

did not matter so much with a drunk in an alley, but finesse was more enjoyable.

She walked behind the group, then quickened her step, passing them . . . by just a few feet, and walking as if she had somewhere to go.

"Ah, mademoiselle! Bonsoir!" one of the men called to her.

"Pieter!" the woman chided. "Leave her be!"

Louisa allowed herself to turn slightly, to survey the group. Hardly la crème de la crème of society. The woman's skirt was too short, her blouse was low cut, and her breasts all but spilled from it. And there was something about the way she moved . . .

Ah, well. A lady of the evening. Louisa did not really judge this at all; a woman did what she did to get by. But alas, this one was somewhat coarse. The breasts were there, and so were the hips. In time, she would be quite large. Not the one to be courtesan to the rich and mighty. And not smart enough, not in the least educated, she would not even know that what she sold so cheaply could have been refined and improved . . . and used for power.

And the men . . .

A bit coarse as well. Past their first youth, but not yet old. Married? They wore no rings. Yet they had the look of men on the prowl for illicit pleasure. And still drinking, and looking for their place, at this hour.

Cheap, oh, yes, very cheap, perhaps, if they could only afford one woman between them.

Not at all the type she would really choose . . .

But then, they had, at least, bathed during the past decade.

"Marie, you sound jealous, the more the merrier!" the second man said.

Louisa allowed herself to slow down. The first man, Pieter, matched his stride to hers. "Mademoiselle . . . I don't mean to disturb you, but you are walking alone, and there is a murderer loose in the environs."

She took a moment to look at him. Ah, yes. A fellow a bit old before his time. Too much drinking. Too much debauchery.

So many entertaining men went this way!

She shuddered slightly.

He took it as a sign that she was afraid.

"You must have some wine. It will keep you warm. I didn't mean to frighten you, only to protect you."

She accepted the bottle of wine and took a long drink, watching the man's dark eyes. She saw the light of cunning and pleasure that touched them. Ah, yes, big fellow, he had made another conquest.

"There is a hotel straight ahead. Perhaps you could spend a little time with us there, until it grows light, and you are not walking alone in the streets."

She took another swallow of the wine.

"I'm Pieter. My friend is Jorge. And our companion is Marie."

Louisa nodded in the direction of the threesome.

"I know where else we can go," she said, her voice silky—and just a touch tremulous.

Pieter looked her up and down, at the obvious fine cut of her clothing. And surely, that of her figure and poise. He must be thinking that he had struck gold.

"You know somewhere else?"

"Oh, I do."

She could see him calculating the money he would save if he did not have to rent a hotel room for his few hours—no, no, with these wine-sodden fellows, it would only be a few *minutes'* pleasure—with his whore.

He smiled broadly, his face appearing all the more fleshy and bloated. Was he married? If so, she'd be doing the poor wife a favor.

"Lead on!" he told her. "Jorge, Marie, this lady has a place for us to go!"

"Mais oui!" she murmured. "Come, come . . ."

The house was not far from the ruins of the old St. Michel. She had seen the signs upon it, but she had known it once . . . long ago.

They followed her. Pieter remained beside her. From behind, Jorge ribbed him, apparently unhappy that it now appeared he had the chubby Marie while his friend had the newfound beauty. Louisa smiled. She could almost *hear* Marie's pout.

They came to the house.

"It is condemned," Pieter said.

"Ah, but I've been in!" she told him. "There is a problem with the roof, and an upper room where a storm has weakened the supports. You must trust me. The grand salon remains . . . quite grand."

She pulled off the boards that had sealed the entrance with so little effort that Pieter talked about the carelessness of the village in sealing a place so poorly. Louisa smiled. He must think what he liked.

"Will we find more wine in there?" Marie whined.

"Well, for me, I can say that there will be plenty to drink," Louisa assured them. She looked the three over. "Perhaps it will not be the finest vintage, but . . ."

"At this point, it doesn't matter in the least," Jorge said.

"No," Louisa agreed, "I guess that it does not. We must all . . . stoop beneath us a bit now and then, n'est-ce pas?"

She didn't wait for a reply, but slipped through the

door she'd opened. The others stepped in. They looked around at the remnants of the beautiful old place, and did not notice that the door closed firmly behind them without being touched.

"This way . . ."

Louisa led them first to the ladies' salon, a small room off the entryway. There was a delightful couch, and a cart with a crystal decanter of brandy upon it. Cobwebs clung around the crystal, but the stopper remained firmly in place over the contents of the bottle.

"Jorge . . . Marie, perhaps you would enjoy the splendors of this room for a moment. I think that I must get to know Pieter on a more personal level . . . first."

Marie clasped her arms around Jorge's waist, laughing with pleasure. "The brandy must be fine, Jorge! And see that little settee?"

"It's too small."

"You haven't seen how I can manage furniture as yet!" Marie insisted.

"Enjoy."

Louisa beckoned Pieter with a crook of her finger. He followed her out, eyes filled with anticipation. She closed the door to the salon and led him across the foyer to the men's smoking room. A huge leather sofa faced a fireplace. Pieter did not notice that a fire burned within it, awaiting them.

"Do you know who owned this place?" he asked.

"Once," she said.

Another cart held a large choice of liquors. Pieter went to it, prowled among the bottles, and poured himself a large scotch. He drank it down in a swallow, then turned to her.

"Let's see what you have."

She arched a brow delicately.

"You first."

"I will not disappoint you."

"No, you will not. I know what I am getting," she said.

He smiled, kicking off his shoes, sloughing off his jacket, then practically tearing off his shirt. He slid from his pleated pants.

He wore some sort of underwear in a ridiculous flag pattern. Tight, skimpy little underwear, designed, apparently, to increase the size of his bulge.

"Pieter . . ." she purred, coming toward him. "You must show me what you've got. Everything you've got."

His grin deepened ridiculously and he made a point of thrusting his hips as he skimmed away the last garment. He spread out his arms. "Now, belle dame, you come and show me what you've got," he said.

"Oh, yes, certainly." She walked deliberately toward him. She slid off one shoe, and then the other. She made an elaborate display of removing her beautiful new clothing, piece by piece, as she came near him. Of course, it was not necessary, but she did love her beautiful new contemporary designs.

She stood before him, smiling, running her hands down the length of her body, pausing at strategic places. "I have got this . . . and this . . ."

She paused, certain that he was going to pop on the spot.

"And this . . ." She rubbed her hands low over her abdomen, pressing with slow eroticism against her mound. "This . . . and . . ."

She walked the last step toward him, just out of arm's reach.

"And I have got these," she told him.

She opened her mouth wide. For a moment, his wine-sodden mind was so befuddled that he did not grasp what he saw.

She heard the inhalation of his breath. And she knew that he was about to scream.

She did not allow him to do so. Her assault was instantaneous. Rich, warm nourishment flooded into her body. She gripped her prey as he shook spasmodically in her grasp. He never let out a sound, for she had dealt with his windpipe.

She allowed herself the luxury of sinking to the floor. Of drinking slowly and surely, savoring every drop, lapping up each tiny bit, all but writhing in ecstacy at the luxurious meal, taken at her full leisure. It didn't hurt at all that this drink was so heavily . . . spiked.

When she had finished, she tossed the remains aside. She would deal with them later.

She stood, and walked with a smooth, sure sway out of the room, closing the door behind her. In the full beauty of her nakedness, she returned to the ladies' salon. She opened the door.

Marie, Marie! She did not speak the words aloud, but thought them with grave disgust. The chubby prostitute was pumping away on poor Jorge with no rhythm, no finesse, no . . . joie de vivre whatsoever. She was sweaty, and in a hurry. And poor Jorge . . . well, the alcohol had the best of him.

He looked up at Louisa, standing in the doorway.

And he practically threw Marie to the floor. Maybe he did not throw the woman, but she wound up on the floor on her fat backside.

"Hello," she said softly.

"Hello," Jorge breathed. Ah, there! He was rising to attention, Louisa thought with some amusement.

She did, at times, enjoy playing with her food.

She walked into the room, breasts and hips swaying.

"Where is Pieter?" Marie asked.

"Oh . . . well, he is down, I'm afraid. No life in the poor fellow."

"Ah," Jorge breathed. "There is lots of life in me!" he boasted.

"So I see."

"Then . . ." He paused, licking his lower lip. "Then you . . . you do enjoy a threesome?"

"Oh, yes. I love a threesome," she told him.

She knelt on the floor between Jorge's legs, and next to Marie. She thought that the woman might have protested, so she reached out and touched her, smiling, and locking her eyes upon the woman's own. A breath escaped Marie. Louisa let her hair fall over her face as she bent low. A little sound escaped Marie as she teased her flesh . . .

A louder sound escaped.

Jorge let out something coarse and guttural, reaching for her.

Which was fine. Marie had already slumped on the Persian carpet. Jorge dragged Louisa on top of him.

She smiled, meeting his bright-eyed eagerness, hoping that he did not drool.

"Oh, baby . . ." he muttered.

Then she moved in.

Twenty minutes later, she was sated, laughing, delighted, and feeling ridiculously powerful. Euphoric. Glutted! The two lay next to her on the carpet, eyes staring to heaven.

"Oh, my pets, my pets!" she said, stroking the hair back from each cold face. "I do, I do, I do enjoy a good threesome."

She was thus engaged when she heard her name called. And sharply.

"Louisa!"

She looked up, startled, instinctive fear clutching at her heart.

A man's form was silhouetted in the doorway to the ladies' salon.

Brent awoke, startled and still, yet uncertain of where he was.

He cursed himself silently, realizing where he slept.

He stood, dusting himself off, angry with himself, and yet asking at the same time just what else he could have done.

Morning light had not yet come.

So much for standing sentinel . . .

He stared through the darkness, toward the house. All seemed well, and when he closed his eyes and concentrated, he felt nothing but the stillness of the night.

But something had to be done. Today.

Château DeVant held the key.

Look at what you have done! At the mess that you have made!

Safe. She was now safe. And would be powerful again. But his words were still ringing in her ears, and she felt a greater fury toward him than she had toward any of the silly creatures who had not known her, and had not known who she was. He knew. And he had treated her as if she were an errant child.

Look at what you have done. The mess that you have made.

After the plans that I have made; everything that I have done.

At first, she had simply laughed. Risen in all her glory, slid her hands over her breasts and the length of her torso, relishing the delicious feel of the coat of red she created. Triumphant and amused.

You've found me, at last. I felt you so strongly, and now . . . Come darling, I've not left much, but you are welcome to what little remains. I would have saved more . . . I could have kept the girl. She was not much, but . . .

Her sultry, teasing words had meant nothing. Nothing.

He had walked in impatiently, ignoring the richness of the beauty and the bounty she offered.

I'd have thought you'd have more sense!

She'd felt as if she'd been slapped. And she had drawn herself to her full regal height.

You forget to whom you are speaking!

And you don't realize to whom you owe your life!

Then . . .

Nothing but impatience, irritation. There was a mess to be cleaned up. There were not many he could trust. There was danger in the city, extreme danger, and he had expected to get so much further before they were discovered, and already, with her carelessness, so many knew.

And what would they do? She wanted to know. What could they do?

She didn't begin to understand, and what a foolish woman. After all that had occurred before, she should have known. They had to go, there was no time; perhaps there were a few things that he could do . . .

And then, of course, there were the servants. But not as they used to be. She must understand that.

And still, he did set about doing all that he felt must be done.

Then, they were away.

And safe.

Her temper somewhat ebbed. He had made great plans. They had gone so much awry, and one of the reasons they must be so careful was that those who had caused her return to be less than magnificent must be dealt with quickly. Surely, she had realized that. He was aware of her movements, he had been just steps behind. But so had the others.

Ah, but, indeed, he had planned, because here she was, in safety, in comfort.

And when she had lain down to sleep, he had at last knelt by her side, and touched her with the reverence and adoration she deserved.

Rest . . . and our night will come.

Rest . . . we are together now, and together . . . we form our own alliance.

Lips upon her forehead. Tender fingers upon her cheeks. Ah, yes . . . adoration.

My dearest beauty, we form our own alliance. And there are others, others who are working with us, it's just that I cannot lose you again, and we must take such care as we gather our strength. You must give me time to implement all that I have planned.

By morning's full light, Jacques DeVant was awake, and feeling strong.

He had awakened very early, having been troubled by nightmares. Life had taught him competence and speed in all natural functions, and he was showered, shaved, and dressed in a matter of minutes, and down in his library.

He pulled down book after book, and he realized,

considering himself a dolt, that he had not imagined the scope of what had been going on.

With his books surrounding him, opened to different pages, he then logged on to his computer.

Ah, what a wonderful invention!

The books gave him the past.

The computer gave him the present.

He might be an old man, and many of his cronies wanted nothing to do with the confounded machines, but he had avidly learned everything he could about many programs, and about the Internet itself. He could break many codes, enter into many records where the various institutions would assure their clients that their information was totally safe, secure, and confidential.

Jacques searched very carefully through all the records that he accessed.

He read them all over slowly, twice.

Katia knocked on the door and stuck her head in, offering him coffee. He thanked her and agreed.

Back at work, he made a number of notes.

Katia brought his coffee, and he sipped it, staring at his information again. He was certain that he was right. Yes, yes, he was right.

He knew what had happened, what had been happening. He could see it all now—the how, the where, the when, the why . . .

Just not the *who.*

He needed help. He was old. The Alliance had been weakened by time and the modern world. The new generation didn't believe. Because they didn't know.

The new generation, ah . . . !

But then, each generation was a new generation, and surely, his own had been the same as this. What mattered, always, was knowledge. And a very careful sharing

of that knowledge. He sat back in his chair and, for a
moment, closed his eyes.

He opened them, a slow smile curling his lips.

He had felt . . . yes!

Oh, yes. He wasn't so old . . . he wasn't all used up
yet.

The time was coming.

Who?

The word rang in his head again.

Who?

And his elation faded.

He should have known, should have suspected. He
should have taken steps, and stopped this from happening.

He leaned his head on his desk.

And began to pray.

CHAPTER 10

By morning light, the world always seemed different.

Her fears from the dark of the night had evaporated, and Tara became convinced anew that any talk of evil and vampires was delusional. It was time to get a better grip on what was really going on.

She was going to the police.

She showered and dressed, thanked Katia for the café au lait and croissant she brought to her room, and determined to leave the house and head for the station in the village.

Ann had left for work already, Katia informed her. Jacques was awake, and working on a new book, she believed. She had brought him breakfast, and he looked very well and industrious.

In fact, he looked hale and hearty.

Katia loved Jacques, and she was pleased.

Tara warned her again that she was not to let the

strange woman in, and Katia informed her that she was not to worry, she had no intention of doing so.

Tara knocked on the library door. She had to knock twice to get her grandfather's attention. He bid her enter.

She poked her head in. "I have a few errands in the village. Do you need anything?"

His computer was open and a number of books were piled around him. He stared at her, frowning. "You're going to the village? I need to talk with you."

"Of course. I won't be long—I'll come in and spend the afternoon with you when I get back, if you like."

He was still frowning. She didn't want to tell him what she was really doing; she didn't want to be dissuaded from going to the police.

"We really need to talk."

"I am always happy to talk with you."

"To talk with me, yes, but as to believing me . . . but, this afternoon will do. You will not be gone too long?"

"I promise, I will not be gone long."

He nodded, apparently very absorbed in his task. "You will be very careful, and you will come right back?"

"Yes, Grandpapa, I promise."

She fought the temptation to tell him that she was over twenty-one and she lived in New York City, had been on her own quite a while, and was very capable.

"I promise."

He nodded again, barely aware when she closed the door. She called to Katia that she was leaving, but would be back. She hurried to the door then and threw it open, then stopped short with surprise and a bit of dismay.

Brent Malone was standing at the door.

"Brent."

"Good morning, Tara."

She stepped outside, forcing him back on the steps. The door to the chateau remained open, an escape route should she feel she needed it. She meant to be entirely challenging, and was alarmed to feel a warmth churning from somewhere deep inside her. There were a million things she wanted to shout at him. She was equally tempted to reach out and touch his face. He appeared tired, and yet, more compelling than ever. He had not worn a jacket that morning. He wore a long-sleeved black silk shirt and chinos. Showered and shaved, hair tied at his nape, bronzed features grave and arresting. Even when she walked away—which she assured herself she would do—his scent would linger in her memory, and the temptation to touch would remain.

She forced her voice to be level and determined. "What the hell went on last night?"

"There were a few toughs in the bar."

"And you took care of them?"

"In a manner of speaking, yes."

"Why did we suddenly have to get out? And why did it seem that . . ."

"That what?"

"That . . . I don't know. That we ran over someone. That someone had jumped on the car."

"Did you see anyone?"

"No. And we went back, and we didn't even see you."

He shrugged. "I'm quick."

Today, his green-gold eyes seemed veiled.

"Well," she murmured, "I can't talk to you now."

"I haven't come to see you."

She took a step back, startled, and admittedly, somewhat dismayed. *Was he hoping to see Ann?*

"My cousin isn't here. She works, you'll recall."

"I'm not here to see Ann, either."

"So—"

"I need to see Jacques."

She inhaled sharply. "No. No, you are not going to go in and upset my grandfather."

"He will be upset if he does not see me."

"All this talk about vampires! All right, so perhaps you believe that you are among their number. Well, then, you must be invited in."

"I don't *think* I'm a vampire. And, if I were, Ann invited us all in last night. But that's far beside the point. I need to see Jacques. And I assure you, your grandfather wants to see me."

"I will not let you in—"

"Tara!"

She was startled when her name was spoken sharply from within the house. She turned to see that her grandfather had come to the entry.

"Tara, there is no need to be so rude. Invite Mr. Malone in, please."

Brent Malone arched a brow to her, his expression one of superior amusement. She wanted to hit him.

"Grandpapa, I didn't think you should be disturbed."

"Nonsense, invite Mr. Malone in. Sir, please, you are very welcome."

Brent extended an arm courteously, indicating that Tara should precede him inside. She shook her head angrily, but her curiosity piqued.

"I have business in the village," she said curtly.

Brent's face hardened. He looked for a moment as if he would argue.

"My granddaughter is insistent upon doing her errands, Mr. Malone. And this time of the morning is definitely the best to be about such business, don't you agree?"

Brent Malone stared at Tara and nodded slowly. "Fine, sir, we shall speak alone."

"Tara will be back soon."

"Ah, yes, and Mr. Malone will be gone then," she said. She was irritated with herself as she heard the slight wobble in her words. Yes! She wanted him gone. Since she had first seen him, everything had seemed crazy.

And nothing was more crazy than her desire to throw herself against him, no, much more than that. She wanted to cast a quick apology to her grandfather, she wanted to forget that she should know anything, that she should be suspicious, afraid, and protective. She simply wanted to take Brent by the arm, insist that he shut up, just shut up about evil and danger, shut up completely, and take her somewhere, anywhere, well, hopefully, private, and just . . .

Touch her. Consume her.

"I'm leaving," she said curtly. "Mr. Malone, I do assume you'll be gone when I return!"

She marched out to her car.

As she did so, she knew that Brent Malone entered her house.

A cold chill swept through her.

"My God," Jacques said, staring at Brent.

"I believe you've known that I was here," Brent said softly.

"I'd thought you might be." Jacques kept staring at him. Then he said sharply, "Yes, you are here, and there are others. How many, I don't know." An inadvertent spasm shook him. Jacques hoped it wasn't obvious. Then he realized that his visitor saw everything there was to see.

But Brent made no comment about Jacques' evident frailty.

"Yes," Malone said slowly, "there're more here, I think, than we begin to fathom."

"The years have been kind to you, Mr. Malone."

"The years have been long," Brent said, his tone flat. "Years spent . . . waiting." There was a note of pain in his tone, and perhaps even hopelessness and confusion. He shook it off sternly, and perhaps, to regain his own sense of strength, he made note of the state of Jacques' health. "And you, my friend," he said, his tone then soft, "you have not fared so well."

Jacques stiffened. "I'm quite well, thank you."

"That's not what I've been told."

"A man's family worries about him. I am stronger than I appear."

"Are there more of you?" Brent asked him.

Jacques waved a hand in the air. "Perhaps. Maybe. But time, you know, the world rushing on. I moved to America. I wrote books."

"Yes, so I've heard. Very good ones. Fantasy, science fiction, the occult. All with a message for humanity."

"You've read my work?" Jacques could not help but be pleased.

"I've had a lot of time on my hands."

Not exactly the compliment Jacques had expected.

"There was not much contact after . . . the end. Perhaps the writing was my way to stay in touch with the world."

"So . . . there is none of the old guard about?"

"I am afraid not. And yet . . . well, I cannot say right

now. Somewhere, the Alliance must still be strong. There were more. But the threat was ended."

"The threat has never ended. It has been low, stirring."

"We are not as gifted with communication as your kind." He felt defensive. "But you—you were there. You were late."

Brent arched a brow. "You forget that I was working on an assumption. A hunch, if you will. But there is more here than we've seen as yet. I believe that the situation in the crypt was a plan, long and carefully conceived, and that we must find the orchestrator of the plan."

Jacques waved a hand in the air. "Come into the library. I'll tell you everything I know."

Tara found herself ushered into a small office and seated before a French detective. He introduced himself as Inspector Javet, in charge of the murder case, and asked her to sit. He started speaking in French, but aware of her accent, slipped easily into English.

He was a big man, not in the sense of armchair-big or youthful muscle gone to fat. He was simply big. Not exceptionally tall, but well muscled and trim, with a surprisingly lean, aesthetically attractive face, dark hair, and very deep, dark eyes.

"I understand that you have some information to give me about the murder at the crypt, Miss Adair," he said, folding his hands on his desk and staring at her.

"Information?" she repeated. "No, I'm sorry. I'm afraid that I've come here because I'm worried about what happened at the crypt."

If he was disappointed that his direct question gave

him no aid, he kept the emotion from registering in his eyes.

"Mademoiselle, everyone is worried about what happened in the crypt. I'm afraid that if you've come here for assurance, you are wasting time for us both." As she stared back at him, he sighed softly. "I am working on this case full time. We have brought in a man from Paris. Every possible piece of forensic evidence is being collected and analyzed. We are living in modern times where science is most helpful. Have you been to the ruins?"

"Ah, yes." The question took her by surprise, and she found herself remembering, vividly and annoyingly, that Brent Malone had repeatedly warned her to keep her name out of the situation. Her grandfather had warned her as well.

"How long have you been in the country?"

"Just a few days. I have family here."

He shuffled through papers on his desk, then stared at her again. "You are staying at the Château DeVant."

"Jacques DeVant is my grandfather."

That brought another long stare.

"Old Jacques," Javet murmured. "Tell me, did he send you to the crypt?"

"No!" she lied quickly, and hoped that her protest was not so strong it betrayed her immediately. "No, I have always been interested in the history of the area. I'm American, as you're well aware. We like to go back and find our roots, that kind of thing, you know. We seldom just say we're Americans, you see. Because we all have a background somewhere else. Except, of course, our Native Americans. But most of us say that we are something. You know, Hispanic-American, Afro-

American, Irish American, French American . . . you
know."

She was babbling. Great. And her cheeks were growing red.

"Yes, of course," Javet said. She wondered if he had
grown suspicious. She wondered what he would say if
she were to break down and tell him that her grandfather was convinced that evil had been dug up, that
vampires were streaking around the village, probably
intent upon the great feast offered not just here, but
just a shade farther west, in the great populous city of
Paris. And that, in her short time here, she had met the
strangest people, also convinced of evil, one of whom
had been in the crypt at the time of the murder.

Where she had been as well.

"Look," she said impatiently, "I'm sorry for wasting
your time. But I'm here for an extended stay. My cousin
is a young woman who travels in and out of the city
daily. Naturally, I am very worried. The papers have
done little except describe the murder. Yes, I was hoping
to come in here and find out that the police were hard
on the case, and that you did have suspects, and perhaps,
that an arrest was imminent."

Javet smiled at last. "Passionate, impetuous, and
determined that justice must be done! Yes, you are very
American—and somewhat French. I wish I could tell
you that an arrest was imminent. I can tell you that we
do have suspects. And that we do not intend to rest
until the perpetrator of this horrible crime is brought
to justice. Now, are you happy?"

"I'd be happier to hear that you have the murderer
in custody."

"Of course," Javet said, "and I'd be happier, of

course, if I didn't feel that there is more that you're not telling me."

She shrugged. "I wish that there was more that I could tell you. My cousin and I went out last night and when we were leaving, I thought that—that we were being followed. That we were, perhaps, intended victims of . . . some kind of an attack."

"Leaving where?"

"La Guerre."

"And what made you feel that you were under attack?"

She realized just how ridiculous she was going to sound before she spoke. "Shadows," she said despite herself.

"Ah, shadows. A dark street, fear in your hearts," he pointed out, not unkindly. "Was there any more than just . . . shadows?"

She hesitated again. "We thought we hit something—or someone."

"Oh? There have been no reports of bodies found in the street this morning."

"No . . . we drove back. There was nothing in the street."

Javet kept staring at her. She felt her cheeks reddening again. She wondered if she should tell him that they had not left the bar alone, and that their companion had held back, telling them to run. But then he'd want to know who the companion had been, and she would tangle herself further and further into the events in the crypt. It had been foolish for her to come.

"Look," she said. "I am sorry. I shouldn't have taken your time. I suppose that I did want some kind of assurance. I needed to know that the police were . . . doing something."

Javet shrugged. "You thought we were a poor provincial police, and that we hadn't the knowledge or capabilities of dealing with such a horrible crime, because we are accustomed to ticketing people who do not come to a full stop at the signs in the street."

"No, no, really—"

"As I have said, we have an excellent man in from Paris, a man who is accustomed to this kind of work. And we are not so poorly equipped as you might think. We are small, on the outskirts of a great city, but even here, there are things that happen. There is a great deal of countryside. We have dealt with the pathetic remains of murders before."

Time to compliment the man, she thought. "From the moment I met you, sir, I could see that you were a serious law-enforcement officer."

He nodded. Flattered or not, she couldn't tell.

She decided to move in. "I understand that one of the diggers at the site is the man who reported the crime."

"Yes."

"I assume he is a suspect."

For the first time, Javet looked a little uncomfortable. He quickly masked his unease. "He has been questioned, and is being . . . watched."

"But he is not under arrest."

"Not yet."

"But he may be? Soon?"

"We don't believe that he could have committed the crime, Miss Adair, and as to exactly why, I am not at liberty to say. He has been told, of course, not to leave the area. And I know that he has not done so because we keep tabs on his whereabouts."

She wondered just how good the inspector's information could be on Brent Malone's whereabouts, since he was at that moment, she assumed, still at her own family home.

But then, again, she was the one person who knew for certain that Malone was not guilty.

"What about Professor Dubois?"

"Dubois," Javet said, shaking his head. "Trust me, mademoiselle, we have spoken with Dubois. He calls daily. His concern is not for the man who died; he is anxious to get back into his dig. He has no intention of leaving the area. He hounds me on a daily basis."

"That doesn't mean—"

"There were witnesses who saw the professor leave the crypt. And witnesses who saw him reach his home. We are following every lead, and cannot let out every scrap of information that we have—if we ever expect to find the killer, we can't have him aware of what clues we have found. And naturally, Miss Adair, and this, of course, is no more than you can read in the papers, we believe that someone entered the tomb for the purpose of robbery, and that they did not expect to find a worker still on the site. Therefore, he had to die. So I assure you, we are investigating the professor's acquaintances, though it is true as well that a scholar who has committed his own funds to research may not be aware of the greed of others who allow him to lead them to a treasure trove, and then steal the treasure from beneath his nose. Rest assured, we are investigating."

She nodded, feeling that she had been dismissed. She started to rise. "Again, I'm sorry for having taken your time."

He rose as well, and smiled at last. "It was a pleasant break. Perhaps you will join me again for coffee, and I can keep you up to date on the events when I am not on duty."

His words startled her. His manner had been not just professional, but almost impatient. She found herself nodding in agreement. "Yes, coffee. That would be nice."

"I will see you out."

He escorted her through the office, opening the door for her. His eyes were very dark and unfathomable as he asked her, "If your tremendous concern for Mr. Malone comes from the fact that you two have met, I would suggest that you be careful."

"What?"

"I told you, Miss Adair, that he is a man we are watching. Did you meet in the tomb when he was working, or was your first encounter with the American man at the café down the street?"

"I saw him when he was working, of course. We didn't really meet until I saw him at the café the following morning." That was very close to the truth, and her voice was even, considering the fact that the inspector had taken her so completely off guard. She smiled. "And yes, of course, since I have met the man, and read in the paper about his discovery of the body, I am concerned."

Javet nodded. "Miss Adair, you should have mentioned that fact from the beginning."

"Since you're aware that we've met, you should understand my concern."

Again, he gave a slight inclination of his head.

"Perhaps I should inform you as well that your grandfather's interest in the tomb is also suspect."

"My grandfather!"

"Our records indicate—along with the testimony of

Professor Dubois—that Jacques DeVant had a tremendous interest in the tomb before it was opened."

"My grandfather is in poor health, Inspector. He
could hardly hurt anyone."

"He is a man of some means, Miss Adair. And he was
adamant about that site not being disturbed. He wrote
many letters of protest, to the church, to the government, even to the police station."

"He is a scholar, a man of history, and also a very
religious man. With sound convictions. But my grandfather is not at all a violent man!"

Javet studied her for a long moment. "Your grandfather came to be known as a hero of the Resistance, Miss
Adair. I assure you, he must have known some violence
at one time of his life."

"He was a soldier in a war, Inspector. All men must
do their duty at such a time."

Javet shrugged. "I'm merely explaining to you that
your grandfather loathed the very idea of the dig, and
that he is definitely a wealthy enough man to have had
influence on others."

"He would never hire a killer. Ever. And you can
bring in every expert from Paris and around the world,
and you'll still never find anything to suggest that he
would!"

Javet smiled, then stiffened suddenly. "Ah, well. Miss
Adair, perhaps this gentleman will make you feel a bit
better about the situation." He inclined his head toward
someone coming their way, footsteps landing softly on
the pavement.

She swung around to see a pleasant looking, light-
haired man with deep eyes and a hard chiseled face.
Taller than Javet, broad-shouldered, with the look of a
long-seasoned police official.

"Miss Adair, this is Inspector Trusseau, from the Paris office. Inspector, Miss Adair. The young lady is an American visiting French relatives. The DeVants."

"Mademoiselle," the Inspector murmured. Low-toned, charming voice. He kissed her hand, as if he were a prince rather than a policeman. She smiled, nodding, drawing her hand back. Smooth. Definitely smooth. Very charming smile. Too . . . suave for a policeman. Maybe not. He had very direct eyes, and she found that she couldn't easily draw her own gaze away.

"How do you do, Inspector Trusseau?" she said.

"Wonderful, thank you. How nice that we have met now."

"Really, sir? Why is that?"

"Well, naturally, I intend on paying a visit to your grandfather."

"Why?"

"Because he is such a scholar, of course," Trusseau said. "I'm hopeful that he can give me some insight into the crime."

She glanced at Javet.

"I've already told her that Jacques DeVant could come under suspicion."

"And I've already told him that suspecting my grandfather of any evil is insanity."

"Then I would go to him simply for help," Trusseau said politely, smiling and inclining his head in a gesture that acknowledged her defense of her grandfather. Trusseau shot Javet a hard stare that suddenly made Tara uneasy. Yes, the man could be charming, but he could also be hard as nails. Well, that was good. He was here to find a murderer.

"Inspector Javet has suggested quite plainly, I think,

that my grandfather paid someone to kill the worker in the crypt, and spirit away the body in the casket."

"That's not quite true," Javet said, his tone irritated. "What I meant for you to understand is that all leads are being followed."

Someone called Javet's name from within the office. He turned, nodded to the officer hailing him, then gave his attention back to Tara. "You'll excuse me?"

"I shall see Miss Adair to her car," Trusseau said. He took her arm. There was strength to his hold, and an electricity about him. He was well suited for his job.

"I'm really quite fine. I'm not sure I'm headed straight home," she told him.

"Then I shall, at the least, bid you a pleasant day, mademoiselle. And may I say that I'm certain we'll meet again."

"When you come to question my grandfather?" she said.

He smiled. "Ah, my dear! Just like Lady Liberty, standing tall, protecting the shores of her harbor! Truly, I have heard about your grandfather for ages. Don't begrudge me this chance to talk with him. When I come, I pray that you'll be there, and that you'll invite me in with warmth, and join in the conversation."

She held very still, imagining this hard-core man listening to her grandfather's tales about vampires.

Jacques would definitely wind up locked away.

"My grandfather is very ill."

"I'm so sorry to hear that. We'll not take much of his time."

"I promise you that when he is resting, we let no one disturb him. No one."

Could she say that in France? Tara realized that she knew little of French law. In the States, of course, they would need some kind of a warrant to insist on speaking with an aging and ailing man. Here, she wasn't certain. But Ann would know.

"Bonjour, mademoiselle. A pleasure," he repeated softly.

He turned to the station.

Tara found herself alone on the street. She had gained nothing, she thought, except greater fears and exasperation.

Jacques!

The police were investigating her grandfather! They knew about his interest, and they knew that she had become acquainted with Malone.

She suddenly hated the man! He'd done nothing but bring trouble and danger into their lives.

And her grandfather had not really told her everything; he had given her stories about legends and fantasy. And if the police kept investigating Jacques and he talked about vampires and evil, he would surely wind up in a mental institution. Especially with a man like Inspector Trusseau insisting on speaking with him.

She stared down the block and across the street. The doors to the present St. Michel had been repaired. A few people were entering and leaving, intent on their daily prayers.

The outer entry to the site remained roped off with yellow crime tape.

There had to be something more that she could do. There had to be a way to protect Jacques. She felt lost, angry, and a little more than afraid.

She started toward the café, thinking a café au lait and a few moments' thought and reasoning might stand her well. How on earth could she get Malone and his friends away from her household?

And more disturbing, why was it that, when she was near him, she wanted to forget the basic facts she knew and the sensible, logical thoughts that should be prevailing in her mind? *He intrigued her,* he had informed her with complete confidence. And, of course, the frightening thing was that it was true, and he did far more than intrigue her. He seemed to have some kind of a mesmerizing hold on her that went far beyond intrigue.

When she was away from him, she was fine. The closer he came . . .

As she stood there, someone opened the police station door and emerged behind her. She started to murmur an, "Excuse me," and step away. The greatest sense of cold swept over her. A chill that went far beyond the touch of the breeze.

And there was no one there. No one at all.

She frowned, staring at the door that still seemed to be closing. An overwhelming sense of fear seemed to come crashing around her, like a cold wave.

Why not? Javet and Trusseau both seemed to be after Jacques.

They were the cops! she reminded herself. Out for justice.

Malone was the one who had brought fear into her house.

She decided suddenly that she didn't need coffee or time to think.

She needed to get back to the chateau.

Brent Malone was there. Alone with her grandfather.

She should have never left.

CHAPTER 11

Ann stared at the piles of manuscripts on her desk, and sighed. She allowed her head to fall on her desk. She was exhausted! They had not stayed out so late last night—in fact, she could have stayed much longer. She had enjoyed herself until . . .

She almost laughed aloud. Why had they been so afraid when they left La Guerre? Shadows! How silly. Fear had bred fear, and they had then thought that they'd hit something, that something had been on the car, that . . .

Malone had stayed behind. Such a good looking fellow. And Tara was all but rude to him. Ah, well, the American from the café had been there. Very sexy. Not that she was really ready to tumble into a deep relationship again so quickly, but . . . well, the fellow was American. And he was giving her the courage and conviction to stay away from Willem.

She didn't even know how long Rick Beaudreaux intended to stay in the area. And yet . . . um . . . he might be just what she needed right now. The attraction was there. Sparks, delicious little tingles of electricity swept through her when they talked, danced, moved together. And that was the thing, of course. It was either there, or it was not. It was possible to know a man forever, a man with all the right qualities, virtues, whatever, perhaps even good looking, well employed, mature, kind . . . and it would not matter in the least if an attraction was not there.

The American might not live in Paris, he might not even be gainfully employed, she didn't even really know.

But . . .

She wasn't sure that she cared. She wanted to see him again. Or, she would want to see him again if she weren't so ridiculously tired. She could imagine a night teaching him about French wines . . . and then time alone. Yes, quite frankly, she didn't need a dinner, more dancing, or anything. She would love just one night alone with him. And then . . .

Well, she wouldn't allow for a heartbreak. She would indulge herself because she was out of a relationship, because he had that very sexy quality and the right sparks, and she was a woman with the right to desires and an affair if it was her choosing.

And, of course, she wanted Willem to know. She wanted him to know that she had forgotten him, could truly live without him, and could be adored and swept into a brief but passionate, absolutely fiery relationship with another man. Even as he tried to make amends.

But she was tired. So, so, tired . . .

"Ann?"

Startled, she looked up. She blinked.

The man of her thoughts had suddenly materialized in front of her desk. He was wearing a business suit. Well cut, it enhanced his height and his shape. The suit was dark, Armani, perhaps, or Versace, very simply cut, clean, and appealing. He appeared very blond and bronzed in it. And he smelled . . . divine.

To her dismay, since she did consider herself a logical and businesslike, competent and assured woman, she stuttered.

"Monsieur Beaudreaux."

"I'm sorry, I didn't mean to startle you."

"How—how did you get in here? Without being announced?"

"I spoke to the receptionist outside. Told her that I was trying to surprise you, take you to lunch."

"Lunch," she murmured, afraid that she sounded a little stupid, as if she didn't comprehend the word in English.

"I'm sorry, maybe a surprise wasn't such a good idea."

"No, no, it's lovely that you're here," she said, quickly collecting herself. "I hadn't thought about going to lunch. I have stacks of work, and I'm afraid that it hasn't been my most productive day."

"Maybe a break will get you going."

She stood up. The hell with work. She gave her job eighty hours some weeks.

"Perhaps you are right."

She collected her purse. The weather was beautiful, a little cool, but sunny. She didn't need a jacket. She walked around her desk. He took her arm, smiling. A warm, wonderful smile.

"Where are you taking me?" she asked him.

"Wherever you would like to go."

A discreet hotel room, she thought. But she didn't

say the words out loud. His smile deepened, as if she had.

She was delighted as they passed by the outer offices of the very contemporary Paris high rise. The receptionist and a few workers were about. They watched her with envy.

She paused by the receptionist's desk. Henriette, young, pretty, and now, somewhat bug-eyed, apologized quickly. "Ann, the gentleman said that he was an old friend and wished to surprise you. I should have rung through . . ." She paused, looking a bit perplexed. "I'm sorry, but I didn't, and I hope . . . I guess . . . that it's all right?"

"Yes, Henriette, it's all right." She glanced at Rick. "My old friend and I are going to lunch. I may run a bit over. But I'll be back for the art meeting this afternoon."

"Yes, of course."

"Thank you, Henriette," Rick said. He smiled at the receptionist. Ann could almost see Henriette's heart flutter.

Then Beaudreaux took her arm. The electricity shot through her arm.

They walked to the elevator. Others were leaving for lunch. She felt their eyes, and knew that she and the American made an attractive and appealing couple.

They reached the street.

Rick looked down at her. Dear God, what wonderful, powerful blue eyes he had. She couldn't have looked away if she had desired to do so.

He asked softly, "So, where would you like to go?"

She met his eyes, and answered simply and honestly. "Somewhere . . . anywhere . . . with . . ."

"With what?" he asked her.

She'd meant to say, *with a nice salad and warm bread.*
Somehow, those words eluded her.

"Somewhere with . . ." he prodded in a warm whisper.

She let out a long breath, her eyes still locked with his.

"Somewhere with a bed," she said.

The library door was closed when Tara returned. She
ignored the fact, and, without bothering to knock,
walked in.

Her grandfather was behind the desk.

And, as she had surmised from the battered old BMW
in the driveway, Brent Malone was still with him. He
stood, leaning over her grandfather's shoulder, as
Jacques made marks on a map of the area.

"What are you two doing?" she demanded.

"Studying a map of Paris and its environs," Brent
said.

Her grandfather was looking up at her, too. He didn't
appear particularly frail—rather, his cheeks were
flushed, and his excitement in his work was apparent.

"You need to leave," she told Brent.

"Tara!" Jacques said firmly.

"My grandfather has been very ill lately. If you tire
him, he could well have a relapse of pneumonia."

"Tara!" Jacques repeated.

"Perhaps it is time that I left," Brent said.

"I have told her exactly what is happening," Jacques
refuted firmly.

"Yes, but she doesn't believe you."

She folded her arms over her chest and walked to
the desk. "If you have come here to further encourage

my grandfather in his belief in vampires, you are certainly not welcome.''

"She doesn't believe," Brent said softly.

"Whether she believes or not, they exist," Jacques said, "and she must not interrupt our work."

Malone gave her a shrug. "Well, then, I guess you're the one who has to pitch in and help—or leave."

"You're telling me that you actually believe in vampires? In real demons that rise from the dead?''

"Some are demons, and some are not," Jacques said.

"However, Louisa de Montcrasset may definitely be described as a demon," Brent told her. His eyes were level on hers. He might have been agreeing that there was definitely going to be rain in a day or two, or that, yes, winter always followed autumn.

Infuriated, and more than a little unnerved, Tara turned on her heel and walked out of the room. The temptation had been to grab Brent Malone by the hair, drag him out of the room, and throw him out of the house.

She wouldn't have the capability. And she was afraid that touching him would be dangerous.

As she left the room, slamming the door behind her, she nearly tripped over Eleanora. The shepherd had come to the door. She didn't try to slip past Tara and run into the room; she stood still, as if she were an ancient Egyptian guard dog, sensing the death of the Pharaoh.

"Eleanora, come, let's get away from here," she said, stooping to pat the dog.

But though she didn't growl or protest Tara's touch, she didn't move, either. And she didn't jump all over Tara with excitement, as she was prone to do, remembering her every time she came and left, no matter how long she stayed in the States.

"Even the dog has gone mad!" Tara muttered, striding across the hall and heading for the stairs. She continued to her room, needing to be somewhere she could pace and explode without making matters worse for her grandfather.

She entered her room, slammed the door, then locked it. She began to pace, and tried to make herself slow down. She had just done the worst thing possible. She had come home and lost her temper instead of sensibly explaining to them both that corpses didn't rise up and kill the living. Greedy people, those with their own agendas, committed murder. And some people were cruel, heedless of human life, and some were psychotic and very sick. That's why terrible things happened. She should have humored them, she should have kept a level tone and a level voice.

She threw herself down on the bed, pounding the mattress in sudden fury. She closed her eyes tightly, shaking her head, wondering what the hell to do.

Did she go back down and have another fit, force Malone out of the house? Or did she go back and try to be calm, rational?

As she lay there, she became aware of a peculiar odor. Looking up, she saw that garlic bulbs had been hung over the doors to the balcony. For a few moments, she just stared at the new adornment in her quarters. *This is too much!* she thought.

"He's been in my room!" she exclaimed aloud.

That was it. Tara jumped to her feet and ran back down the stairs. Eleanora remained before the door. When she strode toward it, the dog rose. To her amazement, the massive shepherd growled at her.

"Eleanora! It's me, Tara, what on earth is the matter with you?" she demanded.

The dog held her ground, proud brown eyes razor sharp.

"If you're guarding Grandpapa, you're guarding him from the wrong person!"

And still, the dog refused to move. Tara took a step to reach over her and pound on the door. The dog began to snarl with a warning sound once again.

"Hey!" she yelled furiously.

A moment later, the door swung open. Brent looked at her, and at the dog. "Silly girl," he told the shepherd, patting her head as if he were the animal's master. "It's Tara. She wants to come in. It's all right."

As gentle as a kitten, Eleanora moved aside, sliding down for a nap by the wall. "So you've decided to join us?" Brent said.

"I've decided to wring your neck! What the hell were you doing in my room? Why is there garlic over the doors?"

"I haven't been in your room," he told her. "And I didn't put garlic over your doors."

"What are you two whispering about?" Jacques called out.

She passed by Brent, standing before her grandfather's desk. "There's garlic over the doors to the balcony."

"Yes, of course," he told her.

"You put it there?"

"No, no, of course not. Katia put it there."

"Great. So Katia believes in vampires."

"Katia has an open mind, and knows that the world in its entirety is not always plain and visible to the naked eye," Jacques said.

She turned away, flinging herself into the ancient armchair between her grandfather's desk and the large hearth. She made a steeple out of her fingers, staring at her grandfather. "Jacques, a man was brutally murdered in a tomb. A tomb that you didn't want opened. That you went to great pains to keep from being excavated."

He narrowed his eyes at her.

She leaned forward, ignoring the fact that Malone was in the room.

"Javet! Inspector Javet. Do you know that they suspect that you might have paid someone to kill that worker to keep any more work from being done at the crypt?"

Jacques was not in the least concerned. "Javet!" he said, dismissing the man with annoyance.

"And not just Javet! The inspector from Paris may be questioning you as well."

"So you went to the police," Jacques said. He was angry. He shook his head with tremendous disappointment.

"The police are the ones who investigate murders," she said flatly.

Brent sat on the edge of her grandfather's desk, neither angered nor amused. "They investigate disappearances as well."

"What are you talking about?" she asked.

"As of today, up to seven people have disappeared in the past few weeks, reported to the main station in Paris."

"Disappearances—of who? And what do the disappearances in Paris have to do with a brutal murder here, in the village? Jean-Luc didn't *disappear*. His body was butchered and left for discovery."

"Paula Denton, British student, a beautiful young

woman, last spoke with her family over two weeks ago, telling them she'd be leaving Paris for home that night. Next, reported about ten days ago, John Bryner, an American. He was due at a school in Nice, and never showed up. Jillian Grieves, a Parisian prostitute, hasn't been seen in nine days. Barbara Niemes, another prostitute, has now been missing nearly a week. The list goes on—the known list. God knows how many people have disappeared who don't have family members who track them—or street sisters who are still able to prove their love by looking for their friends."

"Students have disappeared—young students, running around Europe. And prostitutes," she said.

Brent raised a brow. "Oh? They don't deserve your concern?"

"Don't be absurd!" she lashed out. "Naturally, they are human beings, and deserve everyone's concern. But students roam through Europe all the time. And prostitutes—"

"Prostitutes with drug problems always return to their supply," Jacques said with a sigh.

She stared from one man to the other. They both stared back at her.

"Okay, I get it. They've all disappeared because of — vampires."

Neither one of them said anything or moved a muscle.

"Vampires are supposed to drink blood, they don't consume every inch of a body," she said. "If vampires had taken these people, their pathetic, blood-drained bodies would have been discovered. Their grieving families would have buried them, and then, they'd have risen again and there would be more vampires, and more vampires, all coming out of the walls like cockroaches."

"Vampires drink blood, yes," Brent said.

"There, you see?" she told Jacques.

"They also mean to survive, and therefore, they don't leave discarded bodies lying about. They're also territorial, and seldom fond of competition. They rarely create new members of their own kind. There is actually a code by which they survive," Brent said.

"A code. A rule book. The Vampire Rule Book. Sorry, I haven't read it yet."

"It's not a book, Tara, and you can't read it. But there is a society, and it's ancient, and there are codes and laws by which the creatures exist—and have existed throughout time."

"And you dug up this countess, and now she's a vampire."

"She was a vampire before I dug her up. But yes, now she's loose," Brent said.

She stared at him, then lowered her head, shaking it. "You knew my grandfather before you came here today," she said.

"Yes."

"Tara—" Jacques began.

She interrupted him. "You came here, Malone, way before any of this, and you filled my grandfather's head with a lot of rubbish. You got him to lodge protests about the dig, and because of you, the police are going to wind up questioning him. You are the instigator of this nonsense, this fantasy, you've convinced him that he's part of some kind of an alliance, and what you've done is dragged an ailing man into a nightmare."

"I am not an ailing man who has lost his mind, young lady!" Jacques said with level dignity.

She still couldn't look at Jacques. She thought she was beginning to piece it together. "I don't know what your game is, Mr. Malone. Maybe you're a writer, too.

Some kind of a critic, out to malign Jacques, or make your own name somehow through him. Whatever your game is, though, it is over. I'm going to go straight back to the police and tell them everything I know."

"I can't let you do that, Tara," Brent said. His voice held either a soft menace, or a simple promise.

"Are you going to kill me? Do you, perhaps, think that you're one of them? That you're a blood-sucker yourself?"

Staring at her, he blinked, but his eyes didn't fall from hers. "No," he said.

"Oh, well, thank heavens for that, at least. What a relief. I've yet to see one of these creatures."

"But you have seen one."

"I have?"

"Yes, the other night. Countess Louisa de Montcrasset was here, at this door, when you and Ann returned home. And you must sense far more than you're willing to admit, because you weren't foolish enough to let her into the house."

She wanted to protest instantly, to assure him that she simply never let unknown visitors in to see her grand-father.

But something had settled over her . . .

A chill.

And she was afraid that, somewhere, deep inside her-self, she was going as mad as they were. Because some-where, deep inside, she was almost believing the insanity.

"You know I'm right," he told her.

"Listen, Tara," Jacques said. "I've tried to tell you about this, to make you understand."

"I—I—" She stared at both of them.

Then she flew out of her chair. "No!" she cried

angrily. "No! I will not believe any of this absurdity, and Mr. Malone, I will get you out of this house!" She stood before her grandfather's desk. "Jacques, how can you let this man play with your mind this way?"

"Tara—"

"I will not be a part of it," she said, and turning, left the room.

Ann lay with her eyes closed, sleek and sated as she had not felt in . . . all her life. She curled into the pillow, so aware of the man at her side, and smiling because her thoughts were so clichéd: she felt as if she had died and gone to heaven.

They had chosen one of the loveliest hotels in Paris, despite the fact that she had come out only for her lunch hour.

Luxurious. Clean sheets, drifting white curtains, windows that led out to a beautifully planted courtyard, the slightest touch of an autumn breeze . . .

She turned, burrowing against the formidable wall of his chest, running her fingers over the mat of fine, golden blond hair. They had sated the initial urge for simple appeasement, taken things slowly, swiftly, slowly again, and now—far later than she had ever imagined and still not at all willing to rise and leave and return to work—she was fascinated by exploring the man who had walked into her life like a cataclysmic shift in the earth. She frowned, noting as she ran her fingers down the length of his arm. Though well healed and barely visible, she realized that there seemed to be a great deal of scar tissue on his body.

"The accident," she murmured softly.

"Yes."

She rose over him. "I'm so sorry, and yet so glad that it brought you here, to Paris."

He smiled, putting an arm around her, pulling her closer. "It was quite a while ago now," he told her.

"What happened?"

"I was caught in a fire. Um . . . let's see, I was out with friends. And while they escaped it, I was trapped."

"They left you?" Ann said, indignant that anyone would leave a friend to such a fate.

"It was a strange situation," he told her, "and it doesn't matter; it's over now." His tone was light, but it seemed that there was something in his eyes. Maybe a deep-seated bitterness, one that he didn't intend to forgive. She could hardly blame him.

"You must have been burned very badly."

"As I said, it doesn't matter. I'm healing, and have been healing." He ran a finger down her arm, bringing a tremor to her limbs. "Tell me more about you."

She laughed. "There's not much to tell. You know where I work, what I do."

"Yes, but . . . what about your personal life? This has been a rather mad rush of a lunch hour, don't you think? Is there . . . anyone else out there?"

"I live with my family," she told him.

His magnetic smile deepened. "I meant, is there someone else in your life. Another man. I have to admit to being head over heels, and jealous as all hell, and yet I can't imagine that a woman such as you wouldn't have a lover in her life somewhere."

She didn't pull away from him, but withdrew a little into her thoughts, amazed that not a single thought of Willem had come to her until Rick had specifically asked. She had thought herself so wounded by Willem so deeply in love, and so determined to be strong against him. . . .

Rick inched a shade closer, as if he were trying to assure her that he meant to give her so much more than the taste of flesh against flesh. "There is someone?"

She shook her head. "There was, just as I'm sure there have been many others in your life," she said with a wry shrewdness.

He merely smiled. "There is no one now, I can assure you."

"And I can say the same."

"But what about this man you were seeing?" he persisted.

"Willem. He's the head of sales for my company."

"Um. Scary for me. You see him on a daily basis."

"No, only for meetings. And it doesn't matter—it's over."

"I hope so," Rick said, his gaze sweeping over her. Then he added, "No . . . that's far too indefinite. I intend to make it so."

Ann relished the husky sound of passion in his voice. "Really?" she teased. And added a bit breathlessly, "I am just dying to see what you do with your—intentions!"

"For now, I intend to keep you a bit longer."

"I should go back to work."

"Not quite yet . . ." he said.

And within seconds she was convinced that she needn't go back at all.

There were other signs that the household was far from a sane one.

As Tara went by the front door, she noticed that the

little basket on the old oak stand near the front door, which was customarily filled with flowers, now held numerous small bottles. She paused to pick one up, studying it.

They had come from Notre Dame, and were filled with holy water. Exasperated, Tara set the little bottle back in the basket and continued out of the house. She walked to the stables, but realized when she entered that old Daniel had been let into the pasture. Even as she stood deep within the structure, staring at Daniel's empty stall, she felt Brent's arrival. She turned to find that he had come in after her, and seemed to be blocking the exit.

It was as it had been that first day in the crypt. At first, he seemed just a shadow, a silhouette. Far larger than real, a presence that eclipsed the entry, the daylight beyond, the world. And she felt again the same sense of fear, and she almost closed her eyes, as if she could hear the scream from within the tomb once again.

"I'm going back to the police, you know," she said from her distance. "I'm going to tell them that I was in the tomb, and that I saw you there. I'll be honest, of course, and tell them that I know you aren't the murderer. But I'm going to make sure that they know you are a very frightening and dangerous man, and that you're the one urging my grandfather into . . . trouble and madness."

He didn't reply. He walked in. He was no longer a dark silhouette against the daylight. He was a man again. He seemed no less menacing.

She had meant for her tone to be certain, hard, and a sure warning, but she could hear her own words echoing back at her and they were uncertain and halting.

She took a step back.

"Look, you're dangerous. And you think you have some kind of hypnosis or magnetism and that people will believe your ridiculous words and lies. But we're not all so easy."

He was still walking toward her, lean, smooth, agile, and now, as the silence in the stables and the shadows seemed to surround her, he didn't seem as lean and lithe. In her mind, his shoulders grew with each step. He was coming to slip his hands around her throat and throttle her. He'd been charming at first, more than intriguing, as she had admitted to herself. But he had some strange agenda, and now, he was simply going to kill her.

There was a pitchfork stuck into a pile of hay bales behind her to the left. She saw it clearly from the corner of her darting eyes. As he took another step, she dodged back, dragging the tool-to-be-a-weapon into her hands, and before her, a warning that she would strike if he came any closer.

"I'm not afraid to use this!" she said, and managed to make the threat a real one.

Still, he merely smiled, but actually paused for a minute. Then he told her, "You're not going to skewer me with a pitchfork."

"I will—I swear that I will. Now, I want you off this property, and away from my grandfather."

"It's not going to happen, Tara."

He kept coming toward her. Though she now held her weapon, and knew that she did have the strength to use it, she backed away, watching him with wary, narrowed eyes as he slowly, confidently, took each step.

"You have to admit that you're insane. You need help," she told him.

She could use it, would use it . . .

"You know that I'm telling the truth."

"That there are vampires?"

"You know that I'm telling the truth, because you were there. You heard the cry in the tomb. And you knew when you left La Guerre that something was following you. You knew it. You knew that there was danger in the shadows. There was something that you couldn't see, but you could feel it. And when you came home, and that woman was at your door, you knew there was something wrong. You stopped her from entering."

He was just feet away. She cursed herself, but felt the strange magnetism he exuded, and she denied. Felt his gaze, the strange gold color of his eyes that was really just hazel, but seemed able to touch and burn as surely as any yellow flame of fire. She willed herself to move, mentally arguing against every word he had said to her. *A killer was loose, it was natural to be wary when a killer was loose, she hadn't been feeling any supernatural warnings of danger beneath the surface of light and shadows . . .*

"Get away," she told him.

He reached out a hand. "Give me the pitchfork."

Her fingers tightened around the wooden handle. She bit her lip, desperate to hold on, to prove him wrong. But she couldn't tear her eyes away from his. Her heart was hammering, and it seemed that every breath was an effort.

"You are definitely your grandfather's descendant," he said very quietly. "And you are stubborn and strong-willed. But you are going to give me the pitchfork."

"You're not all that wonderful," she whispered in return. "Don't think that you are."

"But I am right, and that's why you're going to give it to me."

She didn't intend to do so, but as he took the last

step, when she should have pulled her arms back and tensed her arms to strike, she found that her limbs did not seem to be obeying the commands of her mind. Rather, her hands began to tremble, her arms to shake, and slowly, slowly, against her will, she began to extend the weapon to him.

His hands grasped the handle, and the pitchfork was his. For one wild moment, she thought that he meant to turn it on her, to strike and send the tines of the tool shooting into her abdomen and chest.

He flung the weapon far from him. She saw that strange glow of fire and gold in his eyes, and he came closer, now reaching out for her. She wanted to scream. The sound froze in her throat.

She had completely forgotten about work. As Rick Beaudreaux lay next to Ann DeVant, he propped himself easily on an elbow, and watched the woman at his side.

Such a beauty. And so easily his.

Ann DeVant. A woman so very important. And so . . . Perfect.

Time had fled, minutes to hours. And yet . . .

Still time before dusk. She did need to rouse, and return to work. He glanced at his watch, reckoning the arrival of dusk. Twilight. And then the night.

He ran a finger down her arm, leaning over her. His whisper delicately touched her ear. "I hate to say it, but it's late, you know. I . . . want more of your life, so much more, but . . . I don't want to cost you your job."

She sighed, rolling, moving against him again. Her arms locked around his neck. "I know, and I'm such a practical person. Why is it that I hate to leave you so much?"

He smiled, holding his weight above her. "I promise you, I will be around," he assured her. "In fact, you'll be amazed. You won't be able to get rid of me."

Her lips curled beautifully in the contours of her face. He drew his fingers gently through her hair.

As he bent to kiss her, he smoothed a lock from her face.

There . . . on the side of her neck, usually hidden by the fall of her dark hair, were two little marks.

Just pinpricks . . .

Barely visible to the naked eye.

He stared at them a long moment . . .

"Rick?"

He drew her into his arms.

CHAPTER 12

That evening, Yvette Miret was off duty at five.

And at five, she was definitely ready to go home.

Paul had come by at three that afternoon. They had been planning to go to a rock concert in the city that evening.

But now, the rock concert was off, mainly because Paul was such an ass.

Yvette had known Paul since she was a girl. He'd lived down the street in their little village. He was a friend.

But Paul didn't see any farther than the borders of his father's farm. Yvette didn't intend to spend her life working with sheep, or feeding the men who herded them, at the crack of dawn every morning of her life. Though she had encouraged Paul at various points in their stormy years together, she had also told him several times that she did not intend to settle down in the village. She was going places, and she didn't particularly care what she had to do to get there.

There had been a group of British students by that day, too; handsome men on holiday from their university. She had been flirting, laughing, and dropping napkins on the table with her phone number.

She hadn't realized that Paul was across the street, just outside the police tape that still roped off the outer entrance to the old church dig, and that he was watching her. Just as she delivered a second round of drinks to the table, he had come storming over, gripped her arm, dragged her to the wall and called her a whore and a slut. At the end he shouted to her, "You'll be sorry! You'll be so sorry for the way you behave toward me— you bitch!"

She'd longed to slug him, really hard, right on the jaw. She could feel the blood rising to her cheeks.

But then, the owner had come out to yell at Paul. He had been duly chastened, but she had been threatened with losing her job.

And worse than anything, the whole scene had been distasteful to the British boys, and they had departed without so much as an extra franc left on the table. The cocktail napkins with her phone number remained beneath their cups. It was so humiliating she could have cried on the spot, but she'd also been furious.

Paul had called almost exactly an hour later, apologetic. But then he told her that she would wind up becoming a prostitute right on the street if she didn't watch herself; he knew about the many times she had picked up customers, and met them at their hotel rooms late at night. She would come to no good, and it hurt him, really hurt him, because he loved her so much. She thought of him with his wild brown hair and eyes, his endearing face. Somewhat of a handsome face, but too young, too naive for what she really needed from the world.

And he was wrong—she *was* attractive to other men, really attractive, and they didn't all just use her and walk away. She refrained from asking him how he thought she acquired her designer coats and boots, and the earrings and jewelry she sometimes wore. He would only have worse things to say about her.

The phone call left her even more furious. "No, Paul, I do not forgive you," she told him, "and we will not be going to the concert together. We have to end it all now, right now. I do not love you. You stink of sheep, do you understand? You stink, stink, stink, of sheep, and I can't stand it!"

She had hung up. Of course, she was upset all over again, because customers—and her boss—heard the conversation.

She begged pardon from Monsieur François, who had been patient with her many times, she knew, because she was so popular with the customers. He grunted, and she explained that she'd needed to be cruel to be kind— she hadn't wanted young Paul living with illusions and coming to make a scene at the café again.

Monsieur François did not fire her. She wondered if any of her regular customers would stop by, anxious to see if she needed company when her work shift was over.

No one stopped by. Feeling irritable and annoyed, she rued the fact that she hadn't brought her car that day, and that she had a very long walk home.

As she started out, she felt the nip of a wind. She hadn't brought a coat, only a little cashmere sweater.

She hugged it around her shoulders, and started walking.

Darkness came so early! she thought. It was fall, of course, but not yet winter. Yet as she walked, it seemed that a true winter chill settled over the road. She hadn't worn her good work shoes, either, but had worn little heels today, planning to change into the low-slung jeans in her bag for the concert in the city. The roads in the village were rough, and twice, she stepped down hard on stones and nearly twisted her ankle.

She cursed Paul as she walked.

Then . . .

From the darkness, she saw the glare of headlights, coming along the road.

She moved aside, certain that after a day like today nobody would be kind enough to give her a ride.

And yet . . .

The car drove up beside her.

She hesitated, remembering that there had been an awful murder right across the street from the café. But then, what did she have to do with a silly dig in an ancient crypt? She walked over to the car and looked in as the passenger window was rolled down.

Her heart leaped.

"Hello," he said softly. "I'm surprised to see you out here. All alone. It's cold. Why are you walking alone in the dark?"

"I'm afraid I broke up with my boyfriend today," she said with a sigh. Her cheeks were flushing. A bold sense of excitement was growing inside her. The day was not so bad after all. She had not imagined that he, this incredible man, would come by. And he liked her. He found her cute, naive, charming. He didn't really know

her, but then, did it matter? She knew that he was
attracted to her.

And she was more than a little attracted to him.

"I'm sorry to hear that. Come in, and I'll give you a
lift."

Thrilled, she opened the door, and slipped into the
car. A nice car. She should have known that he would
have a new model automobile. Sexy, smart.

"Thank you so much for stopping," she said.

He pulled onto the road immediately, waiting a bit
before replying.

"It's my pleasure—my extreme pleasure," he told
her. Her hand lay on her knee. He covered it with his
own. "You're such a lovely young woman. That fellow
is a cad to have left you to walk home."

"It was best," she said softly. "Really. This has been
coming . . . we just aren't . . . well, we just aren't going
in the same direction in life."

"Poor girl," he murmured.

"My house," she told him, "is about a mile down,
on the left."

"All right. You're not going to go home and cry all
night alone, are you?"

"I told you, it was actually better that this happened."

"Ah."

They passed the road that led to her house.

"You missed the turn," she told him.

"Yes, I did so on purpose. I think I should take you
for a glass of wine, cheer you up."

She tried to keep her eyes on the road ahead, and
not to show her absolute elation. "That would be lovely.
Thank you so much."

The countryside could be very dark at night. Yvette
frowned, wondering where they could be going. They

had driven so far that she could think of little that was
out here. Mainly, ruins of places abandoned after World
War II, countryside, and more countryside.

And sheep.

It seemed that everywhere one went in this wretched
place, there were sheep.

The car moved onto a rutted dirt road. She was
thrown next to him. His arm came around her, then
his hand fell on her knee to steady her.

"You're all right?" he asked her.

"Fine," she said softly. "With you . . . well, I feel just
fine."

He flashed her a white and fascinating smile. She
stared at him, wondering if she was falling in love. He
could have taken her anywhere, done anything. She'd
never felt such a rise of fascination and excitement.

"Where are we going?" she asked after a moment.
She didn't feel the slightest fear; she was merely puzzled.

"Right here. Come along."

He parked the car.

They were far past the pasturelands, she saw with
relief. Into the forest. At first she couldn't see anything
at all. Then she saw an edifice in old stone rising before
her. Once, the place had been a chateau, something
fairly grand, she thought, but it had been abandoned
long ago. There was muted light from within, but she
had barely seen it at first, the windows were so overgrown
with shrubbery and ivy.

"You're staying here?" she asked him.

"It's really quite nice inside."

She didn't get out of the car, but stared ahead, a faint
unease suddenly coming to her. But he stepped out and
came around, politely opening the passenger side door
for her. He reached in and took her hand.

"Come, my lovely little Yvette."

She still felt the unease. But she was so aware of his hand, the way it felt where he touched her, and she was completely fascinated by his voice. She allowed him to draw her from the car. And as she stood before him, he drew her close, holding her to him gently, the suave lover of her dreams. His fingers moved over her hair. "My lovely, lovely, little Yvette," he murmured.

She leaned against him. She could have stayed there forever. Had he wanted her to strip then and there in the dirt, she would have done so.

"Come," he murmured.

She looked up at him and nodded. His hand moved then, over her face. His knuckles brushed her chin. She realized that she was staring up at him like a complete novice, lips parted, breath coming far too quickly . . . she warned herself not to be a dolt. That she must be mature with this sophisticated man, that she must not seem too easy, and too eager.

Apparently she stumbled. They moved through the overgrown path to the house together, he supporting her. He opened the door, and they entered.

It was indeed beautiful within, if somewhat dark. A fire burned in a large hearth, and candles glowed from numerous tables about the large entry. The place was old, very, very old. She stood still, looking around her.

The candles created massive waves of shadows. They seemed to whisper, to dart about, to change angle, substance, and form with each flicker of the flame in the large fireplace.

The slightest unease touched her again . . .

But then, his hand fell to the small of her back.

"This way," he told her.

The hallway loomed dark before her. Alarm still rang

somewhere within her, but she was equally convinced that she could do nothing but keep going. If she willed her legs to turn her around, to run, they would not do so. But she didn't will it. She longed for the seduction of his whisper, his words, his touch.

"Here, my dear, my lovely, lovely, Yvette."

They turned from the hall through a doorway. The room was magnificent. A huge carved bed was in the center. Another fire burned in a smaller hearth. Shadows played with little spurts of flame against the walls. A silver tray with a decanter of wine and crystal glasses awaited.

"Wine, my dear?"

She nodded. He walked away, pouring from the decanter into a glass. He brought her the wine, and she drank.

As she swallowed it, she closed her eyes.

And as she did so, a sense of panic suddenly filled her. For when her eyes closed, she still saw the place around her. And it seemed that it was filled with winged creatures. Demons with horns, with forked tongues and tails, and all in shades of flame red.

She opened her eyes, ready to discard the wine, to scream, to run at last . . .

But he stood before her.

"We're here, beautiful Yvette, because we hunger," he said softly. "Soon, you'll know what is wanted of you."

She nodded. His hands were on her shoulders. He stared into her eyes, then turned and moved toward the fire. She was hot, so hot, and knew what was wanted of her. She shed the horrible shoes and then bit by bit, the cashmere sweater, her silly underwear. It might be strange here, even scary, but she had never wanted anything more . . .

She crawled atop the massive bed with its mound of pillows on silken sheets. She stretched out on it luxuriously, a feeling of her own sensuality sweeping over her. This was so different, so exotic, so unlike anything she had ever known before . . .

She closed her eyes for a moment to experience the smooth sensation of cool sheets and roaring fire.

But she was afraid she would picture eerie things in her mind once again and so she quickly opened her eyes.

And he was there, as magnificent and beautiful as he had ever been, far more real than the tricks of her mind, and coming toward her, standing before her.

Then, he stepped aside. There was someone else there as well.

Yvette started to scramble back on the bed, puzzled, horrified, and then angry.

What had he expected of her?

But he was ignoring her, his total concentration on the third party who had so silently joined them in the bedroom.

"I had thought we'd dine in tonight," he said casually.

Then he did look at her.

Yvette started to scream.

And scream.

And strangely, the last thing that crossed her mind was the rueful reminder of what Paul had said to her today. "You'll be sorry, you'll be so, so sorry!"

* * *

Javet was hard at work, studying the lab reports from the Paris office on the forensic studies done in the tomb. Despite the incredible advances science had afforded law enforcement, there were times when science could still offer nothing, because there was nothing to offer science.

Every drop of blood tested had belonged to the victim. Not that there had been many drops of blood left. And there was the first mystery.

That's when intuition came in. A police officer's gut intuition.

There had been dozens of people in the tomb— workers, onlookers. Footprints in the dust and finger-prints could mean everything—and nothing. Javet hated Dubois, but hating a man didn't make him guilty of murder.

He drummed the desk, then let out a long sigh.

Two things: Dubois needed to be questioned more strenuously.

And it might be time to arrest Jean-Luc's coworker.

"Inspector!"

He looked up from his desk. Millette, one of the his finest officers, was standing at his door, looking in. "What is it?"

"There's a report just in from Edouards, sir. We've found a body by the Eau Gallie stream."

Millette's tense appearance told him there was more to it than that.

"And?" Javet said. "Man, woman, child? Is there an evident cause of death?"

"Woman. The coroner has just been called. But . . ."

"Yes?"

"The victim was decapitated."

* * *

She wasn't going to die, Tara determined.

Not then, at least.

And with the pitchfork cast aside, she suddenly found herself moving forward, drawn inexorably toward her enemy, practically throwing herself against him. She was shaking still, ready to scream or cry and again deny every bit of nonsense this man was telling her.

But she was glad as well to feel the steely heat and security of his arms as they came around her. A voice of warning still screamed within her, but it was overshadowed by instinct and desire; since she had first seen him, this was where she had wanted to be. She was like a moth who had flown straight into the burning flame, but after a moment of being there—feeling enwrapped, ridiculously safe, and more than willing to simply melt into the fire—she drew away, staring at him again.

"You used me to get to my grandfather," she said.

"No. I would have come to your grandfather no matter what after the night in the crypt."

"You talked to him before the night in the crypt— you're the one who convinced him that there are vampires lurking around Paris."

He angled his head slightly, watching her. "I didn't talk to him before the night in the crypt."

"He knew you!"

"We met—before."

"When?"

"A long time ago. Having nothing to do with the current situation."

"And what is my grandfather's part in this travesty?"

"He is a member of the old Alliance."

"And this Alliance?"

"It's an organization that's very, very old."

"Oh, I see. The members of this Alliance are like Freemasons—who believe in vampires."

"They're guardians."

"Guardians of . . . ?"

"Humanity, the sacred right of life. Good over evil. However you wish to phrase the terminology, that is the role of the Alliance."

"And when was this Alliance formed?"

"There has been mention of the Alliance—sometimes obscure—in writings that go back to the Dark Ages."

"All right," she said, hearing his words, denying them still in her heart, and forcing her tone to be as rigid and scathing as any law official might utilize. "And you're part of this Alliance?"

"Not exactly."

"Then what is your role here?"

"I'm on the outside," he said softly, then shrugged. "I had heard rumors about the dig at the church, and through various legends and tales, I knew the rumors about Louisa de Montcrasset. I've studied a great deal of French history. I took the job with Dubois to make sure that I would be there when the coffin was opened."

"But you ran into me instead."

"Yes."

She started to walk by him. "You don't have to feel compelled to hound and protect me because I happened to be there at the time—or because of my grandfather."

He caught her arm. "I am compelled to protect you."

"I can handle myself."

"Well, you can't, not yet, anyway. But the fact that

you feel I'm hounding you . . . well, that has nothing to do with your grandfather."

She stood very still, torn between her desire to cast him off, to run away, and to throw herself against him once more.

"You're lying," she said.

"You know that I'm not."

Once again, she paused. Then she could pause no longer. Outside, the day had gone. Within the stables, the shadows were misting and thick, yet they offered no hint of menace. She slowly took a step toward him, and even more slowly, reached out to touch him. Fingers and palms coursed over the shape and structure of his face. She edged ever closer to him. He held very still, allowing her the exploration. Then she found herself pulled into an embrace so close that it defied the thin barrier of cloth between, found that she was being kissed with an open-mouthed passion that rendered her instantly reeling, blood rushing hot to every extremity, hunger suddenly something that shuddered and thundered with every throbbing beat of her pulse. She kissed back, lips and tongue aggressive, nearly desperate. His mouth drew the total focus of her attention, his kiss in the shadows, in the midst of the stables in the growing mist of the night. She was heedless of her own reckless movements, drawing ever closer still, fingers upon his shirt, seeking buttons, shoulders shrugging from the constraints of her own silk blouse. Then there was a moment of total, staggering awareness when his hand first fell upon her naked flesh, at her waist, fingertips traveling along her rib cage, palm and touch molding over her breast. She made little sounds, desperate little sounds. She wasn't sure when she lost everything else— shoes, jeans, undergarments—only that there was a trail along the scattered hay and grain on the stable floor, leading to the soft stacks of hay. Shadows and mist . . . both of which had been tinged with shades of danger just the night before, now seemed like a surreal blanket of the sweetest privacy. He threw horse blankets over the bed of hay, and as she came down upon it, she felt as if she had never known a softer mattress, never lain upon a surface so welcoming. He was everything she had sensed from the beginning, smooth, sleek, agile, so tightly drawn and hewn, flesh searing, each movement vibrant, every brush against her body by every part of his like an awakening of fire and need and more, a coming together destined by eternity. Something she had waited for all her life.

He was a practiced lover.

His mouth moved over the length of her. Subtle, seductive, aggressive. She drifted on waves of sensation, inhaling the rich clean scent of hay, and that of the man. There were moments so intense and acute she lost all thought except that of the carnal pleasure, and there were those brief seconds when she thought she had lost her own mind, because nothing would ever be the same again, she could never be touched so again, so completely that the liquid spiraling heat could enter and touch what was ethereal as well as flesh and real, and that she was desperate for cataclysmic union with a madman, and no one could ever make her want or hunger in the same way again. And yet, in those brief moments of sanity, there was something deeper as well. The birth of her own madness, for she knew as well that, somewhere in her heart, in the depths of her soul, she was very, very afraid that she believed . . .

Then all thought was gone again. She burned from the center of her being to every extremity, felt the red flame of hunger lapping at her ferociously, intimately, lips, breasts, thighs, sex, stripped, bare, throbbing, waiting. Then they were together at last, in shadow, in shades of fog. She was entwined, tight, surging, close, shuddering, trembling, straining. He seemed to fill her, a part of her, hard and strong, and she longed then never to let go, hungering and desperate, yet ruing the very explosion she sought so fervently with every twist and surge.

In the end, the night itself seemed to conclude with them, shadows burst to light, darkness to implode, mist to shatter into crystalline motes. Again, the rich scent of the hay came to her, along with the dampness of her own flesh, and at last, the prickles of the hay piercing through the blankets here and there. Reality. The stables, the night, her nakedness, her arms twined around the bare muscled torso of a near stranger.

But it didn't matter. There was no going back.

She didn't know what to say then.

That didn't matter either. He was the one who spoke.

"It's full dark," he said, and kissing her forehead, he rose. "I have to go."

Ann stopped back into the office for only a moment. Henriette had gone, and most of the workers were leaving. She didn't care that she might face a severe reprimand from the publisher for missing the meeting. She spent extra hours in the office every week. She took work home every night of her life. She was good at her job, and she knew it, and she would defy anyone who said differently.

The art director popped his head in her office. "You missed the meeting," he said.

"I know. I'm sorry."

"Don't worry—we decided on the plain design and coloring for the new American novel that had been your suggestion. It was no big deal."

"Thanks!" Ann said. "That sounds great. I am sorry."

He shrugged. "I think it's the first meeting you ever missed."

"Yeah, thanks."

"See you tomorrow."

He walked away. Ann moved around her desk and pulled open her top drawer, looking for a rubber band to bind a manuscript to take home with her.

"Where the hell were you?"

She looked up. Willem was standing there.

"Out," she said.

"Where? With whom?"

"None of your business," she told him irritably. What was his problem? Willem hadn't been part of their meeting today anyway—unless he had decided to horn in on it just to make her miserable.

"It is my business," he told her.

"And why is that?"

"Because—because I love you. And because there is a crazed murderer out on the streets of Paris."

She snapped the rubber band around the manuscript. "You don't love me. Certainly not as much as you love yourself. You're merely aggravated because you're not so wonderful that I'm willing to take you back after you've made a fool of me. And because I might have other interests in life. And there is a greedy murderer out there who wanted to steal the riches from a corpse," she said flatly. "Excuse me. I'm going home."

"Wait, you must wait."

She sighed. "Why, Willem, why must I wait?"

"You mustn't be led astray right now, Ann. This is a dangerous time in Paris."

"Willem, it is dangerous for me to care for you. And the amazing thing is that as much as I loved you, I'm over you."

"Ann, I am begging you to forgive me a moment's folly that meant nothing, that was nothing. The girl asked for help."

"Um," she said dryly. "Well, you see, I'm afraid there may be so many more women out there who might need your help in the future! Now, I'm tired. I want to go home. Excuse me."

For a moment, she felt real fear that he wasn't going to allow her to pass through her own doorway.

Then he stepped aside slightly. She meant to march by him, head high, indifferent. She was afraid, though, that he was going to be like a bridge—closing upon her just as she crossed it.

He didn't exactly "close" upon her, but he did stop her, his fingers closing around her upper arm.

"Willem—"

"Ann, you are a silly little fool. And you don't realize that you are mine, and that I will prove it to you, very soon."

Absently, she drew her fingers over her neck, thinking that a stray strand of hair was irritating her flesh.

"Let me by."

He lowered his head toward hers. "No, my love, you'll see. You're mine."

"Good night, Willem," she said firmly.

As she walked out of the office, she was afraid. She knew that he remained where he was, watching her, until she had left the reception area, and closed the door behind her.

She quickly pushed the button at the elevator, looking over her shoulder, more afraid of him than she wanted to let on.

The elevator door opened. She entered the little cubicle, leaning against the back wall. The door wasn't closing.

She stepped forward to hit the lobby button once again. But as she did so, Willem stepped into the elevator.

She backed away. The door closed.

"So, Ann," he breathed softly. "Here we are. Alone."

There were things that he could touch in the twilight period between sleep and wakefulness, when day gave way to dusk, and dusk to full night.

Things he could see.

Images.

That night, he saw her, walking along the street, aware, and yet still seeking those who had called her.

Hungry.

He saw her . . . saw the two men and the woman in the street, and her smile as she joined them, taking the bottle of wine, and then taking the lead. He could even see the street signs as she led her companions through the city.

He saw the old house, saw her work her will as she prepared it, and saw her practice her art of seduction, amused, and yet . . .

Thirsting.

He saw her tease and play . . .

And then he saw her as she came in to kill.

And kill again.

The images faded as he felt something else. A call, a

warning. Words that came to him through the channels
of his mind.

They have touched her, reached her.

Who?

Ann. Ann DeVant. But I will follow. I will follow.

CHAPTER 13

Katia was serving her grandfather dinner in the library when Tara returned to the house. The houseckeeper busied herself getting another setting for Tara, bustling about as she did so.

Tara stood quietly waiting for Katia to be done, watching her grandfather, not speaking. Then she frowned suddenly, remembering the time.

"Where is Ann? She should be home from work by now."

Jacques shook his head. "She called and told me not to worry. She took a long lunch break today and had to clear up a few things in the office before coming home."

Katia smiled at Tara, seeing her frown. "Mais oui, Tara. She is just running late. She wanted to make sure that Jacques went ahead without her. He must eat. He must keep his strength up!" Katia touched her on the shoulder. "Don't worry, Tara. Roland and I have the house and grounds all locked up. We're safe."

Katia left the room. Tara kept her eyes on her grandfather as she took a seat by the side of his desk where her plate had been set. She started to speak, but Katia knocked on the door, bringing in a bottle of white wine to accompany their fish.

When Katia left again, Tara at last spoke. "I still believe that this entire thing is insane."

"Insane, perhaps, but true," Jacques said firmly. He took a bite of his fish and seemed to savor the taste. "Katia is an excellent cook."

"Jacques, excuse me, but I have to tell you. There is a vampire loose in the Paris area."

"No," he said, pausing for a sip of wine.

"There is no vampire loose in Paris?"

"No, no. There are *vampires* loose in Paris," he replied.

"I thought Louisa de Montcrasset was the vampire."

"She is indeed a vampire. But we are quite certain now that it was not happenstance that she should be dug up after all these years."

"We—that would be you and Brent Malone?"

"Yes. And of course, there are others. On the side of good."

"Naturally," she murmured, still watching him. "His friends, of course, are on the side of good."

Jacques nodded solemnly, as if he was relieved that she was understanding the situation at last.

She shook her head. "I do believe that there are very strange things happening. And your friend, Brent, has something of a quality about him that is very . . . that induces trust. But I still don't really understand the connection. You didn't see him here, in Paris, before you became so worried about the dig?"

"No."

"But you do know him. I mean—you knew him . . . before."

"Yes."

She felt as if she was trying to pull teeth. "Okay, so when did you meet him?"

"He didn't tell you?"

"No."

Jacques frowned. "He followed you out to talk to you, to try to make you understand."

"He—he had to leave. Rather quickly," she said.

"Ah."

"Well?"

"We met years ago, here in France."

"But . . . you were living in the States years ago."

Jacques shrugged, giving his attention to the fish. "France has always been my home, I've always come and gone," he said, his eyes not meeting hers.

"But years ago?"

"He may be a bit older than he appears."

"How did you meet?"

Jacques waved his fork in the air. "It doesn't matter now. But yes, you see, I knew him before. Just as I knew before that vampires did exist. But the last time there was real trouble . . . in which I was involved, was long ago. Around the time of the war. And back then . . . there were many in Europe who believed, who knew, and there were many who were part of the Alliance. But the war ended, the world went on. New wars came with new weapons and the world became so sophisticated and high tech that people forgot. I forgot. And those I knew . . . those I knew well are gone now. But there will be a new generation, and times change, things change, people change. Even the undead change," he murmured thoughtfully.

"But Jacques—"

"I am to help them with the country, you see. There is a lair, somewhere. And they have keen senses, of course. But there are so many ruins in this area. So much abandoned and left to return to nature! The Alliance has always been there to know, you see. At one time, there were no powers on the darker side who could really be trusted. But as I said, the world moves on. And the sanctity of life, all life, or existence, whatever it might be, has surfaced, oddly enough, even among the technical mumbo-jumbo of the world today. Even above the fanatics and the insanity of some people who are human—and merely evil. You were right the other day, you know. There are human beings more evil than any imaginable demon. But that doesn't mean that the dark powers aren't out there, and that they aren't cruel, careless, and brutal as well."

"Jacques, you're still not making any sense to me."

"The important thing is that you believe we're in danger. That no one is allowed entry to this house. Katia knows in her heart that there is evil. She doesn't ask questions; she secures this home where we live. We'll move forward with our own investigation, and take care while we are here."

"Jacques, what I told you earlier is true. The police are suspicious of you."

"They are welcome to question me. I am a good and innocent man." He frowned. "What they need to do is incarcerate Dubois. I am willing to bet that he bears more guilt in this—oh, he's not the murderer. But he is working for the vampires. Bribed, he will serve them,

believing in the rich rewards they will give him. The
man is a fool, and always has been a fool. His reward
will be death."

"Jacques—"

Tara broke off as there was a tap at the door, and
Ann stepped in. Her cousin seemed more ashen and
gaunt than ever, yet she was smiling and seemed cheerful. "I'm home—I just wanted to let you know. I'm
going straight to bed. I'm exhausted. Work is getting
to me. But I had a great day. Still, Lord! I need some
sleep."

"You're not having dinner?" Tara asked.

Ann looked at her, preoccupied, but still smiling and
cheerful. "No, no. I had quite—yes, quite!—a lunch.
I'm not hungry, just tired. What a day! I'll tell you all
about it tomorrow." She frowned suddenly. "Were you
out with Daniel, Tara? You have hay in your hair."

Tara reached instinctively for her hair, seeking the
hay, as she felt her cheeks burn. "I, uh, yes, I was out
at the stables."

Ann was too distracted to do more than nod.
"There—you've got it. Hay all gone. Oh, well, love you
both, I'm going up to bed."

She blew them kisses, then turned away.

They heard a growl.

"Eleanora! Bad dog. It's me, Ann!" she heard her
cousin say.

She turned to her grandfather, frowning. Jacques had
put down his fork. His hand, resting on the table, trembled.

"Grandpapa?" Tara said anxiously.

"I'm all right, I'm all right. But I think I must get to
bed."

"Of course."

"Call Roland for me, please."

"Right away."

Tara went out and found Katia who immediately called for Roland who came and smiled and gently assured Tara that Jacques was fine, just worn out. It had been a very long day for him.

She promised her grandfather that she'd be in to say goodnight.

She helped Katia pick up the plates in the library, then wandered up the stairs, thinking she would check on Ann before saying goodnight to her grandfather.

She tapped at her cousin's door, and when there was no answer, she opened it, popping her head in.

Ann's room was dark. Her cousin was already in bed. Tara silently walked into the room.

The balcony doors were open. The garlic bulbs had been impatiently cast into a pile in the corner of the room.

Tara hesitated, trying to discern her cousin's features in the darkness. Ann was definitely and soundly sleeping.

Tara decided that it couldn't hurt to close the balcony doors and replace the garlic. She did so, then tiptoed out.

She went into her grandfather's room. He was in bed, and like Ann, appeared to be sleeping. His eyes were closed. Tara thought of his great age, and his tenacity and passion for life—and determination that he was part of the Alliance, a Resistance fighter for good against evil.

She kissed his forehead, checked his balcony doors and the garlic hung above them, then crept out.

She was tired herself, but restless, and her mind was moving with incredible speed. Aware of her afternoon, longing to go back over each moment, yet not wanting to think and analyze tonight, she drew out her easel and pad, and sat with pencils to sketch.

Disturbing pictures flew from her fingers onto the page.

Images . . .

A churchyard, stones askew, graves split open. She stopped. Another sketch. A wolf. Huge, snarling, teeth gleaming, massive, hard.

A bat . . . flying like a shadow overhead.

The shadows then covered a Paris street, the path they had walked on the night she and Ann had gone to La Guerre.

She paused, then began to sketch again.

A man's face . . .

She frowned. She had drawn someone she had met. She couldn't quite place the image she had created with her subconscious mind.

She glanced at her watch. Late. Time to shower and get some sleep. The tension that was tightening within her seemed to warn that the day to follow would be long and hard. She went in to shower.

Bits of hay still clung to her clothing. There were a few more fragments in her hair. The scent of him seemed to linger about her.

She went to bed thinking that it was still true that she barely knew the man. And yet, if he were to walk out of her life as suddenly as he had appeared in it, she would be disconsolate.

He wasn't going to walk out of her life so quickly. He believed in vampires. Believed that vampires were killing in Paris . . .

She tossed and turned, and at last fell into a fitful sleep.

* * *

Lucian drew the car to a halt. "Near here," he said.

Brent got out on the passenger side. "Looks like a lot has been abandoned in this area."

"There." Lucian pointed to a street sign. "I saw that sign. Clearly."

"Lead the way."

Lucian did. They came to a house set back from the street. A fallen board stated one French word for condemned: CONDAMNÉ.

Brent followed as Lucian crawled over the sign.

"We're too late, of course. Way too late."

They stood in a foyer. Before time had rendered the structure dangerous, the place had been beautiful. There were delicately carved wall panels. The ceilings were covered with now peeling and fading frescoes.

They were both quiet for a moment, listening, waiting. Brent nodded toward Lucian, and moved to the left.

He came to a room where a recent fire was down to cold ash. He stood in the center of the room for a moment, then moved toward the once ornate sofa. He stooped down.

Droplets . . .

Possibly wine.

But not. He reached out and touched one of the tiny stains. Dried blood.

A sense of danger seemed to grip him. He rose quickly, striding back through the elegant foyer to the other side of the house. Lucian was there, black-coated back toward him as he inspected the contents of a desk.

Brent didn't know what he had been sensing. He started to walk toward one of the draperies.

A sudden scream of rage tore through the dark silence of the house.

The creature, naked, wild-haired, wild-eyed, lips snarling and fangs barred, came shooting from the draperies like a whirlwind from hell. Brent was still at a distance. The creature was flying toward Lucian.

Brent took a step forward, pulling the sharpened stake from beneath his coat. The dirty, grotesque figure that had once been human could move like lightning. And still, he could move faster. His speed was natural, honed through the years.

Lucian turned. The vampire was but inches away, intent on slashing and biting, when Brent impaled it from the back. The thing wasn't dead. Caught on the wooden spike, it thrashed and screamed in a frenzy. Brent pinned it to the floor, and bent down, avoiding the teeth. He gripped the hair. And ripped.

The head came free.

There was no blood.

Lucian crouched down, studying the body. He looked up at Brent. "That was quite clean and neat. I was really all right, though, you know."

"You're not supposed to destroy your own kind."

"Those were the old rules," Lucian said bitterly. "The world, and the rules, have changed."

"I don't think there are any more here," Brent said.

Lucian held still, then shook his head. "They wanted us to be here—they meant this one as a sacrifice."

Brent squatted down at Lucian's side, studying the face on the dismembered head.

"What is it?" Lucian said.

"I'm not sure, the features are so distorted . . . but there's something familiar about this man."

"Let's hope he wasn't a friend," Lucian murmured.

"No, it's not an old friend. But still . . . there's something familiar about the face. Or would be if . . . I don't know. Hopefully, it will come to me."

Lucian looked around the room. "This wasn't exactly a setup, but I have a feeling this fellow was left here on purpose. They know we'll track them down eventually. Maybe they're hoping to at least wound us, take us off guard. Rather insulting, however, to think we might be taken by such a raw and stumbling new recruit."

"Maybe they don't have much else," Brent suggested.

"There has to be someone behind this who has known and tasted power."

"Think about your enemies. There must be a few."

"A few? Hundreds, I would imagine," Lucian said. He studied Brent. "What about you?"

"I can only think of one, and that was a very long time ago and he is dead. But you're right. There's nothing else here. We need to start moving."

"Let's go," Brent said.

Ann was hot. She tossed off the covers. The room suddenly seemed stifling and filled with a wretched and horrible odor.

She sat up and looked around. The damned garlic was back at the windows. And the balcony doors were closed.

Impatiently, she got out of bed and walked to the doors, throwing them open. She pulled the garlic from the top, wincing as it seemed that the bulbs had thorns, as if they were roses, and they hurt her. She threw them as far from the open doors as she could and stepped out on the porch.

Ann.

She heard her name. Or didn't hear it. She felt it.

Ann . . .

It was like a caress. The breeze, oh, it was the breeze! So good against her skin. It felt as if she were being held again, teased again, kissed and touched, all over her flesh.

Ann . . .

Yes!

There were fingers in the wind. Fingers that moved over her. They seduced and beckoned. And each time the breeze whispered her name, she felt it anew.

Ann . . .

Yes, yes.

Come! Come to me.

Yes, yes, of course . . .

Officers Surrat and Martine were driving down the street, cursing the lack of light, when they saw the pair.

"Georges!" Martine said to his partner. "There— two men."

"I see them," Michel Martine replied, and he depressed the gas pedal further, then jerked the patrol car up on the curb, cutting off the two men on the street.

"Is it him?" Georges Surrat asked his partner. Martine was an older man who had worked in Paris for years before being transferred to the village a decade ago. Surrat was young, and just learning the ropes.

"Yes, that's him. Brent Malone. The American digger. Javet wants him. Careful, he might be dangerous. Remember the corpse in the crypt?"

Georges nodded grimly, reaching for his side arm as the two simultaneously got out of the patrol car.

"Brent Malone!" Michel Martine spoke, his voice hard and determined. He'd dealt with a hell of a lot on the streets of Paris.

And not even all that had prepared him for the corpse in the crypt at the church, the headless torso they had discovered that day.

"Brent Malone! You're under arrest."

The two men had stopped. They stared at one another, and then at the officers.

"What's the charge?" Malone asked.

Martine felt strangely unnerved. Neither man appeared armed—but then, they were wearing ankle length coats. They were both big men, very tall.

"Murder," Georges said. His voice sounded quavery. Not good, he thought. They were the police. Though the pair they accosted were impressively sized men, they had made no outward moves to suggest danger or resistance.

"Javet knows that I'm not guilty of murder," Malone said, frowning.

"There is a warrant out for your arrest, Malone, and that is that. The bodies are piling up, so if you're innocent, perhaps you can prove it in jail."

Malone stepped forward. "Gentlemen," he said softly. "I'm very sorry. I can't afford for you to arrest me tonight."

Martine drew his side arm up, aiming for Malone's heart. "Monsieur, you are under arrest for the murder of—"

He suddenly found that he had stopped speaking. He found himself looking past Malone to the other man. Then he lowered his gun, dizzy. He was going to black out!

He stumbled back, falling against the patrol car. He shook his head, clearing his eyes.

"Michel!" Georges called out frantically.

"What, what is it?"

"I can't see!"

"Hold still, close your eyes, take a breath!"

Michel had done so already. He blinked, and was greatly relieved to realize that he had vision again.

Vision . . .

With nothing to see. The street was empty.

All around them, he saw nothing but shadows.

From somewhere, however, came a chilling sound. A deep, elongated cry in the night.

A howling . . .

The night's chill suddenly surrounded him. The shadows seemed to be encroaching, like something alive.

"Get in the car!" he commanded Georges. "Get the hell in the car!"

Later, back in the light and bustle of the main square, he felt sheepish. He looked at his partner. "We never saw anything tonight, do you hear me?"

Georges stared straight ahead at the road. "Not a thing, sir. Not a damned thing."

The strangest thing about the dream was that she knew she was sleeping, that she had entered a nightmare realm, and that nothing here could be real.

But it *felt* real.

She was moving from darkness into light, but the light would never become really bright. The dark, she believed, was the safe realm of sleep, where, if she did dream, it was of moments gone by—simple things, strolling down a country lane, walking along the streets of

New York, doing something so mundane as trying to capture the exact mood and feeling she wanted for a canvas, with the paint perhaps disappearing each time it seemed she had touched the paper with the perfect tone. The darkness was deep sleep, restful sleep, a place that was safe. Strange that a shadow realm should promise such a land of peace, while the light . . .

But it wasn't sunlight, not the light of day, or even the friendly light of a street at night flooded with neon.

It was different. Muted, eerie, yellow light tinged with something that threw everything within it askew. And there was a breeze. Not a soft, gentle breeze that wrapped around the flesh and touched with an air of freshness, not a breeze that lifted the hair as tenderly as a touch. The breeze had a chilling element. Not like the wind, not like the cold of winter. It was a chill that seemed to reach with hard and bony fingers, and close right around the heart, and perhaps the soul.

She was walking, walking forward from the safety of the darkness into the unknown dread that would be so readily visibly in the odd and evil light. She didn't want to go, and indeed, tried to turn back. And it wasn't so much that the evil reached in and dragged her out, but rather that she knew she must go forward. It was imperative that she see whatever horrors were to be discovered in the realm of the macabre; she knew only that she must move forward.

For the longest time she simply moved, aware of the chill, aware of the evil. She moved with caution, yet wondered why. She could see her bare feet take step after step, but there seemed to be nothing beneath them. She could feel the silk of her nightgown wrapping around her with the breeze, the fabric itself made cold by the touch of the unlikely wind. Her hair pulled behind her, blown out around her, tangled and whipped, and she could feel each strand as it touched her face. Her fingers were cold, her hands knotted and unknotted with tension, and she could take note of each and every sensation around her. Color . . . the color of her nightgown was light blue, almost ethereal in the yellow glow. Her toenails were painted ochre.

And the house . . .

At last, she stood in the woods, and the glow was coming from a house. There was ground beneath her feet now, earth, grass, stones . . . a path. A little trail, heavily overgrown, that led to the door.

Her feet hurt as she moved forward. She could hear her own exclamation as she stepped on stones and cried out softly in pain. Then, it seemed as if she first stood some distance from the house, staring at the thick, heavy old door.

Before she realized she had taken a step, it suddenly loomed before her. She was there. She wasn't certain she had come willingly, but she was there.

The knob was cold in her hand as she reached for it. Brass. Rounded. More than cold. It was icy.

The door seemed to move, to shudder inward, then outward, as if the house itself were breathing.

Whispering . . .

Come in, do come in, please . . . we've been expecting you.

The voice of sanity in her mind called out with valiant, determined, effort. *No, no, no! It's what they want you to do! Don't go in, don't go in . . .*

She stilled the voice, because there was another. *I have to go in. I have to go in, and find out what is behind the door. I have to go in for Jacques. I have to go in, because . . . the truth is within the house . . . somewhere.*

And it's all right. It's all right if I go in, because it's only a dream.

Her fingers closed tightly over the knob. She twisted, pushed the door open, and the squeaking, creaking sound it made was like the sound of fingernails raking across a blackboard. She could hear it so clearly.

And then . . .

Candles . . . oh, Lord! Candles burned everywhere. They were tiny accents to the fire in the hearth that seemed to roar as loudly as the door had creaked. The warmth was intense, and yet, oddly enough, it seemed that the breeze had followed her in, and she was chilled and warmed, all in one. The flames in the hearth flickered blue, green, yellow, gold, and intensely red. The large flames leaped and danced in a frenzy, as if bowing to the breeze. And all around her, the candles burned with flutters, leaps, and bows, as if they too danced to the same whispered beat.

Gargoyles and grotesques lined the hearth, sat upon the newel posts to the staircase at the end of the room, and graced the arch over the long hallway that went off to the side, where the yellow light seemed to dim with shadow. Not a welcoming shadow, not the warm darkness of safe sleep, but a shadow that wavered and played in strange shapes.

She found herself walking toward it. She paused, staring up at the archway. A horned grotesque seemed to escape its inert stone boundaries and come to life, hissing and spitting down at her as she moved along. She looked up at it, and knew that it could not come down for her, yet neither did she dare come too close to it. From the hearth it seemed that she heard more— spitting, cawing, harsh, cackling laughter that was suddenly only a whisper, a sound that might have been the breeze, or the dance of the fire . . . but was not.

But was not.

She looked down. The hardwood floors had been strewn with woven runners in shades of crimson, black, and gray. Battle scenes were depicted. Tartar armies defeating their foes, slicing them down in a frenzy of death. As she walked, the characters beneath her feet seemed to come to life. The victims shrieked and wailed.

Blood curled beneath her toes.

She looked up, and straight ahead. The runner was playing with her, creating fear. She had to look ahead, straight ahead. The night was illusion, she thought. The house was a house. The gargoyles were fashioned of stone, and they did not move.

Yet still . . .

There was that laughter. Deeper than any whisper. It became a pulse, a beat . . . like a heartbeat. A heart that beat too hard . . .

The hallway beckoned.

She walked.

Doorways creaked open as she trod through the hall. She heard the eerie creaking sound as they parted, as the little rays of evil light seemed to escape from each. She came to the first. It was barely ajar. She didn't want to look in, but she knew that she must. If she didn't look, it had made no sense that she had come.

She had to do it. She had to know. There was truth here, somewhere.

She pushed the door open.

And she saw . . .

There were bodies . . . body parts . . . torsos . . . heads . . . limbs. Strewn about. As she stood there, they seemed to form together, as if drawn by unseen tendons or ligaments. Furious arguments began to take place in whispered anger. *Let go, you've got my foot! That's my hand!* And then, one of the heads rolled to connect to a neck, and the lips moved in the mottled, bony, gray, sexless face. *Give me what is mine! Give me what is mine!*

The eyes of the creature suddenly locked upon Tara. The lips began to move. The tongue was swollen and black, and as it moved, blood began to trickle down the decaying chin. *Why, Tara, you've come! Don't you think I'm right? He must give me my own legs. I was never fat before, and I'll not take his fleshy little knees when my own are right there . . . where are my arms? I must have my arms. The better to hold you, my dear, the better to draw you to me. I must have my hands, the better to touch you. To stroke your neck. What a lovely, lovely, neck . . .*

The thing was almost all together. Limbs danced and angled awkwardly across the room, intent on completing a full body. And the eyes . . . the eyes were still on her, the lips were still moving, whispering her name.

Almost, Tara, almost . . . oh, Tara, Tara, I'm close, so close, you can almost feel my breath against your flesh, your long lovely throat . . .

She stepped back into the hall. The thing was quickly, quickly, melding together. She turned to back down the hallway, return to the great room with the hearth, find the door and escape, but there was something there. Something enormous and dark, winged, clawed, taloned, and more evil than anything she had thus far witnessed. She knew that she could flee into that shadow, and it was the shadow, not the light, that had beckoned her.

Called her, to trap her.

The huge, winged shadow began to whisper.

Oh, yes, my dear, you've been trapped. That ancient mind

has fallen prey to self-confidence, and you have come. You have come, when you should not have done so. You have left that place where you should have been, a guardian, a sentinel. And so now, you, too, will lose, don't you see? I will have those you love, no, actually, I have them now, and in the end, you will come as well . . .

She started to scream, as loud as she could, hysterically, somehow aware that she had to be loud, louder than the fire and the wind, louder than all the cackling, and the whispers like drumbeats. She had to close her eyes tight against the darkness, force herself to know that it was a dream, only a dream, and that she could awaken. She had to awaken, had to awaken . . .

"Tara!"

She was jerked up, suddenly aware of pain, very real pain, in her upper arms. Her eyes flew open. There was no house. She was in her own room.

She blinked. She had thought she was in her own house, but she was staring into Brent Malone's golden hazel eyes, eyes that burned with an intensity like the flame in the house of evil. His fingers were wrapped so tightly around her flesh that she'd be bruised in the morning. And she was screaming, had been screaming, was still screaming, and wildly trying to fight against him, to free herself from his hold, lash out again and strike him, flail against him, anything.

"Tara, stop!"

It wasn't the command in his tone, but the very softness of it that brought her to a trembling rationality.

The sound faded.

She had ceased to scream.

A nightmare. It had all been a nightmare, because all they talked about was vampires, and the Alliance.

"Tara . . ." He moved a hand tenderly against her hair to soothe her.

She stiffened, mistrustful, even as she felt the urge again to throw herself against him. "It was a dream," she said. "Only a dream." But she was still trembling fiercely. And he was there. She closed her eyes, and leaned against him, and felt the comfort and warmth of his arms around her.

Then she stiffened again, drawing back. "How are you here? How are you in my bedroom?"

"I came back," he said simply.

"And how did you get in."

"That's not important. You have to tell me about the dream."

"No!" she insisted angrily. "How did you get in?"

He let out an impatient sigh. "I knocked on the door. Katia let me in."

"I don't believe you!" she charged, but then, looking past him, she saw that Roland, Katia, and her grandfather were standing in her doorway, ashen, looking in on her.

"Oh . . ." she breathed. "I'm sorry. I'm so sorry. I've awakened you all . . . and it was just a dream."

Jacques, looking frail in his pajamas, his feet bare, pressed past the other two and came to her bedside.

"Tell us about the dream, Tara."

She shook her head. It was fading, but it was still too vivid. "I was at a house. In the woods, I think. I didn't want to go in, but I felt that I had to. There was a huge fire, there were gargoyles that came alive. And there was a hallway, and I knew that I had to go down the hallway. Then there was a door, and there were body parts in the room, but they weren't parts, because they started to come together, and the lips in a head were moving. The thing was talking to me, and I was afraid of what would happen when it all came together. So I backed into the hall, but the shadow was there, and it started laughing and telling me that I was trapped, and the shadow was saying that . . ."

She broke off, staring from Brent Malone to her grandfather, and then to the door where Katia and Roland were standing.

"Where's Ann?" she breathed.

Brent stared back at her.

Then he jumped up, racing for the hallway.

Tara, as well, leaped to her feet. She flew after Brent.

He had already reached Ann's door.

Crashing into his back, Tara looked beyond him.

Ann was not in her bed. The balcony doors were open.

The breeze was blowing in . . .

As chill as that which had colored her dream with fear.

CHAPTER 14

Henri Javet ruefully looked in the mirror.

The five o'clock shadow could be easily solved. He kept a razor at work. He had stayed at the station many times before on the cot in one of the holding cells.

But the dark shadows and bags beneath his eyes . . . la, la. They were not so easily concealed. Years of hard work had brought him to his position here, but in such a short period of time, he had come up against something that seemed to eclipse all but the most heinous crimes he had encountered before. What should have been a case of greed and murder was becoming much more. The body found in the water was not going to be the last.

Javet shaved, washed his face well, noting again that the shadows and bags could not be washed away, and walked back to his office. He glanced at his watch, frowning. The inspector from Paris had gone out to bring in Dubois. He and the men sent had not returned.

He looked at the notes he had taken during the task force meeting, calling out to the desk sergeant to let him know the minute the inspector returned. As he did so, the outer door opened. A young man, slender, his clothing rumpled and his hair wild, came barging in.

"I must see the inspector!" he insisted.

"You must explain your business first," the sergeant said sternly, but not unkindly.

"She is gone, she is missing. I waited all night by her house, I had to let her know that I would be her friend, no matter what. But she never came home. She is missing."

"Now, now, monsieur, slow down," the sergeant said.

But Javet stepped forward. "It's all right, Clavet," he assured the sergeant, and turned to the young man. "I am Inspector Henri Javet, in command here. And I am glad to hear your story. But in order. Your name, young fellow?"

"I am Paul Beauvois. From this village, the far outskirts, the farmland. And I . . . I have, for years, been a very good friend to Yvette Miret."

"The girl at the café?" Javet said, knowing the name. A feeling of dread slipped to the bottom of his stomach. He had seen the girl many times, as had most people in the area. Unfortunately, he had often feared that she would come to a bad end. She had used her position at the café far too often as a stepping-stone for another sort of business.

She had never been arrested, because she did have a paying job, and because, anytime she had been asked about her business with visitors and tourists, she had enthusiastically talked about the "friendship" she had formed. What she did could not be labeled illegal, especially since no one had ever lodged a complaint against her.

"So," Javet said. It might be the most natural thing in the world that the girl had slept elsewhere. Though she had a look of purity, she was anything but innocent. That nagging feeling at the pit of his stomach remained. "She did not come home last night, and you watched and waited for her, and so you are very worried."

Paul nodded. "We had a fight, a terrible row. I was angry, so I went into Paris without her, but then . . . I had an uneasy feeling. I was worried, so I left the concert we had planned to attend together, and went to her house. Her parents are gone; she lives with an old crone of an aunt who cares little about her, but the woman is not a liar. She was impatient, telling me that Yvette had not come, and that—" He hesitated, looking at Javet, then continued, "She said that Yvette could find men, real men, and that she did not need to rely on a boy like me who offered nothing when there was so much more in the world."

"And then?" Javet said.

"I sat outside her house all night. She did not return."

"Perhaps it is a bit early to consider the young lady as missing," Javet said. And it was. The likelihood was that the girl had found someone more intriguing with whom to spend her time. But under the circumstances, with so many missing . . .

And a headless body to be identified . . .

"But, monsieur," the young man protested, close to tears. "I am afraid—"

As he spoke, the door to the station burst open. Big, gruff, curly haired François Vaille came in like a whirlwind. He stared at Paul, and Javet thought with a frown that the man had followed him here.

"My girl has not shown up for work. She was to take the early shift, and she has never promised to open the café, and then not appeared. And that—fellow!" he spat out contemptuously. "That fellow came in yesterday, swearing, ranting, and raving—and promising that she would be sorry."

"Now, François!" Javet said. "Calm down, and we'll take things one by one. The girl has not shown up for work, but young Paul here says that she did not return to her home last night. He has come in to report her missing."

The café owner, gone to fat over the years but still a formidable man, lunged at Paul. Javet quickly interceded, stepping past the lad.

"François!" Javet warned.

François wagged a finger around him at Paul. "He has come in to report her missing, because he knows that she has met with foul play. He should be arrested on the spot."

"François, we all know that Yvette has many friends."

"Yvette likes her job with me as well. She has always had her many friends, but she never makes the mistake of missing work."

"We will begin a search for her right away," Javet said. "Though it isn't customary, under the circumstances, we will look for her right away." He hesitated. "We have discovered a body by the stream," he admitted. "I shall have some officers take you both by the morgue, and see if you can identify the girl."

"Oh, God!" Paul exclaimed, burying his face in his hands.

"A body! And now I am to go, too?" François Vaille

demanded. "But what about my café? I will lose money as it is, since I do not have Yvette working the sidewalk tables."

"Your concern for your employee is admirable," Javet said dryly. "This must come first. Sergeant Clavet, call in an escort to take these men to the morgue. As quickly as possible. I know Yvette myself, and will see that there is a bulletin sent out."

He turned back toward his office, then paused, instinct warning him that François was about to strike out at Paul again.

He swung back, his voice bellowing out. "One more move, François, and I'll have you locked up for the day, which will not do your business any good at all!"

That would halt François, he knew.

In disgust, he entered his office again. He had barely drawn out the proper paperwork before his door opened again.

Inspector Trusseau, the Paris man, was there. Naturally, Trusseau thought himself above knocking. He considered himself superior to any of his village coworkers, though his instructions had been to work with Javet.

"What is it?" Javet asked somewhat irritably. "Do you have Dubois?"

"No, I do not," Trusseau said. "Despite the hour of our arrival, Professor Dubois was not in residence. A neighbor, rather temperamental after being awakened in what she considered the middle of the night, informed us that she hasn't seen him in at least a day, maybe two."

"What about the American, the digger, Brent Malone?"

"A strange coincidence. Mr. Malone has not been seen at his apartment in quite some time, either."

Javet nodded. "All right."

He looked back to his desk, ruing the fact that things seemed so out of control. He would find the men, of course. He had waited too long to bring them in.

"So, Javet?" Inspector Trusseau said, a certain mockery evident in his words, and in his lack of courtesy in eschewing Javet's title.

"So, you should be back on the streets, searching for the men," Javet said. He stared pointedly at the man sent from Paris. "Now."

"There are other things that should be done—"

"And I will do them. Thank you, Inspector."

His door closed. Javet picked up his pen and began to write on the forms that sat before him. He picked up the phone as he wrote, informing the morgue that he was sending men in who might be able to identify the headless corpse.

"Ann!" Tara burst through the room, rushing to her cousin's bed, and then on to the balcony. She stopped short, breathing hard, heart thundering, as she saw that her cousin was standing there, staring at her as if she had lost her mind.

A noise behind them alerted them to the fact that others had come in behind Tara. Ann's delicate brows arched high. "My goodness, what is this, a party in the middle of the night? Mr. Malone . . . my goodness . . . !" Her eyes traveled from Tara to Brent, and a slight smile played at the corner of her mouth. "Did you join us for the evening, Mr. Malone? I go to work one day, come home a bit worn out . . . and it seems I have missed a great deal." She was teasing, but there was a still a perplexed look in her eyes as she added, "Grandpapa!"

That was said sternly. "What are you doing out of bed? And no slippers, no robe! You will catch your death of cold, you will wind up with pneumonia once again, and you must not. Roland! What is Jacques doing up so?"

"Going back to bed," Jacques said wearily. His tone was relieved, but still laced with a certain concern.

"I don't know if I need bother to try for a little more sleep or not," Ann said, yawning. "It's nearly time for the alarm to go off, and I really shouldn't be late." She walked in, going to Jacques. She kissed his cheek. "I love you, Grandpapa," she said.

He kissed her back, holding her face between his hands. "Child! You are as cold as ice! You will catch your death of cold. You must get back in bed!"

"I'm going, as soon as I see that Katia and Roland have *you* back in bed," she assured him.

Jacques nodded. Tara saw that his eyes met Brent's then, over Ann's head. She saw assurance touch her grandfather's expression. He seemed to relax enough to be able to go to sleep.

The three left, and Ann stepped forward, shutting her door, leaning against it, and staring at Tara and Brent.

"What are earth are you doing?" she demanded angrily of Tara. "I never, never bring anyone home to sleep here! It is the most disrespectful thing you can do! There's no reason, of course, that you two shouldn't have your little liaison, but not under Grandpapa's nose!"

"He wasn't sleeping here," Tara informed Ann.

"Oh?" Ann remained angry. And skeptical. "Well, I now know why Tara was wearing hay in her hair yesterday."

"I happened to arrive very early," Brent said evenly, staring at her.

Tara was surprised when Ann's eyes fell.

"So tell me, Ann," Brent said. "What were you doing out on the balcony at such an hour?"

She arched a brow. "It is my balcony."

"You shouldn't have your doors open like that."

"I've kept my doors open many a night for years," Ann informed him. She sniffed and waved a hand in the air. "I had to get rid of that ridiculous garlic—the heat and smell created between the closed doors and the garlic was unbearable! What is going on here? Grandpapa has lost his mind. If this continues . . . I fear he may really need care."

"Jacques is doing fine," Tara said.

"Oh, yes. Our house is riddled with garlic, and our grandfather is doing fine," Ann said. She yawned again, slumping against the door. "I am so tired! I sleep and sleep, and still . . . !" She stared at the two of them. "Well, this has been fun, but . . . I may have a half hour left to sleep. You were leaving, weren't you, Brent?"

"He's staying for breakfast," Tara said.

"Right, breakfast," Ann muttered. "Fine, do whatever the hell you like. I have to be at work this morning, there's so much that I have to do."

"What do you have to do that's so important?" Tara asked her.

Ann frowned, as if trying to remember. "Oh, yes, it's the American novel. I must decide if we're going to buy it, and if so, what kind of a bid we're going to put in. And I haven't read the damned thing through once yet, much less given it serious thought."

"Do you have it here? I can read it for you."

"I—you're not an editor or a critic, Tara. You're an artist."

"I can still read!"

"Maybe . . . no, no, I have to go to work."

"Call in late," Brent suggested.

Ann's lashes flicked low over her eyes. "I shouldn't. I really shouldn't. Not after . . ."

"After?"

"I took a long lunch yesterday," she murmured.

"Still, you should call in late," Brent told her.

"No, no, it wouldn't be good," Ann murmured.

Tara was surprised when Brent walked across the room and took her cousin's face gently in hand, meeting her eyes. Ann didn't pull away from his touch. She listened as he said, "They value you very much, where you work. You can call in late. Tara can glance through the book, and she can tell you whether it is good or not. If you can get some sleep, you must."

To Tara's astonishment, Ann agreed. "Yes, I will sleep, if I can," she said. She yawned again, and walked by Brent, then came to Tara, smiling at her. "I am so tired." She touched Tara lightly on the shoulder with affection. "Good night."

With the two of them still in the room, she crawled back into bed, pulled the covers to her shoulder, and closed her eyes. It seemed that she was instantly asleep.

Brent walked over to the bed and looked down at Ann. He touched her hair, smoothing it from her face, and seemed to study her very seriously. A sound like a weary sigh, barely perceptible, seemed to escape him. He walked to the balcony doors, closing them, locking them. And he replaced the garlic bulbs Ann had discarded.

With all arranged, he came back to Tara, eyes hard on her, strange, both defiant and commanding.

"Let's leave her to sleep now."

Tara stared at Brent as he opened Ann's door, indicating that they should leave. Tara preceded him into the hallway. He closed the door quietly behind him.

"What the hell was that all about?" Tara asked him.

"She really needs her sleep."

She kept watching him. "I don't believe that she paid such serious attention to you."

"You don't believe anything yet, no matter how many signs stare you right in the face," he said softly.

"Signs!" she murmured, and started out ahead of him.

He caught her by the shoulder, pulling her back. She wished that she didn't feel his slightest touch so acutely. She stared at his fingers upon her silk clad shoulders then to his eyes, but if he noted any kind of a withdrawal within her, he gave no sign.

"The time is coming when it's going to be very dangerous for you not to believe," he told her. "You with your logic—and your fear that anything you can't taste, feel, or touch is mad and insane, fantastical. And, of course, if you were to accept the fact that there were things beyond your realm of understanding, well then, you would be giving in to madness. There are such things. What do you think that dream was, Tara?"

"A nightmare."

"A nightmare? Or a warning?"

She arched a brow as imperiously as her cousin. "A warning—about Ann? Ann was fine, just cooling off out on the balcony."

"Cooling off? Her skin was like ice."

"When you're very hot," Tara said with aggravation, "it feels good to get cold!"

"You brought her in, Tara! You called to her, just in time."

"In time for what?"

He dropped his hold on her shoulders and walked by her, heading for the stairs in disgust. Katia was just coming out of Jacques' room, and she stopped, speaking to him on the stairs, her French so rapid Tara wasn't sure what she was saying.

But Brent responded to her and Katia smiled pleasantly. They walked down the stairs together.

Everyone trusted him. She had trusted him. So much so that she had fallen into his arms, and more. If she didn't care so much about him, if she didn't feel such a need to know him better, deeper, keep him near her . . .

If she didn't care so much, she might not be so distrustful.

And yet . . .

Something about him just wasn't right. He had told her that there were vampires, and that the Alliance was true and real. He had denied that he was a vampire himself when she had accused him of being one. Her grandfather seemed to know him very well, and hadn't shown the least surprise or alarm when he had found him not only inside his house at night—or the morning—but in his granddaughter's bedroom.

She watched the stairs for a moment, thinking, then turned and quietly entered her grandfather's room. She walked to the bed. His eyes were closed, but he felt her there, and his eyes opened.

"She's in danger," he said softly. "But then, we're all in danger." He fumbled his hand free from the covers, seeking hers. He found it and wound their fingers tightly together. "Tara . . . it is you, you know. It is you, and you must be strong, because I am not the man I once was, and no matter how we are protected, we are in danger. It is my fault, of course, because of what I am, which once brought me such great pride, and now fear."

"Jacques, I don't know what you're talking about."

"You have to trust your senses, your gut feelings!"

She nodded, smoothing back his white hair, growing very worried. "Grandpapa, please, if I really understood just a little bit more. When—when exactly did you meet Brent Malone?"

Jacques closed his eyes. "A long time ago," he said.

"Grandpapa! When?" she said.

But his eyes didn't flicker. He had either fallen asleep again, or he was determined to pretend that he had done so.

Tara left him. She started down the stairs, certain that Brent was still in the house. She meant to accost him herself.

He was there. She found him as soon as she reached the landing. He was standing in the open doorway, staring at the newspaper, which had just arrived along with the first pink streaks of dawn.

"Another body has been found," he said.

With anger, he threw the paper to the floor, and stepped out the door, slamming it behind him.

Paul stood next to the towering and angry Monsieur François and stared at the video screen.

They were informed that they were not to see a body;

they were going to be shown the clothing and jewelry that had been found on the woman.

He waited, tense. A cart was rolled before a camera somewhere else in the morgue.

He stared at the screen, blinked and stared again.

His knees wobbled, he felt faint, like jelly.

He slipped to the floor, sobbing.

He was aware that, next to him, Monsieur François was swearing.

In the depths of a nether region, images of the past swirled in a field of mist.

That day . . . so long ago.

He was weak, incredibly weak. There had been so little food for so very long. With no nourishment, they had been put through backbreaking labor.

Now, they were all together in the camp. The religious and ethnic prisoners, the dissenters, the political prisoners, and anyone that the regime had any reason whatsoever to dislike. At the beginning, it hadn't been that way.

But then he had seen Andreson.

And Andreson had seen him.

It was as if they had known from the very beginning that they recognized one another.

But Andreson had held the power from that very beginning, due to the circumstances. He had been certain that Andreson would see to his immediate execution, but amazingly, it hadn't been that way. Instead, Andreson had set out to break him.

Eventually, of course, he would kill him. He would disappear one night, as so many others had done.

Andreson liked a more subtle form of torture, just as

much as he enjoyed his own more physical pursuits. He liked the fact that the man he so loathed was left to go to bed each night, wondering, fearing, dreading what might come when the sun went down. There had been times, at the beginning, when the prisoner had found strength, when he had tried to explain to the others that they were harboring a monster more evil than they imagined, but his words fell upon deaf ears, and they were surely brought to Andreson, who enjoyed such complete and total power that they were only a greater form of amusement.

There had been the morning when he managed to escape en route to the brutal road work, the time when he had so nearly come upon Andreson, had nearly done what must be done.

Except that Andreson was in charge of a different kind of monster, a corps of men who had been specifically chosen for their inhumanity. And he had been stopped. Then had come the days in solitude.

The nights when he lay awake . . .

Waiting.

But toward the end, Andreson had, perhaps, begun to fear for his own future. Not that he feared death himself, but he was about to lose all that he had gained, lose his force of absolute power. He could feel it inside when Andreson lost his keen amusement in his subtle torture. And he knew, of course, that the end was coming. The only question was whether the Americans or the Russians would come first.

There may have been other places where the promise of damnation made other men relent, and want nothing more than to desert and run, leaving prisoners as they were.

But not here.

Not at this place.

Crowds were drawn to the firing ranges. Men worked night and day to dig ditches.

Crematoriums never ceased to burn . . .

His time was coming. He knew that he was in the lot to go the next day.

But then, a whisper arose in the camp. There had been an escape from the medical buildings, where the experiments were done.

The numbers to die the next day were increased. The guards, unnerved for some reason, were more brutal than ever, making sure their prisoners knew what their fates would be. Soon. So soon.

Yet other whispers abounded as well. Rumors.

There was a rumor that guards—well-trained, crack-shot guards—had been killed. And there was a rumor that Andreson had been wounded.

And that night . . .

They had formed a tight, close-knit group. It included men who had been incarcerated for their birth and their beliefs, Resistance fighters, and even a few so-called "madmen." They drew close that night, determining any chance of trying to overpower the guards, and, if they sacrificed their own lives, perhaps, allowing others to escape.

They were huddled in the dark, discussing what they knew of positions and weapons, when the first shots rang out.

They all leaped to their feet, listening.

Then they heard it. More rapid fire. The guards shouting, arguing . . .

A few screaming, as if the earth itself had come to life to gobble them up, bit by bit, blood, flesh, bone . . .

The door burst open.

It was dark within, while there were pools of light outside, blinding light. And all he could see was a silhouette at the door. An unbelievable silhouette. He cried out.

But a moment later, there was a man inside, and shackles and chains were being keyed and released.

Someone shouted that they had weapons, taken from the fallen guards.

He staggered out into the night. The place had gone mad.

Guards . . . bloodied, broken, littered the yard. Those who appeared now, streaking out into the night, shocked by the commotion, were quickly mowed down by those prisoners who had seized weapons . . . and who had the strength remaining to use them.

He found a new burst of power within himself. Quickly, they shouted to one another—some men carried on the task of freeing others, of going for the women and children. Others had taken up the fight to finish off their brutal captors.

He ran from building to building, remembering everything he had learned in the streets in what seemed like another world and another place. He used the buildings for a shield, learned that he could listen, and discern the footfalls of the guards. Learned that he could still use his weapon.

Building by building, inch by inch, a handful of ragtag men who were little more than walking skeletons began to find victory.

It was when he came to the medical buildings that he was taken by surprise. Backed against the doorway, crouched low, he was astounded when a hand—a hand more like an iron fist—descended on his shoulder.

He nearly cried out.

Nearly lost control, and let his automatic weapon pour fire into the night.

But then . . .

He knew.

Paul was so relieved that he sat on the floor, sobbing.

The clothing did not belong to Yvette. She was not the corpse that was so hideously disfigured that it could not be shown.

He was so happy that he hugged Monsieur François's leg. Monsieur François was overcome with relief, but he was impatient. He was angry. He had lost time at the café.

The police were kinder. They helped Paul to his feet. He was vaguely aware that the police were saying something about fingerprints and perhaps DNA, but since Yvette had worked at the café, they could, and would, make certain that the body was not hers. Paul already knew.

Those were not her things.

No, they were not.

The police drove them back to the village station. Monsieur François huffed and puffed and was nasty to everyone. He hurried back to his work, swearing that he had lost a lot of money. He left the station swearing that Paul himself should be questioned relentlessly— the police could not begin to imagine just how bad the quarrel with Yvette had been. Monsieur François made certain that the officers knew that Paul had threatened Yvette.

But perhaps the police felt sorry for such a pathetic fellow, tears streaming down his face. They did not detain Paul.

He came out of the police station and made it down the street. He felt weak. Very weak. He slipped to the curb, unable to stand.

As he sat there, shaking, he became aware that someone was standing before him. Someone tall. He shaded his eyes against the sun, and looked up, far up.

The man standing above him squatted down to his level and said, "Paul? I'm a friend. I mean to help you. And I need your help as well. We both want to find Yvette, right?"

He nodded, staring at the stranger.

"Come with me, Paul," the man said.

And Paul rose, amazed that he found new strength to do so.

He had seen the man before.

He was desperate to find Yvette.

There was nowhere else to turn, and . . .

There was something about the man.

He had a power.

And Paul believed.

CHAPTER 15

Tara had assumed that Brent would still be there, that he had just stepped outside to have a few minutes alone, that he wouldn't have left the house.

But he had.

Something else was incredibly disturbing. When she had first decided that he probably needed those moments alone, she had determined that showering and dressing and being prepared for the day were important things to do, and she had made a truly odd discovery.

Her feet were dirty. The bottoms looked as if she had been walking barefoot through dirt. There was a blade of grass stuck between her third and fourth toes on the left foot. An unease crept over her that felt like the wash of a tidal wave. She fought it down, assuring herself that there was a logical explanation somewhere. Perhaps there had been dirt on the balcony, blades of grass and dirt tossed high by the night breeze. She knew for a fact that she hadn't actually left the house, so that was the only possible explanation.

She was still trying to deal with logic, trying so hard that she refused to accept the fact that the dream had been a continuation. The nightmare had begun before she arrived here. Just as real. But she hadn't known then what she had been searching for, or what she had feared.

She still wasn't sure what she was looking for in the forest.

She knew why she was afraid.

She knew whose help she had been calling for . . .

And he hadn't been there, as he wasn't here now.

She bit her lip. So much for her feelings . . . for falling in love with a stranger she had met in a crypt. For believing, even now, that she had been waiting. For this point in her life, and . . .

For Brent.

Back downstairs, she went into the kitchen expecting to find him there. She drank the coffee Katia had prepared, but Katia hadn't seen Brent since she had spoken with him on the stairs; she assumed that he had left. Tara decided to look for him outside.

Eleanora had taken up a stance at the front door to the chateau. Tara wasn't certain that she still trusted the dog, but Eleanora was affectionate and sweet, though vigilant, licking Tara's hands, whining for attention. She didn't follow Tara to the door, but stayed where she was, sentinel at the door.

Tara looked for Brent outside, but couldn't find him. There were no extra cars in the drive. The newspaper lay where he had thrown it in the entryway. She picked it up and began reading about the police discovery of the headless body. Scanning to the bottom of the page, she was startled to see that the police were "looking for" Brent Malone for questioning in regard to the murder in the ruins, and their latest discovery.

"Brent, where the hell are you?" she muttered aloud. Determined, she walked to the stables, anxious to see if he had gone there. But there was no sign of him.

Old Daniel was out in the pasture. She called to him and he trotted slowly over to her. Again, she thought that the horse seemed agitated, eager for the soft, crooned words of assurance she gave to him.

"I feel it, too, old boy," she told the horse.

And she was suddenly angry. Now that she had given her trust to Brent Malone—careful trust, but trust at that—he had gone. She felt amazingly vulnerable, even by the light of day.

Giving Daniel a last pat, she went back into the house and looked in first on Jacques, and then Ann. Both were sleeping soundly and peacefully.

She came back downstairs for more coffee, wondering what she should do, deciding that she must do something, and then making a firm decision. She wasn't sure at all about "vampire rules," and she still couldn't quite force her logical mind to believe that any of it was true. If the myths and stories were at all true, vampires either had to sleep by day, or were at the very least much weaker then. They couldn't enter a house unless they were invited in. Garlic, holy water, and crosses were deterrents.

Katia seemed as willing to take care against uninvited supernatural guests as she was to make sure that their high-tech alarm system worked. Tara could safely leave the house. It was important that she find Brent. The police were saying that they wanted him for questioning.

She didn't believe it. They wanted him so that they could arrest him.

Tara prepared to go out to find Brent Malone. Calling last minute instructions to Katia to make absolutely certain that she didn't let anyone—anyone in at all—she threw open the front door.

To her amazement, she found Inspector Javet standing at the entrance to the house.

"Miss Adair, bonjour," Javet said.

Her heart sank.

"Good morning, monsieur." She stood firmly in the doorway, though she felt there was little she could do. He was the head of the police. "Can I help you?"

"Yes, I'm afraid you can. I'd like to see your grandfather."

"You can't see him now, he's sleeping, and he had a very rough night."

"I'm sorry to hear that. Why was his night so rough?" Javet inquired.

"Because he's old, and has been ill, and he sometimes has a bad time, Inspector. That should be fairly simple to acknowledge."

Javet nodded slowly, and told her very softly. "You know, Miss Adair, it's ridiculous for you to stand there so defensively. I only wish to question Jacques."

"You should be questioning Professor Dubois."

"Yes, I'd like to have seen more of the man. However, he seems to have disappeared."

"Dubois has disappeared?"

"Yes, Miss Adair, that's what I just said."

"I'm sorry."

"Do you think we'll be finding the good professor—minus his head, Miss Adair?"

"I have no idea, Inspector."

"All right, Miss Adair. Perhaps if I were to come in, you could offer me some coffee, and in a bit, your grandfather might be awake."

Tara stood there staring at Javet, feeling wary. Far too wary to let anyone in, not when she could help it.

"I'm sorry. I was on my way out."

"There are legal steps I can take to speak with Jacques, you know," he reminded her.

"Then I'm afraid you're going to have to take them. I have to go out, and I'm not letting anyone to see my grandfather while I'm gone."

"All right, Miss Adair," Javet said, and turning, he started to his car. But then he turned back. "You should trust me. I don't intend to hurt Jacques."

"I don't trust anyone, Inspector."

"I hope that's true. I hope that you're not leaving the house hoping to find your new friend, Mr. Malone."

"Inspector Javet, I'm leaving because I have errands to run."

"You know, Miss Adair, I wanted very badly to trust Brent Malone as well. Such an intelligent man, well-read, such a fine face—and even his French is excellent." He hesitated on that, as if considering the fact that a man who had been taught English as his first language managed to speak such excellent French. "But no matter what techniques we have used, no matter how we have tried, we can find no proof that anyone else was in that tomb at the time of Jean-Luc's death. And now . . . so many young people disappearing, and another corpse found—minus the head once again— I'm afraid that it's difficult to clear Mr. Malone."

"I barely know Mr. Malone," she said evenly, meeting his eyes without blinking.

"You should bring me in on everything that's going

on here, and trust in me, Miss Adair," Javet said softly. He looked at her a long moment, then shrugged. "I will be back, you know, with the legal papers necessary. It may all be much more difficult for Jacques then."

"You haven't a thing on my grandfather, Inspector Javet," she said firmly. "He has done nothing, nothing at all."

He was still watching her. She turned and locked the door to the house, facing him.

"I really won't let you in to see my grandfather," she told him firmly, but she realized that there was a note in her voice that begged him to understand.

"All I want to do is help you," Javet said.

"Find the real killer."

"I can't find the killer if I can't get closer."

"I'm sorry." Looking past Javet, as she spoke Tara was certain that she had seen the area around the house change. If it weren't for the fantastic theories plaguing her, she would have thought that the sun had just gone behind a cloud, that the light had faded just a bit.

But as she stood on the steps with Javet, she found herself beginning to believe everything that had been said to her, that there were supernatural forces in the world, and they were coming down upon Château DeVant, like a flock of black-winged crows.

"Excuse me, will you?" she murmured. She stepped past Javet, walking toward the stables. She entered, and looked around and saw that nothing was unusual. Javet had followed her, she realized.

"What is it?" he asked.

She shook her head. "Nothing. Just shadows on the sun."

She still felt the unease. But look as she might, there was nothing in the stables.

She walked back out into the muted sunlight, again followed by Javet.

"I'm here to help you," he repeated again.

She stretched out a hand to him, smiled, and said, "Thank you, really. But there's nothing that I can tell you, nothing I can help you with right now. And I have errands to run."

"I will find Malone," he told her.

"You are an officer of the law. You must do what you feel you must."

"And I will speak with your grandfather."

"Then you must get the proper papers, because as I told you, he is old and ill, and I will not willingly let you in."

Javet sighed, shaking his head. At last he started for his car.

Tara did the same.

She waited for him to turn on his ignition, and start down the drive before gunning her own motor and following him out to the road.

As she drove, she tried to tell herself that Brent must have read the entire article. He would know that the police were looking for him, that they were after him. He wouldn't be walking around the village or sitting casually at the café. As she drove, she felt the same sense of a deepening dread that had seized her before.

It was real. What they were saying was real.

Her dream . . .

Was somehow real. She had never really left the chateau . . .

And yet, she was certain that the place she had gone to was out there, somewhere.

Somewhere near.

*   *   *

Sleep . . . deep sleep was so wonderful. Ann felt the comfort of her bed, and the sweetness of real rest. But even as she lay, certain that sleep without dreams was wonderful and healing, she felt the incursion into her realm of soft floating clouds and security.

Her eye movement was rapid, and though she couldn't wake up, she was aware that she remained in a nether region. And she was equally aware that it had been entered.

Ann . . .

She heard her name, and he was calling to her.

Ann . . . you know that you are mine.

Her mind fought the words whispered so tersely within it.

You are mine, and you will let me in. You will open the doors for me, and I will be with you. You know that's what you want, what you crave, what you need.

No . . .

Shadows filled her sleep. Great sweeping wings, like those of a giant blackbird, hovering over her, folding around her. Encasing her . . .

There was a staggering heat within the caress of shadows. She twisted and turned, and knew that she was surrounded.

No . . .

It occurred to Paul that he was making a serious mistake, trusting in a stranger. He might well be following the same path that Yvette had taken, and yet, it was all that he could do. He loved Yvette. Loved her more than he did himself, more than his own life, no matter how callously she had played with his feelings.

And so he went with the man, and he found himself answering questions, talking about those men Yvette met at the café.

"She is not a bad girl," he said, defensive lest anyone think that she should deserve a sad fate due to her promiscuity. "You must understand, there are many who live here who travel into Paris to work, there are families here, so many who have come since the city is so large, and space so very dear. But there are those who have been born here as well, and those who wish to escape, and maybe they haven't the education for a fine job in Paris, and they have known so little other than the countryside, and the growing fields and the livestock, and they . . . they simply want more. That is Yvette, she wants to fly above our little village, and she hasn't the wings to do so, and so . . . and so . . ."

The man was looking at him, watching him, and he couldn't tell if a small smile curved the fellow's lips, if he was amused, or if he was merely understanding what Paul was trying to say.

"Yvette has sought to fly by catching on to the coattails of others . . . of other men," he said, finishing lamely.

A hand fell gently on his arm.

"We will find Yvette," he was told softly.

They kept driving. Very far. Paul had grown up here, run in the fields as a child, sought out every little place of mystery, but he was unfamiliar with the trails that they traveled through now. The car drove over grass and roots, and circled through trees and more.

At last they came to a halt.

They entered what must have once been a place of riches and great charm. Still, a certain alluring ambience remained. Darkness and shadow, however, seemed to abound, as if the inhabitants shunned daylight and the sun.

"Come, Paul, we need to know what you know. Everything there is to know about your Yvette, and her . . . friends."

At the doorway, he felt a strange hesitance. Then he entered within. And he met those waiting to greet him.

Tara drove to the village. Though she didn't expect to see Brent, she parked near the café, found a table, and ordered café au lait.

She picked up another newspaper, and spread it before her. She wasn't really reading; she was trying to appear as if she was not watching everything that was going on around her.

But there wasn't much going on.

The café was quiet. The waiters were whispering among themselves, and when she ordered her second cup, the man who served her spilled some of the hot liquid. He apologized, and she quickly assured him it was nothing. When he smiled ruefully, she wondered if she couldn't get him to talk.

"I've noticed . . . you all seem a bit distant today," she said, encouraging him to talk.

He was about twenty-five, slim, with something of a buzz cut that was becoming to him, since he had a fine face and deep, dark eyes.

He hesitated, then indicated her newspaper. "Such things simply don't happen here." He leaned closer, mopping up the spilled coffee. "One of our girls has disappeared now. Monsieur François, the owner, went into the morgue in the city to identify the corpse, but it isn't Yvette. At least, she is not the body that was discovered. But . . . we are a small village. It's unnerving to have people disappear, to have bodies found. It was one thing when it was the man at the dig. We could all believe that he was killed because someone wanted the riches from the corpse. But now . . . there are others who are gone—and there is the one corpse that has been discovered. We have not seen this kind of trouble here in . . . in hundreds of years! So naturally, we are afraid. But," he added quickly, "you don't need to be afraid here. We are at the café, on the street, in broad daylight, and the police station is right down the street."

He was trying to reassure her after saying far more than anyone dependent upon tourist francs should have said. But he hadn't frightened Tara, certainly not any more than she was already. He had, however, said something she was anxious to pursue.

"You've not had this kind of trouble—in hundreds of years?"

"Well, there is a lot of legend here, you know. Back in the days of the Sun King, there were all manner of things going on. I'm not a great student of history, so I'm not all that up on the particular events that occurred. But of course, you know, the body that was stolen from the dig was that of Louisa de Montcrasset. She was a mistress of Louis. She had the king wrapped around her little finger, so they say, and she was able to practice great atrocities because the king was so infatuated that he refused to believe ill of her. They say, though, that she kidnapped poor young people—men and women, she was not particular—and used them in strange rites. She bathed in blood, drank blood, lived in blood, so they say, in the belief that it would help keep her young and desirable forever, and add to her amazing hypnotism over others. But at one point, the king could no longer be fooled, but he would not allow her to be humiliated before the people. She was the daughter of a great knight who had fought long and hard for France, and also, no matter what she had done, the king could not completely rid himself of his love for her. He refused to see her, however, after proof was brought against her. Proof of her misdeeds, as well as proof that she had been cuckolding the king with another man. He was not so protective of her lover— it's said that he ordered his men to burst in upon the fellow, stab him to death in his bed, and have his body cut to pieces and cast into the Seine. The king was helped in all these discoveries, forced to see the evil and death perpetrated on the people, by a strange sect composed of a group of religious men who had gathered together for the sole purpose of bringing down Louisa and her evil companion. But even at the end, the king would not agree to Louisa coming before the public, or having her beauty destroyed. By his command, she was buried and sealed into her coffin, and then the terror that had raged in Paris and the village came to an end."

"I've heard the legend of Louisa de Montcrasset," Tara said, "but I hadn't heard that she'd had a lover other than the king, or that he had been killed when she was buried."

"You won't find any of it in the history books," the young man told her. "It is all local legend—but of course, we know that it's mainly true, since her coffin was discovered. Or, should I say, at least it's true that she existed. If, indeed, she was the corpse in the tomb. Hard to be certain, now that she has disappeared."

"Ah, well," Tara murmured.

"Would you like another coffee?" the young man asked.

"No, no, thank you," she said. "Just the check, please."

He brought the check, and she put the appropriate number of francs on the tray. As she did so, she felt a presence near her, and she looked up.

"Miss Adair, how are you?"

Inspector Trusseau was standing there. She definitely didn't want to get into a conversation with him. She had gained nothing at the café, and it suddenly occurred to her that there was something she should be doing— something practical.

She should get Jacques out of the house.

"Inspector, hello, how are you?" she said, standing quickly.

"Well, thank you. And you?"

"Quite well."

She stood there for a moment, feeling awkward as she stared at him.

"I believe we'll be visiting you quite soon," Trusseau said. He was a smooth, tall, and attractive man. He didn't fit the mold of a forensics expert, but then again, perhaps he was excellent at his work. He had a handsome appearance and apparently the social graces that might get him what he wanted when brash authority might fail.

"Yes, I understand Inspector Javet wants to speak with my grandfather."

Trusseau nodded. "I'm afraid Javet is convinced that your grandfather knows something about the murder in the crypt."

"Um—and do you think that my very aged grandfather can also be guilty of decapitating a body and leaving it in the river to be discovered?"

"Miss Adair, I've read about your grandfather for years. I don't believe he's guilty of anything at all. But then . . . I am not Javet. Of course, I mean to see that Monsieur DeVant is not grilled too rigorously. I am aware that he is an old and failing man."

"Well, then, I'm glad to hear that you will make the session as gentle as possible," she murmured, anxious then only to leave, find a hotel room, and get her grandfather out of the house.

"Yes, of course, you'll be glad that I accompany Javet?"

"Naturally."

Trusseau smiled. "I shall see you soon, then, Miss Adair, at the chateau."

"Certainly," she murmured. "I'm afraid I have some errands to run."

"Excuse me, I didn't mean to delay you. It's a pleasure to see you."

"And you, of course. Au revoir."

Tara hurried to her car. She dug in her purse for her cell phone as she drove, cursing as the phone rang and rang.

Louisa slept restlessly, waking fitfully when she should have been calm and in a deep state of relaxation, gathering strength. She needed this time.

"What is it, my love?" he asked her. He never left her for long. He was up against those whose minds he could not touch, and he trusted no one. There were things, of course, which he must do during the day, but he returned to her, always.

She turned to him, sighing as she found some comfort in his embrace. "It is . . . this place."

"This place is safe," he told her firmly.

"Ah, but there is so much else in the world, in Paris, I want to live!"

"In time."

"In time . . . you forget who I am."

"And you forget that the world is large, and dangerous."

"I have the power to take charge of the world around me," she said, her tone both imperious and petulant.

"In time," he repeated. "When those who would fight us are removed."

She drew back. "You should have destroyed them long ago."

"Louisa, I could not. I dared not create a disturbance before you had awakened. There are many forces out there today that you do not understand."

"More powerful than a king?" she said, insinuating that he was weak.

He sighed. "The population is far more vast today than you remember."

"Vast—and stupid."

"Many are ignorant, but not stupid."

"I'm hungry."

"Very soon, you will feast on our enemies, and then you will have the strength you seek, and the freedom you so long to have."

"I'm hungry," she repeated.

"I will find you prey."

"You said that you would bring me prey before."

"The time wasn't right."

"No, you weren't strong enough to lure her here.

Either that, or . . . you have a greater interest in the girl than you pretend."

"There is not, nor has there ever been, anyone but you. There were years while I pined, hating what you did, who you were."

She laughed softly. "You never pined, mon cher. You have always taken your amusements where you would."

"While I waited," he said softly.

She reached for him. Elegant perfection, sheer carnality. There seemed no reason not to indulge. And yet, at the end, when she had driven him to distraction, she whispered against his ear, "Tonight. I want her here tonight. And I want it finished. And if you will not, or can not, bring her, then I will see to it all myself."

"I will bring her!" he roared in return, and then she gave in to him, and far above them, the fire roared to life in the old hearth, and in their maddened embrace, they were consumed.

"You have to tell us everything, everything that you can," the tall man informed Paul.

He had been taken to an elegant apartment in the city and given wine to drink, offered food, which, of course, he was far too nervous to eat.

"There are so many men at the café. And I do not spend my days there, watching her. I wish I could, but a farmer's life is not an easy one," Paul said. He looked longingly at the door, wishing he had not come so easily.

"Think, tell us about them."

"Well, there are the officers from the police station, of course," Paul said. "There have been students, but she seldom agrees to meet them . . . she prefers to see men with . . . with . . ."

"Money?" the second man suggested softly.

Paul hung his head. "Yes, of course. Those who can buy her presents."

"So, have you seen anyone at the café who appears to be affluent?"

Paul stared at the man speaking to him, then pointed nervously. "You have been at the café. You . . . are supposed to be a laborer. But you look as if you have money."

"She did not go with me."

Paul frowned. "There . . . has been someone else. I have seen him frequently. He is tall, a blond man, well built . . . I am not sure what he does. Perhaps I have seen him at the police station. But everyone has been at the station, frightened, asking the police what they are doing . . . you know."

"A tall blond?" The dark haired man looked at the lighter one. "Do you know him?"

"Perhaps," the second man said. "Perhaps . . ."

"Paul, can we get you water, more wine, coffee?" the woman asked.

"I think I should go."

"No, no, you must stay," she informed him softly.

He was afraid.

Tara reached the chateau as quickly as she was able. She came running through the front door, calling for Katia.

Katia just stared at her when she said that they must pack up a few things, and go to a hotel.

"They are coming with the correct papers to insist on entry and question Jacques!" she told Katia.

By then, however, Jacques had come out of his library. "So—they will come and question me!" he told her.

"You haven't listened to me at all, Grandpapa," Tara said. "They think you had something to do with the murders. And if you tell the police that there are vampires out there . . . well, they'll . . . they might . . ."

"They will try to lock me up with the insane?" Jacques said.

"Yes!"

"No, no, you mustn't worry, Tara. They will come, and they will talk to me, and I will not mention the Alliance, or vampires, and I will make them understand that I have not hired any contract killers. And since I did not, they will have no proof against me, and they will not be able to do anything."

"But, Jacques, listen to me. Be rational. We will simply go and spend a few days at a hotel, and we will be safe."

He shook his head, and she was tempted to scream at him that he was a stubborn old man. "Tara, my books are in this house. We are secure here. Katia has seen to that."

"Grandpapa—"

"Tara, I will not go," he said with a soft insistence that was absolutely final. "Katia, we'll see to it that the windows and doors are truly sealed, n'est-ce pas?"

"Mais oui," Katia assured her.

"Grandpapa, the police are not afraid of garlic," she told him.

He shrugged. "And some vampires actually enjoy it, but they are usually the Italians," he told her, smiling. "Tara, I am joking here, please smile for me, laugh a little."

"Laugh?"

"I have such an arsenal here! Stakes, crosses, so many crosses! Holy water."

"Right. And the Italian vampires won't mind the garlic, and perhaps, if they are Hindu, Muslim, or Jewish, they will not mind the holy water in the least!"

"Ah, there, at last, a sense of humor!" Jacques said.

"You're missing the point, Jacques. The police are coming!"

"Then let them come. And you, young lady, you should get some rest. Look at you! You are drawn, haggard, there are huge shadows beneath your eyes. Quite frankly, my dear child, you look like hell!"

Tara frowned. "There's nothing wrong with me."

"You're overtired, and don't know it. Ann is still sleeping."

"Ann is still sleeping?"

"Yes, and I am fine, and you should rest."

"I'll check on Ann," she said, then stared from Jacques to Katia. "Both of you, pay attention to me now, because if you don't . . . if you don't, I'll throttle you both. If the police come, you must get me before you even open the door. Do you understand?"

Jacques sighed, dismayed that she was behaving as if he were a child. But he said, "Naturally, Tara, I promise that we will get you before we open the door. Now, I am working. I can't make you rest, Tara, but it's important that you keep up with your sleep, and be alert and aware."

"I'll see to Ann," was the only commitment she would make.

He shrugged, and headed back to the library.

Katia looked at her, grimaced, and asked, "Would you like some warm milk?"

"No!" she said sharply, then quickly added, "No, no,

thank you." Katia headed for the kitchen. Tara started for the steps, anxious to check on Ann.

Her cousin was still sleeping soundly. She appeared somewhat ashen, but her breathing was deep, and restful.

The balcony doors were closed, and garlic remained around them.

Tara closed her door, frustrated, and went to her own room.

Her easel drew her. She looked at the sketches she had been making, and started another, not sure what she was drawing, then realizing that she was shading in a man's face. She had sketched him before, and now, with some light and shadow added, he was beginning to appear very real. She knew why she was drawing him. She was coming to know him far too well.

Yawning, she suddenly set her pencil down. She was tired. She decided that Jacques was right, and perhaps she had some time before Javet and Trusseau actually arrived. She stretched out on the bed. Her eyes closed, and before she knew it, she was drifting.

She was there again . . .

The place in the woods. Deep, deep woods. This time, as she walked, her footsteps were being followed. She could hear the movement against the ground, a fraction of a second behind the sound of her own feet against the earth. She would stop and turn back, time and time again, and there would be nothing but the shadows, still shadows that swooped like wings, that seemed to have a whisper within them. Shadows that constantly darkened and changed.

She looked forward, knowing that the old house was ahead. She kept walking. Once again, she heard that hint of sound, a whisper of movement. She stopped, but she didn't turn around. The danger was there. She could it feel like hot breath against her neck. A warning. It was close, so close, as close as the shadows that seemed ahead of her as much as they were behind her.

She ran toward the door. She nearly reached it when she heard the whisper take form.

Almost here, you are almost here, I have told you, I have her, and I will have her, *come, yes, come toward the door, come to me, I am waiting* . . .

The shadow was lengthening, widening. In seconds, it would be all-encompassing; she would be engulfed . . .

Wake, wake, wake up! she told herself in the midst of her dream.

She hadn't screamed; she hadn't moved. Her eyes were wide, unfocused. She blinked, and bolted upright.

Ann.

Tara leaped out of bed, and went racing to Ann's room. She was insane, she told herself, her heart thundering. She was simply insane. Ann was sleeping. The balcony doors were closed, and covered with garlic, she had checked them herself.

She threw the door open with a vengeance.

It nearly flew back at her. There was a strong, chill breeze rushing through the open balcony doors.

The garlic had been tossed into a corner of the room.

Tara forced the door open again and stepped in, anxiously looking to where Ann should be sleeping in the bed.

Her cousin was there.

And so was a man.

Tall, blond.

Bent over her cousin, touching her . . .

He was so close to her, fingers brushing aside the

tangle of dark hair around Ann's face. Stroking her throat. Lips nearly against her cousin's flesh.

"No!" Tara shrieked.

He straightened, looking at her. She knew him. She'd seen him before.

"No!" she shouted again, and went flying across the room, pulling at the large, ornate cross Jacques had insisted she wear, not ripping it from her neck, but twisting it to use as a weapon.

"No! No! No!"

She threw herself against his form. It was like hitting steel. It didn't matter. She curled her fingers around the cross.

Fingers curled around hers with a brutal strength, and the man began to swear.

"I will kill you!" she vowed desperately. She found that her own teeth were baring; she meant it. No matter what his strength or his power, she would not let him harm Ann.

She felt an incredible rise of power and strength, and believed that she could kill him—because she had to. She had heard that faced with impossible situations, parents could save children, siblings could rescue one another, lift cars, break down massive doors, and do all kinds of amazing deeds, because of adrenaline brought on by sheer desperation. She was desperate to save her cousin. She would break free. She managed to jerk a hand from his hold and lift the cross high, ready to bring it down against his face, his eyes. If she hadn't the power to really down him, she hoped, at the least, to wound him, blind him, hurt him badly enough so that she could begin a new offense with him at a disadvantage.

"Tara!"

At first, she was barely aware of her name being called. "Tara!"

It might have been coming from elsewhere, a voice in her mind, from far away, but a voice calling out to her, louder as she struggled.

"Help!" The word escaped her lips.

"Tara!"

It was Brent. It was as if he had been far, far away. As if, perhaps, he had heard her from a distance, had sensed that she was in trouble.

He wasn't far away. He was there now, in the doorway.

"Brent! Thank God, help me!"

She was shaking, caught in a deadly game of wrestling, in which, still, amazingly, she was managing to hold her own, yet . . .

Weakening.

"Brent, *help me!*"

He came striding into the room, steps long and sure and determined. She thanked God. He had come to help her, she wouldn't have to try to bring down this deadly giant of a monster alone.

"*Tara!*" The word, her name, was harsh. It seemed to scratch down the length of her flesh.

Then . . .

He had *her.*

He ripped her from the tall blond man, held her in an iron grasp.

A grasp she couldn't break.

"No!" she screamed.

His arms seemed to squeeze tighter. She couldn't see, for shadows seemed to burst before her eyes. She couldn't breathe, she could only hear the thunder of her heart, slowing . . .

Tara . . .

It was as if she heard his voice, a deadly whisper at her nape.

And she knew . . .

He hadn't come to help her. To save her life.

He had come to kill her.

CHAPTER 16

They had brought Paul to a wonderful hotel room. The furniture was old, but grand. They had left him with everything that he could desire—coffee, wine, fruit, cheese, bread, crackers.

The men had left. The woman remained.

She was in the other room, her attention riveted on a computer. What she was doing, he didn't know, but it seemed very important to her that she find whatever it was. She was beautiful, and very kind to him, checking on him now and then.

At first, the novelty of the hotel suite kept him fascinated. He had walked around and around, running his hands over the polished wood furniture, sitting on the plump sofa, rising, sitting again. He adjusted pillows, picked at the fruit, enjoyed a glass of wine. He liked playing with the remote control and the television, but as time wore on, he grew restless. He walked over to the balcony, opening the windows, and looking out at the streets below. It was a wonderful view. He had never really seen the landscape this way. He saw it from working the land most of the time. But here, where the hotel sat on a little hill, the view encompassed much of the countryside, in many shades and colors. Those colors changed as the afternoon waned, and he was fascinated by each subtle variation in tone. It was all very beautiful.

The woman came out briefly to smile, say hello, and make sure he was all right. Or perhaps she was making sure he was still there.

He smiled in return, and told her that the wine was very good.

At last, he tired of wandering and watching the view. He even tired of playing with the television and the remote control. There was no show on that could hold his attention.

He couldn't help thinking about Yvette.

He wondered why he loved her. But he did, and he had, forever and ever, so it seemed. He was the one who had been there for her, so many times. Through the years, there were times when he had been angry and indignant, but she had told him over and over again that she was a free spirit, and would not be tied down, and if he was going to try to hold on to her, like a giant brick around her neck, she simply wouldn't talk to him at all. And they wouldn't be friends. And there wouldn't be those times when she had no other great interest in life, and spent hours with him, doing things that all but made him stop breathing, that escalated life to such wild fields of pleasure that it made the agony of her constant betrayals all the more complete. But still, all in all, in the end, he believed that she would tire of her hunt for adventure and riches. She would remember the times that he had been there for her, rock hard and steady, always waiting. Always. No matter how she turned from him. He had always thought that he would be there for her under any circumstances. He had fantasized about occasions when she had been in trouble, when he had stepped in, swung a practiced right hook at some abusive fellow, and become her hero.

And now . . .

She hadn't been the headless corpse at the morgue, he reminded himself.

There was hope.

He lay upon the sofa, legs sprawled over the elegantly carved end of it, and let the remote control fall to the floor. He listened with half attention to the sports channel that was on, but found himself drifting off as he did so. He dreamed about Yvette. He should have been so much angrier with her. She had certainly emasculated him frequently enough, not with her words, but with a look. Why, why, did she have to run around with other men? Money did not mean so much in life. The way she looked at him with her beautiful eyes, so pityingly . . .

No one would ever love her the way he did.

As he drifted, she came into his dreams. Yvette. So pretty. She was in one of her playful moods, and a sensuous mood, strolling toward him slowly, hips swaying, shoulders somewhat back. There was that look in her eyes that he hadn't seen very often . . . not in the last many months, at least. A look that was all for him, that said she wanted him.

Paul, silly boy, there you are. Such a silly squabble we had. I need you now, you know. I know I've been bad, but you've forgiven me so many times. You're the one I really want, the one I've always wanted in the end. And you know, Paul, I want you now . . .

I want you now . . .

It was such an incredible dream. She was swathed in some gossamer stuff that seemed to lift and swirl around her as she walked. He knew that beneath it, she was naked. There were hints of flesh to be seen, hints of color at her breasts, shadows at the juncture of her thighs. His mouth went dry as he traveled through the dream, a silly grin on his face, he was certain. He shouldn't smile so. He should be like so many of her other lovers. Suave. Sophisticated. Lying back, waiting, musing, assessing, making her play out the full game, tease and taunt as if she was desperate for once . . .

For him.

It was a dream, of course, which made it far easier not to move. And it was strange. The closer she came to him, the more he felt certain that it was Yvette. Really Yvette. She was in trouble somewhere, and she was reaching out to him. The words formed in his mind.

Yes, Yvette, I love you, I'll save you, I'll come . . .

As she moved, ever closer, that gossamer fabric flaring around her as if it were caught in a strange wind tunnel within the hotel room, he felt the strangest uncertainty. It was Yvette, yes . . . Yvette, yet she was different. At times, there would be flashes of something else, and he would think, *that isn't really her face. It isn't really Yvette's face, and yet . . .*

Paul, I need you.

Where are you?

Silly boy, come closer, closer. I need you, open your arms to me, Paul, help me, Paul, save me, Paul, let me love you, ask me to love you. I am close, and afraid. Can you really forgive me, Paul, can you welcome me to you?

He wasn't sure if there was a sudden burst of wind at

the windows, or if he had left them open, and imagined the chill gust of wind.

Perhaps not.

I'm cold, Paul, so cold . . .

So, yes, my love, come, and I will warm you.

Greet me here, I can come no farther. Come, Paul, please, I need your arms around me now, I need your warmth.

She was so near. He was sleeping, he thought, and it was a divine dream. He saw some ethereal part of himself rise to meet her. She was there, framed in the falling dusk, that shimmering fabric still all around her.

Come, Paul.

The breeze swept away the slender threads of material. Yvette, his Yvette, yes, she was there, she had come to him, because she had been lost and afraid and lonely, and now she knew what was to be found in his arms.

He hesitated suddenly, coming forward. Because he had that strange feeling again. Yvette, and not Yvette. A flash of something now and then that was so confusing. The face, in certain fractured sections of time, seemed to be that of someone . . .

She was real. Flesh and blood and real. He could see the pulse beating at her throat. He could even see the moisture as she wet her lips. She was cold, she did need him, her breasts were swollen, the nipples hard. He started to reach for her.

He blinked, wondering how she could be so very real in a dream. How he himself could be standing where he was, and feel the floor beneath his feet, when he was sleeping on the couch. Of course, it was a dream. The balcony was high above the ground. But she was here. And real, real, real . . .

He stretched out his hand.

He touched her flesh . . .

He trembled because he could feel her. He could pull her to him, bury himself against her, smell her, taste her, drown in the woman he loved, such an expert, so much more experienced than he, and though he resented it at times, she was such a lover that he felt time and time, he could die in her arms.

Yvette, oh, Lord, Yvette . . .

Paul . . .

The draperies began to blow in the breeze, surrounding her, wrapping around them both. His trembling fingers reached for her, through the line of the balcony doors. His hands came around her waist. He began to pull her to him.

"Paul!"

It was the woman. Her shout was loud, anxious, warning.

He turned, a sudden anger filling him. Here was Yvette, naked and waiting and wanting him, and she was interrupting. His dream would fade, his beautiful love would vanish.

"Paul, get back! Quickly!" she commanded.

"Too late!" Yvette called to her.

He turned back to Yvette. Yes, of course, this interloper didn't matter. He had only to hold more tightly to Yvette.

"Come in, come in, come to me, Yvette!" he cried.

He heard a throaty laugh.

And then he saw her face. Really saw her face.

And he began to scream.

"One of these . . . one of these . . . right here, in this area," Jacques explained to Lucian. They were poring over the map of the area that lay on the desk. Jacques had X's marked in various places. "It's so hard to remember now where everything lay . . . it was an occupation, of course, and so much of the city survived, yet here, in the countryside, so many places were abandoned after the war . . . left to rot and ruin. And so many men didn't come back. Families left, never to return. The chateau survived, of course, and here is the Dupré house, which still stands as it was . . . there is a new development here, but as you moved into the country farther and farther here to the outskirts . . . there was some heavy fighting, and much was lost, and to this day, the ruins remain. And many of the places were hundreds of years old. If only I had followed more closely at the end . . . but you see, I was ill then. By the time it was all over, really over, I was in such a fevered state that I wound up in the hospital, I was in a coma, I met my wife . . . and I moved to America. There were years when I couldn't come back, and with the illness, there were so many years when I believed that everything in my life, the war, the camp, and anything else that occurred, had been a nightmare. So now . . ."

Lucian laid a hand on his shoulder. "You've remembered everything when it has mattered," he told Jacques.

"No, no," Jacques said unhappily. "There are many more dead now . . . many more dead. I wasn't ready when I should have been. The old Alliance . . ."

"The old Alliance faded years before your time, Jacques," Lucian said. "You've done well. Look, we have been here, here, and here. And you are right—it is somewhere here. When there is a disturbance, I know it. And there are times when I need nothing more than concentration, and I can reach out and know exactly where someone is . . . I can enter their thoughts, bring them right to me. But Louisa isn't alone—and she isn't even the real danger. She is with someone who knows that I am still alive, and very aware. Very old, and powerful, and they are able to block a great deal. I have been able to follow Louisa, but I seem to get where she has been once she has left. She rose alone, uncertain, and traced her old paths first. Though she came into a new world, she went first to what she had known in the past. I believe she traveled first to the Louvre, and from there, she went out to Versailles. She was on her own, but not for long. She was back here . . ." he pointed to the map, "and here. And I know now that their lair is in this area, where you have shown me the places that can be found in the overgrown forest areas. We have gone over much of it, and still, there has to be something that we haven't discovered. You have done more than you can imagine, but we must find them quickly now, before she grows more powerful, like her mentor, because then, between them, they will have tremendous strength."

Jacques stared at Lucian and let out a breath, his shoulders slumping. "I was just thinking of the old days. There was a time . . ."

"A time when we would not have stood together so," Lucian said flatly. "But that was before. When the world was different. And there was a time, of course, when it was the disputes among my own that were brought before me, and when my kind were only handled by the old rules when they were so besotted with their power that they endangered us all. But that was the old world, and this is the new, and survival has become even more difficult. War is open, and sides have been drawn. And so, Monsieur DeVant, we are together in this, as we were when we met."

"We are all strange bedfellows," Jacques said.

"Live long enough, and the world is strange indeed," Lucian agreed.

"The full moon is coming too soon," Jacques said glumly.

"Yes, but of course . . . that gives us distinct advantages as well."

"It's almost night," Jacques said.

"It is night," Lucian said. "Night again."

He frowned, stiffening.

"What is it?" Jacques asked anxiously.

"Something is wrong."

"Here?"

Lucian shook his head. "No, there is something very wrong . . . with my wife." He turned, long strides taking him to the door. "Tell Brent . . . never mind. Brent will know. Stay tight, stay in the house, let no one in—"

"I know this, of course," Jacques said somewhat impatiently.

But it didn't matter.

Lucian was gone. He had been there, and then he was gone. Jacques wasn't sure how he had left. He had blinked, and the man was gone. He sighed softly.

And it was then that the screams began to tear through the chateau.

"Tara, calm down, stop it!"

The serious shake that she received, and the fact that she couldn't breathe, caused Tara to pause in her struggle, gasp desperately for breath, and meet Brent's eyes, her own laced with hatred and determination.

"It's Rick, Rick Beaudreaux," he said.

As if that should mean something to her!

"My cousin—"

"He is one of us, one of us, Tara!"

She looked from Brent, who still held her in an iron clasp, to the other man. He was still breathing heavily, looking at her, wiping at the wounds she had inflicted on his face. He offered a grim smile. "I'm sorry we haven't met. Really sorry." He cast Brent something of a reproachful stare. "But you were suspicious. You didn't want to believe. And someone needed to watch your cousin. And it was rather amazing when I met her . . . I swear to you, I would guard her with my life . . . my life as it is. I have been guarding her."

Tara stared at him, still speechless, feeling as if her mind had been completely numbed, encased in ice, frozen to the core.

"Why isn't she waking then?" Tara demanded, "She is there, still sleeping, she is there . . . almost as if she were . . . dead."

She hadn't realized until that moment that Brent had let her go. She stepped back, rubbing her lower arm where it still hurt from the force of his hold. She looked from Ann, still an inert form on the bed, to the blond giant introduced as Rick, and on to Brent.

"Someone else has been to her," Brent said.

"What are you talking about, someone else?" Tara asked angrily.

Rick started for the bed. Tara flew to it, standing between him and her cousin. "Don't touch her! Don't you dare touch her!"

Rick paused, ignoring Tara's fierce hold on his arm. He pulled back the covers and shifted Ann's hair. "The marks, see the marks, Tara. I believe it must have begun some time ago. It was begun slowly and carefully. But someone else has gotten to Ann."

Tara saw the marks on her cousin's neck. So tiny . . .

and yet there. She felt as if she were crumbling within. As if she were in a nightmare, and it was real, and there was no waking, and no escaping.

"Then Ann is . . . dead?" she whispered. "Dead, gone . . . lost?"

"No, not necessarily," Brent said.

"We have to see that they don't get to her again," Rick Beaudreaux said. He looked at Brent.

"Go on," Brent told him, watching Tara. "She's seen so much, suspected so much . . . and still she doesn't want to believe anything I say."

Tara answered that by going to the balcony doors and closing them. She arranged the garlic around them again. She went to Ann's bedside, fighting tears, assuring herself that her cousin was breathing, that her heart continued to beat.

"She's ill, isn't she?" Tara asked.

"If she doesn't come to soon, she will need a hospital, a transfusion," Brent said. "And we have to keep her safe and—here. And away from the force that has taken her, and certainly has some control over her now."

"There are different ways that vampires kill," Rick said. "They feast—and usually destroy the remains."

"Decapitate their victims?" Tara said.

"Yes," Brent said.

"What about the old stake in the heart?" Tara demanded harshly.

"Good, but decapitation is better. It's the only way to be certain."

"I don't understand this. How did you get here?" she asked Rick.

"Ann let me in."

"Ann has been sleeping."

"She let me in—as she slept."

"I don't understand—"

"Obviously, Rick is a vampire," Brent said.

Tara felt again as if black clouds were surrounding her, as if the world had become surreal, it was all a dream again, but she couldn't wake.

"Then we need to destroy him, don't we?" she asked harshly.

"Real world 101," Brent said impatiently. "There are forces out there, have always been, will always be. There are those who are fighting for a realm of normalcy, for life for all, for peace if you will, for all good things. And there are forces out there where power is sought by some, where needs and selfish gains outweigh all else. Once, and actually still, always, in some place, for some reason, battles are waged. Long ago, tribes fought for space. In the Dark Ages, tribes were constantly shifting and moving. Death and destruction were the general way of life. And later, when the civilized world encroached, warfare generally ruled. Battles have always existed for land, and for power. And in the midst of that kind of death and destruction, more death and destruction was not much noted. Even into the past century, men went to war around the globe. And into this new century, men still fight their battles in their different ways, with death and destruction still the result. So in all this time, it has been easy for many to survive on the spoils of war. But if you will, it isn't exactly true that a vampire is a shell of evil, a soulless entity. Vampirism is like a disease, an ancient disease. One that cannot be cured, but can be controlled. And for some, the true soul remains, and a hunger for something different—eternity, if you will—along with the rest of humanity, a belief in a greater being, something beyond . . . respect for life. Over the centuries, things change.

And now . . . those who come over, who do 'die,' who are not slain but 'turned,' if you will, can be as they were in this life. Those who were prone to bloodshed hunger for greater bloodshed—and power. Everyone 'turned' faces the hunger. Just as we are born with free will to seek peace or vengeance, so is the change.''

Tara stared at him blankly.

"I was a cop," Rick said ruefully.

"A cop?"

"A cop in New Orleans."

"When?" Tara demanded.

Rick shrugged. "Not so long ago," he said softly.

"You weren't brought forth from some musty tomb?"

He shook his head. "I'm a very young vampire," he explained. "Unlike Lucian."

Tara's eyes shifted to Brent. "So your friend Lucian . . . is an old vampire?"

"Very old, yes."

"When was he brought from his tomb?"

Brent smiled. "Never."

"I see. He was born a vampire."

"No, but he was turned when the world was in a constant state of raids and warfare, and he has been as he has been . . . since."

"And his wife, Jade?" Tara asked.

"No," Rick said softly.

"But—"

"She was never 'turned,' " Rick explained, as if that should make sense.

"This can't be real!" Tara said, in a whisper of exhalation.

"But it is real, Tara," Brent said, and he waved a hand impatiently in the air. "Just look at history, at the things that have gone on, at the legends that have been around forever."

"So you are a vampire as well?" she demanded, staring at him. "You lied to me, you said you weren't, but you're among them, and you are one of them!"

He stared at her a long moment. "I'm not a vampire," he said. "I'm—"

She lifted a hand. "Don't! Don't tell me how you're part of my grandfather's great . . . *Alliance.* I don't think that . . . that . . . oh, God! This is so . . . insane! This woman, this one woman, came out of a tomb. Because she wasn't destroyed completely, the king loved her, so he didn't take off her head. And now she's been dug up . . . and she's running around the countryside, and the police don't really know what they're up against— except Rick here, who used to be a cop in New Orleans—so some other vampires are here to stop her?"

"You don't understand," Brent said. "She isn't alone. She was extremely powerful in her last life, because she had the king. She had him in her power, but she didn't kill him, because she needed him for the life she was living. But your grandfather's Alliance was alive and well back then, and the king was forced at last to do something with her. And the Alliance saw to it that at the least, she was contained, with the proper materials, lead, brass, silver, copper, and gold. And she was held fast with these materials formed into the cross on the coffin, and sealed with the molten metals. But she was brought back on purpose, by someone who decided that they must have her. There is another force at work, one that is old and very powerful, and what we haven't managed to discover is exactly who this is, and where they have created their lair."

They were crazy. It was all crazy. The thought struck

Tara again, along with a need to be away from them for a moment, to be alone.

She turned and walked blindly into the hallway and then headed for her room.

She closed her door.

It opened immediately.

The two men had followed her. "Tara, you can't run away from any of this," Brent said. "You have to listen to me, I'm trying very hard to explain, completely, why you have to do everything I say, and exactly who I am, and why—"

He suddenly broke off, staring across the room.

Tara looked as well, and could see nothing, just her room, bed, chairs, desk, balcony doors—closed, garlic around them—her suitcases in the corner, her easel, set up where she had been sketching.

She looked at Rick, who appeared as puzzled as she was herself.

"What is it?" she asked.

"The drawing," Brent said harshly.

She walked over to the easel. "What? The shadows on the building? The wolf? The . . . sketch of the man?"

"The man," he grated out.

"That's just Inspector Trusseau, the forensic specialist in from Paris."

"Tara!" She was startled when her name was called from the doorway by a soft, feminine voice.

Ann's.

She was amazed to see that her cousin was up; she was a classic, fabled beauty, pale and gaunt, clad in a flowing nightgown, holding on to the door frame.

"Ann!" She started to hurry to her cousin, afraid that she would fall, she appeared so ashen and fragile.

Ann waved her away.

"That isn't Inspector Trusseau," Ann said impatiently. "Tara, don't you ever pay attention? Don't you remember? I pointed him out to you at the café! That's Willem."

"Willem?" Tara said.

"Yes, that's Willem."

"No," Brent said, and she had never heard his voice harsher, or seen him so tense, for he stood there, his fists knotted at his side, his eyes transfixed upon the paper. "It isn't Trusseau, and it isn't Willem. It's Andreson," he said, and the word spit from his lips as if the man were the greatest abomination ever to walk the earth. Evil incarnate.

He didn't explain further. He suddenly stiffened as if a bolt of lightning had traveled through him, let out an expletive, and turned, heading for the door.

Tara raced after him, catching his arm. "Brent, wait! What are you talking about?"

He shook her off as if she were an annoying raindrop, but his eyes fell upon hers. "I can't wait, I'll explain later. Your grandfather . . . something is happening. Now!"

CHAPTER 17

Sick with worry, hurriedly Lucian entered the apartment.

Instinct informed him that whatever had happened, whatever evil had been there, was gone.

"Jade?" He called her name, silent prayers filling his heart and mind and he looked around.

He found her, slumped on the ground, by the balcony doors. The open balcony doors. He stooped down, hands shaking as he reached out to shift his wife's hair from her face, to find her throat, feel for a pulse.

She groaned softly as he did so, rolling onto her shoulder and her back, looking up into his eyes, blinking, half rising.

"Oh, God, Lucian! I failed."

"Sh, sh!" he said, drawing her carefully into his arms, eyes searching over her for any sign of injury. "What's important first is that you're all right." There was a catch to his voice, concern as he lifted her hair, ran fingers gently over her collarbone.

"I'm all right, Lucian. I do have experience . . . and I was so certain, so sure of myself. I just knew that I could protect Paul, and I couldn't."

"Jade, it's all right. We're going to make it be all right," he amended. "What happened? I knew . . . I knew you were in trouble. I couldn't move quickly enough. I can't get into the minds of these abominations. They know I'm out here, and they're using tremendous strength to block me."

"I kept checking on him, I kept checking on Paul every few minutes. He seemed to be doing fine. He was restless, but he seemed to understand that we had to sit tight. It was so sad, in a way, Lucian. He loves that girl so much!"

"Then . . . ?"

"He was watching television. I was on the computer, bringing up everything I could find on the area immediately surrounding Le Petit Château DeVant. Anything around the church and the village. There was so much destruction there at the beginning of the Occupation. Resistance fighters had been holing up there . . . and the enemy went after them. I was trying to find the exact sites of the ruins . . . but I kept coming out to check. Paul fell asleep. A few minutes later . . . I felt uneasy. I came back and . . . Lucian, I've never seen anything like it. There was someone . . . something . . . there. But the face kept changing. I didn't know the café girl, I'm not even certain I saw her the day we met Brent at the café. But, of course, it was her, because Paul was going for her, and I screamed at him to stop, and then, it seemed that it wasn't the girl . . . then it was again . . . and I don't know who was out there. I went rushing to the window with the holy water, and tripped in my haste and fear . . . but I sprayed the creature, whoever or whatever it was . . . managed to enrage it, but not stop it! Suddenly there was nothing but black, a huge black shadow, or a shadow wing, and it swept out at me and sent me flying . . . I was dazed . . . I felt it coming again . . . but it paused above me, and couldn't come closer. I have my cross, of course, and I think that I spilled half the holy water on myself, but . . . I heard Paul scream. I tried to struggle up, and I was knocked back down by the wing of the shadow . . . and I knew that Paul was gone . . . and then you were here.''

Lucian sat on the floor, pulling her against him. He held her tight, his chin resting lightly on top of her head.

"They're shape-shifting," he said softly. "It wasn't Yvette, the girl from the café. It was either Louisa . . . or whoever it is that brought her back, who is guiding her, caring for her. He has to be someone old, someone I have encountered, and someone who knows what forces to use against me, and against others who would stop him."

"It has to be the lover," Jade said.

"The creature she was seeing when the king finally realized he was being mesmerized by a monster?" Lucian said.

"Yes."

Lucian was silent a minute.

"Do you know who it is?"

"Supposedly he was destroyed by the Alliance, with the blessing of the Sun King."

"But perhaps he wasn't," Jade said. "You knew him, and about him, didn't you?"

"I knew . . . and at the time . . . the world was different," he said.

At that time, the ancient rules had been followed, she knew. And seldom, if ever, did they destroy one of their own kind. Often, perhaps, they led mortals to the strongholds of their enemies, but the destruction of one's own kind was completely taboo.

"He might have survived," Jade repeated.

"Yes, he might have survived. He was to have been killed, dismembered, decapitated, and thrown into the river. The king's command. But . . ."

Lucian stood, drawing her to her feet, meeting her eyes. He lifted her hair again, worried.

"I wasn't bitten," she assured him softly.

"But you were before," he reminded her. "And didn't tell me."

"Because, if I had entered your world, it would have been fine with me. I'm afraid of life, of the years that will pass, as it is," she told him.

Lucian hesitated, then kissed her on the forehead. The world was a strange place. Life and death were stranger still. He had come to a point amid the centuries himself when he knew exactly what his role would be.

And yet . . .

He didn't know if the end would bring eternal damnation. And he would not risk such a fate for someone he loved with every fiber of his being. She had become more than his lover and his wife, she was his very soul.

"We need to get to Château DeVant," he said.

"Wait. I have all kinds of printouts for Jacques," Jade said.

Lucian waited while she collected the papers. He got her coat, placed it tenderly around her shoulders, then led her toward the door, but there, when he looked worriedly at her again, she spoke with a determined confidence.

"He has the answers, I know that Jacques has the answers, as soon as he is able to get through the tangle of possibilities," Jade said.

He nodded, but they both knew what lay unspoken between them.

Fear.

Lucian was afraid for her. He hadn't doubted that his presence in the area would be known. That didn't matter. He intended to make himself known.

But now . . .

Besides the urgency of keeping the DeVant household safe, there would be another worry.

Jade.

She placed a hand on his arm. "I've been through this. I'm not afraid."

"I know you're not," he told her, and admitted, "I am."

"Don't be."

"We have to end this. Quickly," he told her.

"We will," she said.

"Strange," Lucian murmured.

"What?"

"I think that it's the old man's granddaughter who actually has the answers," Lucian said. "And she just hasn't realized that she has them, that they're there, in her mind . . . or in her dreams."

He locked the door as they left the room. And he wondered why.

It was like locking the stable door after the horse had been stolen.

*   *   *

Louisa stood by the great hearth, leaned against the stone, watching as the flames rose and danced. As he walked into the room, she turned to him, a smile on her face, arms crossed over her chest. "All is well," she assured him.

"What have you done, where have you been?"

"Oh . . . I picked up this evening's supper, that's all," she assured him.

"From—where?"

"Ah . . . well, I picked up a young man. From under the very nose of our enemies."

"Which enemy? From where?"

"I picked up a young man, from Lucian DeVeau's wife."

For a moment, his heart leaped. "And Lucian's wife?"

Louisa's lashes flicked over her eyes and a look of irritation crossed her beautiful features. "What about her?"

"You didn't bring her here?"

She looked at him coolly. "No."

"If we had her—"

"What about you?" Louisa inquired. "Did you do as you said you would? Where is the DeVant girl?"

"She will be coming," he said. Then he reminded her, "It's the old man who must die. And it's the other granddaughter I want."

"Well . . . as I see it, you haven't the old man, or either grandchild."

"Had you managed to be a little subtle upon arising, I would have taken care of everything."

Louisa smiled, and waved a hand to indicate the home

he had chosen so carefully. "Look around you. Since I have come . . . well . . . we are well-guarded. We are safe. And each day, our strength grows. You cannot bring them here—while they spend their days and nights searching for us! Don't worry, my love. I have arranged for such power here, you can't imagine. I have done so. So . . . you mustn't instruct me further. I will instruct you."

"You little fool! You are remembering nothing!"

"I don't need to remember," she told him.

"You were sealed away," he reminded her curtly. "While I . . . the suffering, the healing . . . were agony."

She lifted her chin. "And what of the years in between, my love? You did take your time coming for me."

"It was almost impossible, you know." His irritation died suddenly. "The years in between . . . were nothing. Practice for the changing times." He walked over to her, taking her into his arms. "I learned how and when to use power," he said softly. "Always . . . waiting for you."

She smiled, stretching like a cat within his arms. "I feel so very well . . . our little army serves me when and where and how I command. And now, night again, hours ahead, more to do . . . but more time together."

He bent to kiss her. Her words stopped him.

"You were her lover," she said softly.

He was impatient. "I needed to know her."

"You cared about her, you enjoyed yourself."

"I enjoyed myself. I did not care. I was waiting for you."

"She dies, the second she comes to us."

"She does not die; she is bait, for the other."

"I will manage the second girl," Louisa said icily. "I—alone. Do you think I have never traveled by daylight? That I am so weak I could not follow in your steps on occasion? Did you think at all that I might not see you, as you pretended to be who you were not, as you spoke, so reasonably . . . watched her as well . . . hungered?"

"She is the one," he said simply. "The one who must be stopped."

"Then I will stop her."

"I have been the one laying the trap. I will stop her."

"No, my love."

"Jealousy has no place here," he said firmly.

"Neither does your lust," she replied.

He let out a sigh of impatience. "Louisa! I plotted, I planned, I crept low and carefully in these surroundings, seeking to release you, longing to be with you, to rule and reign with you again, in our secret world. A dangerous world, which must be solved now . . . before we move on. Let's finish them. And then . . . I have always loved the Caribbean in winter."

"The Caribbean?"

"Islands, my love. With gentle breezes. And warmth. And . . . no Alliance," he told her. "It's time," he said with a shrug. "Those fools, even the village police, will figure out soon enough that I'm not an inspector from Paris. Of course"—he gave her a broad smile—"it might be a while, because it will take them some time to find the real Trusseau."

She laughed, the sound husky, and in her throat.

"Don't you think it's time, then, as well, to take the offensive?"

He stroked the flesh on her throat. "Perhaps . . ."

"Perhaps?"

"Yes, then, if you wish. If you wish . . . when the shadows of night have fallen, fallen really deeply."

She smiled. She allowed his kiss. The fires burned, the passion between them roared to life along with it.

"What about the other one?" she inquired. "The— outsider."

He was silent. She heard his jaw working. "He is part of this, don't you understand? Dogging every step, ruining your re-entry to this world. He is the enemy and that is part of why the DeVants must not die too quickly."

"You knew him before, didn't you? You have met, and tangled, before."

He was bitterly silent for a long moment, staring at the flames. "Oh, yes, I knew him. And he should have died then. Just as the old man should have died. But they will die now. I will make certain. They will die now."

"I know nothing of this man," she said. "Other than the fact that he . . . he wounded me, when I was determined on entry to the DeVant house."

"He will die a worse death, for what he has done."

"He will not die easily," she said, reflecting on her encounter with the man in question.

"You forget—I know what he is. And I know how to kill what he is—so actually, when I choose, yes, he will die easily enough. This time. I am prepared."

They were both somewhat startled by a thumping sound. They stared at one another, and then Louisa laughed.

"Dinner is growing restless, I'm afraid," she said.

She stood in all her beauty before the fire, and reached her hand to him. "Come love. Shall we dress for supper? Or be casual tonight?"

"Casual, I think," he said.

For a moment they locked together in an embrace. She drew away.

"Casual it is," she agreed. "I confess, childish though it may be, I do so love to play with my food."

Though she ran in his wake, Brent was down the stairs long before Tara. And when she came down to the great hall and entry, he was nowhere to be seen.

Jacques, however, was there, standing at the open door.

Javet had come.

Tara raced up behind Jacques, putting her arm around his shoulder, staring indignantly at the police officer. "What—"

"I have all the necessary papers, Miss Adair. And I am not here alone. I have six patrolmen with me. Now, you will let me in."

She stood her ground. "You are not coming in. You have been fooled, Inspector, and this is not where you should be looking! Your man from Paris isn't who he says he is at all. If you want answers, go question him."

"What are you talking about?" Javet demanded.

"Inspector Trusseau isn't who he has said that he is. He—he works at my cousin's publishing company. He's not even a salesman. He took that job only to be around, to watch what was going on. He is some kind of a monster."

"A monster," Javet repeated, shaking his head. He looked at Jacques again. "You're going to have to start talking, Monsieur DeVant."

"Javet, if I told you what I know, you wouldn't believe me," Jacques said wearily. "I didn't know anything about this Inspector Trusseau, but if my granddaughter says that he is not who he claims to be, then he is not."

"This is rubbish. He came with all the proper docu-

Shannon Drake

ments. If he had been lurking in the village, I'd have seen him.''

"He wasn't in the village most of the time—the publishing company is in Paris," Tara said with aggravation. "He is an imposter—"

"A monster?" Javet said again.

"You are up against monsters," Jacques said, and hesitated. "Monsters . . . murderers."

"You knew about this, this . . . this plague upon us! Knew about the murder in the crypt before it took place," Javet said angrily.

"Not exactly," Jacques said. "There is nothing I can tell you that you would believe."

"I'm sorry, Jacques. But I have the papers and authority to arrest you. Unless, of course, you know where the American is. Perhaps, if you were to turn him over to me . . . ?''

"What?" Tara said in disbelief.

"Your grandfather is under arrest, because I am going to get somewhere with this investigation. Too many people are dying or disappearing! Now, no more excuses or fairy tales. You're coming to the station with me, Jacques.''

"No! He is not coming with you—" Tara protested.

"I will use force, if I have to do so," Javet said. "Damn you all, there has been another headless body discovered, and the investigation in the city has come up with even more missing people. You know about this, and whatever is going on here, it must be stopped. Jacques, you are under arrest. At the station, we may get to the bottom of this!''

"No!"

Tara didn't know where Brent had been, but now he walked in the door. He stared at Javet. "Take me in.

You wanted me, Javet? Here I am. Bring me in. Let him alone."

"Hell, yes! I'll take you in. I suspected that you were lurking here," Javet said. "Yes, yes . . . Jacques can have a reprieve. I will bring you in."

"Good. I'll confess to the murder—to any murder. Just leave Jacques alone."

"He is not guilty of any murder!" Jacques said indignantly.

"I can arrest you both," Javet told him.

"Leave Monsieur DeVant," Brent said. "Take me. I will talk to you until you are weary of listening. Javet, Jacques is ill. If he dies in your custody—"

"All right," Javet said. "You come with me." He stared at Tara and Jacques. "But if Monsieur Malone cannot convince me that he—and he alone—is a killer, I will be back. And then, there will be nothing to stop me until I get to the absolute truth."

"Brent can't go," Jacques said. "It is better if you take me."

"We're not bartering here, or choosing straws!" Javet exploded.

"Jacques," Brent said, placing a hand on his shoulder. "It will be all right."

Tara was frightened. What would happen when he left? She would be alone then, with these terrible things going on, with a stranger who had been introduced as a vampire, who had been bending over her cousin, who was now ashen and failing.

But as she stood there shaking, desperate for something to say or do, he turned his eyes on her. And she was startled by the gold fire in them, filled with both emotion and strength, and the assurance she needed.

"It will honestly be all right," he said firmly.

She moistened her lips, trying to nod. Javet took Brent by the arm, leading him out, calling to one of his men for handcuffs. When they were nearly at Javet's car, she ran after him. She ignored the other officers and came before him, placing her hands on his shoulders, rising on her toes. "I believe in you," she whispered softly. "I don't understand you . . . I don't know why you left us . . . I love you . . . rather assinine, since you walked away this morning . . . I'll do something . . . I'll get you out, quickly, somehow."

She was startled by the smile that curled his lips. "You were never alone. Rick was always watching. And you're actually more important than I am. And I love you, too. Don't worry about me. Lucian will come . . . and I will get out myself. I promise."

"What is this?" Javet asked with aggravation. "Miss Adair, I'm about to arrest you, too. And you won't be in the same cell, I can assure you!"

She stepped back. She watched as they got into the police car. Then she realized that her grandfather stood alone in an empty doorway, and she rushed back. He was shaking. "Come on, Grandpapa, come on, let me get you into a chair, get your feet up, get you some brandy."

"Ann?" he inquired.

"She's—she's okay. A friend is here."

"Ah, the new one . . ." Jacques murmured. "Rick. Another American."

She frowned. Even Jacques had known about the man.

She paused, closing and locking the door, placing the garlic around it. She walked slowly with him back to the library, wondering why Javet had chosen a time of darkness to come and make an arrest at the chateau.

She had to admit to being very afraid. She couldn't let Jacques know.

Katia came running in from the kitchen then, aware that she had missed something, and at a loss as to know what. "Help me get my grandfather back to the library, please," Tara said.

"I will get brandy for him," she assured Tara, once Jacques was seated. When Katia returned with the brandy, Tara found herself uneasy about the two upstairs. She asked Katia to stay with Jacques for a moment, swearing that she'd be right back. She raced up the stairs, going first to her room, but neither man was there. She went running back to Ann's room. Her cousin was back in bed. The tall, blond, muscular American was seated in a chair by her side, his hands folded prayer fashion as he looked at her.

He gazed at Tara as she entered, gave her a grim smile. "She is all right," he said softly. "But she mustn't be left alone. Not for a minute."

"They've taken Brent in—the police have taken him in," she said.

Rick nodded. "I know . . . I saw some of what happened, but I couldn't . . . didn't dare leave Ann. He'll be all right, you know."

"But—he isn't a vampire."

Rick seemed to skip a beat before answering her. "No, he isn't a vampire."

"What can I do?"

"Nothing. He'll be all right. He'll manage on his own, or Lucian will step in."

"Lucian isn't here," she said.

"But he'll be back."

"But—"

"He's old. Very, very, old. And can sense trouble. He can enter into minds . . . he'll know, trust me."

She stared at him. She didn't even really know him—and she was supposed to trust him. But these bizarre things were growing easier. Because, she had, of course, gone completely to the flip side of sanity.

She believed.

"What do we do now?" she asked.

"We wait. See to your grandfather. I'm watching Ann."

As Tara started back down the stairs, there was a knock at the front door.

Katia came rushing out from the library. Tara shook her head at her. She walked to the door herself and looked through the peephole.

She exhaled, fought with the demons of logic and sanity still lurking within her mind, and opened the door.

Lucian and Jade entered.

Tara opened her mouth to speak, to explain the current situation, but she didn't need to do so.

Lucian spoke. "They left just minutes ago?"

"Yes."

"Jade will stay here. I'm going. Listen, it's imperative that you all be incredibly careful. Every window, every door, must remain sealed. Don't leave. You understand?"

She nodded.

"Rick is here, of course," Jade reminded Lucian.

Lucian glanced at his wife. "Rick needs to stay in, too. He's got incredible courage and spirit, but he's still so young . . . inexperienced," he added, looking at Tara. He smiled. "It will be all right. I'll be back with Brent. And while we're gone, just sit tight. Get in there with

Jacques, and . . . Tara, I think that you can perhaps find what we're looking for."

"What?"

"Jade will explain. I'll be back," he said.

He turned, and was gone. Jade closed the door behind him. She looked awkwardly at Tara, shrugged and smiled. "Well . . . what we need to do is find their lair."

"Their lair?"

"Lucian can . . . feel where others are. But, naturally, they're blocking him. Probably setting all kinds of traps, but it doesn't really matter. We have to find them. We've spent a great deal of our time here looking. Following their trail. But . . . we haven't found the right place yet. It's going to be what appears to be an old ruin, but is actually sound. And hidden, far off the beaten path . . . hidden by nature, trees, vines, foliage. Do you know such a place?"

"I . . . I think I know of several. When we were children, sometimes we'd take turns riding our horse, Daniel, into the woods. We'd come upon all kinds of places."

"Let's go in with your grandfather. And start studying the maps again."

"All right," Tara said softly. She led the way to the library door, and they entered together. Jacques looked gaunt, but determined. He already had maps spread out on the desk. He greeted Jade with a question in his eyes.

"Lucian has gone for Brent," she said, smiling. "I'm sure he would have been fine on his own, but . . . it's important that we're all together. Lucian will bring him back quickly."

Jacques stretched out a thin arm, curling his fingers around Jade's hand. "And you're all right?"

She nodded. "Humbled, but unhurt," she assured

him. "I—I lost one of our witnesses," she said sorrowfully.

"We'll get him back."

"I don't know what you're talking about," Tara told them both.

Jade explained what had happened at the hotel, whom she had been guarding, and why. And how she had failed.

"Perhaps we can save him yet," Jacques said.

"Perhaps," Jade said.

Jacques looked up. "Now that my granddaughter has joined us, I know that we will find the truth."

"Grandpapa, how can you be so certain I can help?"

"Because it's you," he said.

"What is me?"

"It's you . . . I'm old and failing now. And there is always one in the family who is meant to come . . . and the new strength in the Alliance. It is you, Tara."

She shook her head. "I . . . I don't think so at all, Grandpapa! I barely believe any of this, as yet!"

He smiled and shrugged to Jade. "Tara, look at the map. What do you think? Tell me what you know, what you remember, from the time you were a child."

She came around his shoulder and pointed. "There's what we all called the Giant Rock. It really isn't giant at all—it's just what we called it as children. Here, here are ruins," she told them. "But truly crumbled."

"We've been there," Jade said. "And the basement is caved in."

Tara looked at her.

"I looked it all up on the Internet. Found the owners, the date when it was condemned, and the original blueprints."

"Oh," Tara said. "How logical." She looked back at

the map. "Here . . . this . . . if I remember correctly, this is the old Dupré House. We couldn't even reach the house itself on the horse, the area in front is so overgrown." She fell silent, closing her eyes, as a rush of ice seemed to envelop her.

The Dupré House!

Suddenly, childhood memories combined with the haunting images of her dreams. The shadow wings had thrown her off . . . she had only ever gone there in daylight as a child. They'd never been allowed to stay out with the horse in the countryside when it was close to dusk.

She started to open her mouth, to explain the past, and her dream, but she never got a chance. From outside, with the suddenness of a bomb explosion, noises began to rattle the night. Eleanora began to howl as if she were a wolf pack in herself, baying, barking, letting out a cry to the moon once again.

And it sounded as if the stables had imploded; old Daniel was kicking at his wooden stall.

"What in God's name . . . ?" Tara whispered.

Katia came bursting into the library, wringing her hands. "I have told him no! I have told him no, but he ignored me! Roland grabbed the gun and went running out. And it's out there, I know it's out there . . . I saw it! What do we do, Jacques, what do we do? Roland has gone out."

Tara rushed to Katia. "Katia, calm down, please— what did you see?"

Even as she spoke, Tara saw something . . .

Something she couldn't describe. It was as if the room darkened. Lamplight flickered, and grew dimmer.

As if great shadow wings were sweeping over the house . . .

"Katia, please, what did you see?"

Katia drew away from her.

"Evil! I saw evil!" Then the housekeeper clutched her shoulders. "Evil, Tara, and you must feel it . . . I can feel it . . . it is as if it has entered the house!"

As she spoke, the lamplight fickered.

In the hearth, the flames suddenly rose high . . .

And then died.

At the same time, the flickering electricity gave a last faint glow . . . and then went dead as well.

They were cast into darkness.

Just as the stygian night fell upon them, an ear-shattering scream sounded from the courtyard beyond the door.

And the dog began to howl and bay again . . .

Until that sound, too, was suddenly silenced.

CHAPTER 18

Brent sat quietly in the back of the police car, keeping still, offering no resistance. When they arrived at the village station, he followed along as he was told. He wasn't directed to take the chair in front of Javet's desk as he had previously done. He was led to a room with a table and chairs, no windows, and just one door. He was aware that the side with the one-way glass led to another chamber, where other officers could watch his movements and hear his words.

He was left there alone for a moment. Then Javet came in and sat across from him. "Coffee, cigarettes?" He asked.

"Sure," Brent said.

Javet pushed a pack of his own brand across the table. He motioned for one of his officers to go out. The man returned with coffee. Javet still stared at him.

At last he spoke.

"All right. Tell me what happened. Start with the night in the crypt. Or before, if you wish. But, perhaps it will be easiest if you begin with the murder of Jean-Luc. You had to have had an accomplice. That's the only way you could have gotten rid of the contents of the coffin that was excavated."

"The contents of the coffin excavated themselves—and killed Jean-Luc," he said.

Javet paused in the lighting of his cigarette, looking over at him. "The contents of the coffin . . . the corpse, after hundreds of years, rose and killed your coworker?" Javet said with disgust.

"Yes."

"You admitted to the murder. You are here to confess."

"I'm telling you what I know."

Javet rose, swearing, knocking his chair over as he did so. "That is bull!" The man was furious. Every vein in his neck stood out, and Brent was well aware that the police officer was doing everything in his power not to jump over the table and throw his fists against him.

But he was a good police officer; he found the restraint. Hands balled into fists, he turned away.

He spoke at last. "For tonight, we will leave Mr. Malone in his cell, and give him time to think about his answers. If he can't find more information than such ridiculous lies to give me, I will have to bring in the old man."

His back straight, he walked out of the interrogation room. A minute later, one of his officers took Brent's cigarette and coffee, and indicated he should rise.

That night, he was the only prisoner at the small station. His cell was spare, but clean and neat. Once he was inside, the door was locked. The officers left him.

He sat on the bunk for a minute, waited, leaned his head back, and hoped that Javet had left for the night.

He couldn't stay. He hadn't Lucian's powers, but even he was suddenly afraid that they were running out of time.

He lit one of his own cigarettes, smoked it, crushed it out.

Then closed his eyes.

A moment later, a terrible sound erupted from the cell. In the anteroom, two of the skeleton night crew in the station, standing at the desk, stared at one another. Officers Deauville and d'Artoine were both young, new to the force, thus drawing the late night hours.

They drew their weapons, and went rushing into the hall where the four small cells were situated.

"He's gone!" Deauville said.

"No . . . no, there's something in there," d'Artoine said.

"Where?"

"At the end of the cot."

Deauville unlocked the door to the cell. Both men walked in cautiously, their weapons aimed. Deauville stared where d'Artoine had directed. He saw nothing but . . .

Eyes. Gold. Glittering. Lethal. Like the eyes of a . . . demon.

He swallowed hard, wetting his lips.

"What is it?" he whispered.

"A . . . dog?" d'Artoine said hesitantly.

"That's no dog."

"It's an animal."

"Where's the prisoner?"

"Escaped?"

"What do we do?"

"Shoot it?"

As they debated, the creature in question suddenly sprang to life. All d'Artoine knew before the thing landed on him, knocking his weapon to the floor, was that it was huge and powerful. He screamed, certain that he was about to be killed.

The weight lifted from him. He was aware of noise. It was Deauville, at his side, still screaming.

He hit Deauville. "It's out!"

They both leaped to their feet, rushing to the front of the station. Other officers were milling there, looking around anxiously.

"What is it?" someone called.

"A beast!" d'Artoine said, and realized how ridiculous he sounded. "I don't know, some kind of an animal."

The door to the street suddenly opened. The men all straightened as the man from Paris walked in. Trusseau. He looked around at them, contempt in his eyes. But then, he always seemed to have contempt in his eyes. He was from Paris. They were just villagers. Inept.

"What is going on here?" he asked.

Deauville had accompanied Javet and his arrest warrant to the DeVant chateau. And he narrowed his eyes suddenly, remembering that the American granddaughter had been saying that Trusseau was an imposter.

And now, he wondered. It wasn't impossible, even if the girl had been saying anything to save her grandfather, and her lover.

Of course, it was the American digger, the woman's lover, who was now gone, and who had somehow left some kind of a beast in his stead.

Still . . .

"We are looking for a creature, some kind of beast,

which has gotten loose in the station," he said to Trusseau.

"Ah," Trusseau said. "A beast."

"Yes. It is here, somewhere. You must take care."

"Oh, I will," Trusseau said.

"Do you need a weapon, Inspector Trusseau—that *is* your name, *sir*, correct?"

"Is it my name?" The man seemed amused, but he didn't reply to the question. Instead, he said, "I carry my own weapon. Where is this beast?"

"Here . . . somewhere."

Whether he was an imposter or not, Trusseau seemed willing to look for the beast. He drew his weapon, a gleaming silver pistol of a make with which Deauville was not familiar, and backed against the wall.

There was silence as they barely breathed, and waited.

There was a clanking sound from the far wall. They all spun around. Two men fired. Chunks of concrete and stone spewed from the wall.

Then there was a sudden burst of . . . something.

Something huge, moving with the speed of light. It leaped over and past them, charging straight for the station door. They were all taken by such surprise that instead of firing too quickly as they had before, they fired too late.

All except for Trusseau. His gun went off.

The door, however, had gone down.

The creature was off in the street . . .

Leaving a trail of blood.

Trusseau smiled at them. "Don't worry. I'll hunt down your beast."

Deauville decided to take it upon himself to discover the truth. He kept seeing the American girl. Tall and slim, so beautiful, and so indignant and well spoken, even as she argued so passionately for her grandfather.

Something wasn't right.

"I don't think so, sir. I think we can catch the beast on our own. You've been accused of being an imposter, sir. I'd like you to remain here while we give a call to the Paris office."

Trusseau lifted a brow. He smiled.

Then he lifted his weapon, and aimed at Deauville.

"Sir, what the hell—?" d'Artoine began.

Trusseau's bullet exploded in the night.

Tara fumbled at the fireplace, finding the long matches that lit the logs. As she did so, Jade DeVeau produced a flashlight.

"Roland!" Katia said in a wail.

"Don't worry; I'm going for him," Tara said.

"I've more experience," Jade said. "I'm going out. You're too valuable here right now, Tara. I'll find Roland."

"And Eleanora," Tara said softly. "But you can't go out there alone."

They all jumped as a rich masculine voice with a deep Southern accent suddenly interrupted them. Rick Beaudreaux made his way into the room. "Don't be ridiculous, I'm going out. But Tara, get up there with Ann right away. And Jade, you stay here with Jacques and Katia."

Both Tara and Jade were ready to argue.

"You know I'm the best one for the job!" Rick said.

"I'm going up to Ann right now," Tara told her grandfather. She cast Rick a glance, then went racing up the stairs. She tripped, trying to go too fast in the darkness. She had to catch herself on the stairs.

She stopped at the hall closet, feeling her way to open it, and finding the large battery-powered lantern they kept there for emergencies.

Her hands curled around it. She quickly turned on the light and headed for Ann's room. The door to the hallway was closed. She reached for it, then felt a sense of dread filling her. She paused, then threw it open.

She didn't need the lantern in Ann's room.

The balcony doors and drapes were open. Moonlight was pouring in.

The drapes drifted in a ghostly field of moonlight. The air that rushed in was cold.

The bed where Ann had lain was empty.

She walked to it disbelieving. "Ann!" she cried softly, looking to the balcony. But her cousin was gone.

Just barely gone.

There was a note on the bed. Next to several drops of blood.

It read:

> *She has perhaps ten minutes to live. Unless she is saved, of course.*
> *By the new Alliance.*
> *Such sweet blood. Perhaps I cannot wait so long.*

He limped, cursing himself, gritting his teeth, praying for the strength he needed—just for that night.

Well, at last he had seen him again. And while he hadn't known that Andreson had been behind the evil in the village, Andreson had definitely known that *he* was there. He had come prepared with the right weapon.

The only weapon . . .

He slunk into a side street. After his escape, it seemed that all hell had broken loose at the police station. Officers were running all over the street. The only thing he could do was find the darkest alley, and pray that he could stanch his own wound.

But as he sat against the wall, listening to the shouts and pounding footsteps all around him, he became aware of the shadows overtaking even the darkness. For a moment, he tensed. If Andreson were to find him now . . .

"What the hell happened to you?"

Lucian was there, kneeling beside him.

"Andreson is here, and damned bold at that," Brent said dryly. "Walked right into the police station—and took a shot at me."

"I thought you'd done something yourself to rile them all up," Lucian said. "You're bleeding like a stuck pig."

"Well, hell, he got me with a silver bullet."

"You're slowing down, my friend."

"Just get the damned thing out," Brent said.

Lucian pulled a knife from his jacket pocket, flicked it open, and dug in. Brent gritted his teeth, nearly crying out at the pain.

"Got it," Lucian said.

"None too gently."

"You needed it out, right?"

"I did."

Lucian sat back on his haunches. "He isn't around here anymore," he said softly.

Brent struggled to his feet. "We've got to get back to the chateau."

"You're going to be about worthless."

"No . . . and anyway, about worthless isn't totally worthless."

"Still . . ."

"You said that he isn't around here anymore. The chateau . . . well, Rick is there, I know, but Andreson knows a hell of a lot more tricks than a young fellow like your Southern friend. We've got to get back."

"Yeah, take my hand."

Brent struggled to his feet. He swallowed hard. "Go— ahead of me. I'll catch up. I don't want them there alone."

Lucian didn't argue with him.

"What the hell is it? You know there's something wrong there, right?"

"I've a sudden sense of darkness. I know the man as someone other than Andreson, but if he was here . . ."

"Then she might have been at the house," Brent said. "Go!"

Lucian was already on his way.

Brent paused, bitterly resenting every moment it took to summon his strength. At last, he closed his eyes, and found the power to move. He went silently through the village streets, avoiding the prowling officers. At length, he came to the outskirts beyond the square, started out along the road, and felt the light of the moon upon him.

He began to run.

Tara shot back down the stairs, not pausing to find the others in the library, but bursting outside the front door, shrieking her cousin's name.

There was no answer. The driveway was locked in shadow; clouds covered the moon. She called and shouted. There was no sign of Rick, Roland, the dog, or anyone.

She raced back into the house, bursting into the library. Jade stood guard, literally, straight and tall, posed behind her grandfather's desk chair.

She paused for a deep breath, wet her lips, and told Jacques, "They've got Ann."

She was so sorry. His entire face went gray, and seemed to sink within. He might have been a skeleton with leftover flesh, watching her.

"Lucian will be back; Brent will be back."

She shook her head. "We can't wait. I'm going."

"Tara, no!"

"They're going to kill her if I don't go."

"You're not going alone," Jacques said.

"Grandpapa! You can't come with me. Then I'd have to worry about your life as well as my own."

Jade was shaking her head. "You know nothing yet, Tara. You know nothing at all. You haven't the experience—"

"Then you'd better give me a quick lesson."

"I'm coming with you—"

"You can't. God knows where Rick is, or what happened with Roland, and I'm still certain that Jacques is in terrible danger. And now . . . now that we've come to this, I'm not afraid." It was the most preposterous lie she had ever told in her life, but she could see no other way to get her cousin back. "Look, supposedly I'm genetically primed to do this, to go after these people. So if you want to help me, tell me quickly what I need to know. Jacques—I drew a picture upstairs. It turned out to be a man Ann had been dating, as well as the man who claimed to be from the Paris police, as well as someone Brent seemed to know from somewhere else. If you can—"

She had thought that her grandfather looked half-dead before. Now, he was the color of pure ash. "Andreson!" he breathed.

"Andreson . . . who is Andreson?" she asked.

"A true monster. He was head of the medical experiments when I was in the prison camp during the war. He ran the place. Naturally, of course, I knew later. He was constantly glutted, there was a chance for such rich carnage during the war! No crueler commandant ever existed, no one, not even among a field of monsters, was so heinous. But at the end . . . his cruelty brought about his death. Or so I had thought."

"The war . . . Jacques, how does Brent know about this man, then?"

Her grandfather looked at her.

"Brent Malone was Andreson's favorite experiment, and there was nothing he enjoyed more than trying to solve the riddle of his survival, and what he had become."

She felt ill. Brent had lied to her. It was impossible. If he wasn't a—vampire, one among them, how could he have lived back during the war?

"What do you mean? Tell me quickly. Brent couldn't have been in the war. He'd be old now, really old now. He said that he wasn't a vampire, he told me twice that he wasn't a vampire—"

"He's not," Jacques said.

"Then—"

"He's a werewolf."

"Oh, God!"

*   *   *

Ann DeVant lay on the sofa, eyes open but unfocused. Louisa stared down at the woman, hating her.

She longed to strike right then and there. Slide her teeth deep into the woman's throat—so white against that spill of dark hair—tear into her, rip her to shreds, draining every last drop of blood from her body.

She forced herself to move away from the girl.

Gerard had said that she must live, and it was true— she was the bait to get the other, and now, Tara DeVant would have to come, of course. She was certain that Gerard would have killed the wolf by now. And Lucian was busy seeking the body of the wolf . . .

It had all been so well planned. The only torture was now . . . waiting. And hating the girl, of course.

She stood over her again. Jealousy was eating at her, consuming her. Actually, when the time came, she wanted to kill the girl in front of Gerard. Wanted to see that she meant nothing to him, that she could be drained, used up . . . and discarded like refuse.

She felt his arrival. Sweeping black shadows that she knew long before they touched her.

"Did you kill him?"

"Yes," he said, but there was a hesitation.

Louisa said angrily, "Did you kill him?"

"Yes, of course, I struck him with a silver bullet."

"And you saw his body?"

"No, I did not."

"Then—"

"He's dead! Don't you understand? I hit him with a silver bullet."

"I understand," she said, "that he was the one to ruin things when you should have been there to welcome me from the coffin. That he wormed his way into a job with Professor Dubois, and was watching, waiting, all along.

He was the one who summoned Lucian, and the one determined again to find Jacques DeVant and seek out what information he had . . . and he is the one who has created so much trouble all along. And you did not see his body!"

"It does not matter, I tell you. I struck him with a silver bullet."

She studied him for a moment. "I thought you would have been more determined on being certain that he was dead. After what you tell me that he did to you . . ."

"It was ten years before my injuries even began to heal," Gerard said bitterly. "He tore me to shreds. He came back for the prisoners. When they were freed, they stabbed and shot me, hung me up like a slaughtered steer. DeVant knew that I should have been decapitated, and he would have seen to the deed himself, but that's when the fires began, and he was forced to run. To take that traitor, Weiss, and get the hell out. Weiss! I never found that sniveling little coward, either. He was never prosecuted—prisoners defended him! He went to America and lived in peace and plenty and died at the age of ninety-nine. Yes, I loathe and despise Brent Malone! I should have finished him off when he was brought in, but he was the only one to withstand the onslaught of the wolves. There were many more then. They attacked both the Allies and Axis soldiers, heedless of their uniforms. They left a field of devastation worse than that of any bomb or slaughter. But he was alive. And I knew he'd be one of them. And I wanted to know what caused it—what made him stronger, what made him weaker. What caused him the most pain . . . he is dead! I know that I hit him. And . . ."

His voice trailed away. He saw Ann prone upon the

couch. He walked over to her. Louisa was certain that he stared down at the girl with the greatest affection.

Louisa sat on the couch, running her fingers along the bare length of Ann's arm as she looked up at Gerard. "Let me kill her . . . now. Watch me kill her . . . now. We can share her, but I must confess. I tasted her blood when I shape-shifted to you, luring her to the balcony. Delicious. And I'm still so hungry. But if you wish . . ."

He drew her to her feet. "Not now!" he said. "This is our chance to take them, one by one. Tara DeVant will come. She will have to come alone . . . the others will be too far behind. You left the note—as I told you."

"Of course. So there is no reason to keep her alive."

"There is every reason. She may have real talent. An instinct deeper even than that in the old man. She's young—"

"She hasn't the least idea of her own powers. She doesn't know what to do."

"She may know if her cousin is dead, and then she may not come."

"I think that she is coming already," Louisa said, licking her lips, looking at Ann.

"We have all manner of creatures from which you may take greater nourishment—or entertain yourself. Leave her be. For now."

Louisa returned to the fire.

"Fine. But when Tara arrives, I will deal with her. You will wait for Lucian's arrival—and he will arrive."

"What if she is not so easy as you seem to think?"

"My love, we have a little army ready to greet her when she arrives. She will be half-dead when they finish. I will merely deliver the final blows."

*   *   *

Jacques had spoken quickly, almost tonelessly, trying to explain how he had come to know Brent Malone. How Brent Malone, under the care of Doctor Weiss, had survived, how he had returned to the camp to rip it apart before anymore prisoners could be executed, and how he and Weiss had, in turn, taken care of him.

Taught him the ways of the Alliance.

She had listened for several minutes, listened as if hearing an impossible fairy tale. Then she had glanced at her watch and said, "None of this matters. They're going to kill Ann."

"I know that Lucian will be here. Any minute."

"Then when he arrives, you must send him after me. You know now exactly where to send him. But I must get there first."

The argument had already been won, she knew. Katia had been useless—she had taken a seat in an overstuffed chair where she sat and moaned and rocked to and fro, almost as if she were catatonic. But Jade had acquired everything her grandfather had said she needed, and she was ready. Her faith would always be her greatest protection, Jacques told her. Her faith, and her gold cross. Unless she had buckets of holy water, she could only burn and scald them with it, but not bring them down completely. She was armed with a stake that Jacques had owned since his father had given it to him when he was a boy, and a newer weapon for backup. She was also armed with his army sword, sharpened to perfection, as apparently he had kept it, always. She had understood that heads must be removed, or that corpses must be burned beyond recognition.

Afraid, she set out, driving as far as she could.
Then she set off through the woods.

And it was her dream again . . .

Darkness, incredible darkness. Shadows broken only
by the light of the moon, and that disappearing far too
often, as if the clouds were conspirators along with the
vampires.

She felt the wet grass against her ankles. Felt the
coolness of the air, which wasn't the natural coolness
of the breeze. Something more.

Some part of the darting, changing, shifting shadows.

With each step, she felt a greater dread. She knew
that the house lay just before her. That she was walking
toward it, though she longed to run away.

A silent plea escaped her.

Help me, please, come, help me . . .

She knew now, knew far too much. Knew what lay in
the shadows, stretching before her. Knew to whom she
cried for help.

*But he was in jail. He had gone to jail to keep them from
incarcerating her grandfather. She had realized, so late, that
they hadn't just known each other. They had formed a bond.
They had saved one another's lives. They had taught one
another, they had learned to live through one another. He had
let them take him, so that they would not hurt Jacques. He had
said that it would be all right, that he would be all right . . .*

But he wasn't here!

And she was walking . . .

Walking alone . . .

A strange birdcall sounded in the night. Not a birdcall
at all. It was the breeze picking up. Growing stronger,
colder, louder.

Her name came to her on the breeze.

Tara . . . Tara . . . Tara . . .

Darkness descended deeper . . . deeper . . . deeper . . .
There were footsteps behind her. Furtive. Stealthy.
She walked, she stopped, she turned. And there was
nothing, no one, just the fleeting shadows.

Cold, she shivered. She gripped the stake she carried
fiercely in both hands, so fiercely that her fingers were
knotting and cramping. It was harder and harder to
walk, to make herself go forward. There was darkness
ahead, and then light, and then shadow wings falling
over the illumination, and laughter, and her name . . .

Close, she was so close to the house.

She heard whisking sounds that chilled her, for it felt
as if the shadows were real, real and cold, and they
passed by her and touched her, an evil, menacing caress,
calling to her, taunting her, teasing her.

Her dream, her nightmare, oh, God, she was living it . . .

She nearly stopped, ready to drop to the earth, throw
her hands over her head, and do nothing but scream
and pray for the light.

But Ann was in there.

And so she kept following the footsteps . . .

Of her dream.

She reached the house. Ivy hung around it, nearly
obscuring the facade. But a fire burned within. A fire
that soared in the hearth, ripping and tearing against
the walls, and creating a new realm of shape and form
and shadow.

As she neared it . . .

The door opened.

The breeze whispered her name again.

Tara, Tara, Tara . . . come in . . .

We've been waiting. Waiting for you.

CHAPTER 19

The house was as she had seen it. Exquisite ancient furniture. Paintings on the walls. Paintings of depraved scenes and acts, executions, bloodshed, orgies . . . paintings in vivid colors, paintings with fires that seemed as real as that which burned in the hearth.

She looked around her carefully, for the strange noises and brushes of air seemed to sweep by her and touch her with an ever greater frequency. She knew that she had to go down the hallway.

Saw it.

Saw the dark, and saw the light.

And the first door that she knew she must open.

Her hand trembled upon the doorknob. The feel of her own flesh against cold metal was real. But everything in the dream had always been real as well. And still she knew that this was different, and for a moment, she stood trembling, seized with an absolute panic. She hadn't believed any of it . . . and here she was, alone, facing fears beyond comprehension, and it was ridiculous that she was here. Ridiculous that such creatures could exist, that there could be vampires . . . and werewolves, and that she was desperately praying that one of the two would arrive quickly, because it seemed that it was all true, and she was horribly afraid that she wasn't up to the task.

Jacques seemed to have faith. She was the one to inherit the strain of the Alliance. And what did that give her? A determination to die foolishly?

If she ran now, they would only come after her. Even if she escaped, she would fail, and her cousin would die.

Or worse.

She forced her fingers to twist the knob. The sound of the door creaking open was hideously loud, ripping and tearing her nerves.

She stepped back quickly, certain that something would spring at her, that the body parts would be waiting to form together, to come after her. But when she opened the door, she at first saw nothing. Then, from beside the bed, a woman rose.

Young. Not Louisa. Tara had never seen her before.

She was naked. She looked at Tara as if it were the most natural thing in the world that someone had walked in on her. She stretched, lifted her long hair to let it fall back again upon her shoulders. Then she looked at Tara, smiling salaciously. "Hello . . . shall we play? I love to play, love to play . . ."

One sultry step after another, she came toward Tara. Tara stared at her, tense, afraid, wondering if she was a prisoner, poor, pathetic, needing an escape, or if . . .

When she was almost upon Tara, the girl opened her mouth. An eerie hissing sound escaped from her.

She had fangs . . . the size of a saber-toothed tiger's, or so it seemed. Tara prayed desperately that she wouldn't falter.

She slammed the stake into the girl's chest, bit her lip, nearly doubled over. She forced herself to take the sword into her hands. She had to look away to deliver the first blow.

It didn't sever the head.

She had to take another whack, and as she did so, she heard herself protesting. "No, no, no!" was coming from her own lips. A slow keening. And then . . . the head rolled away.

She stared at her own handiwork, shaking once again. There was very little blood. She hadn't known what to expect. That the body would become a pile of ash, and disappear in a sudden breeze? It did not. It lay on the ground in its mangled pieces.

Even as she stood there, staring, she felt the tension, the cramping in her fingers, for she still held Jacques' war sword. She swallowed hard, bent down, and pulled the stake from the girl's torso. She had to tug hard upon it. It came free with a sickening sound.

Tara, Tara, Tara . . .

She heard her name being called again. The tone was soft, sultry, amused. She knew then that she had accomplished very little. The girl was just a piece of a shield. A foot soldier, not at all valued by the real enemy; totally expendable.

She stepped back into the hall carefully, trying to see in every direction. She couldn't allow her panic to take hold.

She looked down the length of the hall, wishing that

she dared call out her cousin's name. She couldn't, she needed to move quietly, though she was certain that Louisa and her consort—whatever his real name was— were well aware that she was here.

As she moved along the hallway, looking ahead, she became aware of a creeping sensation at the back of her neck. She paused, turning. At first she saw nothing.

The chill continued over her. Deep dread seemed to freeze her in place. Slowly, she looked up.

Flat against the ceiling was a man. He had curly dark hair, appeared young, and grinned down at her imp- ishly.

"Hello, there."

Even as she stared up at him, he fell from the arched ceiling, like a spider dropping down upon its prey. She fumbled with frozen fingers for her stake. She managed to lift the point just as he came down upon her. The impetus brought them both to the ground. Caught on the wood, his face was just inches from her throat as he suddenly began to snarl and snap. She struggled to force the point more deeply into his body, to throw his weight from her own. Saliva dripped from the fangs that nearly touched her throat. Gasping, heart thundering, arms trembling, she at last managed to cast him to the side. She scrambled to her feet, shaking still. He lay on the ground like an animated figure with a faulty battery, arms and legs thrashing. She slid the sword from beneath her coat and lifted it high again, bringing it down against his throat. Sobs escaped her. It wasn't easy to sever a head. Once again, she had to strike several times. At last, the head rolled away. And this time, as she watched, the flesh seemed to wrinkle, then wither, turn gray . . . slowly become ash and bone.

She fell against the wall, staring at him, fighting the

hysteria that threatened to overwhelm her and the tears that rose in her eyes.

As she sat there, she became aware of the whispering sound again. A whooshing that made it seem as if a thousand voices were hissing in her ears. She forced herself to rise quickly, to look around, to rescue the stake from where it had fallen in the bone and ash upon the floor.

She was still being called down the hall by an invisible draw.

There were doors along the way, but she didn't pause. The door at the end of the hall, with the strange light emanating into a field of dancing shadow, was where she needed to be. Resolutely, she walked on.

She came to the door. Her fingers again tensed and froze on the knob. She forced herself to twist it.

The light was coming from a massive blaze that burned in the hearth. And at the hearth stood a woman.

The woman who had come to her house.

She was elegant in form fitting black with trailing, gossamer sleeves. Her features were classically beautiful, framed by a wealth of sleek dark hair. Her skin was pale, her lips were very red. She seemed pleased by Tara's appearance, those lips breaking into a slow, secret smile.

"Welcome, ma chère!" she said softly. "Welcome . . . you see, you are most incredibly welcome here, though you turned me away from your home. Ah, well, the Alliance has never been known for its diplomatic tact. But . . . what does it matter? You're here now. And such a smart girl, clever girl! You knew the way down the hall, and that every door was but a roadblock, before you came to me. Of course, however, I was calling you, but . . . that's because you're so very welcome. Isn't she welcome, mes amis?"

Tara started. Her attention had been so focused on the creature at the hearth that she hadn't looked around the room.

People . . . or creatures . . . were all about. A young couple huddled together against a wall, pale, anemic looking. A bearded fellow in Victorian attire was seated in a wing chair, just to the left of the fire. Two women, the one resting upon the other's lap, were on the bed, while another man was lasciviously stroking the long blond hair of a teen-aged girl.

"Children, my dear children, look who has come! The newest member of the Alliance." Louisa moved away from the hearth as she talked, strolling casually in Tara's direction. Hands on hips, she surveyed Tara. "She doesn't look the part, does she? A tall, slim blond . . . not much muscle to her. Ah, and that face! Such a lovely face, fine features, excellent bone structure, actually. And what does she do for a living? She's an *artist*. An artist, can you imagine? Not a police officer . . . a young service woman. Ah, well, your grandfather let you down. He might have seen to it that you had fencing lessons, or something in the new Asian methods of defense. Even some kick-boxing might have stood you well. But an artist . . . what are you going to do, dear? Paint us all to death?"

Tara ignored her words. "Where is my cousin, Ann?"

She was amazed to see a look of annoyance briefly cross the woman's features. "You'll see her soon enough. But first . . ."

Louisa had been purposely drawing her attention. In the nick of time, Tara realized that the couple from the bed had risen from their lethargy. Both of the women hovered behind her.

The stake wouldn't help her when it was two against

one. She gripped her grandfather's old war sword in both hands and swung around in an arc. The razor sharp steel cut across the midriff of the first and the waist of the second. Neither was dead, but they both fell back.

The man with the beard had risen; he too was coming toward her. She held the sword at the ready as he approached her, her heart sinking. She had managed against them one by one. She had been methodical. Stake the creatures, remove their heads. But she couldn't do it when they were coming at her from all sides.

And now, her arms were burning. She was tiring. Muscles not accustomed to such movement were beginning to scream and groan. She had to ignore it, or she would not survive. As the man came toward her, she decided on the offensive, lunging forward to pin him in the stomach with the sword. She missed, and the sword struck bone, bringing a smile to the man's face. One of the women behind her, wounded but alive, and all the more furious for her wound, was coming back. Tara spun again, trying to inflict all the damage she could with the sword.

Arms suddenly slipped around her. The man who had been stroking the blond's hair had come up, and she hadn't been prepared. His fingers closed around her wrist, like hot iron biting into her flesh. She was desperate to hold on to the sword, but she couldn't. She let it fall, but as she did, she grasped quickly beneath her coat for the stake, ramming it backward with all her strength. She heard him hiss with fury and pain; he fell back from her. But in front of her, one of the others was already reaching for the sword. "Yes, yes, disarm her! Guillermo, don't whine so, you will survive, get the

stake now, come, come . . . she mustn't be carrying those
weapons when we go to find her cousin."

The room suddenly seemed to become a rage of shadows. A great, rising, flapping sound began to fill the air,
as if a host of giant winged creatures was descending.
They were everywhere, all around her. Her hair was
being pulled, torn. Wild breezes seemed to rip around
her. She was surrounded, and they were touching her
everywhere.

She saw shadows, faces, wings, hands, reaching, grab-
bing. She held on to the wooden stake as if it were a
lifeline, but fingers were tearing at hers, forcing them
one by one from her grip upon the wood. At last, the
stake clattered to the ground. Both her main weapons
were gone.

The flapping subsided. She stood alone, coat torn
and ragged, hands empty.

Louisa approached her again.

"Ah . . . well, I think just a taste of your blood for the
moment. Then, I'll bring you to your cousin. And you
can watch . . . while I watch as well, as she is finished.
Consumed, of course. Such a delicious young thing. But
then, I suspect, you will be even better.

Despite herself, Tara felt her eyes locking with Louisa's. The woman was smiling, so aware of her power.
Coming closer, and closer.

Tara forced her mind to work. And as Louisa stood
just before her, hands resting on her shoulders to pull
her in and bare her throat, Tara reached quickly for
one of her last weapons.

A small paint gun, loaded with holy water.

She brought it up to Louisa's face. And fired.

Louisa screamed and shrieked, the sound of a thousand banshees wailing in the night. Her hands flew to

her face, and she shouted out in rage, "Kill her, kill her!"

The flapping sounded again. Rising in a cacophony. Surrounded, Tara began to spin around wildly, aiming the water wherever she could.

At best it was a stalling measure. She would lose . . . the shadows hovered closer and closer. Screams rose and fell. Hands and arms were on her, tearing at her . . .

Then, the first of them was wrenched away. She heard a thunderous noise as a body went slamming against a far wall. There was a second sound . . .

The body's head landing in the wake of the corpse.

She turned, her fingers still on the paint gun.

"Don't aim it at me!" came a command, and she turned quickly again, shaking.

She was no longer alone. Lucian had come.

He had freed her from the grip of the bearded man, who now lay in pieces against the wall. She had a brief moment to retrieve her sword as Lucian reached for the next enemy; she didn't watch, she didn't want to see, as he dispatched the woman.

Instead, she ducked and grasped the sword from the floor, and scrambled onward, desperate to procure the stake as well. As she did so, one of the women went flying above her head. She turned, there was someone else, stalking her like a zombie. She raised her sword. A hand caught her arm. She turned again in dismay and terror.

But it was Lucian.

"No," he said softly. "He's still alive."

He stepped forward and sent a fist against the young man's face, causing him to crumple to the floor in a silent heap.

The room had gone still, except for one groaning

figure on the floor. Lucian took the sword from Tara's hand. He looked down. With a single, forceful sweep, he lopped off the man's head.

Shaking, Tara stood still. Lucian looked around. "She's gone. She's managed to get by," he said wearily. He started for the door. "Are you coming?"

Jacques did not look well. Katia remained in her keening state. Jade DeVeau felt her muscles tighten and ache, but she remained at her post. She was ready. Vials of holy water littered the desk in front of her. She had torches ready, should she need defense of fire. She had fashioned more stakes from pieces broken off chairs.

Regrettably, antique chairs, but then, their lives were in danger.

There was nothing for the longest time . . .

And then . . .

She heard a whining sound, coming from the front.

Jacques, white, tense, and gripping the arms of his chair, sighed softly. "It's Eleanora. The dog. She's hurt."

He started to rise.

"Sit, please, Jacques," she said softly. She grabbed one of the stakes, and slowly made her way from the library through the great hall, and to the door. She hesitated, still. Then she heard the soft whining again. She opened the door. Indeed, it was the shepherd. Bloodied, limping, yet wagging her tail. Jade smiled. "Good girl, brave girl, come in, I'll bandage you."

She bent down to pet the dog. Then she screamed, for a huge shape suddenly came lumbering toward her. She started to slam the door.

"Jade! It's Rick, for the love of God!"

She threw the door open.

Rick was more beat up than the dog. And he was carrying the body of a man over his shoulder. "Let me in, quickly!" Rick said.

Jade did so, hesitating, looking out into the night.

"Jade!" Rick said.

She felt the strange breeze that touched her face.

Quickly, she shut and locked the door, and turned.

Jacques let out a hoarse call.

Jade went flying back to the library.

Lucian DeVeau went through the door, heading for the hallway.

Tara, numbed, looked around her. She stared at the empty doorway, then sprang to life, scrambling over the fallen to follow Lucian.

She saw him moving, the sway of his leather coat, ahead of her in the hall. She quickened her pace, trying to catch up. One of the doors burst open and it seemed that a harpy flew from it, a scraggly, white-haired old witch of a woman, landing upon her like a giant chimp. She struggled against the strength of the creature, again desperately trying to avoid the slash of the snapping fangs. A second later, the creature was torn from her.

Lucian reached a hand down to her, pulling her to her feet.

"You have to expect things like that," he told her, and started walking again. She followed in his footsteps. As they moved along, a second door opened. She swung around with her stake in a death grip once again. A giant of a man stepped from the room, exceedingly tall, with long, gleaming blond hair. She gasped, getting ready to strike.

Lucian set a hand upon her arm and shook his head. "This is Ragnor, Tara. He's with us. What did you find?" The question was directed to the blond man.

"Three, novices, dug up and released, I'm assuming. Mindless, unintelligent creatures; thugs from another century—nothing much."

"The foot soldiers, more than expendable," Lucian said softly, echoing Tara's earlier thoughts to a T.

He started down the hall again, the tall man at his side. Tara followed, hurrying to keep up with their strides. "They've got . . . like a nerve center?" she asked, gasping for her each breath. "And these . . . people . . . or things . . . are like the outer defenses?"

"Yes."

"And there's a room, another room with a hearth and a sofa and . . ." She broke off, stopping where she stood. "It's where they have Ann, and it's where they want us to come?"

Lucian glanced at her, a wry but grim smile beginning to curl his lips. He nodded. "Yes. You see, you didn't want to believe, but it is you, and you are . . . Alliance."

He stopped as well, staring at her. "Remember, you have a strength you don't even know."

She nodded, and moistened her lips. "Where is Brent?"

"Wounded, but on his way."

"Wounded?"

"He's on his way."

They had started walking again. She raced along behind them. "I don't understand all this. You all can be killed, of course . . . and Brent?"

"He will be along."

"How was he wounded?" she persisted, following closely.

"Silver bullet," Lucian said.

"And he's still coming? He's only wounded? He can't come . . . who had the bullet?"

"Gerard," Lucian explained briefly. "Willem . . . or Inspector Trusseau, as you came to know him."

"So he knows . . . who . . . what . . . Brent is."

"Oh, yes, he knows. He knows well," Lucian said. "Just as we all know one another."

She swallowed hard, following them. They returned to the great hall, and there, the fire in the hearth was burning with an ever greater intensity. Something about the room had changed, Tara thought. The shadows created by light and fire had shifted, risen somewhat. And then she knew why.

They were meant to see now.

A snap and crackle brought the fire burning ever higher, and she saw Trusseau—or Gerard, as Lucian had called him. He was now by the fireplace. He held a rifle at his side. He smiled as the three of them entered, shaking his head.

"Well, Lucian, here you are at last. I must say, since you're the great 'king' of our kind, it took you long enough to get here. And considering as well, that you have this fresh, young, vampire huntress at your side—and Ragnor! Of course. The Viking of old! And that's it? You didn't summon a host from around the world? Ah, well, I have always been underestimated. But then, you thought that you'd have your friend, Mr. Malone here, with, perhaps, a few of his own. Ah, but sadly perhaps, his kind have been all but brought to the brink of extinction. Farmers do hate it when the wolves ravage their herds . . . and that old fairy tale has certainly done a lot to keep the population of those predators down. Actually, it's so easy to kill a werewolf. All you need is a silver bullet. Now as to vampires . . . well, Lucian. Your command is a joke. You aren't supposed to be killing your own kind now, are you? What happened to the rules?"

"You broke them, Gerard. Freeing me to do the same. This is a new world. New rules."

"Not so new, not really. Names, faces, and centers of power change. Luckily, human beings remain greedy, power-hungry creatures, so there are always pockets in the world where my kind can thrive."

"Thrive? After the war, Gerard, you were in pieces."

A flash of anger crossed the vampire's face. "Ah, yes, and you see, I haven't forgotten. I even hope that wretched Malone is just limping along somewhere—I didn't want a quick death for him, not after all that I suffered at his hands." He glanced at Tara, eyes sweeping her up and down. "And here we have her! Heiress to the old man. He was a harder nut to crack than I had imagined, but then, I'd something more in mind for him than a simple coup de grâce. The wretched old fellow. Once he and Malone got together at the debacle when the armies were closing in . . . well, let's just say that I don't want either of them dying easily."

"I think they'll oblige you in a bitter fight, Gerard," Lucian said. "And consider this—the extraordinary power Malone has is all thanks to you. All those steroids and such you pumped into him when he was in your power. He already suffered the tortures of hell at your hands. I think you should actually hope that you end your pathetic existence before he arrives," Lucian said.

"You think that you will do that, do you?"

A figure suddenly rose from the depths of the sofa, the back of which faced them, and had been hiding her. It was the elegant Louisa, with a skein of her long hair now covering her face. She moved it back to show the horrible blisters and burns caused by the holy water Tara had cast upon her. "You're all dying here tonight—dying for good. If there's to be royalty among us, I do believe that I far better fit the role. You have created a travesty of what we are, Lucian! You would make us into a pack of lambs when we are, in truth, the greatest birds of prey."

"I would have us survive, and live within our world," Lucian said. "Your excesses, Gerard, brought about centuries of death for yourself and Louisa years ago, and caused hundreds of others—innocent and defenseless—to face execution as well."

"We are meant to rule over the weak, and slake our thirst on the blood of innocents," Gerard said coldly.

"Ah, yes, the weak!" Louisa said. And she reached down, dragging Ann to her feet from where she had lain hidden on the old Victorian sofa. Tara gasped. Ann's eyes were open; she could see them all. But she didn't register their appearance. She simply stood in Louisa's hold, ashen, apparently sightless, listless, and ready to obey every command issued by her new masters.

As she stared at them, Louisa brushed aside Ann's hair, and smiled at Tara. "Such easy prey . . . she fell for Gerard—or Willem—the moment he came to her. And she! The granddaughter of old Jacques. I think she might die now, no matter what else we do . . . she is so very tired and, of course . . . drained."

Tara was startled to hear herself speak, grasping at the subtle hint Louisa had given earlier. "Ann was weak?" she inquired, taking a step forward. "How strange you call her weak. It seems to me that Willem fell rather hard himself, and still, no matter what the power, Ann would not invite a monster into her home, and she could resist him when she discovered simply that he wasn't a man she wanted in her home or in her life."

She had struck home. Louisa shot a glance at Gerard where he stood by the mantel. Her hold on Ann was weak.

Tara sprang forward, determined to seize her cousin. But even as she came close, Louisa turned, staring at her with a force that sent her sliding back, falling to the floor. Her hold on Ann tightened. "Now, now is the time when I finish this wretched creature!" she exclaimed.

Tara screamed, surging against the force, like a wind, that was holding her away. Lucian and Ragnor moved at that time as well, leaping forward, immune to the force. Lucian reached Louisa a split second before she could tear into Ann's flesh. As Lucian began to grapple with Louisa, Ann began to crumple to the floor. Tara reached her cousin, catching her, trying to hold her up. "Ann, Ann, please, snap out of it, you've got to fight what's happening!"

She felt a hand upon her shoulder, drawing her upward. Lucian. "You've got to get her the hell out. Now!" he said.

She looked at him, and beyond him, then gasped. The room was filling. Gerard and Louisa hadn't begun to call on all their resources. Even as Lucian spoke to her, two men who must have once been bikers were striding quickly toward his back. "Look out!" she said, trying to hold Ann—and fumbling for her paint gun at the same time. She brought it up, blinding the creatures over Lucian's shoulder, causing them to stagger back.

But Louisa was rising in all her fury, and the room had become pure bedlam. In the midst of it, Tara heard the explosion of a shot. And Gerard's mocking voice. "Amazing, isn't it? Mortal men—and women—can be killed by silver bullets as well."

"Get her out!" Lucian repeated, heading toward Gerard. The gun exploded again, tearing into the fabric of the sofa, just inches from Ann and Tara.

Tara was no longer gentle. She grabbed her cousin by the arm. "Get up and move!" she commanded.

Dragging Ann, she headed for the door, staying as low as she could. An old man suddenly stood in her way. He looked like a bum off the streets of the city. But he smiled, and displayed his teeth, and moved toward them, arms outstretched. Tara found a reserve of strength she didn't know she had, seizing the hilt of the sword with her right hand as she supported Ann with her left. She gathered all her strength and aimed straight for his throat. She didn't sever the head completely, but he fell away, hands clasped to his neck.

She made it out the door. She shook Ann firmly. "We've got to run, run! Do you understand. We've got to run."

Ann didn't seem to understand, but neither did she fight Tara's hold. Still, the going was not easy. They were trying to escape through a maze of trees and underbrush. The ground beneath Tara's feet was strewn with rock and bricks and old building materials. Branches and tree limbs seemed alive, tugging at her hair, her tattered clothing.

She screamed, thinking that one of them had come upon her, as a particularly prickly, bony-fingered, leafless branch tangled into her hair. She freed herself, pushing Ann along, and at last broke into an open field.

Yet even as she ran toward the place where she'd left

the car, she felt the eerie sensation that had come to touch her with danger.

With the presence of her enemies.

A great shadow seemed to fall over the night, and the sound of whooshing winds came again.

The shadow was behind her . . . sweeping over her. She felt the darkness, felt the fear. And then . . . the shadow loomed before her. Huge, giant wings, rising . . . and then falling. And it seemed that the wings folded, and Gerard stood before her once again.

She halted, arms tight around Ann, staring at him.

He smiled. "So . . . here we are. I have both the lovely granddaughters of the learned and knowledgeable Jacques DeVant standing before me. Ah . . . a bit like smorgasbord."

"I will kill you if you come one inch closer," Tara told him.

He laughed, tremendously amused.

"I'm not so sure I want to destroy you at all, Miss Adair. So much spunk and fire! You can join with us, you know."

"I don't think Louisa will like that."

"Alas, I'm not sure Louisa is going to survive the fight in which she is currently engaged."

"Lovely. You left her to fight Lucian and Ragnor, and you came after two mortal women."

"There are many ways to win," he said softly. "I loved Louisa, truly. Yet, in all those years, I had forgotten how demanding she could be. And then, of course, in the midst of all, I am forced to recall that it was she—trying to save herself—who gave my name to the Alliance at the Sun King's court. I suffered cataclysmically. And yet . . ." His eyes narrowed. "Not quite so badly as I did at the hands of your grandfather—and Brent Malone."

Tara's arms were aching. Ann leaned against her so that she was standing with her cousin's form weighing her down, and causing new aches in her muscles. Keeping her eyes locked with Gerard's, she eased Ann down into the high grass. She drew the stake from her coat.

"Come near me, and you're dead."

"I don't think so."

He took a step toward her. She felt a sudden agony in her arm.

"Yes, a creature of spirit, courage, and beauty! But such a novice. Oh, yes, of course, you dealt well with the silly young creatures and dumb bandits I created and dug from graves to test your strength and skill. But you've yet to be up against something like me."

He took another step toward her. "I should make use of a much greater finesse!" he said. "But . . . time . . . we're going to have to end your resistance here and now, I'm afraid. We'll see where the future might lead once I have tasted your . . . deliciousness," he said softly. "When truly hungry, of course, we will dine on just about anything. But a young woman such as you . . . I'm salivating already."

The entire length of her shook. She could barely hold the stake. She wanted to reach for the last of her holy water, but she couldn't force her arms to move. She had to tear her eyes away from his. She could not, and he was coming closer, closer, closer . . .

She prayed in desperate silence and willed herself to break his hold. At last, she tore her eyes from his, keeping the stake in her left hand, and reaching for the water with her right. But it was too late. Even as she tried to aim the gun at him, he reached her, and her bones were nearly broken as he forced it from her hand.

Still, she struggled with the stake, but he wrenched it from her as if she were a child waving a tinsel wand.

Then he stared down at her, holding her shoulders. Smiled suddenly, and lifted the fall of her hair. She found one last inch of strength, and brought her knee up with a vengeance, wondering if she could move him in the least. He fell back, shrieking a guttural cry of pain and fury. But he was instantly up, instantly on his feet, ready to come after her again.

But then . . .

They both heard it.

A baying sound. A sound that rose and rose into a cacophony, cries to heaven, a shrieking, a howling borne on the wind.

Beneath them, it seemed that the earth began to tremble.

Gerard let out an expletive, reaching for Tara and his rifle at the same time.

And then, from the tangle of forest and trees, they appeared. There seemed to be a hundred of them— silver, huge, wolves, and not wolves, for as they moved, they couldn't truly be seen, they were like a spin of motion, film out of focus, a thunder of illusion that spilled across the landscape. Tara struggled wildly to free herself from Gerard's steel hold. She started to shout in warning. "He has silver bullets, he has silver bullets!"

Gerard began to fire, wildly.

It seemed that the wolves were a wave. A wave of howling, baying, snarling death. They barreled on toward them. Gerard took aim. Tara used all her strength, forcing the gun up, the bullet to burst into the air.

And as she did so, the first of the wolves was upon

them. Far larger than life, standing taller than Gerard, taking him down in a fleeting glimpse of time.

She could hear Gerard. "Damn you, damn you, damn you, die!"

Tara, released, gasping, staggered away, trying to reach Ann, to cover her from the immense pack of wolves thundering over them. But though she heard the howling, growling, snapping . . . tearing, gnashing of teeth and ripping of claws, nothing came near them. She kept hearing Gerard's curses, and then a gurgling sound. She closed her eyes, ducked over Ann, praying, and then . . .

She realized that she heard nothing. Nothing at all. Except the soft whisper of the breeze, and a rustling of trees.

She lifted her head, and rose slowly.

There were no wolves in the field.

Only a man.

The moon had risen high in the night sky. The clouds had dissipated. And against the natural shadow of moonlight and night, she saw him standing there, tall in his silhouette, reflecting upon something that lay in the grass.

The body of his enemy.

She swallowed hard, needing to speak. She was shaking. Sound wouldn't come to her lips.

Then at last. "Brent?"

He turned to her, and started walking across the grass to her. He was limping. She found her own strength again, warmth to make her frozen limbs burst into motion. She raced across the grass and into his arms. He encompassed her in the strength of his hold, drew back, smoothed back wild tendrils of her hair, searched her face with his anxious golden gaze, and trembling himself, kissed her lips.

She leaned against him. For a moment, they held there, feeling the sweetness of the night air, the caress of the breeze, and of the moon.

Suddenly, the night was shattered by the sound of an explosion. Streaks of fire soared into the sky.

Brent's hold tightened around her.

"It's the house in the woods," he said softly. "It's over."

She drew back. "Lucian," she murmured worriedly. "And his . . . his friend. Ragnor!"

"It's all right; they're out."

"But how . . . ?"

"I would know if they were not," he said simply. Then his arm slid around her shoulder and he lifted her chin. "We need to get Ann, and take her home now," he said.

And she nodded, for though fire filled the sky, the world seemed strangely right once again.

EPILOGUE

They sat at a table at the same café on the Champs Elysées where they had come that first morning when Tara arrived in Paris.

There were three of them, though, this morning, Ann, Tara, and Jade DeVeau. Jade had been trying to make sense of everything for Tara, though she had gotten most of the story from Brent and her grandfather.

Brent had been attacked during the war, but discovered by the one enemy general who had known and recognized his exact condition the moment he had seen him. Calling himself Andreson at the time, Gerard was too impressed with his own power and superiority to fear the mangled man he had at his mercy. He had become fascinated with medicine during that phase of his existence—and the human capacity to endure pain.

He'd never realized he was creating the creature who would undo him, cast him into years of pain and healing.

Doctor Weiss had been a truly good and gentle man, and it was through him—and the rescued political prisoner, Jacques DeVant—that Brent had first been brought to a woman in Paris, Maggie Montgomery, a friend of Lucian's, and someone with knowledge and a healing touch. Brent had learned what he was, but Maggie had saved him from despair. He would be different, because of the things done to him in the prison's experimental lab. He would have greater powers. And perhaps, at times, greater agony, learning to harness the violence and needs that tore at his physical being. But such had been the case, and as such, he had, in his way, become part of the Alliance.

There were differences in the world beneath the known society, Tara learned. Brent could not shadow-shift, as the vampires could. But his strength went beyond that of even the oldest and most practiced and learned vampires. Nor was he prey to saltwater, which meant certain death to vampires. He couldn't mind read, or focus, the way Lucian could, but he was learning.

The night had ended with a victory that went beyond expectations. Even the police had been satisfied.

Javet hadn't totally ignored Tara's words. He had been checking into his man from Paris. He had discovered that the specialist had not been who he said he was, and he was more than willing to believe that the false inspector had been the thief and the evil murderer who had brought his victims to the ruins in the woods, satisfied his sick needs, and tortured and killed them there. He believed that "Trusseau" had died in the fire, and even that he had been the one to kill Jean-Luc and steal the corpse—for on a pile of bones among the rubble, incredible riches in jewels were discovered. Jewels that had belonged to the Sun King's mistress, Louisa de Montcrasset.

An even better note had been that not all had perished.

The café girl, Yvette, had not been killed. She must have endured terrible events at the hands of the two, but they hadn't killed her. Nor had they killed Paul, who had retained something of his sanity, his will to protect her and his love for her stronger than the power of his captors. The two, like Ann, had emerged from it all very ill, but getting better every day.

And, Paul had told them all proudly, Yvette had asked him to marry her.

Rick Beaudreaux had been in worse shape than Ann, ravaged in his fight with five of the "young army" Louisa and Gerard had created to be the front line of their battle. He had saved Roland, however, from certain death, with the help of Eleanora, even after she had been attacked by the creatures. Old Daniel had even helped out, Rick said, kicking the "holy shit" out of two of the attackers.

Ann, though mending herself, let no one else tend to Rick. The two were actually quite adorable, not seeming to have so much as a single argument between them, ever.

Jacques, too, was doing well, gaining strength with each new day. The fact that he now had his family around him, believing in him, seemed to be the greatest medicine in the world.

Healing had been the first order of business.

And now . . .

Tara leaned forward in an attempt to get Jade to explain more fully. "I'm trying really hard to make sure I've got everything straight. The Alliance is as old as . . . ?"

"Organized civilization, I guess," Jade said. "I'm not really sure of that myself. It is, of course, a secret society. If it weren't, most of its members would be locked away for their own benefit. In years gone by, the society was more accepted. People had a greater belief that there could be more that went beyond the realm of the everyday senses. And of course, in past times, such beliefs have caused absolute horror as well—look at the Inquisition, the witch burnings, more."

"And Lucian is very old, almost as old as the society."

"Not as old as the society. Just very old."

"But you're not?" Ann said curiously, joining in the conversation.

Jade shook her head ruefully. "Just as old as you see me. I met Lucian a few years ago. He saved my life." She flushed slightly. "He believes that I saved his as well."

"But . . ." Ann murmured. "You'll age, and he will not."

"We've not really worried about that yet. He was deeply concerned at first, knowing that I wanted a family. But by happenstance . . . we've adopted a son. And he's gorgeous."

"I don't understand," Tara said. "Every time I think I do, I get confused again. Lucian is a vampire—a good vampire, a part of the Alliance now."

"Not really a part. He has known about it, and in our current times, it's a natural coalition."

"Crosses don't bother either of them because at heart they still have a deep belief in an afterlife and the sanctity of God and man. If I have this right, it's kind of like hypnotism—if you're not an evil person, you can't be talked into doing evil under the power of the hypno-tist?''

"Kind of," Jade said, "but the question of free will comes in often. A vampire can be driven by natural instincts, just as man can be driven. It's a question of what's right, and what's wrong, and learning to exist by a code that respects others. The world is always shift-ing—our world is always shifting, new fears, new friends, new enemies. It's the same in the world we can't really touch. The rules have changed in the new order. But yes, I suppose it boils down to the classic fight man always wages within himself, a battle between the capabilities of doing good and doing evil."

"Why doesn't Lucian change you then?" Ann asked.

"Because he doesn't know what the end brings," Jade told her. "I'm willing to take any chance. Lucian isn't. I was bitten once, but like you . . . I healed. And he still doesn't really know about the immortal soul, and so . . .''

Tara plunged in then, asking frankly, "What about werewolves?"

"What about them?"

"Do they live forever?"

Tara sipped her coffee. "No. But they age far more slowly than an average man. They have their weaknesses, and their strengths. And like any other creature, they learn with age. At the beginning, as I understand it, Brent had little control. He was subject to the pull of the moon, losing all power over himself when it was full, having little ability—unless he was under extreme duress—to change when there was no moon. But he's learned over the decades. He has tremendous abilities. And in his desire to inflict torture, Gerard endowed him with incredible strengths." She leaned forward, a slight smile curling her lips as she told Tara, "We all have to make decisions, and choices, you know. But then, I'm not really sure that you do have as many choices as someone else. You must realize yourself now that you have been born to the Alliance. There are many more who are Alliance across the world. They may not all know it yet . . . and usually, in times of need, they somehow find one another." She looked at Ann. "You have a choice. Perhaps it's already been made."

Ann shrugged and asked Jade, "Is there . . . has there ever been a cure for vampirism?"

"No . . . well, yes, but I only know of one case where a vampire returned to a mortal life. And that was rather a different case. Back home, in Charleston, where Lucian and I and our . . . group is centered, there's a woman. Maggie. Brent knows her well. She was here, in France, after the war, and she was a great source of help for him at that time. And now . . . well, long story, but she's married to a cop in New Orleans, and I'm sure that Brent will tell you all about her, except, of course, that you should all come and visit. There are really too many stories to try to explain by simple conversation."

Tara stared at her, smiling suddenly. New Orleans. She loved the city. It would be wonderful to visit—and understand.

"Strange," she told Ann, "to think that the last time we were sitting here . . ."

"I was bemoaning the loss of a monster!" Ann said with a shudder.

"Yes, but you came through."

"And now I'm debating a life with a different vampire," Ann said.

Tara laughed. "At least you know a little more . . .

Jade, you said that vampires can't have children. What about—werewolves.''

"Brent Malone is really a man like any other—with a few special abilities. Oh, there are so many arguments! Are these things all illusion, chemical changes? What are the true properties of matter? Throughout time, I'm afraid, no one has had the real answer.''

"If my cousin marries Brent,'' Ann said with stern practically, "is she likely to have a litter?''

"Ann!'' Tara said.

"Well, it's what you're asking, isn't it?'' Ann said indignantly.

"You'd be most likely to have lovely children,'' Jade said.

Tara didn't say any more. She could see that the men, who had been in the airline office in the middle of the block, were returning.

"We're all set,'' Lucian said. "But I'm afraid we leave now.''

Rick looked at Ann. "You're sure you're coming?'' he asked.

"Definitely,'' she told him.

"Time to say our goodbyes then,'' Lucian murmured.

And so they did. In a very natural way, hugs and kisses all around, American style, French style.

And it was strange, of course, because Tara was staying on in France for a few weeks while Ann was going to the States on vacation with Rick.

In the end, the promise was that they would all see one another soon.

Then the others were gone, and Tara was left at the table with Brent. He ordered a coffee, and smiled at her ruefully across the table.

"So . . .''

"A werewolf, eh?"

"I'm afraid so."

She was silent, watching him.

"I can go away," he said softly. "Walk away from your you, and your life, and leave you in peace."

She leaned close to him. "Don't even think about trying it. I'm Alliance, you know. I'd hunt you down to the ends of the earth." He lowered his head, but not before she saw the light that touched his eyes. Shimmering. Golden. She loved it.

He looked up. "So what shall we do?"

"Um," she mused. "Let's see . . . you don't actually fly, do you? I'd kind of had this fantasy about being swept away to the highest spires in the city, and ravished there, of course."

"Very uncomfortable," he told her, shaking his head. "I could kind of fly with you into the deepest forests, up the highest mountains . . . but you're facing the same problems there. You know, stones, rocks, twigs, scratchy things. Not exactly what I had in mind." He was joking, speaking lightly, but he took her hands, looked down at them, and then into her eyes. "Actually, it doesn't matter to me where I am, if I'm with you. But you've had a tremendous amount to grasp and understand lately, and to me . . . well, I'm asking a lot of you. You're an incredibly beautiful, talented woman. You left a full life behind you—it's waiting, if you wish to return."

She smiled slowly, choosing her words. "My old life is waiting . . . but before then, I was waiting. I knew that there was something else out there, waiting for me. The Alliance, what happened here, yes. But something else. I never told you, but the dream began long before I came here. The dream, the nightmare, the premonition, whatever it might be called. And from the beginning, within it all, I was calling to someone. Brent, you're what I've been waiting for my whole life. And if you were to walk away from me, I'd spend the rest of my life waiting for you to come back."

"You really do understand all about me?" he queried.

"I've been around a long time, you know. I wouldn't want to pretend. There have been others all along the way, but never . . . never like this. I never felt . . . all right, in all honesty, at first I was so afraid for you. There was the terrible need to be with you. And then I knew that it was more than fear, the need to protect. It was, perhaps, the same. As if there could be nothing . . . until I saw you that day in the crypt, and from then on, every move I made cast me deeper and deeper into longing . . ."

"I like that. Nice to hear I was really desirable."

"Well, that, yes. But longing for much more. It was the same . . . as if I had been waiting."

"But I'm afraid that my appearance gave us serious problems. You might have stopped Louisa from ever rising."

He shook his head. "If she hadn't escaped that night, we might not have known about Gerard being here. I'm not anywhere near as old as Lucian, so I didn't really understand what happened during the Sun King's day. Nor would I have envisioned that her legendary lover might have been the man—the man who caused me such agony during the war. He had been so careful here, as well, kidnapping or seducing his victims, hiding the bodies . . . until he grew careless. He could have gone on for months, years, undetected. I don't know . . . I believe in the free will of man—a free will even when the normal course of a man's life is disrupted.

And yet . . . it's hard not to think that it was destiny, when you appeared in the crypt that day."

She smoothed a finger over the top of his hand. "Well, then, if it's destiny, we should accept the fact that we're meant to be together."

"Well, then . . ." he murmured, repeating her words. And he met her eyes again with a rueful grin. "Rocky hilltop, elegant hotel room. Hm. My vote is for the Ritz."

"The Ritz . . . sounds lovely."

"A short stay, or extended?"

"Extended, of course. Katia and Roland are with Jacques . . . he's quite all right. And you seem to think that I need time . . . and I do. Endless days, and nights, of course."

"Life will never really be normal again, you know," he said softly.

"What is normal? No one ever knows what each new day will bring," she said. "And who wants normal? Who on earth would want to give up extraordinary for normal?"

He stood so quickly that he nearly knocked the chair over.

He reached out a hand. "The Ritz?"

"Definitely."

Hours later, they ordered champagne. They lay on a gorgeous king-sized bed piled high with pillows and satiny-smooth sheets."

"So . . . you really think I'm extraordinary?"

And she laughed. "Beyond a doubt. Oh, my God, yes, beyond any doubt."

Night fell, and a full moon rose over Paris. High atop the elegance of the landmark Parisian hotel, the balcony doors were open to the breezes of the night. Within the hearth, an electric "fire" burned. It might as well have been the real thing, for it seemed that the flames rose and fell, rose and fell, and burned with the fever of the night.

Burned . . .

And burned.

After all, they had both decided . . .

They had been waiting all of their lives.